Hiding Behind The Couch

by
Debbie McGowan

Beaten Track
www.beatentrackpublishing.com

Hiding Behind The Couch

Second Edition
Published 2017 by Beaten Track Publishing
First published 2012
Copyright © 2012, 2015, 2017 Debbie McGowan

ISBN: 978 1 78645 125 5

Cover Design by Debbie McGowan
Cover Background Image:
'View through Freud's study',
Freud Museum, London.

Beaten Track Publishing,
Burscough. Lancashire.
www.beatentrackpublishing.com

For fabulous Paul:
my colleague, my therapist, my friend.

***

This novel is a work of fiction and the characters and events in it
exist only in its pages and in the author's imagination.

Contents

"I really believe, or want to believe, really I am nuts, otherwise I'll never be sane."

Allen Ginsberg

Prologue

To know people, that is, to know them well, one must spend time with them, go where they go, engage them in conversation, be an enduring part of their daily life to such a significant extent that one might feature in their diary or journal. The back stories of friends intersect frequently, though narrative style will vary according to the magnitude of those shared experiences in the context of the individual's history. Nonetheless, there remains a mutuality that an onlooker cannot readily circumvent; confusion ensues.

Of course, this puts you, our newest acquaintance, at a distinct disadvantage. You join us on an ordinary evening in our favourite restaurant, preferred for its affordability and the excellent service the regularity of our custom brings. We will remain until the staff intimate we are about to outstay our welcome, but we will worry about that later. For now, let me briefly introduce you to my closest friends.

Fittingly, Dan has taken a position at one end of the table, although I daresay his position as our leader is more concrete in his mind than in reality. He is an absurdly good-looking fellow: angular facial features, chiselled, one might say, and a musculature defined by dedicating many hours to physical leisure and labour. His brother sits to his right and pretends that he is not listening.

Andy, the older and arguably more handsome of the siblings, lacks Dan's easy charisma and looks beat. Some would contend that he is disorganised and devoid of ambition; on the contrary, his strength lies in his capacity to follow his instincts, to live for the present. As if to demonstrate, he runs his hand up the inside of Jess's thigh in spite of the company and at best a fifty-fifty chance of a positive outcome. On this occasion, she slaps the hand away whilst continuing to converse across the table.

Had Jess failed to achieve a first-class degree in law, a lucrative career as a glamour model could still be hers. With her long, perfect blonde hair, large breasts and slender legs, she alludes to everything that she is not, satisfied to be in a friendship with benefits, albeit one which is not without its drawbacks. Sometimes I wonder how she came to be friends with the rest of us, for on an intellectual level, there is only one who comes close.

Eleanor: my dearest friend, carrying the weight of my world on her shoulders with ease. Still greater are the trials she creates herself, for her life does not need to be so difficult. It is beyond me to know whether she is beautiful, so I will leave you to decide, as you observe her skilfully flitting in and out of conversations with everyone here, ever the diplomat, which is why tonight, we find her sitting between Dan and Adele.

Note the perfect tip of that nose, the symmetrical geometry of those eyebrows, the flawless skin and precise placement of every hair. There are times I fear she is lost within that painted, delicate shell, but every now and then, less often than a blue moon, say, a hairline crack appears, and the real Adele seeps through. Even then, I find her disappointingly simple but love her dearly, admire her, perhaps, for her capacity to maintain a superficial glaze of interest. See that flutter of eyelashes? Kris believes she is actually listening.

What a strange mismatch of artistic passion and forthright Nordic sensibility! Kris has 'contradiction' running through him like the place name in a stick of seaside rock. This animated gabbling about his work is a ruse, and if you have fallen for it, then you are forgiven; most people do. Here is proof positive that it is impossible to be everything to everyone and maintain an integrated sense of self. Watch his reluctance in switching his attention from one love to another: Shaunna wants a drink, and she rubs his arm gently to alert him once again to her presence.

Life has not been so kind to Shaunna, although you wouldn't know it. I envisage that she frequently falls to pieces behind closed doors. She is an excellent, devoted wife and mother, noteworthy in that she was involuntarily thrown into both. What would she have made of her life in the absence of childbirth? Maybe no more than she did in its presence, and to ponder such possibilities denies the value of motherhood.

And here to my left is George, who loves me, but we ignore it. Alas, as his love grows, I fear that mine dwindles. He fusses so and tries too hard to please me; and everyone else for that matter. Is there something to my leaving him until now?

Lastly, I am Josh. There is little I can add that you will not discover in time.

Chapter One:
A Dream of a Wedding

Josh didn't like heights, a fact he was more acutely aware of in this context than in any other, because it was a very high platform over a body of water that did not appear vast or deep enough to take the fall. This, he had concluded long ago, was not phobic, in the sense that it was entirely rational, based on the only possible outcome of plummeting from a great height, which at the very least would involve a certain element of pain or injury.

That said, damage of the physical sort was perhaps more akin to a phobia for Josh. He could fix most kinds of mental anguish, real or imagined, through a variety of tried and tested procedures, adjusted to take account of the particular foibles of the individual in question. He accepted that those often did harp back to a past event, related to some extent to the basis of the fear, and he had himself fallen down the odd flight of stairs, including those from the upper deck of a school bus.

He could recall exactly the sensation of losing his footing at the top, sliding down the first couple of steps relatively slowly, grasping for the rail as it slipped into an impossible distance, before free falling the rest of the way. He had landed on a couple of younger students; his diagonally strapped bag stayed behind him and provided an effective cushion. No major injury, just embarrassment and the unforgettable wave of laughter that accompanied the rest of his journey home.

Now, he was standing on this platform; in front of him a long, wide, blue, winding tube, gushing a torrent of chlorinated water through its belly to carry each and every soul safely to the pool below. Never in his life would he have willingly chosen to engage in such an adventure, and had it not been for the impatient queue of revellers forming behind him, right at this moment he would be turning on his heel, clambering back down the ladder that he must have ascended in order to be there, staring into the gaping mouth of the plastic abyss. Grunts and grumblings aside, this was something he had to do.

"For God's sake, get on with it."

"This place shuts at six, you know."

"What's that man doing, Mummy?"

Josh edged closer to the mouth of the tube and peered as far into it as he could see: about fifteen feet, he estimated, at which point it twisted sharply to the left. He felt the unfamiliar surge of adrenaline, as water splashed against his bare legs, and glimpsed down to his feet, in time to realise that firstly, he had been pushed from behind, secondly, he was now tumbling headfirst into the tube, and thirdly, he wasn't wearing any swimwear. No trunks, no shorts, nothing whatsoever. The light turned sky blue around him, his head started to spin, and he awoke with a start.

***

"That's got to chafe terribly," Eleanor remarked, as she selected a breadstick from the buffet table, dipped it in garlic mayonnaise and bit off the end, all without paying attention.

"Yes, I imagine so, but I never got that far, and anyway, what on earth does it mean?" Josh was following closely behind, armed with a small plate, so overloaded with miscellaneous chicken portions and pastry based finger foods his wrist was ready to give, and he wasn't anywhere near done yet.

"No idea," she replied vaguely, shoved several objects out of the way so she could put down her own plate and proceeded to hack chunks from all of the cheeses on the cheeseboard. "You're the therapist."

It was true, but then in that capacity Josh had made, if not his fortune, certainly a decent living out of the notion that no patient could effectively comprehend the symbols of their own unconscious. There was a reason they resided there, hidden from the day to day amblings of conscious thought. As his best friend, Eleanor usually indulged him with a little layperson's analysis. Indeed, she had the paperwork behind her to give a partially qualified interpretation, but that she ever believed there was any meaning or value in dreams to begin with.

A clang of silver on crystal marked the need to return to their table; Josh quickly grabbed a couple of slices of French bread and a butter curl and followed Eleanor back across the hall. The best man had never been a patient one, and he was well into his opening commentary before they reached their chairs.

Dan: always the best man, never the groom. This was his fourth wedding as such: the good-looking brother, the most loyal friend, the stepson who never judged and now the bride's ex-boyfriend. His speeches were as well-rehearsed, heartening and original as those of a Pentecostal preacher, although thankfully somewhat shorter in duration.

"Nice cravats, eh?" Eleanor whispered.

Josh laughed, or at least snorted quietly so as not to disturb Dan's monologue, which was being received in customary awed silence. "A fifteen-grand wedding? I would bloody think so too."

7

"How much d'you reckon they cost? Have a guess."

"No idea. Probably a couple of hundred each."

"Two hundred quid?" Jess, who was sitting next to Eleanor, leaned in to their conversation. "Seriously? Who's gonna pay that for a posh tie?"

"My thoughts exactly." Josh adjusted his collar for effect. "Mine's been driving me mad all day."

"Actually," Eleanor explained in a hushed tone, "they were only eighty-five pounds each, and they were on 'BOGOF'."

Her companions nodded and mouthed an 'oh' in understanding.

"Just don't tell the bride," she added, unnecessarily, as everyone present knew Adele only too well. As it was, most of the guests were invited to boost numbers and not because they had a right to be there, nor any obligation, as friend or family. Adele was all about appearance; this marriage was no different. It was only the groom who didn't know it, or at least would not allow himself to see it. Adele had gone straight from Dan to Tom, someone outside of the friendship group, thus not entirely aware of the heartache and how it repeatedly caused her to drop her guard.

She had crafted a shiny, perfectly formed shell for herself, through surgical endeavour, hours at the gym and a career that afforded her luxury cosmetics at wholesale price, for she was no mere window dresser; every display was her own catwalk still shot, and she did it extraordinarily well. After all, this was the pinnacle of 'appearance only': in a five-storey department store filled with dreadful, over-priced garments and unfashionable perfumes, there had to be some way of presenting the place to bring in the money. Plastic Adele was the right woman for the job.

The only true exception to the pretence was her previous relationship, and even now, as the best man spoke with a kind of indifferent passion about the luck of the groom, she watched him, transfixed with love and maybe a hint of regret, until Tom squeezed her hand, hard.

"Did you see that?" Josh elbowed Eleanor.

"Of course, but it doesn't take the work of skilled people-watchers like us to know she's still carrying the torch."

Adele would never get over Dan, and for all the wrong reasons. He wasn't just the best-looking brother of three, he was the most handsome man in the room. He had style, popularity, eloquence, humour, humility and wealth. Perhaps those were not the wrong reasons to fall for a man, for he was perfection personified for more than Adele. As much as all the guests knew the stuff she was made of, they also shared her fascination, even those in the friendship circle. That was not to say Dan was conceited—far from it; nor that he did not know his own worth. Whenever they went out as a group, it was Dan that the women, and men, would chase. It was Dan who could get them into anywhere through a simple word with a doorman, not because he had happened on being well connected. The associations were all his own making.

"You do realise he's been at it for fifteen minutes already," Eleanor complained, slumping ungracefully into the red and gilt chair. In any other situation, it would have been comfortable enough, but they had been there, eating and listening, virtually all day. The ceremony had been finished by eleven, followed by wedding breakfast, speeches, time to socialise, change into evening wear, drinks, more socialising, a sit-down meal, speeches again, photography, buffet and now more speeches. There was only the dancing to go, and she had eaten so much food she was convinced she would drop through the dance floor.

"Surely the great Dan hasn't finally managed to bore someone?" Josh whispered in mock astonishment.

"Of course not! But I'm stuffed and fed up with being in this rotten hotel. And once he's done, we'll have to listen to Tom, then Adele's dad will no doubt want to add something about not losing his beautiful little girl, et cetera et cetera."

"Ah yes, we know the drill all too well." Josh switched off for a moment, to contemplate the considerable number of weddings they had attended, mostly as guests, during the past ten years. Their friendships were cemented in high school and proved remarkably resistant to their nomadic adventures, in and out of higher education, for they had all returned and more or less picked up where they left off. Not even marriage and family commitments could drive the friends apart. Josh was thirty-five, a little younger than the rest of the group; some remained single, some travelled for their work, but always they came back to the flock. It was strangely enduring and a commitment that most would flee from if it were formally imposed.

First, there was Eleanor's wedding, to an outsider, a small and civil affair, which essentially described the marriage that followed as well. He was a nice enough guy, a fellow doctor at the hospital during their eighty-hour stints. Whilst that was the reality, their marriage was stable, but it crumbled as soon as they had time to spend together. Nothing in common save their careers, and Eleanor had long since moved on from that.

A round of contained applause brought Josh back to the present and signified Dan was done. He handed over to Tom, who rose unsteadily from his chair. Adele had the grace to shift her gaze.

"This should be joyous," Jess mumbled. "Have you considered that if he makes it past a year, he'll be the first?"

"I was just thinking that," Eleanor said, for she, too, had been pondering her own short-lived marriage. Jess had followed suit, via a brief encounter with a barrister in her firm. He was much older and a stoutly, not overtly attractive man, who wooed her into agreeing to a partnership ceremony—to all intents and purposes, a wedding. She dressed up for the occasion, brought along a retinue of small female relatives in cute, peppermint frocks and flowers, and her dad reluctantly passed her to a man who was his equal in both years and girth.

When confronted with his enduring infidelity, the wayward barrister reasoned that their relationship was irretrievable due to a conflict in interests. Jess secured alternative employment and dissolved the partnership without recourse to legal intervention, by stating that maintaining several affairs simultaneously equated to nothing less than polygamy. Once the dust settled on that ill-fated romance, she and Eleanor concluded that none of them was kitted out with what it takes to be a good husband or wife, and that was why the nine of them had remained friends for so long.

Only Kris and Shaunna proved able to withstand the test of time and the trials of friendship, and they were both part of the group. Their relationship remained unsullied, regardless of what was thrown at it, for there they were, after five years of marriage, on top of many more spent in blissful cohabitation, so truly besotted with each other that throughout the speeches, they continued their intense dialogue, sitting close, clasping each other's hands, foreheads almost touching, unaware of the sarcastic commentary taking place behind them. They were always the same, something Krissi—Shaunna's daughter—still gave a teen treatment of flicked-back-hair disapproval, even if she was twenty years old.

To his credit, Tom accepted Adele's lifestyle with grace and patience. He took no issue with her friends, but then, Dan had laid it before him in absolutely certain terms. This was a thing that could not be broken, and it was nothing to do with their prior intimacy. He loved Adele like he loved them all, would go to the ends of the universe for any of them. Tom could either accept it for what it was, or not.

As Adele's manager, Tom had cautioned her many times for gossiping on the shop floor with whichever friend happened to be visiting that day. She smiled her sweet apologies, and it went no further. Had it done so, it would have been to the detriment of the store's window displays, and she would no longer have been in his life every day. To even embark on their romance was a risk he had been afraid to take, yet something he had always privately hoped for.

Adele's adoration of Tom was real. True, it was nothing compared to her love for Dan, but when things became awful, it was Tom who listened, hugged her, took her to dinner as distraction. He'd known Dan himself a fair few years and concluded that the obsession was mostly one-way, for Adele rarely came up in conversation. As far as he could tell, it was the pairing within the friendship group that had been predicted, the one that was expected, and that was the only reason why it came into existence.

As friends, Dan and Adele got on tremendously, fought ferociously, but always made up. As a couple, they were beautiful, perfectly matched in looks and glamour. However, as lovers, they were selfish, secretive and hurtful. To have confided in any of the group would have been to betray each to their best friends, and they were still the best of friends. Thus, Tom was Adele's saviour, and she loved him for it. He had given her the strength to battle through the break-up without losing everything else she cared about.

"And Adele's friends: 'The Circle'. You guys are the best." Tom raised his glass warmly in their direction.

"Pay attention now, people," Eleanor muttered through smiley, gritted teeth. "That's us!"

All heads turned, raised glasses, sipped in unison, and onwards. Tom returned to his seat; the anticipated short burst of applause subsided, and finally the bride's father stood to deliver his speech. Josh stifled a yawn and glanced at his watch.

"Where the hell has George got to?" Jess whispered.

"I don't know, but no doubt he'll arrive right at the end of the speeches," Eleanor grumbled, because that was what usually happened.

Of all of them, George was the only one to have moved away permanently and lived deep in the middle of nowhere in the US, which was no excuse for his habitual late arrival at weddings and such. He knew how long it took to travel home. Still, he would arrive when all the ceremony was done with, and there was only fun to be had. Then he would stay longer than he planned and engage in as many social activities as he could, before another teary farewell at the airport.

"He sent me a text message an hour ago to say he'd just left the terminal. And no, he hasn't ordered it yet," Josh explained, to which Eleanor and Jess rose their eyes to the ceiling.

Josh and George had the most complex of all the relationships. George claimed that Josh was the reason he moved away, and it was true, although it was not every day that an estranged father left two hundred acres of ranch to his son. It hadn't occurred to George that a degree in agriculture would ever serve him any use, and he had no justification for choosing such a route, yet that was where his life somehow directed itself. When it came to leaving, he begged Josh to go with him, refusing as always to accept that they had no future together. Josh loved George, but only a little more than he loved Jess, Kris, or any of them, other than Eleanor. She would always be his very best friend.

Among them, there was an enduring closeness, a pairing between those most alike that was more special, yet still part of the group. For Kris and Dan, their high school friendship was further strengthened during their time in London, at different universities, but geographically nearer each other than anyone else. Adele and Shaunna reached a similar arrangement, albeit somewhat less meaningful in comparison to the others, as evidenced by Shaunna failing to stay at the top table even in her capacity as matron of honour.

For Jess, it was Andy, Dan's older brother, missing the wedding because he was in hospital following a car crash, compound fracture and surgery; hence, she was feeling a little left out. The two brothers were alike in many ways, not least of all that they were prepared to take chances.

However, where Dan found it to be the root of his success over and again, for Andy it was frequently his undoing. He failed at sixth form because of it, dropped back a year and became part of the group, toed the line, scraped through university living fast and looked likely to continue existing that way until one of his schemes killed him. He loved the sense of danger, surviving on the edge, and his younger brother would always bail him out, because that was what Dan did.

The final round of applause signified the end of the speeches. The lights dimmed, and several hotel staff, still in blacks and whites, excused themselves as they shuffled the tables to the edges of the hall. The DJ fired up the lights and music, and the bride and groom took to the floor, followed by their parents, then by Shaunna and Kris, still physically attached at all possible points.

"You'd never guess she was four weeks pregnant," Josh remarked, watching Tom spin Adele, her skirt fanning gracefully outwards from her delicate frame. The pair of them appeared to know what they were doing, which was some kind of waltz, meticulously learned and rehearsed over several weeks, at Adele's insistence.

"She was gutted you know—wanted to do everything traditionally and in the right order," Eleanor disclosed.

"Oh, well, you can't have it all ways," Jess said. "Mind you, she's not going to look pregnant yet, is she? Not even the tiny size she is." Adele twirled in front of them, a dancer's smile fixed to her face. Jess smiled back, then added, "I'll tell you what she does look like—the toilet roll cover my nan used to have on her cistern."

That made all three of them laugh, as they recalled the crocheted bodice and skirt with the little plastic doll head and arms sticking out of it.

"Right then." Josh shifted his head in the direction of the dance floor and looked expectantly at Eleanor.

"There is no way on this planet I can possibly consider getting up and dancing," she protested. "In fact, I think I have become a planet."

"You misery guts! You've got to. Come on." He tried to pull her up from her chair, but she resisted.

"Go dance with Jess," she ordered. Jess shrugged and allowed Josh to take her hand.

"Fine. You just sit there 'being fat' and we'll go burn off the buffet," he admonished in jest, as he and Jess headed for the dance floor.

"And the dinner, and the breakfast," Eleanor shouted after them.

"Mmm. Food." George had finally arrived. He dumped a large bag on the chair next to Eleanor, and gave her a tight hug.

"Ouch! Watch it!" She hugged him back with her arms whilst refusing to move otherwise. "I'm totally stuffed."

"Well, *I* am starving, so I'm off to get a plate-load and a drink. You want one?"

"No, I'm good."

George nodded his understanding and went in search of food, leaving her rubbing her uncomfortably bloated belly.

"Never again," she muttered to herself. "Never, ever again."

Chapter Two:
The Johanssons

When Shaunna was fourteen, she did that thing that all the girls at school talked about. She was the party slag of urban mythology, the one who got too drunk, went to the bedroom where the coats were piled high on the double bed, and had sex with a stranger. She didn't know who he was, could only vaguely remember where she'd been and what she'd been up to, and tried to let the memory slip away with the hangover. Four weeks later, she was certain that night was going to be with her forever.

She didn't tell Adele, who was lovely and loyal and the best friend in the world. They went shopping together, read magazines every night in Adele's or her own room, both of which were decorated with virtually identical wallpaper and furnishings, all in pink. They talked about boys they liked, girls they didn't, sometimes they even worked on school projects together, but not this. She missed a period, and knew, long before the test result, that their innocent and carefree girls' nights in were over.

It was Kris, who at the time had convinced himself and everyone else that he was gay: he was the one who took her home from the party, carried her upstairs to her room and carefully laid her under the duvet. He even fetched a glass of water and placed it by the bed before silently slipping out of the house and returning to his own home. He alone was aware of what she had done; he'd heard the noises, *heard everything*, as she protested uselessly against whoever had climbed on top of her.

Then nothing was to be said of it, but he continued to watch over her through the weeks that followed, and he saw the changes. Finally, he took her away from her other friends one Saturday afternoon, and they went into town to drink super-thick milkshakes. He asked her straight out if she was pregnant. She said she didn't know, but then the first tears escaped and there was no going back to the lie. For two hours, he held her hands across the table while the milkshakes melted to normal consistency. She cried, they talked, she cried some more, and when the tears stopped, she declared that she would not be wasting the milkshake. After all, she needed the calcium.

Kris offered to take responsibility, to say he was the father, that it was he who was drunk and she had said no. She didn't order him not to; instead, she remained silent. He was with her when she told her parents, and they assumed what he was saying was true. Surely their baby girl would not have done such a thing of her own free will? They screamed at him, ordered him to leave immediately and never come back. He left, and Shaunna's guilt gave way to the truth, delivered in staccato bursts interspersed with sobs. She needed her mum to stop shouting and just cuddle her, tell her it was OK, kiss it better, and once her parents absorbed the shock,, her wish was granted. It would never be all better, but they would make the best of this bad deal.

When the baby was due, Shaunna said she wanted to be alone for the birth, and of course no-one listened. The friends had suffered sickness, heartburn, intolerance, phone calls at two in the morning when she couldn't sleep. They had felt first kicks, watched as that bump got bigger and bigger until she looked as if she could be cracked open with a spoon. They'd scammed coursework, demanded cushions on classroom chairs and flat out refused to 'just sit at home waiting for the call'. The antenatal ward staff were very patient, for the waiting room was not designed to hold so many teenagers, who went into a kind of rugby huddle when the new grandmother emerged to proudly announce the birth of a beautiful, healthy baby girl.

In pairs, they went into the delivery suite; Adele and Kris went first.

"Meet Krissi." Shaunna beamed, not once taking her eyes from the blanket-swathed bundle in her arms.

"Krissi," Adele and Kris uttered in unison.

"Hmm." Shaunna's mum walked around the bed to look again on her granddaughter. The poor woman was not yet forty. "Are you sure she's not yours, now?" she asked Kris, a twinkle in her eye. Shaunna, like her mother and her mother's mother before her, had thick, red hair, always worn long so that it cascaded in huge auburn waves over their shoulders. The baby's hair was jet black, and whilst it was too early to say with certainty that she was also of dark complexion, it proved to be the case in the long run. Kris was Scandinavian, with fair skin and light-brown hair, more or less ruling out any possible genetic association to the baby, but from the day he had saved her, Shaunna loved him. Krissi was the right name; he was as close to a father as this baby girl would ever have.

When finally Adele and Kris could be dragged away, Josh and Eleanor met their niece, for that was what she was to all of them. Eleanor went completely gooey—a totally unexpected response because she didn't like small children at all. She had so many younger brothers and sisters—her mum was expecting her seventh child and showed no signs of stopping there—but this baby: she was different. She was so beautiful, and she was part of them.

Josh ribbed Eleanor mercilessly for years about walking her around the hospital grounds whilst she got the whole 'I want one' thing out of her system. Meanwhile, George and Jess paid homage, followed by Dan and Andy.

"Here she is!" Shaunna announced again over the newborn grunts and wails of a baby tired out, hungry and fed up with entertaining visitors. "Although she's not feeling very sociable at the moment."

Dan and Andy stayed long enough to give their congratulations and then got out of the way of yowling infants and experiments in breastfeeding. Looking back on that time, which she did frequently, Shaunna noted how uneasy Dan was especially. He had always been so good with people from every walk of life, even as a teenager, but babies were definitely not his thing. It was small wonder that he and Adele had never worked things out. All she'd ever wanted was a big house and a whole brood of little ones to care for.

Not that any of the others ever told Shaunna or Adele, but they had long ago agreed that it was inevitable the whole teen pregnancy thing would happen to one, if not both, of them. A couple of years after Krissi was born, Adele also became pregnant in very similar circumstances, although she miscarried early on and didn't want to talk about it, or didn't need to. Either way, she threw herself straight back into her social life and continued her design course at the local college.

Meanwhile, Shaunna devoted herself to achieving motherhood perfection. She was determined Krissi would not suffer for her mistakes, to the extent that she refused her parents' offers of help and rejected Kris's invitation to accompany him to the sixth-form leavers' ball. He begged her to reconsider, even went behind her back to get her parents on side. They bought her an outfit in secret, hoping they would succeed in changing her mind. Everyone else was going, it was only one night and Krissi would be asleep anyway. Dan invited Adele, even though she had left school and they were not officially seeing each other; Eleanor and Josh paired up, as did Jess and Andy.

In Shaunna's absence, Kris was left with little choice but to tag along with George, an arrangement that was complicated by their once intimate relationship, now reduced to little more than an embarrassing interlude in light of Kris's fixation with Shaunna. For this and more altruistic reasons, they all endeavoured to persuade her, stressing that it would be the last night out together for a long time, possibly ever. She stuck to her guns.

After finishing sixth form, Kris reluctantly accepted a place at a London college. He was an actor—a very good one at that—and the best drama schools were in London. Shaunna reminded him that he had no real responsibility to her or Krissi, but that wasn't his perception. Initially, he came home every other weekend and spent entire days at the park with the toddler, feeding ducks and pushing swings. As time went by and his course became more intensive, there was no choice but to ease back on his visits, and Shaunna put on a good show of not minding.

In truth, she missed him so much, although to Krissi there was little difference between two weeks and six. She would soon forget about him, busy as she was painting indiscernible shapes at playschool, pedalling around the garden on her tricycle and refusing to use cutlery even once she'd mastered the art of picking up food with a fork.

All of those things children did happened so fast; Kris could hardly keep up with the changes. He hated being away from Shaunna and Krissi, although Dan did his best to keep his friend occupied, meeting up two or three times each week and clubbing at the weekend, if they could spare the time and money. Inexplicably, Kris had become sexually attracted to Shaunna—the first girl to have this effect on him—and he had been certain he was gay. He didn't tell Dan for a long while, because going to gay clubs seemed a much safer way of avoiding a one-night stand with any random girl, a momentary lapse in judgement and self-control that would betray everything he and Shaunna had.

Many opportunities came his way while he was in London, and not just to sleep around. He was offered work with theatre companies, succeeded in almost everything he auditioned for and undoubtedly could have stayed there, making a good living as a TV actor. But he couldn't do it. Shaunna and Krissi were his family, and he had already missed too many years.

By the time he went home for good, Krissi had started school. They were still staying with Shaunna's parents, who were always trying new ways to tempt her into living a little of her own life. Her mum, a teacher, offered to go part time; her dad, in early retirement, told her to go and enrol at college, take days out to go shopping, anything she wanted, but always she declined their offers. Either of them could collect their granddaughter from school each day, without any inconvenience, they reiterated uselessly against Shaunna's defiance.

Eventually, she picked up three mornings a week in a hairdressing salon, mostly to shut them up but also because it was in the same road as the school, so she could still take Krissi first. And if she was honest, she loved that job; she was appointed to wash hair and brush up, but she was that bit older and more grown up than the trainees; whilst they were learning she was, too. Simpler cuts and styles were easy accomplishments and the owner advised her to register on a recognised course, which didn't have quite the intended consequence, as Shaunna realised the job was becoming too important and had to go; she gave her notice, regretting it even as she did so. It was a miserable decision, yet she knew why she'd made it. Josh had confirmed it for her. Krissi must never feel that she was a mistake, that she was not wanted.

Kris registered with an agency in town and managed to gain regular work as an extra in a regional soap opera, along with voiceovers for radio ads. It wasn't great pay, but it was steady enough to count as a salary and gave him the chance to save a deposit for a flat. That was what he had aimed to do all along, although, as he saved he decided it wasn't good enough. They would need a house, with a garden, somewhere to play with the dog. Where all the traditional stuff and nonsense came from, he had no idea, as it certainly wasn't something he would ever have imagined for himself.

He made it in time for Shaunna's twenty-sixth birthday, when he presented her with two jewellery boxes. One was a ring box; the other was slightly larger and flatter. Krissi got one too and tore it open immediately. Inside was a tiny gold pendant of a cat with emerald eyes, a symbolic gift that she understood straight away. Passing the boards in shops or reading the local papers was a nightmare, with her always eagerly peering over his shoulder on the lookout for 'kittens to good homes'. It was a given that one day they would live together as a family, and Krissi persisted with the request for a cat when they did so.

"Pleeeaaase?" she would say.

"I tell you, Missy Kissy, I won't stop sneezing ever again," Kris would respond, although he was *severely* allergic to cats, and his reaction went far beyond mere sneezing. He had always called her Missy Kissy because she couldn't say her name properly until she was five. However, here was the cat she'd always wanted, and Krissi knew it meant they had a new home. Kris signalled to her with a finger on lips, and she complied by putting her own finger across her lips, but continued to bounce up and down, making little squeaky noises of excitement.

Shaunna was a little slower to take it in. She'd opened the small box first, impatient and easily drawn in by romantic things such as diamond rings, which this was. It came from a passing remark, when pushing the pram along the high street seven years ago, and Kris remembered: three diamonds in a row to represent the three of them, with Kris in the middle and his girls either side. He slid the ring onto Shaunna's finger, kissed her gently, and placed the other box in her hand, still maintaining the proximity of their faces.

"You might want to open this one, too, before someone explodes," he said, indicating with his thumb to Krissi.

"Oh. OK." Shaunna struggled with the hinged top of the little box, her hands shaking. Finally, after several attempts, she popped open the lid and lifted the key from inside, looking at Kris in puzzlement.

"Want to see which door it fits?" he said, taking her other hand with its glistening stones, and pulling her to her feet. Shaunna allowed herself to be led, out of her parents' house and on down the street, with Krissi skipping ahead.

"It's not too far away," explained Kris. "Far enough from your parents for us to have a life, but close enough for them to never miss out on their granddaughter growing up. I know how that feels and I am not going to lose any more time with my little Missy or her beautiful," he walked around in front of her, taking both of her hands, "hot," interspersed words with kisses, "mummy, who is going to be my wife."

"Ha ha," Shaunna laughed, "and I have to say yes, seeing as I turned you straight. You really need to look where you're going, though." She said this just in time for Kris to avoid a lamppost, and they rounded the corner, where a few yards down a 'Sold' sign poked over a garden wall. This was it. Their new home.

The house-warming was great fun, although a little sad, as it was also George's leaving party. Krissi made chocolate-chip cookies cut in the shape of cows, like the ones on his ranch, she said, which made him cry. He went outside and sat next to Eleanor on the patio.

"Have a cow," he sniffed and offered up his tray of biscuits.

"Oh, bless you, poor love," she comforted, rubbing his back. A moment later, Krissi followed with a small box containing more cookies.

"Uncle George, stop crying, right now! You'll make my little cows all soggy! Here's some to take with you. Kris said the sniffer dogs would find them and gobble them all up, so I put Sellotape all around the lid, look." This only made it worse. George laughed, but the tears kept rolling.

"Thank you very much. They are lovely and I will make sure those greedy dogs don't get anywhere near them!"

"Can you let me have a chat with Uncle George please, sweetie?" Eleanor asked tactfully.

Krissi complied immediately and trotted off in the direction of the house. "And Mum said can you bring the box back next time you come?" she called cheerfully as she disappeared through the patio doors.

"Man, that child is something else." George sighed, wiping his eyes on his sleeve.

"She is indeed. But anyway, talk to me," Eleanor prompted. George had been desperate to confide all evening.

"This is the hardest thing I've ever done, Ellie." He picked at the sticky tape wrapped abundantly and untidily around the plastic box of cookies. "I don't even know that it's the right thing to do, but I can't stay here anymore. He's tearing me apart, and he doesn't realise. I'm such an idiot."

"Well, yes, you are. To think that Josh doesn't understand or care about how you feel. He loves you a great deal, just not—well, not how you want him to. He won't let himself, and not just with you. With anyone."

"Maybe it will pass. It'll go away once I'm over there."

"You think so?"

"I hope. I can't carry on like this, that's for sure. I'm going to miss you all so much." He stopped, choked by sentiment, and Eleanor stroked his cheek.

"We'll miss you too, but it's not goodbye, and we'll always be here. Plus there are such things as telephones, you know. Not to mention email and good old-fashioned letters. You won't get rid of any of us that easily, mate!"

George managed a smile and quickly wiped his eyes. Andy was heading their way.

"Mind if I join you?" he asked, sitting down next to George. "And before you grunt at me, Ellie, I know he's a miserable bastard who's having a good old whinge, which is why I came over. I was going to say earlier, me and Dan go over to the States a lot, as you know. So you'll see more of us than you do now, I reckon. In fact—" he turned and swung a leg back over the seat so that he was straddling it "—I'm hoping to get me a lil of that ole rodeo thang going on. What d'ya say?" He mimed flicking a whip at the bench, and George and Eleanor giggled.

"Anyone less like a dusty old cowboy I've yet to meet, but it sounds fun. We will all have to visit. A lot!" Eleanor promised.

"You must all come together," George agreed. "That would be really fun. And yes, Andy riding rodeo. That's got to be worth anyone's dollar!"

***

When everyone had gone home, all the dishes were washed and Krissi was tucked up in bed, Shaunna and Kris snuggled up on the sofa to watch a movie. It was whatever was on at midnight, and neither took much notice. They talked as if they had never talked before. Shaunna started off with the usual ribbing about turning Kris straight, and wondered how they had arrived at this situation, not that she was regretting it. Kris confessed he was still attracted to men, probably bisexual, but hadn't wanted anyone else since they first got together, whenever that had been. They agreed they would get married but would wait until Krissi left school, at Shaunna's request. She still refused to act in any way that threatened to push her daughter out of her life. She was seriously underestimating the love that the child had around her, but if it was what Shaunna wanted, then it was what she got.

Chapter Three:
Three Plus One

The friends frequently dropped into one another's places of work, and not only when they required the specific professional services that each could provide. Certainly, whenever Adele was working, anyone who needed an item that could be purchased in the department store would go there rather than an alternative outlet. In her case, maybe it was a little more to do with the staff discount she passed on to them than her expertise, although she was pretty good at handing out advice on exactly what to wear for any occasion, what the latest colours and designs happened to be, or the newest names in cosmetics and perfumery.

Jess returned the dress to the wardrobe and cursed yet again—Adele for being on her honeymoon, and herself for not pre-planning for the dinner she'd been told she had to attend. Her firm was international, and whenever visitors arrived in the UK, she was trawled out to entertain and enthral. She didn't see herself as especially entertaining or enthralling, but there were certain perks, and pitfalls, to being a single, successful, female lawyer. In Adele's absence, she instead sought Josh's counsel, not that he was any use when it came to fashion.

Josh leased the top half of a building just outside the town centre, where there was some limited parking and fewer people to happen upon someone visiting a therapist. He initially started out in his living room, but it became a place where he could no longer relax, and financially there was no reason to continue with the inconvenience. The rented offices were a good space: two small rooms, a kitchenette and a bathroom. He fitted out the smaller of the two rooms for consultations, with a couch, but not the proverbial, clinical sort. It was plush, covered in deep-blue fabric, and so big that even his tallest of clients could easily lie upon it, if they chose to do so, which most did not. He did, however, keep the shelves stacked with books, all of which he had read at some point and concluded that most were useless. Therapy was never an exercise that could readily be consigned to a hardback volume.

The cost of the lease was covered entirely by Josh's work at the university, and his living expenses were covered by his private clients—the ones who paid. He had always been the ear, the shoulder, to everyone, hence his career choice, which at times he wished had been different, but he didn't know what else he could do, so he just stuck with it. He didn't perceive the time spent listening to friends as part of his work, even if they often expected the aloofness and confidentiality of his profession in these interchanges. That said, only Dan had come to him specifically requesting that he deal with a matter in such a way, and Josh remained true to his word in doing so. Dan even wanted to pay for the consultations, but the offer had been rejected.

Jess sat on the couch, sipping coffee and scanning the bookshelves, whilst Josh tidied papers on a desk diagonally across the room.

"I'm just passing the time, you know?" she said self-consciously.

"Yes, I figured that much out for myself. And since when did you need an excuse to come and visit? Fashion advice? I mean!"

"Well, that bit is true. I have got to find something to wear for this dinner. They've visited before, and for the life of me, I can't remember what I wore last time."

"Hence you have this need for a new outfit."

"Ahem. Yes," Jess coughed nervously. She knew as well as Josh did that her need to buy anything was a sign of something more serious. Josh banged the edges of the papers to form a neat pile and sat down opposite.

"So," she said, "now you're in your therapist's chair, what's the verdict?"

"You tell me. You're the one passing time, so why would there be any more to it?" That was always how he dealt with Jess. She knew for herself precisely what was going on; it took the questions and permission to think.

"Bloody Adele. If she were here, I could have been in and out of the shop in half an hour with exactly the right things." She drew her finger around the top of the coffee mug, stopping to wipe out the lipstick with her thumb. "I bet she's having a fantastic time."

"Bloody Adele—for that reason?"

"Yes. No. Well." She stopped. Josh remained silent. "Don't you feel that life is kind of beginning to pass us by?"

"Why? Because one of us tied the knot?"

"Not just that. Shaunna and Kris, too. It's always been OK because we were all in the same boat. Now George has his ranch. Adele's married. People are starting to move away."

"That's not entirely true," Josh challenged, as it wasn't true at all. He continued, "George left years ago. Shaunna and Kris have been together forever—they only formalised it. Adele was always going to get married. She's the marrying sort. Needs a husband, a significant other. Do you need a significant other, Jess?"

"No, thanks. But it's not just me. Look at Andy, strapped up in traction at his age. It's a bit of a joke, isn't it?" She paused momentarily, and Josh made to answer, but then thought better of it.

It was a rhetorical question, possibly, but either way, he couldn't lead the discussion any further down that line. There were many times lately he'd found he was thinking the same, that somehow he and his friends were stuck in the past, not moving forward with their lives. Yet his clients, with their tired, old marriages, were the very people they were measuring their own achievements against. He could not honestly describe any of those individuals as successful.

"Are you jealous?" he asked, instead of all that was in his mind to say.

"Of Adele and Tom? Maybe a little. I wouldn't mind experiencing that blind love thing again, but once you have and you know it's not what it's cracked up to be there's very little point in going there again."

"That's the thing, though. At our age we know falling in love is a myth."

"I think Adele would disagree."

"She's not really our age, is she?" Josh contended. "Not on the inside."

"I guess not. God. At our age. Is this all life has to offer? Careers and loathing of the very notion of love and romance?"

He had nothing to say to that, being as he'd always hated the idea of love or anything else that implied a long-term, legally enforceable obligation. Based on his experience by proxy, it was all a bit too much like a prison sentence.

Jess lay down on the couch. "It's a very vulnerable time, your mid-thirties, don't you think?"

"Yes, I agree, but only if we're going to get all nostalgic and regretful about it. You know what I think?"

"What?"

"We should go to Ellie's and eat pizza till we're sick."

***

The pizza restaurant was part choice, part accident. When she'd decided that she no longer wanted to be a doctor, Eleanor took the first job that came up, and even with her credentials, outside of healthcare, it was still about working her way through the ranks. So she started as a waitress in The Pizza Place, completed a shortened version of management training and now ran her own restaurant.

It was a hard job with terrible pay, compared to what she could be earning, but she didn't care a bit. It filled the days and nights and was a curious contradiction that kept her diet under control. Having watched her customers eat the quantities of junk they did day after day, most of the time she simply could not bring herself to eat in anything more than a functional way.

Josh and Jess were immediately recognised by the waitress, who seated them at what had become 'their table', given how often Josh sat in with a pile of paperwork at the end of the day, waiting for closing time. Once the place was shut for the night, he and Eleanor would head off to a quiet bar and chat. They did it so frequently that most people would run out of things to say, yet they never did. It had always been that way. Neither of them could recount what they talked about for hours at a time, but anyone looking on would see an intense and trusted dialogue that relied as much on non-verbal communication as it did on words.

"Hey!" Eleanor called over cheerily, as she wiped a glass with a cloth. "Bit early in the day, isn't it?"

"Jess wanted to go shopping," Josh explained.

"Oh, dear." Eleanor went over to their table. "What's up?"

"Has it ever occurred to the pair of you that sometimes I might just need to go shopping?" Jess protested. Her companions looked at each other and shook their heads. "OK, OK." She sighed. "Sometimes I really do just need to go shopping, and…" They waited a moment before she continued. "This isn't one of those times. Ah, crap."

"Well, pizza's always good," Josh redirected, casually picking up a menu—a pointless exercise as he always ordered exactly the same thing: cheese garlic bread. He didn't even like pizza. Jess ordered a Caesar salad, and Eleanor came over with a coffee on her break. They continued the conversation that had started in the surgery, but with Eleanor's perspective it took a very different turn.

There was, she argued, nothing bad about being thirty-six and single, nor having friendships as close as theirs. Many would give all they had for such things. They lived their lives by their own rules, with no imposition from husbands or wives, each answerable only to his or herself, and how could it ever be lonely when they always had each other?

She finished by pointing out that Adele—should her marriage last, and Eleanor truly believed it might—was likely to find that at times she felt trapped by her idyllic life. It would be a superlative existence, where she would be treated like a princess. All that she wished for, Tom would provide, and Adele was shallow enough for her feelings for Dan to transition over time, if she let them.

Josh and Jess knew Eleanor was right; she had an uncanny way of just knowing some things, like she had predicted George's migration long before his father's death.

After they had eaten and Eleanor returned to work, they went their separate ways. Josh had an evening appointment with a client; Jess decided she would leave the purchase of an outfit for another day. It was a step in the right direction, however short-lived. She returned to her office, collected some case notes and went home to review them over a bottle or two of red wine. This, as Eleanor rightly pointed out, was living by her own rules, and she could not in all honesty see a day when she would again be tempted to pass it up for love and marriage, however lonely she was feeling right now.

Josh arrived at his surgery with minutes to spare before his client, a young man named Richard, was due to arrive. Richard was invariably punctual, indeed he was consistent in all manners, which was why he was a client. It was apparent that Richard had a mild form of autism, perhaps Asperger's Syndrome, but had not received a formal diagnosis, and Josh was only qualified to speculate and advise.

Richard absolutely refused any kind of referral, instead choosing to focus on the symptoms of his difficulties, which, at the current time, revolved around his fascination with a certain girl at college. It didn't appear that his obsession was based on physical attraction, but on his observation that she sat in a different place for every lecture.

Josh concurred that this was unusual, as people, being territorial in nature, tend to select a seat at the beginning of a course and return to it, or the immediate vicinity, thereafter. However, to have such rage about it was abnormal, thus was the basis of Richard's treatment.

There were many times when Josh had felt slightly unsafe in the presence of clients. At any given time, the odds were that he was going to have at least one or two really crazy people on his list—the sort who could as easily chat about their troubles quietly over a cup of tea as they could leap from the couch and lock him in a stranglehold. Thankfully, that didn't happen often, for at all times he kept the air of confidence and control that he had owned before any training tried to instil it.

Richard was most bizarre, but not one of the crazy ones, even if he did demonstrate a certain amount of aggression at some point during every session, usually in the form of shouting or, on occasion, hitting himself.

Things were no different during this visit. For the first twenty minutes, Richard sat bolt upright on the couch, exactly in the centre of the middle cushion and as if wearing a back brace, pummelling his left palm with his right fist, saying nothing at all and scanning the expanse of carpet between them. That was the worst type of consultation, where a client refuses to speak, and there is so much to do, yet a book can't be read, case notes cannot be glanced over, it would be insensitive to get on with a bit of vacuuming, turn on some music, or otherwise engage in any activity which might detract from the paid-for silence.

Josh noted, after ten minutes or so, the pummelling had a steady rhythm that any metronome would be proud of; it lasted for a count of six. Beat one: the fist hits the palm; twists left to right for two to six; a six-beat rest; and on again, and again. Every attempt he made to provoke discussion hung in the air like evaporating breath on a cold winter's morning; he was unsure whether he'd just asked the question or thought he should. Twenty minutes of easy money, some would suggest, but they would be the ones who had never experienced this kind of financially secured boredom.

Finally, asynchronous with the ticking of the desk clock but in perfect time with the pummelling, a grunt. Nothing more than a gruff letting of air, but still, an opportunity to venture within the pause in motion that followed.

"Richard, we have very little time left this evening, and evidently you are struggling with something."

Another grunt and a return to the six-beat rhythm.

"Last time, we discussed the girl in your French class. You also mentioned a problem with your housemates. Can I ask if either of these difficulties is in your mind now?"

Still nothing but the incessant rhythms of hands and clocks. Josh also noted that the water pipes clanked at quite regular intervals. Undoubtedly, those would not be predictable enough to please his client.

"There is a square pattern to the weave of this carpet," Richard stated, finally and clearly.

Josh held on to a sigh with all he had. "Really? I hadn't noticed."

"Yes. I know it is a plain carpet. The manufacturing process must cause the square pattern, every ten centimetres, ten centimetres."

Josh turned his attention to the beige carpet and could see Richard was right. There was a slight dip in the pile, creating squares that, he was certain, if he were to take a ruler to them, would be exactly ten centimetres in length and width.

"She does it every time, the girl," Richard continued, as if the carpet and the girl were connected in some metaphysical sense. "Every time a different chair. Not the same chair ever."

"This still makes you angry."

"Yes. Very angry. Two hundred and fourteen chairs in the room. She will not ever sit on the same chair twice."

"What makes you think that?"

"She comes in and looks at the chairs. She thinks about it for five or six seconds. She chooses a place. Always a different chair." Richard stopped pounding his hand and held eye contact, only for a fleeting moment, not even a second. "You think I am mad. I know that I am not like everyone else, but the girl. She does it on purpose."

"It is very strange behaviour, I grant you. However, we still need to understand why it bothers you so much. You told me last time it was not because she was unpredictable."

"She is not unpredictable. She is very predictable. She always sits in a different chair. That is predictable. You know I like patterns. There is no pattern to where she sits." Richard's clipped sentences had replaced the rhythm of his hands.

"What worries you most about this girl? Is it that you think she will sit in your chair?"

"No. I get there nine minutes before the lecture starts. Three is a good number. Three minutes would not be early enough. Three times three is nine. Nine minutes is long enough."

Josh waited for more. It was the most Richard had ever talked without constant prompting. He didn't have to wait long, and again, knew for sure that the elapsed time would meet Richard's requirement for patterns.

"She does not sit in the places others have made their own. The class has only thirty-seven students. She will not ever need to sit in the same place twice. She will not ever need to sit in someone else's place. Someone else's place that they have made their own. Not ever."

There was always a monotony to Richard's tone. Even in the height of an emotional exchange, the pitch was constant, and Josh had become accustomed to listening for slight changes in volume, a little shakiness, or the tiniest increase in the speed of its delivery. The latter was what he sensed, and he thought he knew why, although quite what he was going to do with it was another matter.

"Can I speculate here?" Josh paused, for exactly six seconds. He knew this by the tick of the clock. *Damn, now he has me at it.* "Would I be right in saying what worries you most is that one day she will accidentally sit in a chair she has sat in before?"

Richard grunted and remained completely still. Josh continued his analysis.

"And you are worried about this because you don't know how you will cope with it, because at the moment you have recognised that she is someone like you?"

Richard resumed his earlier scanning of the carpet. Josh even detected a slight rocking motion, which told him he had hit the nail right on the head. He was a little irritated with himself for making diagnostic assumptions, for this was the seventh consultation he had held with Richard, and not once did it occur to him that it young man might be in love.

For most people, the experience of being in love was one that could be made a lot easier with the services of a therapist; for Richard it was the only way he could deal with it. This was a breakthrough, and it was one that had been delayed by Josh's arrogant belief in the rules and principles governing his discipline, the ones he'd shunned at university, when he instead chose to pursue what his professors referred to as wishy-washy pop psychology and a licence to print money.

Having mentally kicked himself in the shin, he adjusted his approach and noted down a couple of ideas on where to take the treatment next. He had thought to himself, and recorded several sessions ago, that the girl was as nuts as his client, although not in those terms. It was time for some straight talk. That was what people like Richard required—the sort of questions where there was no possibility of misinterpretation. Once he had established for sure that Richard was indeed attracted to this girl, further research in the area would be necessary. Still, it made a change from self-harming teenagers, oppressed housewives and paranoid husbands who invested heavily in the concept of the mid-life crisis.

"OK," Josh resumed, "I need to ask you some questions. You can choose not to answer if you wish. However, if you want me to help you, then it would be best if you can be honest and open with me. Is that all right?" The clock ticked the passage of six seconds.

"Yes," Richard replied. Josh respectfully waited another six seconds before venturing onward.

"Are you attracted to the girl we have talked about?"

"Yes."

"Do you have feelings for her?"

"Yes."

"Do you want to talk to her about this?"

"No."

Bugger. Stumped again. And he'd not been counting the seconds, but Richard had.

"She doesn't know who I am. I cannot talk to her."

Back on track again, Josh thought it safe to strive on in the same direction.

"So, what you mean is you would like to talk to her but can't, because you believe she hasn't even noticed you exist." Richard nodded his agreement and Josh went on. "This is a very normal feeling. Most people experience it when they like someone the way you do. Sometimes even people we have known for a long time as friends. As soon as we start to feel differently about them, we believe that it is one-sided and they still only see us as a friend."

And oh, how that was based on something of a personal experience, not for Josh, exactly. George on the other hand, for so many years his friend, and no more than that, suddenly declares that he loves him, always has, always will. He could honestly say in all that time he had never felt the same way about George, nor noticed that was how George felt about him. In his defence, none of their friends seemed to have picked up on it, either. It had been a further ten years since George's admission, and it got no easier for either of them.

The session was officially over, and Richard was already standing up, getting into his jacket. That was one of his best aspects as a client; others required a little encouragement to leave, sometimes even pushing towards the door.

"I am pleased that what I feel is normal," he said, fastening his buttons, three of them, Josh observed. "Thank you, Josh. It has been most helpful."

"Good. You have done very well. What I will do is have a look at some research before I see you next."

"It is strange that being in love is something that can be studied like that."

"Yes. I agree with you, but then every aspect of human experience can be studied. A lot of the time, I feel the scientific approach is a little useless to what we do here. However, on this occasion I don't know the area too well, so I will definitely need to do some reading up."

"You have never been in love," Richard stated.

"No," Josh answered. "I haven't."

Chapter Four:
After Effects

It seemed so much less than two weeks since Adele's wedding, and George didn't feel like going home—nothing new there. He always stayed longer than planned and had learned long ago to keep the date of his return flight open. The downside was that travelling economy class with an open return cost almost as much as business class; if it were a toss-up between the two, then a few extra days with his friends won every time.

Before George went home, though, they had to go out as a group, even if they were depleted in number. They went to an all-you-can-eat buffet at a Chinese restaurant up town—a frequent haunt because it was cheap with excellent food. When Krissi was little, they'd gone a lot earlier in the evening so she wouldn't get too tired, although even as a teenager, she had acted more like a grown-up than some of the friends. Now she was almost twenty-one, officially an adult, and to a greater extent accepted as such, but she would always be Shaunna's baby.

With Andy still in hospital—they'd promised him a doggy bag—and Adele on her honeymoon, they booked a table for eight, at eight, instead of a table for ten.

Eleanor returned from the washroom and to her seat between Josh and George, who briefly paused to acknowledge her before resuming their conversation with ease. It was one of those conversations that skirted around the edges of anything meaningful, because George's feelings for Josh persisted wherever he was, endured across thousands of miles, being ignored for entire evenings, unanswered emails and unlifted telephone receivers. He didn't harass Josh at all, but sometimes each felt for their own reasons that he did.

George was no different from the rest of the friends in wanting to confide in Josh; only Adele did so to a lesser extent, and sometimes it genuinely was just to chat about life in general, though there was nothing interesting or new to say after ten years. That was how long George had been on the ranch, and life was pretty mundane. Everyone knew what it was like, but it still made for good small talk, and George was, as always, ribbing Josh, and the others, about what they were missing.

The promised visits only happened twice: once in the middle of summer when it was warm, dry and dusty, and once for Thanksgiving, when they were snowed in for two weeks and all had to plead for mercy from their employers and clients as soon as the phones were back up and running. It was quite an adventure on both occasions.

On the first visit, in the summer, the girls in particular were astonished to see how George was living. They had imagined that the house would be a large homestead, like the *Little House On The Prairie*. Instead, they found a rundown shack, with boards nailed diagonally across the horizontal timbers that made up the exterior walls. The once-white paint flaked away, revealing rotting, infested wood and the interior was no better, consisting as it did of one giant room downstairs and three smaller rooms upstairs. The shower and toilet were in an outbuilding, which was in a slightly superior condition to the house, but required a twenty-yard dash across semi-baked earth or frozen mud, depending on the season.

"I am going to rebuild it," George assured them, then in a quieter voice, as if anyone else would hear him anyway, he added, "They build their own houses here, you know. I don't have a clue where to begin."

"Unfortunately, it's the one thing none of us can help you with," Jess sympathised, and it was mostly true. Between them they could have treated all his ills, medical or psychological, found him the best deals on the market, cared for his children, represented him in a court of law and made sure he was dressed stylishly and appropriately for the event. Andy, who had scraped through a degree that theoretically qualified him for the task, also claimed he didn't have the know-how required for building an entire house, even if it was more of a glorified shed—something they discussed at length over warm beer during their first evening at the ranch.

***

"Couldn't you at least get a fridge?" Adele grimaced as she swigged from the bottle.

"And why?" Josh stated rather than asked. "Why build timber houses in the middle of nowhere when a tornado could just come right along and whip them straight up in the air?"

"I only just got the electricity sorted, Adele, and I don't know, Josh. I'm sure there is a very good reason for it," George slurred. The beer was unrefreshing, but still effective and as the sun dropped, so, too, did the temperature, making it somehow more palatable.

"Actually, good seasoned timber is stronger than concrete," Dan chipped in.

"So what you're saying is that these old shacks are stronger than our brick houses back home? I don't think so." Josh always got a bit bolshy with alcohol and, as usual, directed it at Dan.

"I didn't say that."

"Oh no, sorry. You implied it."

"Anyway!" Eleanor interjected.

"Yes, anyway." Jess gave Josh a nudge with her elbow.

"What?" he protested, but let it go.

"Andy and I know this guy," Dan continued, now that the girls had silenced Josh.

"Do we?"

"Yes. Bill Swanson? Swanson Homes?"

"Ah, yeah." Andy wasn't sure who Dan meant initially. "Yeah, we do."

"He might be able to help you out with the rebuild supplies. I can call him now, if you like."

"That's the thing, though. What am I going to do with a big pile of timber?" George sighed hopelessly.

"Well, when I say 'rebuild supplies', what I mean is Swanson just brings a ready-made house on the back of a big truck and dumps it where you tell him to."

"Oh, I get you," Shaunna said. "I've seen it on the telly."

"Now that could work," George pondered.

Josh made some sort of noise between a laugh and a snort, got up from his chair without saying a word, and went walking off, past the outhouses into the black beyond. No comment was passed; it was just him being his usual self. He was a very tolerant, patient, caring man, but every now and then, he would flip out, and if he was gone too long, Eleanor would go after him, and they would return together, acting as if everything was as it should be.

Needless to say, by the following year and their second visit at Thanksgiving, George was still living in his dilapidated house, as it became one of the many constants in his life. It was therefore customary to start every communication, face to face or otherwise, with the question, 'Have you ordered your new house?' to which George always responded, 'No, not yet.' It was all to do with machismo; and Josh.

***

The waiter didn't rush the friends, who inevitably stayed for several hours, picked at the food constantly and bought plenty of drinks. They were good for business, so it really wasn't in the restaurant's interests to get rid of them, nor do anything which might dissuade them from frequenting the place. However, by half past eleven, all the other customers else had left, and the tables were set for the next day, which proved to be enough of a hint.

"Right, let me see that," Dan said, taking the bill from the waiter.

"How much each?" George asked, getting out his wallet. "Split seven ways is…"

"Eight," Krissi protested.

"Ah, yeah. I forgot you're in the money these days."

"Well, I didn't have any wine, just a couple of Cokes," Dan thought aloud, oblivious to the discussion going on around him.

"Oh, shut up. You're not really going to start calculating what we each owe," Josh remarked in curt disbelief. "We've always split it evenly between the ten of us."

"Nine," George protested.

"Or eight tonight, at least," Jess added.

"That's what I mean. It's too confusing." Dan was still trying to calculate his own contribution.

"That's what we've always done," Josh stated again.

"Not always," George said. "Krissi's only just started paying her own way."

"That's not helpful, George," Eleanor muttered, reading the signs.

"Oh, just give it here!" Jess snatched the bill from Dan, leaving him looking puzzled and like he was holding an invisible piece of paper. She paid with her credit card and told them to give her their share once they'd stopped fighting about it. She'd talked herself into a fair old state of misery and just wanted to go home.

She hadn't intended to spend the entire evening berating the dreadful dinner party her employers had forced upon her, but it was almost one of the greatest disasters of her career. It was held at a senior partner's home: a lovely, vast house befitting his wealth. His wife was pleasant enough and assisted in the kitchen as the guests arrived—for the sake of appearances. It was clear she never did any cooking, or cleaning. She was well groomed, toned and in fine condition for a woman in her late fifties.

The dinner also progressed reasonably well, with the usual introductory chitchat, which led on to business matters and concluded with brandies and coffees and cigars for the men. Jess had given up smoking long ago, but the smell of a lit cigar was still a beautiful thing.

By the end of the evening, she was feeling a little bit drunk. Too many glasses of wine, topped up with a double brandy— not a wise combination—and her requirement for a get-out was immediate in order to ward off the attentions of her boss, the senior partner whose house they were in. He had likewise had too much to drink and didn't appear to care that his wife was within earshot, as he went beyond mere flirting. Everyone was acting as if all was well, and to her credit, his wife could see that Jess was playing no active part in her husband's antics. In the end, it was she who came to the rescue.

"I'll give you a lift home, love," she offered, then added, "I haven't been drinking."

Her husband gracefully bowed out and went to join the rest of the men. Jess quickly said her goodbyes, and followed her boss's wife out to the garage.

"Thank you for this, Mrs. Sharston," she said gratefully, as she climbed into the passenger seat of the gold Mercedes and pulled the seat belt across her lap.

"Please, call me Angie," the woman said, fastening her own seat belt and starting the engine, which automatically raised the garage door in front of them.

"That's cool," Jess remarked in awe.

"Oh, yes, I love gadgets. I have so much stuff that does things like that. All pointless, really, but it makes life easier. Less broken finger nails, and all that." Angie drove forward, advancing along the floodlit driveway towards the double gates that, again, parted of their own accord.

"Charles is very generous—and a faithful man," she continued, as she manoeuvred the giant car into the dimmer light of the private road. "Just no control over his groin. They all get a bit like that at his age."

Jess laughed lightly. Yes, she had seen that this was true. It was the ever-repeating story of her love life, and she got the distinct impression that Angie's sensing of this was why she was being taken home. There were a few moments of silence before this was confirmed.

"I know you had an affair with Alan," she stated. Alan was the other senior partner. "His wife doesn't know, though, so no harm done."

"It's not…I don't…" Jess started to explain, but the words were not there, not with the alcohol muddling her thinking.

"You don't seek them out. They come to you. You are an attractive, successful woman. Younger than them and still in need of a man to take care of you. They are lured by this, and you know it. Still, you don't resist, do you?"

"No. I suppose not."

"Well. As I say, no harm done, is there? Incidentally, I don't know where you live."

"Oh. Of course." Jess proceeded to direct Angie, and nothing further was said on the matter.

She felt better for sharing her ordeal with Shaunna, but as she talked it through, it became apparent that she would need to seek alternative employment. A week had passed since the post-dinner pep talk, and still Charles seemed intent on bedding her. Aside from being utterly terrified of Angie, Jess had promised herself that she would not let this happen again.

She blamed Andy, who'd have been with her at the dinner, had he not been so idiotic as to smash up his legs. The eldest in the group and still acting like a seventeen-year-old; racing his mates along country lanes in fast cars, for goodness' sakes. And the consequence of his accident? He was going to start rallying instead, because it was safer. She didn't need to worry, he said; they wear crash helmets and drive reinforced cars. When he was bored with that escapade, he would move on to something more dangerous, but for now she was to 'just chill'.

Chapter Five:
Group Dynamics

Adele returned from her honeymoon, floating on a high that looked set to last. She was finally starting to feel for Tom what she felt for Dan, although it would never be entirely so. Dan was her first true love, someone she had cared about all of her life. They were at primary school together, and neither could remember the time before they knew each other.

The countless occasions he had pulled the ribbons off her pigtails had merged into one, not to mention when he'd stuck PVA glue in her hair, or drawn cat's whiskers on her face in permanent marker. They were forever in heaps of trouble, being kept in at playtime, given detention at high school and always the same thing.

"It was her, Miss."

"No it wasn't. He started it, Miss."

Afterwards, they would laugh about it, still usually throwing stuff and playful insults at each other.

When Adele felt her relations with others drifting into romance, Shaunna became her confidante. Adele's love for Dan was beyond all else, towering miles above the dates and boyfriends. It wasn't going to conveniently fade away, just because she'd married Tom, who, like those who had gone before him, knew precisely where he stood. Still, a man could not be put down for trying, and he was set on giving her everything she wanted, and more.

He wasn't Dan; she didn't want him to be, for the exquisiteness of that affection was matched with an equally sharp pain that thrust deep into the pit of her stomach every time Dan walked away. They could have made it work, if either could stop being arrogant and selfish long enough to make the other happy.

Adele decided to avoid Shaunna for a few days, mostly because she was still annoyed with her for not spending the wedding reception at the top table. It was almost perfect: the white satin dress encrusted with tiny pearls and appliqué lace; the silver-and-white stiletto shoes that left her four inches shorter than Tom and only just taller than Shaunna; a dangerously long train; six bridesmaids. She'd spent all she had on the wedding, and her father had matched it pound for pound.

To have her best friend let her down was something Adele hadn't anticipated, although she was aware she was making a far bigger deal of it than was necessary, which Tom suggested— cautiously—was due to her hormones. However, the seven deep-pink dresses alone had cost a fifth of the budget, and her matron of honour hadn't really shown hers off to full effect.

By the time she did contact Shaunna, three weeks had passed since the wedding, and Adele had calmed down considerably, almost seeing the whole situation rationally, with time to unpack and savour all of the wedding gifts, which were exactly as requested on the list, so no surprises in general, although as always, Josh and Eleanor couldn't help but put their own twist on things.

The list stated precisely which set of cutlery Adele wanted, and they had bought that one, but they hadn't actually delivered it yet. Instead, they'd wrapped up a set of plastic-handled, second-hand cutlery bought from a car boot sale, knowing

Adele would not complain to them directly, but she would bitch about it to everyone else.

As predictably as ever, it was the first thing she said to Shaunna, after checking there was no gossip to catch up on. It had been a very quiet time: no bust-ups, the usual get-together, no events between Josh and George to speak of, and Jess had 'done a Jess'. Adele was pleased to have missed out on that part, even if she was somewhat disappointed by the general lack of anything interesting to talk about. She moved on to describing, at length, her wedding presents, her honeymoon, and all other Matters Of Significance To Adele but of little importance to anyone else. If Shaunna was disinterested, she didn't show it.

"The hotel was spectacular. Our room, or should I say suite, had a balcony overlooking the bay."

"Wow, that sounds fabulous."

"Oh, it was. The water was so clear, we could see the golden sand below. I felt terribly sick the last few mornings and sat on the balcony, watching the fishermen go out. I even saw some dolphins once."

"Don't tell Krissi that. She's got a thing for dolphins."

"And there was this little village up in the hills, where they make cheese, though, of course, I couldn't try any..." She continued, oblivious to her friend's responses, until there was nothing left to talk about.

Next, Adele visited Andy, who was just home from hospital and still immobile. She was off work for a few more days and offered to help out where she could. He was grateful, of course, and if she was being genuinely helpful, then it would be ungracious to refuse.

However, it crossed his mind that she was only offering in order to stay close to Dan. The last breakup, like the ones preceding it, had been terrible for both of them, with Dan going to see Josh on a weekly basis—something he thought he'd kept well hidden from everyone.

If they had not been in the same friendship group, it was unlikely Andy and Dan would have been close as brothers, considering they were the most distant of all the friends as it was. That said, there was still a connection between them that allowed for second-guessing and created certain obligations regarding staying in regular contact. Between their genetic and business connections, it was enough to ensure that they saw a lot more of each other than either would have chosen to.

This, Andy speculated, was what Adele was banking on with her offer of assistance. Still, he didn't turn her down, just in case he was wrong, and she performed dutifully for two full days before giving up, or maybe he was just being mean.

Adele usually steered clear of Josh, even though she liked him and respected his opinion. However, since he'd trained as a therapist, she was convinced he could see right inside her head, so she avoided eye contact when forced to share a confined space, where possible doing everything in her power to not be in that confined space to begin with.

Thus, she wasn't too happy when he and Eleanor popped round with the cutlery, because Tom was at work and Eleanor received an emergency call from her assistant manager. She wasn't going to be long, but it left Josh and Adele sitting together in the living room, and there was absolutely no escape.

Josh, being the sort of person he was, and being able to see right inside Adele's head, knew exactly why she was so uncomfortable in his presence. Every now and then, in situations like this, he even considered addressing the matter, to reassure her that, in spite of her being as transparent as glass, he would never trespass into her mind.

But then he always concluded that it was pointless. She would just see it as some sort of psychological game; a bluff to cover the fact that all the while he was probing her brain for her deepest, darkest secrets. Instead, he opted for a topic of conversation that meant revealing his own psyche, not that she would appreciate it, which was probably why he felt safe doing so.

"I've had a dream about a waterslide about six times now."

"A waterslide? What do you mean?"

"One of those big tubes they swoosh water through so you don't get friction burns on the way down."

"Oh, yes. We went to a water park with those in Italy."

"It's definitely not my idea of fun."

"They're dead good, although Tom wasn't happy about me going on them, not in my condition. Why don't you like them?"

"I don't know, really. It's just not something I've ever wanted to do. I can swim and all that, but there's a big difference between popping to the local pool and going to one of those places. The only time I did, Ellie tried to force me down a massive slide, and I bottled out. Not my cup of tea at all."

"Each to their own." A few moments' silence passed, and Adele started to fidget.

Most people, when engaged in conversation with Adele, would indulge her. She was the sort who could bring every event back to herself, and as there was little else to talk about, it usually provided some fuel to sustain the dialogue. Josh never played up to this and was more than comfortable sitting in silence. He was used to it, but eventually, she had to say something.

"So, what happens in this dream of yours?"

"Not much, actually, although it does change a bit each time. Basically, I'm at the top of one of those tubes, waiting to step into it, and there's a queue of people behind me, getting impatient. I can't get down off the platform, and then I realise I'm naked. The next thing, I get pushed, I think, into the tube, but that's when I wake up."

"Ooh. How weird. My dream book says loads of stuff about dreaming you're naked. But then, you know more about that than me, obviously."

"Not necessarily. What does it say?"

"I'll go and get it." With that, Adele sprinted off to another room. For a minute or so, there was a lot of banging about and the sound of tape being torn off boxes, before she returned with the tiny, hardback book.

"Let's see, N…N…naked, page…Right. Dreaming you are naked: you are worried you are going to be found out about something. Oh, no, this is it. To suddenly discover you are naked means you are feeling vulnerable." She returned to the book's index to see if waterslide was listed.

At least the book was in agreement with everything Josh knew about dream symbolism, but he wasn't the vulnerable sort. Or maybe on a subconscious level he was, and if so, what was he suddenly feeling vulnerable about? That was a big question, and he didn't have an answer.

"Water." Adele found the page. "There's nothing here about waterslides, or running water, what about boiling water? Was the water warm?"

"I have no idea, but it was bubbling, so it's close enough."

"OK, well, it says you are either going through emotional turmoil, or you are ready to deal with something in your unconscious."

"I see," Josh said flatly, but he really couldn't. It was like reading one's horoscope—sweeping generalisations that were supposed to apply to millions of people who happened to have been born in the same month, or in this case, because they'd had a similar dream.

"So, Josh, are you going through emotional turmoil?" Adele was quite enjoying herself.

"Ha! What do you think?"

"When did you have the dream for the first time?"

"The night before you got married. But I think that was more to do with kebab at three a.m. than anything else. And I was thirsty, which was probably what the water was about."

"But then, why do you keep dreaming it?"

She had a very good point there, he had to admit. However, he was getting a bit fed up with Adele's turning of the tables on him and wished Eleanor would hurry up and get back.

"You don't think it was a premonition about me and Tom, do you?" Adele gasped in horror at the possibility.

"I'm not psychic, so I very much doubt it. Mind you, maybe it was a bit about you and Tom."

She looked mortified, and Josh silently reprimanded himself. It was a dangerous thing to say to Adele, of all people, however true it might be. He, like everyone else, worried that the marriage was a rebound from Dan. Even Tom had said as much on the stag night. The question was, not if, but *when* it failed, who would be there for Tom? Adele would still have them, and he would be on his own.

Eleanor's timely arrival killed the opportunity for Adele to probe further, and she was clearly disappointed.

"Miss me?" Eleanor asked, throwing her keys onto the sofa next to Josh.

"Not really." He winked and held his hands up to protect himself from the gentle cuffing he would get for saying it. "Adele's been analysing my dream."

"Which dream?"

"The one about the waterslide. I did tell you."

"Oh, that dream," she dismissed it. She loved Josh but hated all his psychobabble. Dreams were a function of sleep. That was that. She wasn't interested.

A short time later, they made their excuses, accepted a peck on the cheek and hug of thanks for the real cutlery, and left. It was a dreary Saturday afternoon, with nothing much to do, but there was only so far a conversation with Adele could journey, so they went for a coffee, before Eleanor headed towards home and Josh to his surgery to retrieve some case notes he needed to read before Monday.

Chapter Six:
Insight

Dan's new girlfriend was called Alison. She was exactly what everyone expected of him—as blonde and skinny as he was dark and muscular—and she looked good on his arm. That was also true of Adele, but knowing her as he did had taken all of the fun out of using her as a fashion accessory. Alison, on the other hand, didn't seem to care. She liked a man who acknowledged her looks. She liked flowers and fast cars, and Dan was gorgeous, her friends agreed. He said and did all the right things.

Except what they saw as 'the right things' Dan did because it paid off quickly. He was more than happy to join up with her and the girls later in the evening, if it meant he got to take her home and get what he wanted, without having to spend too much time with her. He wasn't really that shallow, but their relationship was. Even so, he introduced her to 'The Circle'— as Tom had referred to them in his groom's speech—and they tolerated her.

Alison could just about hold her own with Shaunna and Adele, but the rest of them, deliberately at times, talked about things that floated right over her head. Eleanor, in particular although by no means exclusively, had a snobbish disregard for latest conquests that were, inevitably, going to be short-lived and not worth the effort.

She'd initially treated Tom the same way but was prepared to admit that she might, possibly, have been wrong on that one.

He and Adele had already been together longer than any of the others had managed. Now they were married, things seemed to be going well for them, and that was usually the bit where it all started to fall apart. It had held true for Eleanor, and for Jess—the only ones to have endeavoured into the realms of what should have been long-term relationships with outsiders. It occurred to her that, for all the wonder of their friendships, there was also something distinctly destructive about them.

One night, they went out to a club and were standing at the bar. It was Eleanor's round, and Dan had volunteered to help carry the drinks, seeing as it should really have been Andy's turn, but he was still on crutches.

"You don't like Alison, do you?" Dan asked, picking up three glasses with one hand.

"I can't stand her," Eleanor admitted, disappointed with herself for not being able to lie about it.

"Fair enough." Dan's reply was muffled by the bag of peanuts hanging from his teeth. He picked up the other two glasses and let go of the peanuts, using his forearm as a shelf to carry them. "She's not a keeper," he said.

"I'd gathered that much, but watch her. She might act dumb, but she's the type who'd accidentally get pregnant for the trophy."

Dan laughed at the idea; he couldn't see it himself. Admittedly, if his friends didn't know better, they would have assumed that she was playing him for all his worth. She loved staying over at his flat, which was very stylish, with its solid oak flooring and pool of Japanese koi. His bedroom was painted maroon and gold, with coordinating throws, cushions and rugs. All of it was Adele's doing, when she lived there—other than the koi. They were Dan's babies, collected for their status rather than attachment.

For women like Alison, it was about status—good-looking men with money and style. Dan's car, pearlescent blue-black in finish, with leather seats and a top-notch stereo, converted to an open-top at the press of a button, and when he dropped her off at work, everyone heard him and looked to see where the wide-bore-exhaust boom and thumping bass were coming from. Thus, they would see Alison kissing a gorgeous hunk and climbing out of his hunkmobile. She loved it, because it made her workmates jealous. She didn't love Dan, though.

The relationship lasted six weeks exactly, from the day they met and shared a lift through twenty storeys, to the day they separated in that very same lift. Alison folded her arms, stated it wasn't working, pushed the button for the next floor and was gone. If Dan picked up girls just because they were attractive and easily impressed, then there was only so long he could carry on the pretence of being interested in all their pointless little bickerings with friends, and woes about which shade of lipstick worked best with sunbed-tanned skin. No further commentary required, no need for a post mortem, Dan went to see Josh.

It was unusual for the waiting room to be occupied by more than one person, but then Josh tried to keep at least fifteen minutes free between appointments, and Dan had turned up unannounced. The young man sitting there looked somewhat uncomfortable, perched as he was on the edge of the chair, knees tight together, hands clasped, eyes staring into the mid-distance. He muttered a disjointed 'hello' in Dan's general direction, and Dan responded likewise, before taking a seat as far away as he could possibly get.

Occasionally, he caught a wisp of conversation from beyond the closed door to the consultation room—a woman, mid-forties, he guessed, talking and talking about children and, what sounded like bikes, but could have been blinds, or bites, or anything really. The room wasn't entirely soundproof, but not much got beyond those four walls, and the fact he could hear anything at all came from Josh and his client being only inches away, standing just the other side of the door.

Dan's mobile phone bleeped, indicating he had received an email. He pulled it from his pocket and began to read, noting out of the corner of his eye the other man's irritation.

"Sorry about that, I'll put it on silent," he said and did so before he replied to the message. The door opened and Josh ushered the woman out—he had been right—she did look to be in her mid-forties and a little rough around the edges, on account of the children, he imagined. She bustled away towards the stairs and disappeared from view.

"Hey, Dan!" Josh greeted him. "I'll be free in half an hour."

"Righto. I'll go online and have a look at share prices, or read the news, or something."

"OK. You know where the coffee is. In fact, if you're making one, I wouldn't say no. Richard, sorry about the wait. Would you like to come in?"

Richard dutifully rose from his chair, hands still clasped together, and followed Josh into the room. Dan watched him all the way.

"It takes all sorts, I suppose," he said to himself, heading off to the small kitchen to make coffee. Feeling his phone vibrate against his thigh, he took it from his pocket with one hand, and lifted the kettle to the tap with the other, but had to put it down again to turn on the tap.

"What is she playing at?" he pondered aloud, reading the message that filled the entire screen. This time, he didn't reply, instead filling the kettle with water and preparing two mugs. Josh's surgery was a nice little place; it had a good vibe about it, although whether it came from the building or the therapist, it was difficult to say.

The kettle boiled quickly, and Dan made the coffees, took one through to Josh, knocking loudly on the door on his way through, before returning to the kitchen to drink his own. It was likely the other client had been able to hear bits of the previous consultation as well, and he didn't wish to pry. He lifted himself onto the cupboard top and booted up the internet on his phone—an easy way to pass the next twenty-five minutes or so.

***

Richard had not yet got around to talking, although the pummelling of fist in palm was absent this session, which was surprising, seeing as he'd had to wait almost a quarter of an hour, completely disrupting his requirement for regularity and routine. Josh made a note in Richard's file and sipped at his coffee. It was exactly how he liked it, and but for being Dan's therapist, he would have wondered if there was anything the man couldn't do better than everyone else. However, he knew the real Dan, the one he kept well hidden. True, it was essentially the same persona he presented to the world, other than the terrible things he carried around with him, and mostly of his own making.

It suddenly dawned on Josh that several minutes had passed since he had asked Richard whether he'd found out the girl's name, and he had yet to move, let alone answer the question, so he tried again.

"I see you are a little more relaxed today than the last time we met. I take it things have gone well?" Richard still didn't respond to the question, but he did break his silence.

"The man out there. Dan, you called him. He is your friend."

"Yes, he is a very good friend of mine."

"You have known him a long time."

"I have. We went to school together and we left school, erm, eighteen years ago."

"Do you like the same things?"

Josh thought for a moment before replying. "No. Not really. He likes adventure sports and money and cars. I like books and walks in the park."

"I like walks in the park. When there is nobody else there. I like walks in the park at night."

"So do I," Josh agreed, "although it's not really a good idea to go there on your own."

"Why are you friends if you don't like the same things?"

"People can still be friends, even if they don't share the same interests. Why do you ask?"

"The girl's name is Laura. She is nineteen and lives in halls. She likes rock music and collects shells. She goes to the Students' Union rock music night every Thursday with her sister. She goes to the beach on Sunday to find new shells." He stopped abruptly, and the previous silence was renewed.

Josh envisaged that Richard would be horrified by the possibility of even trying to appreciate rock music, but all relationships required a certain amount of give and take.

"How did you find out about Laura's interests, Richard?"

"I talked to her before the lecture. I asked her questions, and she answered them."

That was an amazing breakthrough. Only a couple of sessions ago, when Richard first confirmed his feelings, Josh had noted in his post-consultation reflection that he was unlikely to gain enough confidence to speak to the object of his…fascination. Now, there he was, reporting back on a full-blown conversation with the girl.

"How do you feel about it?"

"I am pleased I have talked to her. But I don't like rock music, and I don't collect shells. There is no point in collecting shells."

"But you do have hobbies. We've talked about them. You have your gardening, and you like walking in the park. Walking on the beach isn't much different. As I said, friends can have different interests. Even boyfriends and girlfriends."

Josh paused for a moment to give Richard a chance to speak, but he didn't take the opportunity.

"So, what's next? Do you want to meet up with her away from the lecture theatre?"

"Yes. I would like to do that. She says I should go to the rock music night next Thursday. I should go to the rock music night next Thursday."

"That sounds like a good idea. Of course, you don't have to stay all night. You can just go along and say hello."

"But if she is not there I will be on my own. Will you come?"

Josh was a little taken aback by the forthright request. He could justify his response either way and saw no issue with it as part of Richard's treatment programme, even if he really wasn't very fond of rock music himself.

"Yes, I will come. I'll be bringing a friend, though, because if Laura is there, then it will be me all on my own." For the sake of personal and professional safety, he thought it best to take someone else along, but he didn't want to explain his reasoning to Richard.

"Good. I will tell her I can go to the rock music night next Thursday. Thank you, Josh."

It would be inaccurate to suggest that they engaged in light-hearted chatter for the remaining fifteen minutes of the session, but the conversation was far easier than usual. The pauses between interactions still persisted at six seconds, and every now and then, Richard would ask questions that Josh had to explain were personal and inappropriate. He had learned long ago that the quirky young man was not intentionally rude; it was just his way of speaking. After exactly thirty minutes, Richard thanked him again, confirmed the arrangement for Thursday, and left.

Dan watched on from the kitchen doorway. "Interesting guy," he remarked, as the door at the bottom of the stairs quietly closed itself behind Richard.

"That's one way of putting it. Want another coffee?"

"Go on then. I'll make it. You go write whatever it is you write when you're done with us."

Josh accepted the offer and returned to his consulting room, calling back to Dan, "You can see your case notes, if you like. There's nothing you don't know, and legally you can request access to them."

"Oh, really?" Dan thought it was probably not the best idea. He had worked through a lot in those sessions, and it would serve no useful purpose to dredge it all up again. The kettle came to the boil; he filled the mugs and carried them through to the other room.

"Thanks." Josh took the very hot mug, cursing under his breath as he turned it to grasp the handle. Dan sat on the sofa.

"I like it here. I've decided, after all these years."

"Why's that?"

"It has a nice feel to it. I was sitting in the kitchen before, thinking how welcoming it is. I don't know if it's you. Probably."

"Well, I don't know, either, but it does explain why some of the clients are so reluctant to leave. There's only one of them I don't have to literally push out of the door."

"Let me guess—Richard?"

"You got it. He just asked me if I'd go to a rock night with him up at the university."

"Part of his treatment or socially?"

"Treatment, obviously."

"Nice. What's up with him anyway, or shouldn't I ask."

"Well, I can't tell you much, but what you saw of him—you should be able to work it out yourself."

"Except I did industrial psychology, not clinical."

"True. However, you didn't come to talk about Richard. What's up?"

Dan flopped back into the sofa and took a big gulp of his coffee. It was still far too hot to drink, but he didn't react. He stayed silent for a minute or so. Josh waited. It was like Dan had to switch modes in his head from business-like, super-confident, self-sufficiency to needing someone else to care, if only for a while.

A conversation had been overheard, during the last meal out, when George was over. He shouldn't have been listening, however fortuitous it might have been. If this was the way it was going to be, he could do nothing about it, but for saving face, because hadn't he been there? Hadn't they all been there? They'd discussed it so many times before.

Josh listened intently, without interjection, mainly because he didn't know what to say. The consequences could be disastrous for everyone, and he had been in on it for a very long time.

Chapter Seven:
Insomniac Resolution

3:15 a.m.

The clock scorched luminous red numbers onto Josh's retinae, and he partially closed his eyes so that the lashes shielded him from the brightness of the display. That damned dream again, only this time he wasn't entirely sure he was pushed. He was definitely naked, though, because the first thing he had done when he awoke was put his hands down to check that his pyjamas were still in place. They were.

At first, he tried to turn over and go back to sleep, but that didn't work. He got up, used the bathroom, poured a glass of milk, drank that, and tried again, with no joy. Finally, he gave in, put on his dressing gown, went back downstairs to the living room, switched on the TV and opened his laptop. There was no point in trying to go back to sleep until he was at the stage of fighting to keep his eyes open.

As always, there was an email message from George. He rarely had anything new or of interest to say but still felt the need to make contact by some means every single day. On this occasion, the information was slightly more intriguing, and not what anyone would have anticipated, because he had finally bought a new house, due for delivery in eight weeks' time. Josh smiled to himself and wondered what new thing they might find with which to torment him. Checking the time, he calculated that it was mid-evening on the ranch. Uncharacteristically, he decided to give George a call.

The phone rang on and on. Just as he was about to hang up, he heard a click at the other end. For a moment, there was only a hum in the background, and it sounded like the answering machine had picked up the call.

"Hello?" Not the answering machine.

"Hey, George, it's Josh."

"Hey, yourself! What on earth are you doing calling me at—must be four in the morning?"

"Yes, about that. How are you?"

"I'm great. I sent you an email this morning. Did you get it. I finally ordered a house!"

"I know. I got it. About time, too. Bet you were fed up with us taking the piss."

"There is that, plus when I got home after Adele's wedding, I discovered a termite infestation."

"I see. Not good."

"No, not good at all, being as I discovered it when I poked a wall with a pitchfork and the whole thing fell in on itself. So I decided that was that. Got it cheap, too, on account of Dan and Andy knowing the guy and everything."

"Great stuff."

"Yep. So," George paused. He knew there was more to this call than small talk. He'd have rather liked it to be Josh telling him he was wrong, and he did want to be with him all along, but that wasn't going to happen. He continued carefully. "What's up then? You not sleeping too well, I guess?"

"I'm sleeping OK, other than I keep having this dream. It started the night before Adele's wedding, and I've lost count of how many times since then I've woken with it still in my head." He recounted the dream to George, who hummed and commented every now and then, just to confirm that the line was still active. It took twenty minutes to explain the dream in its original form, plus all the variations he could recall, right up to tonight, when he thought he might have taken the plunge into the water tube of his own free will.

When he was done, George considered a suitable response. "Well, you're the therapist."

"That's exactly what Ellie said." Josh's voice was not without exasperation.

"What I mean is, I can't say what it might mean."

"I didn't tell you so you could interpret it for me, George!"

"But, there again," he continued, "it might not mean anything. I remember something you said about us being meant to forget our dreams, and if we dream about what we've been up to, then maybe you're just dreaming about the dream, if you get me."

"I'd never thought of that."

"You called me because no-one else is up, didn't you?"

"No. Not at all. At least, no-one else is up, but I saw your email, and I thought I should give you a call. I did always like being your friend, you know. Nowadays we don't seem to get the chance to talk like we used to."

"Nowadays? We haven't for years. In fact, not since I came over to the States. Ten years, that is. Not my doing, though, is it?"

"Don't go blaming me!" Josh said defensively, but George was right. He was always trying to keep in touch—the ignored email messages, unreturned phone calls. It was all one-way, and he did love talking to George. They had been really good friends, until the 'thing' happened.

"How about you just try answering my emails occasionally. I know it must be hard for you."

"I don't respond because I don't want to give you the wrong idea."

"Ah, man, not that again. I got my head around it a long time ago. I can't change how I feel about you, but I do accept you don't feel the same, and I'm fine with that. Really."

There was a very long pause, for a telephone conversation, at least. Josh chewed the inside of his cheek as he considered what George had said. It was an age since they properly, honestly talked to each other.

"Ten years, huh?"

"That's right. We should have done this then. Mind you, I wouldn't have been quite so sensible about it."

"Me neither. I'm sorry, George, truly I am. It is my fault. Look, next time you're over we should go out, just the two of us. Go clubbing or something."

"That's a great idea. Maybe not clubbing, though. Dinner or a movie, perhaps?"

"Excellent. Well, I really do need to try and get back to sleep. I have a whole day at the university tomorrow. It's hard enough without feeling like I'm going to fall on my face."

"You do that. I'll let you know what's going on with the house and send you some pictures. You can tell the others if you like."

"Right you are. Night, then. And thanks."

"For what?"

"For listening and accepting my apology, I hope?"

"No need for thanks, and yes, I accept your apology. See you now."

With that George hung up. Josh stayed where he was a while longer and then closed his laptop and went back to bed. The next thing he recalled was the seven o'clock news playing from his clock radio.

Chapter Eight:
Disbelief

"So let me get this straight. *You* phoned George?" Eleanor put two glasses of cola down on the table and took the seat opposite. "Am I hearing right?"

"Yes, Ellie, I phoned George." Wearily, Josh picked up the glass and sank the contents in one go.

"Blimey. Didn't see that one coming."

"And he's bought that house, you know? The one Dan told him about."

"Yes, I got that. But you called him. That's bloody unbelievable, that is." Eleanor shook her head. She was stunned by this news.

A few days had passed since the conversation in the early hours of the morning, which made it seem even more suspect, as if Josh was hiding something important from his best friend. That wasn't entirely true, in that he did need time to prepare himself for her reaction, but it was based on the importance he had placed on George finally buying a house. Now he wasn't sure which of the two facts surprised him most either. In the middle of the night, he'd needed someone to listen, and he'd turned to George, and it really wasn't just because there was no-one else, as he'd spent the greater part of a weekend talking to him online and emailing him as well.

Nonetheless, the two had always been inextricably linked, as if George's purchase somehow signified acceptance of the state of play between them. Perhaps that was why he had decided to call him, believed it was safe to resume contact.

For several minutes, Eleanor intermittently renewed her surprised expression and sipped her drink, until Josh huffed loudly and slammed down the glass.

"Anyway," she continued, wholeheartedly seizing the opportunity to change topic, "Shaunna came by this afternoon. She's in a bit of a state."

"Why, what's up?"

"Krissi's twenty-first."

"Which is not for ages."

"I said that. She wasn't reassured, so I volunteered our services. Suggested we could all take on a task or two and ease the burden." Eleanor paused and waited for Josh's reaction.

He hated it when she roped him in, but in fairness, if she didn't organise things, sometimes they would never happen, or they'd be a complete fiasco. She was heavily involved in most aspects of Adele's wedding, not that anyone was officially allowed to know, because she had been sworn to secrecy. Had it been anyone's wedding but her own, Adele would have been in her element, taking measurements, arranging fittings and looking through catalogues of shoes.

As it was, Adele just about managed to sketch some ideas—way beyond what anyone else could have managed as fully-fledged designs—before succumbing to the panic, thus Eleanor stepped in to oversee communication between dress shop and bridesmaids, caterers and venue, florist and church, and so on. Now she was taking the helm for Krissi's birthday bash, and without the confidentiality clause, she could delegate to her heart's content.

Josh scowled at her. "So what am I doing, then? You're such a bully."

DEBBIE MCGOWAN

"Don't know yet, probably something to do with the music. I said I'd sort out the food, and by that, I mean I will order it and make sure it arrives. And I'm not."

"Are so." The mention of music reminded him that he still hadn't sorted out an escort for his evening with Richard. "Speaking of volunteering, are you working on Thursday night?"

"I am, but I can swap with Karen," she replied suspiciously. "Why?"

"A client asked me to accompany him to a rock night at the university and I, that is to say, we, would be most appreciative if you could come with me. Us, I mean. Please?"

"Are you mental?"

"Possibly?" Josh flinched as if she might hit him. "Please, Ellie. I wouldn't ask only—"

"There's no-one else."

"And I'll make it up to you. I'll do whatever you want for Krissi's party, and I won't complain."

Eleanor momentarily considered offering up a suddenly remembered reason why Karen wouldn't be able to swap. She thought it was ridiculous that he'd agreed to begin with, but she couldn't abandon him. He didn't ask for much, and at times she had to admit she could be a bit of a bully, assuming that he would do whatever she asked him to, although the likelihood of him fulfilling his promise not to complain was zero.

"All right then, I suppose. I'll have to call Karen to check it's OK with her."

"Thanks, Ellie. You're the best." He hugged her.

"Yes, yes. I've agreed to go with you, so you can stop it now," she admonished, pretending to fight him off.

They arranged times and places, and he hugged and thanked her again, before she shoved him out onto the street.

72

It was probably for the best; between talking to George, extra-curricular support for clients and it being a busy week for work anyway, he had more than enough to occupy him.

Sometimes his monthly, fortnightly and weekly appointments coincided in such a way that it would be as well to take a sleeping bag and camp out in the surgery for a few days. For all his busy-ness, he still remembered to send Eleanor a quick text reminder of their arrangement and received a terse response to the effect that she hadn't forgotten, but she was still optimistic for a cancellation.

***

After all that, the rock night went rather well, considering the volume and genre of the music and how out of place they looked, and felt, in a student bar. Richard was 'progressing well' with the task of getting to know Laura, given a little help from Josh and two pints of lager. Eleanor didn't even seem too freaked out by the way Richard communicated, which was, as always, in short bursts of repetitious speech.

Laura wasn't a whole lot better, with similar issues to Richard, as Josh had suspected, which was why she was accompanied by her sister, Sarah. It was clear from Richard's description of the girl who took a different seat each lecture, and there was a pattern to the behaviour; it didn't fit into threes, which was why Richard hadn't recognised it. Laura had to sit on the next row back each time, and when she got to the back of the room she would no doubt start again at the front. Josh thought it likely that either he was about to lose a client, or gain another one, depending on how things went from here on in.

Sarah stayed with Josh and Eleanor for the evening, not wishing to get in the way of young love, strangely blossoming amongst banging heads and flaying hair on the overcrowded dance floor. It was far too noisy for conversation, but at the end of the night, when Richard went outside to say goodbye to Laura, Sarah confirmed that her sister had been diagnosed with Asperger's Syndrome when she was five. She thought that Josh was Richard's support worker; confidentiality meant he couldn't tell her that was not so, nor comment on the absence of a formal diagnosis.

They stayed a few more minutes, before the three of them followed Richard and Laura out and all said goodbye.

"I haven't been in a Students' Union since I was at uni," Eleanor commented on the walk home. "Don't change, do they?"

"Not a lot, no. Although I can't imagine you went in much for that, anyway. I seem to recall that you were too wrapped up with what's-his-face to enjoy any socialising," Josh remarked, thinking back to their weekends, home from university, when she could talk of nothing but her first great romance, to be replaced by her second, third and then the guy she married.

There was no middle ground: either she was totally single or one hundred percent committed to a relationship and every other aspect of her life took a back seat. Eleanor was fiercely independent, or perhaps co-independent. She was strong and confident, but only if there was a backdrop and a supporting character to pick up her missed lines. Josh was her safety net, not that he minded. After all, she was his best friend. She always did the same for him. However, he believed that one day, she would find her real great love, and, like those who had gone before, this man would take her away from him and everything else that mattered to her now. When it was 'the one', meant to be, that would be it, forever.

They walked in thoughtful silence, quickly reaching Eleanor's apartment building, where Josh paused at the gate.

"Coffee?" she offered.

"Not tonight. I'm shattered." He wasn't making excuses; the dream was starting to lose him sleep on a regular basis.

"OK." Eleanor hugged him, and they kissed cheeks. "You know, I gave up on all that marriage stuff a long time ago. I love you all too much to risk it. Especially you. If Mr. Right comes along…well, he will have to be very, very right indeed, but I'm not going looking for him, and I promise I won't lose my hold on reality this time. I'm much older now. Oh, God, I'm so old!" She laughed.

Josh laughed too and gently squeezed her arms. "See you tomorrow, probably," he said and watched until she was safely inside before he went home himself.

When he awoke the following morning, there was the familiar, vague and fading memory of the dream, but at least he had made it through an entire night without recourse to warm milk, lettuce sandwiches or any other quack remedies for insomnia.

He didn't see Eleanor that day, nor for the rest of the weekend, as she had been pushed into attending a family christening in Scotland, not that she needed a lot of persuading, as she did rather enjoy a nice religious get-together—weddings, christenings—it didn't really matter so long as it involved some sort of long and pompous ceremony. On this occasion, she hadn't bothered to ask him to go with her, because he hated going to church and would have moaned the entire time they were away.

When they next spoke on Monday evening, she was feeling 'spiritually refreshed'—Josh snorted coffee out of his nose, and she slapped him for being horrible. He never did quite understand what was so appealing about musty old churches and priests droning on for hours. Eleanor gave up trying to explain and continued writing out order chits. It had been a very quiet evening, so she easily caught up on all the paperwork by closing. This time, it was she who was too exhausted for a nightcap, which suited Josh, so they went their separate ways, each to have an early night.

***

Andy threw the remote control at the armchair in frustration. Daytime television was so depressing. The physiotherapy was working out well, but he could still only hobble about, relying heavily on the crutches that were causing calluses on his hands and making his hips ache. He hopped to the kitchen, made a sandwich, filled a glass with water, hopped back through to the living room with the sandwich, back to the kitchen for the water and then back again, spilling half of it along the way.

Someone so active should not be confined to their home; it was only ten-thirty, and he was already eating lunch. Jess was in court, Dan had flown to Belgium the previous evening…in fact, everyone would be at work, with the possible exception of Josh, whom he hadn't seen for weeks. He contemplated calling him up, but immediately dismissed the idea. It would be grossly unfair to impose his boredom-induced misery on someone else.

It was all his own fault, and how stupid it had been. He was lucky to be alive, the doctors said so, not that he needed them to tell him. And the car? Well, even if the fire brigade could have freed him without first removing the roof, it would still have been a write-off. Hitting a tree at ninety-five miles an hour—OK, not quite, he had braked, so maybe about seventy miles an hour. Even so, hitting a stationary object at that speed…and his first thought? *Bastard! He's gonna win!* He watched Jay become a distant speck as the screaming engine of the Porsche faded into the distance, audible in the silence of Andy's demise.

He'd hit the tree with such force that it had to be felled, which was what brought about the decision to go rallying instead from now on, just as soon as he could walk properly again. He could have come off the road and hit a house, a person, a group of kids. Luckily, it was only a tree, but it was now a dead tree. He wasn't self-destructive, whatever Jess thought; he just loved living on the edge. However, that was his risk to take, or to avoid. In his thirst for adventure, he had no right to put others in danger. It had taken the accident for him to understand, and whilst he was certainly not the kind of man to get all sentimental over killing a tree, it had been a major emotional eye-opener.

Hence his requirement to get out and about as soon as possible. Any more insidious morning chat-show hosts, not-quite-famous guests, phone-ins about washing machine repairmen, pathetic cheated-on American women giving it their all in front of studio audiences, while their scumbag husbands smugly defended themselves, *Because She Weighs Three Hundred Fifty Pounds*, methods of adding twenty percent to the value of your house, tips on cooking salmon, apple pie… and he may as well book into the funny farm right away.

Here was a man for whom the experience of watching his life flash by was like *The Wizard of Oz* at Christmas: on perpetual re-run. Why he did it, what he craved most, was the sensation of survival. After university, he went on expeditions to remote places, where the journey alone, as the occasional long-abandoned, wind-tattered tent or frayed safety cord could testify, was enough to kill a man. That feeling of achievement, nearing death from hypothermia, barely able to breathe, standing on the edge of what seemed like the precipice of World's End? It couldn't be beaten.

However, reaching the highs took far too long, and so the adventures began—skydiving; snowboarding; swimming with sharks and stingrays—the number of previously healed fractures the surgeon had to work around was testament to the joys and sorrows of each and every voyage. Now, here he was, for eight weeks on a sofa, watching life-beaten old hacks and drunks scrounge a living off other people's misfortune.

Also why he did it was Dan, whom he loved and respected more than any other. The youngest of the three of them, yet the wisest, most intelligent and best-looking, ever popular, smiling, successful. When Michael asked Dan to be best man, of course Andy was jealous and furious that he had been passed up once again. But he wasn't angry with Dan. A few months ago, when they had celebrated Michael's fortieth birthday, such as it was a celebration, his older brother tried to smooth things over between them. It wasn't an act of affection; it was because he hated that Andy gave him no respect. He believed it to be his right, as eldest brother.

Again, when their mother remarried a second time, it was Dan she chose. Andy had been in the Philippines at the time, so he could at least justify his mother's decision. Unlike Michael, he did not covet the favouritism, which was the root of the conflict between them. Andy was happy to accept his place in Dan's shadow; Michael loathed them both—Andy for his admiration of his younger brother, and Dan for everything that he was.

Thinking back, he could recall only two occasions where he felt anything close to hate for Dan, and the first was during high school. He'd wanted to ask Shaunna out for a long time, but he had not been quite confident enough, and it was never the right time. Finally, he mustered enough courage and figured there was nothing to lose, but she declined gracefully. She wanted Dan—they all did—and in spite of Andy sharing his brother's dark, rugged looks, she said it would be unfair on both of them. Andy would be a substitute, and anyway, she wouldn't pursue Dan, for Adele's sake. Her honesty saved their friendship.

Only once since then had that destructive sensation returned, and that was when Krissi was born. He and Dan went in last, and in fairness, neither was interested in this baby, nor anything to do with fatherhood since. It didn't sit well with their lifestyles. Still, he couldn't help but think that it was wrong that someone else should have had Shaunna; if not him, then it should have been Dan. He didn't really understand why that made him hate his brother, but as quickly as the ugly thought had entered his mind, he pushed it out, and he'd refused to let it surface since. Krissi grew on them; she was one of them now—not that tiny, dependent reminder of what could never have been in any way, shape or form.

Back to the matter in hand: he was torn between a garden makeover and an all-women chat show, either of which had the potential to turn him, as it had their hosts before him, to alcoholism. He hobbled across to his DVD collection and selected one at random: *Four Weddings And A Funeral.*

Please don't anyone visit for the next couple of hours. Easing his plaster-cast leg up, he settled back onto the sofa, pushed play on the remote control and succumbed to the wimpy romantic within.

***

Andy needn't have worried. Josh, like everyone else, was hard at work, or at least, he was sitting in his chair, listening to the woman in front of him wailing like a small child. She was, in fact, making a noise not dissimilar to that emitted by his neighbour's dog, who had a penchant for standing in the middle of the garden at around eleven each night with nose in the air, howling at the sky. It would usually start off two or three other dogs in the immediate area. Fortunately, it lasted less than a minute, and most of the time he found it rather entertaining to watch and listen from his bedroom window.

The dog was called John, apparently, based on his neighbour's hollering over the howling. She was in her thirties, with a brood of about six children, the eldest of whom was at most eight years old. There didn't appear to be a partner around, and Josh admired her absolute patience, because the only time he ever heard her raise her voice was to John the dog, at eleven p.m., and the houses weren't particularly soundproof.

The woman in front of him was an entirely different breed. He wasn't one to judge; it would be unprofessional to do so, and suffering was a subjective experience. However, when he considered what some of his clients went through on a daily basis, or had endured in the past, this woman's plight paled into total insignificance. She was reasonably attractive, well dressed, evidently well kept by her husband, however inattentive he was. If life really was as bad as she was saying, surely the sensible thing to do would be to cut one's losses and move on?

Part of him wanted to say that, the part that didn't want to be a therapist anymore. And so, he struggled on with interpreting the alternating sniffs, sobs and words as she lamented the husband's latest crimes. At appropriate junctures, he requested she reflect back on each statement.

It was the tyranny of middle-class, middle-aged womanhood that did it, he was convinced. Not so much about empty nests, but the sudden realisation that the dashing and wealthy young chap they had married was a balding, spreading fifty-year-old, and all his redeeming qualities had been tied up in his looks. Now it was too late to move on, no maintenance payments now the children were all grown up, being somewhat bald and spreading themselves, or too lazy and comfortable in their misery to be bothered with all the upheaval.

'Have you considered marriage guidance counselling?' had become a kind of mantra. It was a very lucrative trade for those who could stomach it, but Josh thought he'd stick with singular loons—as little conflict as possible. He'd once had both members of a couple on his books at the same time, and it wasn't fun, with each twisting his words to match their own agenda. Trying to explain to a cheated-upon husband that, yes, he had actually told his wife that her behaviour was a projection of her own perceived inadequacy, for which her husband was responsible...well, it didn't go down too well. Thankfully, they moved far, far away, and they even paid their bills first.

There was no let-up, either. His one o'clock was with a woman, if not of similar disposition, certainly in the same situation. However, there was a real grace to the way she dealt with it, a quietness to the sufferance that only Josh was allowed to view. She marched forward, appearing unmarred by impotence and infidelity, yet she was exhausted. It was no expression of wretched learned helplessness. She had no desire to leave him; she just wanted a break, for him to stop the infernal game he had played all of their married life.

Josh helped her identify the behavioural patterns associated with the game, and bit by bit, she was starting to win. Just a few weeks ago she reported that it was he who had broken down this time because she took control. There was regret for the poor girl who was the pawn in this battle victory, but Josh reminded her that she was not responsible for the consequences. She had to focus on the central objective, and that was to arrive at her husband's retirement with her sanity intact.

Even if Josh had known that the poor girl in question was Jess, who had started her new job for the Crown Prosecution Service and was hating every minute of it, his advice would have no doubt been the same. That dinner party was the final straw for Angie, and she grasped the opportunity to try and turn her marriage around with the desperation of a dying soul. Without knowing it, Jess not only saved a marriage but also a life. By comparison, it was of little consequence that she didn't like her job, because there would be others.

Chapter Nine:
Anew

Josh pushed the button, just in case by the power of superstition or magic it would work this time. Once again, the PDA's screen lit up, the logo displayed, and then nothing. And it had been on charge all night. He cursed and rolled over in bed, pretty sure he didn't have any appointments but unable to confirm if that were the case, because his PDA was also his diary. Until now, it had been reliable, if not a tad ancient.

He stared at the clock for a while—it was only eight a.m.—time enough to register that if the nesting house martins piped down a bit, he might catch up on some missed sleep, and then he was doing so.

The single mother of six next door stood impatiently on the pavement, a double buggy loaded with babies and assorted bags in front of her, waiting for her gaggle of children to make it down the garden path. She caught the biggest on the back of the head with a sweep of her hand, and off they went, towards the local primary school.

The milkman, running two hours late, stopped to apologise on his clanging voyage down the road and waved at the woman delivering the post. She waved back, leaned her red and white bike against the gatepost shared by Josh and his frantic neighbour, fought bravely against John the dog's efforts to push the letters back out of the letterbox, and breathed a sigh of relief when no animal attempted to snatch Josh's post from her hands.

There was a towel hanging over the rail of the platform, just out of arm's reach, and the floor was slippery from wet feet. He tried to move towards it, knowing, without the need to look, that he was naked. The usual voices sounded behind him, and he felt himself begin to fall, his phone now ringing in his pocket, except he didn't have a pocket, because he wasn't wearing any trousers. He was about to turn to look for his phone on the platform, when he realised he was awake, and it was actually ringing on his bedside table.

Four missed calls, all from the same number, one that neither he nor the phone recognised. Josh swung his legs to sit on the edge of the bed, yawned loudly and stretched. He picked up his phone to return the missed calls, just as it started ringing again: same number.

"Hello?"

"Hello. Is that Josh?"

"Yes it is."

"Hello, it's Briony. I'm waiting outside, but the door seems to be locked."

"Oh, Briony. Damn." Josh rubbed his hair, the static making it stand on end. "I'm really sorry, but I'd forgotten our appointment. My PDA's died, you see."

"Who's died?"

"Ah, no. My palmtop computer? Organiser?" Briony still didn't seem to know what he was talking about.

"So what shall I do?"

"Would you mind awfully if we reschedule. I can probably be with you in ten minutes, but I'm still at home, so if you're free—"

"Can I see you tomorrow instead?"

"Yes. Great. Same time?"

"That's OK. Yes."

"Thanks. And again, my apologies. Bye."

"Bye."

Josh waited for the line to go dead rather than ending the call, as he already felt bad enough without Briony thinking he had hung up on her. There was nothing else for it. He was going to have to buy a replacement for his PDA straight away…just as soon as he'd showered and eaten breakfast.

***

The shopping centre had only been open half an hour by the time he arrived, yet the car park was almost full already, and he took the stairs rather than stand with the hordes of mums, toddlers and prams waiting for the lift to the shops. By the time he reached the electronics store, he was ready to kill the next person who dared, without provocation or warning, to change direction and get in his way.

The sales assistant was trying his best to be helpful, suggesting that the PDA was outdated yet repairable, but Josh couldn't cope without it, even if it did only need a new battery, which would take a matter of days, no more than a week. The man looked at him as if he were committing some terrible crime by wishing to dispose of the trusty old thing.

"Look. If you're that bothered, you have it," Josh suggested, taking the small plastic bag containing his new purchase.

"I really can't do that."

"No, you really can. Have it. Get it fixed and get some use out of it, sell it as a collector's item or whatever."

"All right, then, I will, thanks. Once it's fixed, I can call you to transfer the information to your new tablet."

"Don't worry about it," Josh replied dismissively. By the time he'd cycled through a week or two of appointments, he'd have them all set up again anyway. He made a solemn vow to remember to synchronise his shiny new tablet to his laptop every night and went straight on to the surgery.

The rest of the day was a bit of a mystery, sitting in his chair, waiting to see who turned up next. He was confident that, at the very least, Wednesday was one of the days when he had no appointments between four and seven, so he chanced a visit home to eat. No sooner had he put a forkful of Bolognese in his mouth, than his phone rang: another client waiting outside the locked surgery.

By the end of Thursday, Josh had only missed three of his eight appointments, including the one he had double-booked Briony against. He'd moved on from the guilt, but he felt less in control than usual and spent the entire day sitting in the surgery, going through his clients' case notes to see if he could piece together the times of sessions for the following Monday to Wednesday, some of which he was certain were right, although most were pure guess work.

He wouldn't normally have had a problem remembering and put it down to lack of sleep. For once, he was pleased that tomorrow he was at the university, as his schedule there was put together by the student support staff. That said, Friday proved as gruelling as ever and, having already spent two days not really knowing what he was doing, it left him utterly exhausted. He went home, ate cheese on toast, and was asleep before the end of the nine o'clock news.

***

Another 3:15 a.m. wake-up call: George was online. *Good.* They had chatted via instant messaging a few times since Josh had telephoned in the middle of the night, and it was cheaper, although he had some problems understanding what was being said. George tried to keep the shorthand to a minimum, and

Josh was learning, but he still preferred more old-fashioned methods of communicating.

JustJoshing: Pleased you're online - can't sleep.
JustJoshing: Again!
Geo1972: It's getting to be a habit.
JustJoshing: I'm not doing it on purpose.
Geo1972: Glad to hear it but it's nice to chat to you - bit selfish that, huh?
JustJoshing: Meaning?
Geo1972: I kinda hope you carry on not sleeping - much catching up to do, me n u...
JustJoshing: Menu?
Geo1972: No - me and you.
JustJoshing: Ah!
Geo1972: doh! I'm trying not to use 'txt spk' as well!
JustJoshing: Thanks - you know how it confuses me. Although we don't talk about anything really.
Geo1972: No we don't you're right.
JustJoshing: So what do you want to talk about?
Geo1972: Not much - btw a couple of the guys want to say hi...
JustJoshing: btw? Oh - by the way - I understand now - OK.
[RaymoJack has joined the conversation]
[Wildcard4188 has joined the conversation]
RaymoJack: Hey Josh!
Wildcard4188: You guys. Coooool.
JustJoshing: Hey back!
Geo1972: Ray and Joe (aka wildcard) work on the ranch.
JustJoshing: Oh I see.
Geo1972: You know I told you about leasing some land?
JustJoshing: Yes?

RaymoJack: We got us a rodeo school here.

JustJoshing: Great - sounds like we might get roped in next time we visit.

RaymoJack: Ha ha sure Josh - you'll get roped in!

Wildcard4188: Good one Josh.

JustJoshing: What did I say?

Geo1972: Ha ha

Wildcard4188: See what you did there?

RaymoJack: He don't get it Joe.

Wildcard4188: Hey G! Thought you said this guy was all brains!

JustJoshing: You said what? That's a laugh!

Geo1972: Look what you wrote Josh.

JustJoshing: Hang on…

JustJoshing: Ah yeah - I see - get roped in ha ha.

Geo1972: Brilliant!

RaymoJack: Anyway dudes gotta get on. See ya.

[RaymoJack left the conversation]

Geo1972: Ray's a great laugh - you'd like him a lot.

JustJoshing: Kind of hard to work people out on here, when you're me anyhow - only just got 'lol' - lol!

Geo1972: Yeah - know what you mean but he is just like that…

Geo1972: Always up for a laugh - and really loud!

Wildcard4188: Real loud for sure.

JustJoshing: Well I'll look forward to meeting him.

Wildcard4188: Don't let him get you Josh.

JustJoshing: What do you mean?

Wildcard4188: Ray likes a practical joke.

Geo1972: He does too.

Wildcard4188: Had me good a few times!

JustJoshing: Oh, OK - like what?

Wildcard4188: You know - hiding things from me…

Geo1972: Tripping you up…

Wildcard4188: Yeah - totally.

JustJoshing: Sounds interesting!

Geo1972: Joe tell him about the stable door.

Wildcard4188: Oh yeah - still got the bruises from that one!

JustJoshing: What happened?

Wildcard4188: I was leading Star in, she's real cute.

Geo1972: Oh! Real cute!

Wildcard4188: Beautiful chestnut, 15 hands.

JustJoshing: How big is that?

Geo1972: BIG!

Wildcard4188: I wasn't looking where I was going…backed through the stable doors…Ray pushed the top half shut…Star reared…got me square in the ribs - daresay she broke half of em.

JustJoshing: Ouch!

Geo1972: He's a big baby!

JustJoshing: Yeah - because you wouldn't flinch if a horse kicked you in the chest!

Wildcard4188: Ha Josh, G don't go near the horses - or the cows - heck if we kept chickens he'd still hide inside!

Geo1972: That is so not true!

JustJoshing: Whatever!

Wildcard4188: G, you gonna say anything to the feller? Or you want me to bow out first?

Geo1972: No no, it's OK.

JustJoshing: Hmm - what don't I know here?

Geo1972: Well…

JustJoshing: Actually George, I think I do know already.

Wildcard4188: Really? Ha ha!

Geo1972: Yeah, he will know.

Wildcard4188: Jeez, you said he was good and all, but that's unreal!

JustJoshing: Am I right then? You two?

Geo1972: Yep. :)

JustJoshing: Wow!

Wildcard4188: Wow??

JustJoshing: Yeah just - wow! In fact WOW!!

Geo1972: You surprised?

JustJoshing: A little bit - we can talk about that another time though - so how long etc.?

Wildcard4188: Been a couple months now, right, G?

Geo1972: 7 weeks.

JustJoshing: Cool – was that just after Adele?

Geo1972: When I got back and the house was wrecked. Joe helped me 'fix' things up.

Wildcard4188: Told him to order a new damn house

Geo1972: Yeah - made me do it.

JustJoshing: Nice work Joe - we've been telling him that for years - does he ever listen?

Wildcard4188: I hear ya!

JustJoshing: Well G (lol) you know I need my sleep.

Geo1972: It's Friday night - Saturday morning for you, obviously.

JustJoshing: I still need to sleep!

Wildcard4188: Well I'm going anyways. Catch ya later.

JustJoshing: Nice to 'meet' you Joe.

Wildcard4188: You too Josh. Bye now. xx

JustJoshing: Bye Joe.

Geo1972: x

[Wildcard4188 left the conversation]

JustJoshing: Well, well, well!

Geo1972: Go on.

JustJoshing: Nothing.
Geo1972: nothing?
JustJoshing: I have nothing to say.
Geo1972: Really?
JustJoshing: OK, nothing right now.
Geo1972: OK?
JustJoshing: No - I don't mean it like that...
Geo1972: I don't get you.
JustJoshing: Can't judge people on here, I told you, but even so, you two sound like you're getting on well, easy-going etc.?
Geo1972: Yeah - it's pretty good at the moment.
JustJoshing: You didn't tell me.
Geo1972: Hadn't got round to it, but...
JustJoshing: But?
Geo1972: dnt tell ne1 else yet pls
JustJoshing: Hang on - Ah! Don't tell anyone else! OK.
Geo1972: thx - agh - I mean thanks!
JustJoshing: I got that. Can I ask why not?
Geo1972: I don't want them to know yet, that's all.
JustJoshing: Why - what are they going to do?
Geo1972: Nothing I suppose.
JustJoshing: Look - I won't say anything, though I'm sure everyone will be really happy for you.
Geo1972: You OK about it?
JustJoshing: Course!
Geo1972: Phew!
JustJoshing: You know I love you - as a friend!
Geo1972: I know!
JustJoshing: Believe it or not I want you to be happy and if Joe makes you happy...
Geo1972: He does.
JustJoshing: Well then, all's fine - plus...

JustJoshing: You get a new house!
Geo1972: Yay!
JustJoshing: lol!
Geo1972: I think that's what I'm worrying about with the others.
JustJoshing: They'll be fine - Ellie knows - she'll moan when I tell her it was because Joe said, not because she did!
Geo1972: I can almost hear her now!
JustJoshing: Dan will be happy to have been the one to put you in touch with someone.
Geo1972: Andy'll be happy cos Dan is.
JustJoshing: Shaunna and Kris wouldn't notice if their own house fell down round their ears!
Geo1972: lol - too busy snogging!
JustJoshing: Yes. That's so true!
Geo1972: Adele won't care anyway as long as it's got a bathroom inside (which it has btw).
JustJoshing: I should think so too - welcome to the 21st century! And Jess will side with Ellie.
Geo1972: Yeah - they always did gang up on me.
JustJoshing: On us, actually!
Geo1972: True.
JustJoshing: You remember that time we went to the beach and they bought ice creams for them and not us?
Geo1972: Never forgiven them for it - it was boiling!
JustJoshing: I know!
Geo1972: Then that time we went to the water park…
JustJoshing: Agggh!!!
Geo1972: Oops! sorry!
JustJoshing: It's OK.
Geo1972: Still dreaming then?
JustJoshing: Yep - and still no trunks!

Geo1972: See now, I could make some rude comment - but I won't!

JustJoshing: Not funny!

Geo1972: Must be awful!

JustJoshing: A bit of a pain but I think I can manage on 5 hours sleep.

Geo1972: Which is half of what you always used to get.

JustJoshing: When I was 12 or something!

Geo1972: lol - fair enough.

JustJoshing: Right - I'm definitely going now.

Geo1972: Will talk later then.

JustJoshing: Yes - night G lol lol

Geo1972: Ha ha. Night Josh. xx

Josh shut down his software.

Chapter Ten:
Tension

Shaunna had accompanied Adele to her first antenatal appointment and was now enduring the second, because she'd said she would a long time ago. In actuality, she was struggling with her own life to such an extent that the last thing she wanted to do was sit, for twenty minutes at a time, in different rooms at the clinic for an entire morning. But a promise was a promise, and after Adele's last pregnancy, she really needed the support through those first three months. She had convinced herself that she could bring on a miscarriage through sheer terror alone, something Shaunna insisted, hopefully, wasn't possible.

Adele came out of the first cubicle with a small pot of around four centimetres in diameter.

"How in God's name am I supposed to pee in this?" she asked, intending her query for Shaunna's ears but exclaiming it so loudly that every person in the waiting room looked up from their magazines, many clearly empathising with her plight.

"I know." Shaunna examined the pot. "But at least it will be your own pee you get all over your hands. Wait till you have to change the first solid foods nappy. This is nothing by comparison!"

"I suppose it's still kind of your own, though. Anyway, best get on with it, stupid people, they are." Adele mumbled her way to the toilets at the end of the room. She returned a minute or so later, with her pot filled to the brim and a disgusted expression on her face.

"Yuck." She grimaced, wiping her dry hands on her coat. "How revolting. I hate all this stuff. Blood tests, urine tests, scans, drink all this water and then don't go for two hours. It's torture, that's what it is. And for what? I'll never be a size six again! What am I doing?"

"You're convincing yourself you don't want this pregnancy, that's what you're doing, in the event that something goes wrong," Shaunna responded without shifting her gaze from the tired-out pages of an old and not-so-glossy magazine.

"You sound just like Josh, do you know that?"

"Charming!"

"It's true. That's exactly the sort of thing he'd say, and it has nothing to do with me talking myself out of it, or whatever you said. I'm just being realistic."

"No you're not. You're being pessimistic, expecting the worst."

"Tom said they should be keeping me in for observation, just in case."

"Adele. You had one miscarriage, what, nineteen years ago? You hadn't even stopped going out drinking every night, not even after you found out you were pregnant."

"So?"

"So you're past the dangerous stage, and they're not going to keep you in hospital for your entire pregnancy."

"But what if something goes wrong?"

"Like what?"

"The baby might not be growing properly, and how would they know without scanning me?"

"Look at all these other women. Do you see any of them asking to stay in hospital or get scanned every other day 'just in case'?"

"Well, no, but—"

"Oh, just stop it! You're being pathetic."

"Next time, I'll come with Tom. He'll talk to the midwives for me."

"Good. Next time come with Tom. I don't even want to be here. I came for you."

"Well, don't bother!"

"Fine. I won't!"

Shaunna still wouldn't look at Adele, although everyone else was doing so, and had she asked any of them, they would have agreed that Shaunna was being very unkind. Pregnancy was a terrifying experience, passing as it did from one overwhelming worry to the next. Alas, Shaunna's own somewhat vague recollection of what it was like was even foggier, on account of her current predicament.

Adele pivoted hopefully on the edge of her seat, holding her little golden pot high in the air, as if it might explode with any sudden movement. After a few minutes, she was called through to another's room, where a midwife examined her internally and astonished her by proclaiming that she was sixteen weeks pregnant. She decided there was no way the midwife could possibly know that, based on one examination, and stuck with her own dates, which were two weeks earlier.

The midwife departed, and a doctor arrived, bringing more discomfort in the form of prods to the abdomen, orders to lie down, sit up, bend one knee and so on. At the end of it all, the doctor confirmed that all was well and told her to make another appointment for six weeks' time, when they would be able to tell her the sex of the baby, if she wanted to know. She hadn't thought about it but was confident she was having a girl, in part because having to deal with boys' bits, even those belonging to her own child, was something she didn't like to think about.

After she'd put her clothes back on, she returned to the waiting room to collect Shaunna.

"All OK?"

"Yep. It felt a bit like I was doing the bloody 'Okey Cokey' in there, but everything is fine—so far." She crossed her fingers. "They didn't do any of that stuff last time."

"I'm really sorry about being horrid before."

"I forgive you. Just be there for me, OK? I can't do this alone, especially if…"

"You mustn't think like that. It will all work out this time. I'm certain." Shaunna gave Adele a quick hug. "Let's go and eat ice cream."

"Can't. Not allowed."

"You can, just not soft ice cream."

"Actually, I'd quite like a hamburger."

"OK, hun. Let's go and eat hamburgers, then. Just don't be putting any raspberry sauce on them."

"Eh?" Adele looked baffled.

As if she wasn't ditzy enough to begin with, now her hormones have frazzled her brain. "Pregnant women? Weird cravings?"

"Oh yeah." Adele giggled.

They set off towards the hospital main entrance, with Shaunna sharing some of the more bizarre things she'd wanted to eat during her pregnancy.

By pure coincidence, they arrived at the reception area at the same time as Dan and Andy, the former pushing the latter in a wheelchair. Andy's plaster cast had been removed, so he was back to wearing shorts, sports socks and trainers. Even with the level of atrophy caused by weeks of inactivity, his legs were a sight to behold, and both women instantly reverted to giddy school girls in the company of the good-looking brothers.

"Alright?" Andy acknowledged. Dan nodded a greeting.

"Here for physio?" Shaunna asked.

"Yep. I told him I could walk, but he wouldn't let me."

"It's too far," Dan snapped.

Andy shrugged. "What can you do? He's the boss."

With that, Dan pushed on, past Adele and Shaunna, and down the hospital corridor. The two friends looked at each other, perplexed by his offhandedness but not so much as to forget their mission. They linked arms and headed for the closest place that sold hamburgers.

***

"What's up with you?" Andy asked as they waited by the lift.

"You know I hate hospitals." Dan jabbed the button for the second floor. "The sooner you recover, the better. Got a job for you."

"Good stuff. Can't wait."

Usually, it meant Andy going off to some remote location to make contact with the locals and survey the area for existing technology, and he assumed that his next assignment would be no different. Dan wasn't in the mood for explaining, and Andy imagined it would be another couple of weeks at least before he was strong enough to properly get back to work. In fact, at the moment Dan was stopping him from doing anything physical at all, in spite of the physiotherapist's advice that he should now be going for short, gentle walks and could resume his visits to the gym as long as he avoided leg weights. It was almost as if Dan wanted him to stay dependent, whilst at the same time hating him for it.

The lift finally arrived, loaded with several people, who, like Andy, were paired with wheelchair pushers. One of them, whose name was also Dan, had been in hospital at the same time as Andy.

"Alright, Andy, how's it going?"

"Alright, mate! Pretty good, as it goes. Dan—" Andy gestured to his friend "—meet Dan."

Dan the brother shook the other man's hand. "Nice to meet you."

"This is my dad, by the way." Dan in the wheelchair turned slightly and thumbed in the direction of the man behind him.

"Hello again," Andy said, remembering him from when they were on the ward together. Dan had been in a far worse state, with spinal injuries that were likely to leave him paralysed from the waist down. Andy hadn't figured out how the injuries occurred, other than that Dan had fallen down several flights of stairs and didn't want to talk about it. Instead, they'd spent their time competing at virtual skateboarding and the like on Andy's games console.

"Anyway, good seeing you. Give me a call once you're back on your feet," Dan in the wheelchair called, as Andy was pushed into the lift.

"Will do, mate," Andy called back. The doors closed, and he and Dan disappeared from view.

"You know, Dad," Dan in the wheelchair said, "Andy's brother never came to see him when he was in hospital. Funny that, being as he said they were so close."

Chapter Eleven:
Craving

Adele's requirement for hamburgers persisted, and she wasn't at all happy about it. They were definitely not something she chose to eat the rest of the time, but she couldn't get enough of them, and it didn't stop at plain hamburgers either. She'd pretty much exhausted the menus of all the local fast food outlets, trying each variation as would a connoisseur or food critic. She was searching for perfection, and the closest so far had been a double cheeseburger with every possible ingredient—salad, ketchup, pickle, salsa, mustard—if they had it, she wanted it in the bun.

Every night after work, she stopped to buy one, ate it on the way home and sent Tom out at least once more before bedtime. She was sure it was the burgers that were making her feel sick, like having a permanent hangover: slight headache, toxic feeling and the sense that throwing up would possibly make her feel better, but it wasn't enough to curb the craving.

***

It wasn't just Adele who was suffering at the hands of junk food outlets. Josh's sleep patterns, though still regular and predictable, had slipped to such an extent that he was living a semi-nocturnal existence through the week, with a total day and night flip at weekends. On the occasions where he did make it home early enough to get the equivalent of a full night, it was in dribs and drabs, and he was awake by three in the morning, unlikely to get back to sleep before six. He was too tired to cook and not remotely interested in food, so he was existing on coffee, cheese garlic bread and an average of three and a half hours' sleep.

Some nights, when George wasn't online, he passed the time reading studies, hoping that sheer boredom would send him off. Other nights, he would type up case notes, print them off and delete the files before reading them through so that he would have to type them all over again if he found a mistake. He never kept case notes on his laptop, as he had once left it in Eleanor's restaurant, from where it was stolen. Not that he'd thought it fortunate at the time, but a virus meant he'd only just wiped it and reinstalled all the software, so there was no client information to end up in the wrong hands.

The times George *was* online, he tried his best to help, by telling Josh he couldn't stay for long, hoping it might encourage him to go back to bed. After several nights of this, Josh asked George if he'd rather he stopped calling, and George came clean. He loved talking to Josh, even through the sterile medium of instant messaging, and told him that Joe was always busy tending to the horses. Josh wasn't sure if that meant Joe didn't know that they were spending hours chatting each evening, or he didn't care.

As the caffeine and sleep deprivation took their toll, Josh became so forgetful that once again he left his laptop in the pizza restaurant. This time, it was at the end of the evening, just before closing, so it didn't get stolen, and he realised what he'd done as soon as he got home.

Eleanor wasn't impressed at having to go back and open up, particularly when the regional office received a call from the police the following morning, regarding a possible break-in.

Her manager was a lovely woman, who left Eleanor to get on with the job and accepted her explanation without question, before announcing that she was moving to another region and the new manager would be in touch soon, to introduce themselves. Eleanor wished her good luck and hoped that whoever took her place would take the same laissez-faire approach.

The restaurant didn't serve hamburgers, something Eleanor was very pleased about. She didn't dislike Adele, but she didn't fancy seeing her every day, either. Even at school, she'd rarely had to endure that, with Adele being a far more creative type than she, Josh and Jess. Kris and George were the link between the sporty, arty and academic subgroups within.

Their continued closeness to certain people within the main group came from that time—the formative years of their adult personalities, sexual identities and vocational choices. Certain aspects of it still fascinated her, and she often reminisced during the quieter periods of the day, when there were few customers and the only other member of staff was the chef. Sometimes she wished she had gone off to study psychology with Josh, rather than medicine, not because she regretted where her career path had taken her, but so she could better understand herself and the people she cared about.

Dan, for example, always did stand out as being different, partly because he was endowed with natural charisma, but also because he had matured faster than most, his nearly black hair producing a shadow on his chin by the end of the school day. Andy had been the same, yet reaching puberty early had been far less of an issue for them than it had been for Jess, who had significant breasts from the age of twelve or thirteen. Whilst Dan and Andy soldiered on being 'men', Jess spent the time readjusting to her physical presence, quickly learning to use it to her advantage. It was her undoing, because now all she wanted was to be recognised for her career success on its own merits, rather than because she was both beautiful and intelligent.

Kris was always a grown-up, even if he didn't mature physically until he went to university, and he and George had clearly experimented a little together, with Kris declaring his homosexuality in third year of high school. At that age, Eleanor thought people only had sex to make babies, which she later defended on the grounds of her Catholic upbringing. It was a valid justification, considering her parents were the only people she knew who never missed Sunday morning mass. She'd hated it when she was little, but these days, just now and then, she found herself in the church, lighting a candle or saying a prayer for some terrible world event.

When it came to her own sexual development, it was a bit of a horrible mess really. She was bewildered and terrified by the way her body had started to change shape: hips rounding, waist slimming in, bust forming. It was all too much, and it was the start of her issues with food. She wasn't overweight now and hadn't been then, but believed that if she didn't take control of what she let in and pushed out of her body she would end up the size of a house. It wasn't rational. Deep down, she'd always known that.

George was the first to spot Eleanor's purging and immediately went to Josh—not maliciously. It was what George did. He had fallen in love with Josh during sixth form, and it was the only secret he'd managed to keep from him, until it damaged him to such an extent that he had to say something.

He was a funny one to get to know, George, ever contrary. On the surface, there was this over-sensitive, gentle, passionate person who raved about films, books, poetry and visits to art galleries, whilst underneath he was the rough and ready type. He'd worked on a farm at weekends and loved every minute of it, but then, during university, his horse had to be shot when it panicked and failed to jump the paddock gate.

The mare was two or three years old at most, bought as an eighteenth birthday present by his father as a first attempt at making amends with the son he'd abandoned. The effect was profound, and he immediately surrendered his ambition to own his own farm. Thus, when he announced he was emigrating to the ranch, everyone was truly astonished, except for Eleanor, who had always known he would leave someday.

As for Shaunna, Eleanor had only really come to know her via Kris, not long before the pregnancy. At the time, Kris told everyone he was the father, it was the result of too much alcohol and a lapse in judgment. No-one doubted the truthfulness of his claim, for although Kris had been accepted as gay, there was nothing to be gained from making up something like that. When Shaunna confessed to her parents she didn't know who the baby's father was, Kris finally admitted to his friends he had done it for her sake and the baby's.

If anyone outside the newly forming friendship group asked, they maintained the lie, so much so that over the years it had become a truth. Kris was universally honoured as a brave and responsible young man, standing by the girl he got pregnant, and could do no wrong from that day onwards. He was the most loyal friend Shaunna could have asked for, her own natural development hijacked by pregnancy, childbirth and parenthood. She'd done an amazing job of it, and still she wouldn't allow herself to start enjoying life again.

Finally, there was Josh. He was Eleanor's closest friend, the one who refused to lecture her about food, came dashing to her rescue when her marriage didn't work out and didn't judge her for giving up medicine after more than six years of training. Not once in all the time they had known each other had he ever confided in her about having a crush on someone, or falling in love. If it were simply a case of him keeping it to himself, she wouldn't have worried. But the reality was he hadn't had any love interests at all. There were plenty of people who would happily have paired up with Josh, for anything from one night to the rest of his life, but he either didn't see it, or wouldn't let it happen.

Maddeningly, he seemed quite content to live that way. He wouldn't talk about it, changed the subject if she raised it, but there was no noticeable ill-ease caused by Eleanor's attempts to bring it up. She loved him and wanted him to be happy, and although he did seem to be so, she couldn't help but think something was not quite right. He'd dispatched George's affections in much the same way as he did when clients demonstrated transference. It just wasn't healthy; Eleanor was certain there was more to it.

She also felt a little jealous that he was contacting George when he couldn't sleep at night. He'd mentioned their conversations a few times in passing—'George was telling me such-and-such' or 'when I was chatting with George the other night...' There was nothing sinister to it, and Eleanor had to admit, he would receive the sharp edge of her tongue if he phoned or turned up at three-thirty in the morning.

What it boiled down to, she reasoned, was that Josh and George's friendship had been broken by George's love confession, something she envisaged would require her help to fix. Instead, they were busily repairing the years of damage without any input from her whatsoever, plus she had a feeling that Josh wasn't telling her everything. He would be mid-sentence, narrating some thing George had said or done, and then he would pause and change direction. He sounded like he really wanted to share but had been told not to. If that proved to be the case, she was going to be having serious words later.

The whole thing Jess had been talking about weeks ago was beginning to make sense now, the feeling that somehow life was meaninglessly ambling on. People were changing, relationships were drifting, not necessarily becoming more distant, but certainly morphing into something new. Perhaps it was the natural evolution of such things. It made sense that this age, like adolescence, would have more of an impact. Now was the twilight, especially for the females in their midst who wished to bear children. Maybe that was all it was. Ride the storm. In a few years, things would return to normal. It was a comforting thought, and for the first time ever, Eleanor decided that reaching forty was actually something worth celebrating.

"I think the table's clean now, Ellie."

She jumped, not realising Andy was standing behind her and had been for quite some time. All the while she had been deep in thought, wiping this one tabletop.

"You frightened me!"

"Sorry. You were miles away there."

"Yes, I was. I was thinking about us."

"Us?" he asked, pointing at her and then himself.

"No, you nutter. Us, as in you, me, Josh, Jess, George…"

"Oh, that 'us'."

"Do you ever do that?"

"Occasionally. To be honest, I've been thinking about me recently. I'm a bit self-obsessed, huh?"

"Not at all. Not after what happened. Are you staying? Shall I get us a coffee?"

"Now, is that 'us', or us?" He indicated to the two of them again.

"Ha ha, funny man." Andy sat at the table she had been clearing, which she took as an affirmative to the coffee. "Then you can tell me all about this self-analysis you've been doing."

"Awesome," he replied and shuffled along the bench seat, wincing a little. His leg was still painful, especially as he had walked from home into town.

It was Saturday, and it was mid-afternoon, but there were very few customers, all of whom had not long been served. Eleanor returned with the coffees.

"There you are, sir," she said, putting the cup down in front of him. "So, what gives?"

"Ooh, it's all deep philosophical stuff." Andy laughed, his gold hooped earring catching the light from above the table. It was something he'd worn for years, so as not to be confused with Dan, he said. He lifted himself with his hands so that he could put his foot up on the seat opposite.

"How is your leg?"

"Sore today, but I've been walking, so it's to be expected. However—" he adjusted his position slightly "—it was a real touchdown with reality, this fracture."

"Fractures, you mean."

"Fracture, fractures, same diff. It's what could've happened that got me thinking. I mean, if a group of kids had been where that tree was." He winced again, but this time, the pain wasn't physical.

"You mustn't think like that, Andy."

"I'm trying not to. So, anyway. I promised Jess I'd never do it again, and I really mean it. No way."

"I'm glad to hear it. She was so worried about you—as were we all."

"I'm OK, other than the smashed leg."

"And I don't want to make you feel any more guilty than you do already, but if you'd been at that dinner with her…"

"I know. I feel terrible about it—kind of made me realise how much people depend on me. God knows why. I'm not exactly a responsible adult. And that's the other thing I was thinking about. I'm going to start working, properly working."

"Surely not. A real job?"

"Yep, a real job, with a wage packet and regular hours and all that jazz. Don't quite know what yet." He was slowly revolving his cup on the table, focusing on the movement of the liquid. This was a big step for him, bigger than Eleanor was aware of.

"You and Dan haven't fallen out, have you?"

"Nah, nothing like that, although he's been damned impatient while I've been laid up. I think he must've had some things lined up for me. Plus, conceited as it may sound, I am his brother, and it might have given him a bit of a scare, too. Anyway, what made me decide was talking to Jess the other night. She really hates that job at the CPS."

"Tell me about it." When Jess was miserable everyone got to know, and Eleanor had heard plenty about how tedious her new job was. Jess was used to reading up on previous cases, but criminal law was not her area of expertise. She felt out of her depth, and whether she was or not, she chose to sink rather than swim.

"She wants to set up on her own. An all-female practice," Andy explained.

"Yeah, she mentioned that."

"Except she needs to re-mortgage to do it and can't afford to. So, I was thinking, if I get a regular job then maybe I could buy half of the house from her."

"Or…" Eleanor paused, unsure how he was going to take what she was about to say.

"Or what?"

"You could get a job you really want and stop trying to be something you're not."

He didn't respond, instead maintaining eye contact, pushing her to explain.

"You couldn't do a nine-to-five job, not for Jess or anyone else. It's just not you. I know you have to break away from Dan at some point, and maybe from the rest of us, too, but not like that. It's admirable you want to help, but Jess doesn't need you to do this for her, and I'm not sure it will do her any favours in the long run."

Andy thought about what Eleanor was saying for a moment and nodded. "You're right."

"You're obviously up for making some big changes in your life. Now's the time to do it. You and Jess need each other's friendship and support. You can give her that without sacrificing everything you are."

"I let her down, Ellie."

"Yes, you did."

"What if I get it wrong again?"

"So you get it wrong again. Start over. You always get back on your snowboard. Why should this be any different?" Eleanor drained her cup. "More coffee?"

"I think I might need it!"

Andy stayed until early evening, when he took a taxi home, stiff from sitting for so long after his burst of exercise. It had been a great help sharing his thoughts. The beauty of having a circle of friends like theirs was that they could turn up at each other's homes or places of work any time they needed to and would be welcomed, cared for and heard. Aside from

Josh, Eleanor was the most brutally honest of all, and that was exactly what Andy needed right now. There were decisions to be made and people to tell.

Chapter Twelve:
Facing Facts

Kris popped out to the newsagent's, picked two Sunday papers at random, and returned home to cook breakfast, hoping all the while that Shaunna would have made it out of bed by the time he got back. She enjoyed a lie-in, but it wasn't like her to stay in bed so long. Alas, when he returned, there was still no sound from anywhere in the house, so he fried eggs and bacon, prepared a pot of tea, and took the loaded tray back upstairs. Krissi was at work, which would give them a chance to talk.

Shaunna had at least turned to face Kris's side of the bed, but her eyes were closed tight. He blew gently on her face, then a bit harder, then licked the end of her nose. She smiled, in spite of herself.

"OK, OK! I'm up."

"No, you stay right there! I've brought newspapers, tea *and* breakfast."

"I still need to go to the loo first, bossy boots." She got out of bed, stretched and headed for the bathroom, returning a couple of minutes later, smelling of toothpaste, her red hair scrunched up in a big hairclip. She climbed on top of the duvet and picked up the plate of breakfast.

"Mmm. I love the way you cook bacon." She prodded the crispy rasher with a fork. "You know just how to win me round."

"Years of careful observation and well-executed plans, my sweet." Kris grinned and tended to his own plate. "Now, I want you to forget about things for a little while, eat breakfast, drink tea and read the paper. Then, if you like, we can make love."

"How about—" Shaunna pushed the tray aside "—we do that in reverse order. Sort of." She clambered to her knees and leaned over, kissing him, as he reached up to remove the clip. Her hair tumbled onto her bare shoulders, where it bounced and came to rest on her partly covered breasts. She unfastened his shirt, his belt, and then his jeans. He pushed the straps of her nightdress off her shoulders so that it glided over her breasts and down to her waist. Lifting her arms out of it, she sat astride, kissing his lips, cheeks, neck, chest, writhing slowly. The jeans were scratching her bare legs, and after a short while she climbed off, removed them, along with his boxer shorts, stepped out of her nightdress and returned to her previous position. He allowed her to control the action, and slowly, they moved together in perfect tandem.

It didn't take very long for them both to climax; the tea was still warm, although the breakfast was not. Shaunna pulled her dressing gown around her and proceeded to eat hers anyway, while Kris went for a shave. He really didn't want to broach the subject of Krissi, but it needed to be addressed sooner or later, and sooner was better. Shaunna knew it was coming and was even more reluctant, so when he returned to the bedroom, she promptly left to go for a shower.

"I know what you're doing," he shouted after her.

"So? What you gonna do about it?"

He could just hear her over the sound of the running water. "I'm going to follow you around all day, till you talk to me." He arrived at the bathroom door.

"Great." She turned her back on him and rubbed shampoo into her hair.

"Shaunna."

"La la la, la la la, can't hear you."

"Shaunna! We have to deal with this," he pleaded. He put down the toilet seat lid and sat on it but said no more, because he could hear her, sobbing quietly, her back still turned against him. She conditioned her hair, covered herself in shower gel, shaved her legs, all the while still gulping and sniffing. He waited, holding a towel ready for her once she could delay no more and finally turned off the shower.

"I don't want to deal with it, Kris. I don't want to. How can I tell her that?"

"I'll talk to her, if it helps," he offered. She snuggled against his chest, wiping her face on his shirt. "What do you think?" He nudged her with his shoulder. She nodded.

"I'll pick her up later, and we'll go to the pub or something. You don't have to do anything. OK?" He lifted her face up to his own and smiled gently. "OK?" he asked again, wiping the tears away with his thumbs.

"OK," she replied.

***

Jess and Andy had gone to the beach, not that the weather was right for it, but Jess said she didn't care, so they'd borrowed Dan's car and left in the early hours. Now they were walking, barefoot, along the wash, holding hands. Jess brushed her hair out of her face with her free hand and stopped to pick up a shell.

Andy stopped, too, gazing out to the horizon, recalling with joy the last time he had been surfing. It was a wonderful feeling, free falling from the top of a wave, stomach rolling, arms outstretched, trying not to overbalance. And to come through the other side still standing—no wonder surfers had made the term 'awesome' all theirs. It really was.

Jess held the shell to her own ear, then to his, and he listened, carefully, in case this was the place where his destiny could be realised. He took the shell from her and put it in his pocket before they strolled on.

Their friendship had evolved into this over the years. They could spend hours together, saying absolutely nothing and yet everything at the same time, they were so tuned in to each other. She understood he was trying to figure out his next move; she'd watched him and Dan drift even further apart of late, not that he had actively spoken about it. She knew as well as he did that wherever his life took him from here onwards, Dan was likely to play a far smaller part in it.

It wasn't just down to the changes in Andy, although since his accident, he was different in many ways. Forever self-confident, happy to take a chance on success, regardless of how remote it might be—to an extent, that was still the same—but he somehow seemed more certain and content, less likely to act on the sudden impulses that usually led to a disastrous change of direction. There was a quietness about him that she'd not seen before, as if he now accepted some great truth.

They were nearing a pier and started to cross the beach towards it, their feet sinking into the drier sand as they moved further inland. There was a little ice cream shop on the pier, and Andy's leg was starting to ache a little, so they bought ice creams and sat on the edge of the sea wall to eat them. It was quite chilly, now they were still, with the force of the wind battering the revolving sign outside the shop and whirling around the pier's struts. That and the waves crashing gently onto the sand were the only sounds; it was a beautiful, noisy, kind of peace.

Jess shivered. Andy stretched his jacket around her, and she huddled closer, her blonde hair blowing into his face, catching on his light stubble. He gently brushed it away and kissed the top of her head, inhaling the glorious blend of the scent of her perfume and the salty coastal air. There was no need for words or the angry diversions and possible misinterpretations they invented.

**

"Do you want more tea?" Kris asked.

"Mm? Oh. Yes please, hun," Shaunna replied without looking up from the supplement she was reading. They were sitting at the kitchen table and had been for some time, the traumas from breakfast temporarily shelved to make room for a touch of Sunday normality. She pushed her sleeve up, rubbed her wrist across the open pages and sniffed at it. "Oh, yuck. That's horrid." She grimaced. Kris came over and lifted her wrist, holding it to his nose.

"It's all right, but not for you. Hang on." He spun the magazine to face him. He laughed. "That's aftershave."

"Ah, yeah, so it is. That'd explain it then." Shaunna laughed, too. Kris sneezed. "Oh dear. Sorry about that," she said, as he sneezed again, and then again. She turned the page so that no more of the awful smell could escape, her own nose feeling a bit irritated also, and went to the sink to wash her wrist. As she did so, she spotted something black out of the corner of her eye. It streaked across the kitchen and down the hallway, closely followed by Casper, their Labrador.

"Kris," she explained slowly, "it wasn't the perfume."

"Aftershave," he corrected, the force of his next sneeze jolting the open door of the cupboard where he kept his allergy pills.

"Whatever. I suggest you step outside for a minute."

With that, the cat came tearing back into the kitchen and leapt onto the table, tail held high, lashing from side to side. There was the sound of the large dog, half running, half skidding up the wooden floor of the hall, before arriving, more or less on all fours, at the table, where Kris intercepted him and, with all his might, dragged him by his collar out to the garden, sneezing all the way.

"Here, kitty," Shaunna simpered, edging closer to the cat. It was hissing furiously, its back arched into a complete inverted U. "Nice pussy cat. Come to Aunty Shaunna." She beckoned the animal closer, but instead it backed off further. "Oh, come on now, there's no need to be frightened." She stopped for a second and shook her head. "What am I doing, sweet-talking a cat?"

A change of approach was in order; she took a brazen step forward, and the animal lunged at her. She darted out of the way, but not quite quickly enough to avoid the claws as they scored the bottom of her cheek and shredded her t-shirt, at which point all niceties, fear, or whatever else had motivated her prior caution, were cast aside.

She grabbed the cat and carried it down the hallway towards the front door, with it still hissing and making some sort of howling noise all the way.

"Yes, yes, you're angry. So am I. That's a fifty-quid t-shirt ruined, you stinky so-and-so. And I know Casper frightened you, but it is his house, after all." She opened the door and put the cat on the step, where it took one long, vindictive look back, and prowled away.

Shaunna rubbed her hands together and closed the door. "It's gone," she shouted, going back to the kitchen to wash off the cat odour. She dabbed at the wound on her face with a dampened tissue; it didn't seem to be bleeding too much.

"Kris?"

He still hadn't come back inside, although Casper was now scurrying around the place, sniffing at the cat's previous locations.

"I said it's gone," she called out again. "You can come back in now." No response.

"Kris!" Shaunna peered out of the window, but she couldn't see him anywhere and started to panic. She ran to the patio doors, dreading what she might find, yet at the same time knowing it to be true. Casper dashed past her, and she followed him out, breaking into a run as soon as she saw the dog had stopped and was licking and pawing at Kris, lying unconscious across the garden path. Shaunna put her ear to his mouth. He wasn't breathing. She felt all of his pockets.

"Damn." She sprinted back to the house. They kept a spare epi-pen in a cupboard, but in all the time they'd been together he'd not needed it. She found it immediately and slammed the cupboard door with one hand, picking up the nearest mobile phone with her other. Trying to dial 999 and take the lid off the epi-pen at the same time, she raced back to Kris and stabbed it hard through his jeans into his thigh.

It seemed an age before the operator answered, by which point she'd put the phone on loud speaker and started CPR, something they had all learned to administer years back but had never needed to, apart from Dan, and it was so long ago that he and Kris were on a night out from uni the last time it happened.

"Casper, get out of the bloody way!" Shaunna yelled at the poor dog, who thought she was playing and kept mouthing at her hands and licking her. She was almost hyperventilating, and the chest compressions were getting harder and harder, with her fists clenched together, virtually thumping Kris in the chest. Finally, he gulped and spluttered, and she pushed his dead-weight body with her back so that he was now on his side, shouting to the operator all the while.

The whole series of events, from the cat's entrance to Kris regaining consciousness, took less than five minutes, but it had gone on forever. As Shaunna waited for the ambulance, she found Dan on quick-dial.

"Hey, it's Shaunna, can you come over please? It's Kris. He's in anaphylactic shock." She hung up and dropped the phone, collapsing backwards against Kris and praying that the ambulance would arrive soon.

**

Andy had contemplated turning his phone off for the day but had instead set it to 'silent'. It vibrated in his pocket. He took it out, clicked a few buttons, peered at the screen and handed it to Jess to read the text message. They jogged back up the coast road to the car park and drove home as quickly as was possible, in light of the number of Sunday afternoon amblers on the roads and Andy's newfound caution.

Chapter Thirteen:
Fallout

By the time Andy and Jess arrived at the hospital, it was over. Dan was sitting in the reception area, staring into an empty plastic cup, which he was rolling between his palms. He didn't seem to have noticed them arrive. Andy looked to Jess, and she gave him a worried shrug. They were both expecting the worst.

"Dan?" Andy walked over to his brother and sat on the edge of the chair next to him.

"You took your time," Dan muttered, without shifting his gaze from the cup. "Hope my car's still in one piece."

"We were at the beach. What's going on? Is everything—" Andy stopped, hardly daring to ask.

"Apparently, Shaunna says, that fat dog of theirs chased a cat into the house. Kris went into shock, just like last time."

"Oh, hell." Andy slumped back in the chair.

"Anyway, she pulled a blinder. I must admit, I didn't think she had it in her, but she saved his life."

"So he's OK, then?" Jess asked.

"Yeah, he's fine. Got to stay in overnight for observations and more meds. That's normal procedure."

"Thank God." Andy sighed and rubbed his hand through his dark, curly hair, still not cut since his accident, giving him a distinctly Romani look, especially with the earring. "Where is he?"

"That way." Dan pointed along the corridor to the left. Andy got up immediately and went in the direction indicated. Jess shook her head.

"You can be a real shit at times, do you know that?" she snarled, following Andy without waiting for a response, but Dan gave one anyway.

"Hey, he's my best friend. How do you think I feel?"

"Who knows anymore?" she called back without looking and disappeared around a corner at the end of the corridor.

Dan scrunched up the cup and launched it at the bin, missing by a long way. He walked over to pick it up, but instead kicked it around the floor before laying into the bin, cursing until he got it out of his system enough for the pain in his toe to register.

***

Andy—like Dan in slightly diluted form, and without the anger issues—could charm his way in or out of anything, so the nurse agreed they could go in, but only for a couple of minutes, and only because it was quiet. Shaunna was sitting next to the bed, Krissi on the end of it. Kris was lying back against the raised bed-head, looking uncomfortable and like he was going to get up and leave at any second.

"Alright, mate?" Andy asked, edging along the wall of the very small room.

"Andy. How're you doing?" Kris responded—far too cheerily for someone who had almost died.

"Not so bad. So you want me to get a gun to that cat, then?" Andy winked.

"Don't even joke about it." Kris indicated in Krissi's direction. She had been twiddling her cat pendant the whole time, knowing from her mother's reaction that this had been a close call.

Shaunna was, at times, a bit of an airhead who overreacted to things that didn't matter. But in times of crisis, she went into some other mode, becoming cold and over-rational, until it was all over, and then it would hit her. Krissi remembered that from when Grandma died. All through the illness and the chemotherapy, her mother picked up shopping, tidied, cooked, did the laundry—did everything for Grandma and Grandad. But she was functioning on a practical level and shut off emotionally. After the funeral, she had come home and trashed the living room, throwing ornaments, shoving furniture and smashing photo frames, before finally falling into a heap. For almost a week, she refused to speak to anyone, and in the end, it was Adele who pulled her out of it.

Right now, Shaunna was somewhere between the two states, trying to stay focused until she could get out of the hospital, knowing that Kris's heart was still racing and beating erratically. Any further stress could be fatal.

"Did you see Dan on your way in?" Kris asked.

"Yeah. He's sitting in reception," Jess said.

"Oh, right. He's OK, I take it?"

"A bit shell-shocked, but yes, he seems fine. Stop worrying about him. Get yourself better."

"I'm fine. It's all 'just in case'. But I will do as I'm told." Kris looked to Shaunna as he said this. When the doctor first advised that he should stay overnight, he had refused. He wouldn't have backed down at all, had it not been for Shaunna's expression of pure terror. She needed him to stay in hospital, because she couldn't go through any more emergencies today. Kris promised he wouldn't go anywhere until the doctor said he was fully recovered, at which her shoulders had visibly dropped as she relaxed a little.

The nurse poked her head through the door. "Sorry, folks, your time's up. We're going to be moving Mr. Johansson to the ward shortly."

"Cheers. Right, mate, I'll see you later," Andy said, turning to go. "Oh, and if they offer you the Chicken Supreme tonight, well, all I'll say is that describing it as 'supreme' might be a bit of an over-statement."

Kris laughed. "Thanks for the warning. And sorry for disturbing your Sunday. Dan said you'd taken his car and gone out for the day."

"It's fine," Jess assured him. "We were about to head back, anyway." She gave Shaunna and Krissi a quick hug and followed Andy out of the room.

"I think they meant us too, hun," Shaunna said, once Jess and Andy had gone.

"OK. Well, go and get some rest. I'm fine, honestly, and the other stuff can wait. You did good." He kissed her on the forehead.

She stroked his cheek. "We're going to go home and wash the mutt." The cat had sprayed Casper, which was what caused the severe reaction; Kris knew it as soon as he grabbed him by his collar.

"Now then, Missy Kissy." He poked her with his blanket-covered toes. She almost protested, but reconsidered. "You look after your mum. She's been a very brave lady."

She nodded solemnly and gave him a hug. He really was her dad in every sense but one, and she still needed to know.

"How cool," she said as she disappeared through the door. "We can go home and eat prawn puris."

Kris laughed and gently pushed Shaunna to confirm that she could go.

Dan was outside the main entrance, waiting to give them a lift. Other than moaning about the sand in the foot wells, he said nothing else all the way home. Had he been in a better state of mind, he'd have been able to reassure Shaunna that this was what had happened the last time, to the letter. It was only the third ever severe allergic reaction Kris had experienced, the previous two both being caused by shellfish.

Instead, Dan drove on, silently seething at the fact that he would have to vacuum and thoroughly clean his car, in the dark, so he didn't put Kris at further risk when he collected him the following day. He'd have avoided that, too, if he hadn't been specifically requested for the task. But then, Kris was his best friend, so he was being unreasonable. It was happening a lot of late.

Chapter Fourteen:
Dread

Josh was exhausted and utterly fed up. He'd been up half the night talking to George and overslept by two hours. Hence, it was half past eleven, and he hadn't yet consumed enough caffeine to thoroughly get going. On the plus side, his client hadn't turned up, although freaky as the man was, he did make the day a whole lot more interesting. He had a thing about vampires—fantasised he was one, in fact—and it was no vague sexual fetish. He imagined a personal history of almost four hundred years, during which he had learned to control his hunger so that it need only be satiated once a decade.

The resulting consultations far surpassed the average entertainment score of common or garden vampire fiction, and in their absence, Josh was left pondering over how he was going to pass the hour before his next appointment. He made another coffee and took his laptop from its bag.

The first thing he'd done when he'd leased the office was put in a wi-fi connection, coming to an arrangement with the dentist who owned the surgery downstairs to share both the service and the bill. They were on a great package, which included two phone lines, although the connection itself was prone to dropping out. Still, he decided to go and browse for information on vampirism, seeing as he was missing his weekly fix.

Alex, the vampire, had a very vivid imagination, and each session consisted of some saga he had endured in his search for the perfect victim. At times, Josh worried there was a little too much realism to the fantasy, inasmuch as it was a narration of actual meetings with real people. However, the dates seemed innocent enough, even if the women themselves became unwitting characters in Alex's curious autobiography.

Josh's previous research suggested that vampirism was indeed related to oral needs—even the most inexperienced Freudian analyst could have identified that—but the studies also contended that the specific nature of 'the vampire delusion' was related to schizophrenia. Josh had already devoted considerable time to trying to establish whether, on occasion, his client truly believed he was a vampire. He'd concluded the man wasn't delusional; he was fully aware of the fantastic nature of this other personality, and it didn't intrude into his daily life. Bizarrely, he was also a strict vegetarian, and this, Josh had once tried to explain with as much tact as he could and because it was as good an explanation as any, was probably adding fuel to the fantasy.

It was certainly worthy of further investigation, but instead of continuing his search for evidence on the neurological effects of iron deficiency, Josh got caught up in reading the accounts of other 'vampires', including those of a therapist who authored vampire romance novels, based on the fantasies of her female clients. *Now, if only Alex could find a woman like that, it would be a match made in heaven.* Josh wondered if any of the women he counselled had such fantasies but refused to share them because he was a man. As his mind drifted, the laptop slipped to the edge of his lap and fell to the floor with a loud clunk.

"Crap!" The noise startled him and instantly brought him to his senses. "Stand up. Walk around. Open a window, that'll do it," he muttered to himself, following his own instructions.

He closed the laptop and put it away again. Deciding that he still had time to go for a refreshing walk around the block, he pulled on his jacket and went to pick up his keys, but they weren't on the desk, which was where he was convinced he had left them. Five minutes and no keys later, the buzzer sounded, indicating a visitor at the bottom of the stairs. Josh pressed the intercom button and spoke.

"Hello?"

"Hi. Is that Josh Sandison?"

He didn't recognise the voice, and had it been a client, they would have known the PIN number. It wasn't the most secure way of doing things, but it saved him interrupting a session to press a button, and he changed the number once a month, to be on the safe side.

"It is," he confirmed.

"The name's Phil Spencer. I wondered if I could arrange an appointment with you."

"Sure. Come on up," Josh agreed—reticently, now he'd psyched himself up for a walk in the fresh air. He released the door catch and listened as Phil ran up the stairs, missing every other step on his way. This action itself told him a lot about the person now coming in to view.

"Thanks," the man smiled broadly, holding out his hand for it to be shaken. Josh went along with it and then quickly broke away. He picked up his tablet.

"Now...I have quite a few free appointments during the daytime, if you're available then. How soon do you want to come in?"

"There's no rush. I just need to chat through some things, and a guy at college said you were the best."

"That's nice to know. How about next week? Wednesday afternoon, say, two-thirty?"

"Yep. That's great. Yeah, this guy Richard, said he'd been coming to you for a while, and you'd helped him sort out a relationship thing. I'm having the same kind of problem, you see."

Josh didn't respond, for to do so would have confirmed that Richard was a client; there was only one person on his books by that name.

Phil thanked him again and left Josh to ponder over the mystery of how Richard—who never spoke to another soul at college, until he mustered the courage to talk to Laura, a girl like him—could be friendly with someone like Phil Spencer. On first impression, he seemed incredibly arrogant, but also far too extrovert to be acquainted with someone like Richard.

The interlude had kick-started Josh's brain, and he was feeling a little lightheaded, not quite himself, no doubt from excessive caffeine, mixed with lack of both sleep and proper nourishment. It was also rare for him to take a strong dislike to someone, and the feeling lingered. He took off his jacket again and went to the kitchen to make more coffee.

Still mulling it over, he spooned coffee granules into a mug, reached for the fridge door and paused for a moment. *Perhaps Richard has taken his newfound confidence to the next level and started making new friends...but wouldn't he have said something?* The last time he'd come in, he'd definitely been the happiest and most outspoken Josh had ever seen him, although the interaction still only moderately resembled conversation. *No, there's something very suspicious about this. I'll have to tread carefully if—*

"What the hell?" Josh stopped and stared in disbelief. There, in the door of the refrigerator, where he had anticipated finding a milk bottle, were his keys.

"OK. So I'm going mad," he stated aloud, lifting the cold keys out and quickly placing them on the cupboard. "Now then." He pirouetted on the spot, looking all around the small kitchen. "What in God's name have I done with the milk?"

With no visible sign, he checked all of the cupboards, and finally located it, concealed behind the teabags, sugar and coffee that he had only just used.

"Man, I need to get some sleep," he muttered, and then slapped his forehead with the heel of his hand. "Instead of yattering to George half the night. I'm even starting to sound like him." The thought of going home and climbing straight into bed was so tempting, and he decided he would do exactly that, just as soon as his next appointment was over.

**

Dan checked the locker next to the bed; it contained nothing more than a paper bag and some gauze squares.

"I think these must be standard National Health Service issue. Andy had the same stuff in his when I picked him up. Well, those, plus a games console, about fifty games, more magazines than a doctor's waiting room and enough dirty socks to keep a launderette in business for a month. I wouldn't mind, but he was only wearing one at a time!"

"I wasn't here long enough to make myself at home," Kris said, shutting the locker door again, its sprung hinges making it slam at the last minute. There were no bags to carry; Dan had bought a toothbrush and some paste on the way in, remembering, from the drunken sleepovers of their university days, how obsessive his friend was about cleaning his teeth.

It made Kris laugh, watching Dan check the ingredients— "In the event that they might contain shellfish or essence of feline? I would be thinking about changing my toothpaste, if I were you."

Dan managed a chuckle, but he still wasn't himself by any stretch of the imagination, uncomfortable silence superseding the usual social ease.

On the way home, for the sake of conversation, and because he needed to tell someone, Kris gave him the edited highlights of what was going on with Shaunna and Krissi. "She wants to know who her natural father is."

"Right. How d'you feel about it?" Dan asked flatly whilst over-attending to the task of indicating and turning left.

"I'm not bothered, to be honest, or at least, it makes no difference to me directly. She's always known I'm not her dad."

"How on earth is she going to find out anyway?" Dan momentarily looked away from the road ahead, but quickly checked himself. One written-off car in the family was more than enough for the year.

"We have a yellowing piece of file paper stashed away," Kris explained. "When Shaunna found out she was pregnant, she made a list of all the boys at the party."

"Ah. Well, that's a start. Good old Shaunna, thinking ahead as always."

"Do you remember Zak?"

"Zak?" Dan frowned as he tried to place the name. "Spotty Zak in Andy's year?"

"Yes. What do you think?"

"About what?"

"Him being Krissi's father."

"Well, I guess it could have been him, and I s'pose she did look at bit like him when she was younger."

"Plus, he was always hanging around Shaunna and Adele."

"Yeah, I remember that, now you've said it. But where do you go from there? 'Hi, Zak. Long time no see. By the way, is this your daughter?'"

"Paternity tests."

"Really? How do they work, then?"

"A DNA sample from Krissi and the father, but she's going to have to test everyone who was at the party. That would be the only way she could find out who is, or isn't, her biological father, and she's researched it. She even spoke to Jess about the legal implications."

"I was gonna say, you can't just go and steal someone's blood."

"It's done with cheek cells, but Jess didn't say much, other than, as you say, you can't normally force someone to have a DNA test. However—" Kris paused for a moment "—there is one way."

Not even Shaunna had realised what had happened that night. Kris was the only witness, and he had heard her say no, over and over again. He'd told no-one, even tried his best to protect her by claiming he was the father. Then, when Krissi brought up finding her father a few months ago, Kris found himself in a terrible dilemma. There was no middle ground; to establish her father's identity, she needed DNA samples, and if those who were at the party refused, then the only way was to tell Shaunna what he had heard, why he had stayed by her side all these years.

A police investigation would secure the samples and the identity of the father: the rapist. Now Kris needed to confide in his best friend, to seek his advice, and as he struggled to find the right words, Dan continued to drive, patiently, in silence.

"Shaunna was raped," Kris said finally.

"Shit! You're kidding." The revelation made Dan look away from the road again, only this time, it was the horn of an oncoming car that alerted him, and he had to swerve to avoid a collision.

"I heard it all."

"And you never said anything? Why the hell didn't you tell me?"

"I didn't tell anyone. She didn't know. She still can't remember anything about it."

"I guess that's something to be grateful for. I take it you've told her now?"

"I had to. Maybe it won't even come to it, and they'll all give their samples willingly. But if they don't, then Krissi will need to be told the truth. I had to prepare Shaunna for that."

"Well, Kris, I'm here for you, mate. And you know Andy and I will happily provide our DNA."

"Thanks, although it's the rest of them we've got to worry about, but what I've said—keep it to yourself for now. I don't know how this will work itself out. One thing's for sure, though. Nothing good can come of it. I only hope Shaunna and Krissi get through."

***

Josh estimated he had time for about five hours' sleep, a shower and a snack, before his evening appointments. He wasn't good at napping during the day, but he was so tired that he quickly drifted off into a state of half-sleep, half-wakefulness. Little noises disturbed him: the house martins feeding their young in the gutter outside; John the dog growling merrily, no doubt tugging at a rope toy with a four-year-old attached to the other end…

He guessed he'd been lying there for no more than an hour when the phone rang, and he chose to ignore it, figuring it was probably only a telesales call anyway. When it rang a second time, he threw off the duvet in despair. He reached the phone just as it stopped ringing, and raised his hand, as if to smack it really hard. It started to ring for a third time, and he snatched the receiver up.

"Hello?"

He waited, listening to the scripted pitch at the other end of the line. The woman very politely explained what her company did, what the fantastic offer was, and when she finally stopped, Josh took a deep breath and responded.

"You've called three times to try and sell me books. You've woken me up for nothing at all. You tell me how I think your offer sounds!"

With that he hung up and stormed back upstairs to the bathroom, stepping under the shower at the exact same moment his mobile phone started up, resounding through the entire house.

"Fuck, fuck, FUCK!" he shouted, lifting one leg out of the shower but then changed his mind and put it back in again. "Balls to them, whoever it is."

Chapter Fifteen:
Feel Good

Jess crossed paths with him in the doorway while attempting to balance her boxed ham and pineapple pizza on one arm and push her way out with the other. The man kept the door open for her and smiled. She smiled back.

"He's mine," she mouthed to Eleanor as she backed out of the restaurant, poking an index finger in the direction of the good-looking stranger. Eleanor laughed and waved.

"Good afternoon, sir," she said, eyeing him up and down. He was wearing a well-tailored, dark-grey suit, with a white shirt and maroon tie; a matching handkerchief protruded with triangular precision from his breast pocket.

"Hello." He smiled warmly, and his big, brown eyes twinkled. "I'm James. James Brown."

"Nice one." She giggled.

"Yes, my parents thought so, too."

"So, James Brown, how can I help you?"

"I think, perhaps, that it works in the opposite direction. I'm your new regional manager."

"Ah," Eleanor said, turning slightly pink. "And that probably wasn't the best introduction!"

"Don't you worry, Miss Davenport. I'm used to it. You are El-e-a-nor Davenport, I take it?"

"I am, indeed, Eleanor, ahem, Davenport, yes," she confirmed nervously. The way he said her name, his accent breaking apart every syllable, was just divine. Never in her life had she felt this kind of instant physical attraction to someone, and judging by Jess's reaction, he definitely had 'it'—whatever it was.

"I thought as much. Liz told me great things about you. You are just how I imagined."

"Liz described me, did she?" she asked, doubting there was any truth to that at all. Liz had been the regional manager for the whole time Eleanor had worked for the chain, and she regularly called by phone to check all was well but rarely visited. She'd suggested a long time ago that Eleanor should consider going for promotion—something she had no desire to do—but that was about as deep as her relationship with her line manager had ever gone.

"So, El-e-a-nor," James repeated, melting her on the spot. "Show me your kingdom." He extended an arm and swept it around him in a semicircle, his jacket sleeve rising to reveal small maroon and gold cufflinks. Eleanor, knees wobbling, led the way to the kitchen.

"Now, you'll have to excuse Wotto," she explained, as they approached the swinging doors. "He's a big fan of seventies disco and funk and likes…music while he works."

They entered the kitchen, and as predicted, Wotto the chef—real name Carl Watkinson—was boogie-ing his way between the oven and the pile of pizza dough he had just mixed, singing along to a playlist of seventies disco classics.

"This is Mr. Brown, our new regional manager," Eleanor informed him, at which he slid out of his moonwalk and halted abruptly in front of the pair, removed his latex gloves and brushed his sweaty palms on his apron.

"Hello, Wotto. Pleased to meet you." James smiled, shaking the floury hand held out to him.

"Alright?" Wotto grinned a giant, cheesy grin revealing all of his teeth, pulled his cap straight and went to get new gloves from the box on the shelf behind him. He had very big hair and it tended to push off any headgear, other than what he called his Jamiroquai hat—a giant, leather, peaked cap.

"My word, that is some afro you have hiding in there." James flashed that smile again. Wotto beamed back and continued kneading the dough. Evidently, Mr. Brown's charming ways didn't just win over the women.

Eleanor indicated that he follow her, and they walked the perimeter of the kitchen, looking into boxes, and out to the storage room. All was in order, as was to be expected, for it was very much her realm. Everything had to be just right, which could have made her one of the most irritating people to work for. However, her staff retention was excellent, in part assisted by the slightly higher pay at The Pizza Place compared to other chains, but mostly because she treated them with respect.

After the tour, Eleanor and James sat at a table, and he took out his tablet to make notes on any matters that she felt needed addressing. There was nothing really that was a problem she believed she should bother a regional manager with. The company allowed her to choose her own local suppliers, providing that their produce met the quality assurance standards. As usual, Dan said he could put her in touch with plenty of people who could give her a better deal, but she declined his offers. Eleanor did things her own way.

This was the quietest afternoon of the week, and she and Wotto were working alone. The busiest time was early Saturday evening, when there were six staff on duty, and the pattern was so predictable that the personnel was as streamlined as it could be. Supplies arrived on time, and she always ordered exactly the right amount, so there was never any waste.

"I can see my supervision will be very easy when it comes to your restaurant, Miss Davenport." James smiled and slid his stylus back into his pocket. "I will, of course, visit once a month, and you have the number for the regional office." He pulled out a business card and wrote on the back. "This is my personal mobile number."

"Oh!" Eleanor blushed.

"I should very much like to take you to dinner some time, if that would be acceptable, El-e-a-nor."

"Oh!" she said again, turning an even deeper red. "I mean, yes. That would be lovely."

"Call me." He gently shook her hand, scooped up his briefcase, and strolled out of the restaurant, this time passing Josh in the doorway. Eleanor remained where she was, standing absolutely still, holding the business card.

"Hmm. Now then. Who's that who has just swept you off your feet?" Josh asked.

"James Brown," she declared dreamily.

"Interesting. Give me coffee. Now!" he ordered.

"Yes, Your Majesty." She passed him the business card and did as she was told. It was a joke, always the same with him, and if she had ever taken it any other way, then he'd have stopped pretending to tell her what to do instantly. Truth be told, she was and had always been the one in control.

"What's this? His mobile?" Josh turned the card over and back again.

"He wants to take me out."

"And you said?"

"'Oh'. Then I think I accepted. I'm not sure." She was still a little giddy. It was a feeling she hadn't had for so long that she wondered if she was beginning to come down with flu or something.

"Look at you!" Josh laughed. "All flustered. Bless. He is quite cute, though, I'll give you that."

"Quite cute? He's bloody gorgeous! Charming, too. But enough of this nonsense. I want to talk to you about something." Eleanor suddenly became serious again.

She'd been worrying so much about the situation with Josh and George that she had to be up-front about it, so she told him everything, starting with how it was to do with her own insecurities more than anything else. Josh listened intently to all she had to say—about him always needing her when it came to dealing with George. The fact that he'd sorted it out all by himself made her feel like a spare part that he no longer had any use for.

She watched him the whole time, looking for any clues as to what he and George had talked about, but this really was about her and not just an attempt to glean information, even if there was still that sense of there being something she wanted to know and didn't.

Josh gave out no signals about George's new love interest, nor how he felt about it, for he was still sworn to secrecy. He'd tried to cajole George into permitting him to tell Eleanor, because he trusted her not to say anything but had to agree that it was likely that she would tell Jess, who would tell Andy, who would tell Dan, then Kris, Shaunna, Adele... Before they knew it, everyone would know on a 'don't tell anyone' path of Chinese Whispers. George had joked that by the time it got right around the group, Adele would be telling her customers that one of her friends was cohabiting with Billy Ray Cyrus.

At the end of Eleanor's monologue, Josh drank his coffee and wiped his mouth slowly, trying to find the best way to word his response.

"First off, you're right," he began. "You are being insecure and paranoid. You are my best friend, and if it hadn't been for you, George, or I, or both of us, would have gone totally insane long ago." Eleanor nodded her understanding.

"Secondly," he continued, "you are not a spare part. I tell you about the conversations I have with George because I want to share with you, and I care what you think. I'm a bit cross you haven't told me before that you've been feeling like this, but that doesn't matter." He took her hand, shaking it gently to bring her back from the guilt she was feeling for not confiding in him.

"Thirdly, I'm all grown up now, Ellie, and I had to make the first move. I love George too much to carry on any longer. We wasted ten years acting like strangers, and although you are my best friend, I had to go to him."

"So what are you hiding?" she probed.

Still he held his poker face. "Hang on, I haven't finished yet."

"Sorry. Are there many more to go?"

"No. Just one. Can I get on with it?"

"Go on."

"Lastly, when I told you about my dream, what did you say?"

"Dream? The big slide thing?"

"Yes."

Eleanor shrugged. "I don't know. What did I say?"

"You said 'you're the therapist' and promptly changed the subject. Then, the next time I brought it up, you totally ignored me."

"Did I? Well, I apologise. I didn't realise it was that big a deal."

"It isn't, but in the middle of the night, when it wakes me up, I have to talk to someone."

"I understand that now," Eleanor conceded. This was partly her own fault; however, there was still more, she was sure of it.

"OK," she said, "now the other bit. I know you, Josh. You're hiding something."

"Yes. You're right." He sighed. "But I can't tell you what it is, regardless of how much I want to."

"Is it to do with George?"

"Yes."

He knew exactly where this was going next and could have just quashed it, but it was fun seeing the possibilities flicker across her face, her eyes wide and enquiring, like a child prodding at the wrapped gifts under the Christmas tree, trying to guess what's inside.

Of course, she was totally wrong, but for the moment, he was enjoying watching her fabricate the truth as she saw it. He and George had talked it through and safely boxed it off as a thing of the past, however regrettable that might be to their friends, especially Eleanor, who was apparently hoping he'd relent and tell her what she wanted to hear. Instead, he sat back and folded his arms, waiting for her to pluck up the courage to ask the question outright.

"Is it to do with George and you?"

"No! Stop it now," Josh commanded, making sure he sounded quite serious this time, because there was a small chance that he might crack under the pressure of interrogation. She took the hint and said no more on the matter, even if she did look somewhat disappointed that it wasn't what she'd hoped, but it had got her curiosity back in check.

"So," he said, switching the conversation back to Eleanor James Brown, "when's this date with Mr. Dreamy?"

"Dunno. Got to ring him and arrange it, but I don't want to come across as over keen."

"Oh, in that case, I'd leave it another half an hour or so, at least."

"I shall be ringing him tomorrow at the earliest, Joshua, if I ring him at all."

Chapter Sixteen:
Biting Back

Regardless of her constant worrying, Adele's pregnancy was progressing normally. She now had a noticeable bump, which irritated and pleased her at the same time. It meant that none of her clothes fitted anymore, but she was trying not to think about it. She was experiencing a bit of discomfort in her pelvis and hips, as the baby began to take up more room, which was more of a concern. She was petite and slim, and the midwife had already suggested that she should consider an elective caesarean rather than a natural birth.

Adele didn't want the scar associated with the surgery but was tempted by what seemed a less painful option, despite being told that there were possible risks to her health, not to mention the challenge of coping with a newborn baby whilst recovering from surgery. Still, she had another twenty weeks to go, and they didn't need a decision until she was around thirty-five weeks. Maybe it would turn out to be a small baby, like she was, and, Shaunna said, the aching in her hips was probably only caused by increased elastin. Adele had no idea what that meant but took her word for it.

Although Shaunna was slightly better during the latest ante-natal visit, she was still quite snappy, and Adele tried her best to be patient, all the while thinking that things should be the other way around. It had to be difficult for Shaunna, she reasoned, who had been so young, and scared, when she was going through pregnancy. Adele recalled sitting outside the doctor's surgery and hospital many times, when she should have been in school. It had been much further on than Adele was now before Shaunna had told her she was pregnant, let alone talked about how it happened.

A party, too much cider and who knew what else—Adele couldn't even remember whose party it was, not that it mattered. For Shaunna, memories and questions of that night subsided further with each stage passed, kick felt, finally abandoned in the throes of labour. Adele couldn't wait to experience all of that for herself and was starting to pick up on the tiny movements of new life inside her, the joy and fear of giving birth—something she allowed herself to anticipate now she was at the halfway mark.

Tom was equally excited and very over-protective: he was spending so much time standing in the windows, watching her work and ticking her off for over-stretching or hulking mannequins and pieces of equipment about, that the general manager threatened to transfer him to another store. At any other time, he would have resolved to hunt down the member of his staff who grassed him up, but he was still revelling in the honeymoon phase. He'd married the woman he loved, and she was having his baby. Life was pretty much as perfect as it could be, and since he hadn't seen or heard from Dan in weeks, he'd even stopped worrying that he might still lose her.

Tom also resisted utilising the slight distancing of Adele from the rest of 'The Circle' as an opportunity to break the links for good. It wasn't that he didn't like them; quite the contrary. Even by association, they were the best friends he'd ever had. Of course, he'd known Dan for years. It was he who'd suggested Adele go for the job, and put in a word to ensure she was successful in her application. Back then, Tom thought she was just as stunning—before the nose straightening and chin reduction—but he didn't care if this pregnancy left her fat and covered in stretch marks. He would still find her beautiful.

Adele herself was mortified by the prospect and spent vast amounts of cash, even taking into account her employee's discount, on lotions and gels that claimed to stop stretch marks before they appeared. The first time she spotted a couple of silvery lines extending from her bikini line, she almost died from the horror. Tom kissed her tummy and put his ear to it, telling her the baby said 'she' just wanted to be comfortable in there, so she mustn't worry. Adele wasn't amused, but she appreciated his efforts to make her feel better.

The first real kick wasn't long coming, and within a couple of days, she was regularly seeing and feeling little irregularities in her perfect bump. It was so hard to imagine that there was a person growing inside her, and it made it all the more real, and scary. She started to panic again, calling Shaunna several times a day to ask if some thing or another was normal if it was to do with the baby, or reversible if it involved her body changing shape. Shaunna responded with greater exasperation each time, much more on her mind to worry about than what Adele could do to keep her boobs pert.

The allergic reaction Kris had experienced had several consequences, the first of which was that he agreed to have treatment aimed at reducing the severity of his allergy to cats. It had not been a major concern for him in the past, but Shaunna was seriously affected by it, to the extent that he couldn't sniff or cough without her nagging him to check where his epi-pen was, while she scoured the vicinity for any possible allergen. She had always been house-proud, but the cleaning was becoming an obsessive ritual, and poor Casper was being subjected to daily baths. Shaunna even stopped eating prawn cocktail crisps, which were her favourite and contained no prawn or prawn-derived ingredients whatsoever.

More sensibly, they kept the back door closed as much as possible, only opening it to let the dog in or out, and Krissi or Shaunna would thoroughly check him for feline scent or hairs before he was allowed back in again, although the cat did seem to have learned its lesson and hadn't been seen in the garden since the day Shaunna scragged it. She was still contemplating sending the neighbour a bill for her ruined t-shirt and Dan's petrol expenses.

However, the most significant outcome of the event was that Kris still hadn't found the time to talk to Krissi about her quest to find her father, and if he was honest, he was glad, because he didn't relish the task at all. He justified his inaction by reminding himself that she had only mentioned it once, on the night out when George was over, and they had done a spectacular job of keeping her focused on her twenty-first birthday, which was what the conversation was about to begin with.

Kris knew that once he explained how much it would upset Shaunna, Krissi would give up, he was certain of it. Her friends who had reached twenty-one before her all demanded expensive presents, yet she had asked for small gifts, knowing that their income was limited; she was a caring, compassionate girl. Kris refused to accept any responsibility for how well she had turned out, even though he had been there throughout her life.

And he had been saving to buy her something big, without telling Shaunna, who would have insisted he didn't. He had enough to buy her a little, second-hand car, pay a deposit on a flat, or book her an all-expenses-paid holiday. He wanted to surprise her, but she wasn't helping at all, because she had no real hobbies or interests, and when he asked what, if she could have anything she wanted, would it be, she just sighed and said, 'I don't know. I'm still thinking.' Four months back, that left plenty of time to plan. Now it was less than four weeks to her birthday.

***

Meanwhile, thanks to Eleanor, everything else was under control. The cake was ordered, as was the buffet. Josh had assured her that the music was sorted; Shaunna had booked the Royal British Legion's function room; Adele had organised a collection and made sure everyone came good on it before buying a selection of expensive perfumes, cosmetics and accessories.

Jess, Dan and Andy were awaiting their orders, knowing that sooner or later, Eleanor would collar them for something. She'd even phoned George and convinced him to come to the party, although the delivery of his house had been delayed, and it was due to arrive at around the same time. He said he could probably get one of the men on the ranch to supervise. Eleanor tried him with a couple of questions to see if she could prompt him into telling her the secret he had with Josh, but to no avail. All George would say was that he was going to do his very best to be there for the party, but he was making no promises.

***

It was only a matter of time before Krissi raised the issue again. For now, Kris and Shaunna were happy to pretend nothing was wrong and hoped that if they kept her preoccupied until after the party, she would let it go. She'd only recently finished a business management course and started a new job, so it wasn't difficult to keep her mind on other things. Shaunna used work as a focus of conversations during the evening, enthusing about the little stuff that happened and asking far too many unnecessary questions.

Now that she'd absorbed what Kris had told her, she felt slightly better about what had happened to her that night, because it meant it wasn't her fault, not entirely. All those years she'd blamed herself for not giving Krissi the right start in life, for being so drunk that she consented to sex with someone she didn't even know. Even if she had known them, there was no-one at the party she even wanted to date, or at least, she might have considered going out with one or two of her closest friends, but she certainly wouldn't have slept with them. Her 'next time' had been with Kris, a good five years later, and that had been a real trial. It felt very much like the first time for both of them, for Kris had only ever been with men before, and she had little recollection of losing her virginity or anything associated with it.

She was considering making a proper appointment with Josh, if only to get it all out of her system. They didn't see each other much, and she knew she could trust him to keep anything she said to himself. When Dan let slip with some passing comment that Kris had confided in him, she'd been a little annoyed, but then Dan was Kris's best friend, and he had to talk to someone. Dan also promised to help locate the eleven fifteen-year-old boys—now men in their mid-thirties, scattered around the world—if that was what they agreed would happen, and when they found the bastard, Dan said he would hold him down while Kris kicked the living daylights out of him.

Much as Shaunna appreciated having people on her side, Dan's anger was hardly cathartic, for there were aspects of that party she did recall, and he hadn't helped matters. He and Adele were too busy getting it on, and Shaunna didn't know any of the other guests that well. At that point in time, Kris was someone she'd seen around school, spoken to once or twice in the canteen while they waited for their respective best friends to finish arguing or kissing, depending on the phase they were in, but he wasn't a friend as such. Maybe, if Dan hadn't distracted Adele at the party, if Shaunna hadn't felt pushed out, then maybe she wouldn't have wandered off on her own.

The more she dwelled on it, the stronger her desire to seek Josh's counsel; she gave him a call and arranged to go to his surgery the following week. It would give her time to change her mind if she wanted to, he said.

The ill-ease between Shaunna and Adele had been spiralling for weeks, so it was no surprise when it finally came to a head, given that Shaunna's imagined recollections had now placed Adele as an unwitting accomplice to the crime. She realised it was absurd and tried desperately to rationalise, but it wasn't helped by the persistent phone calls detailing the ins and outs of every single experience, however trivial, as if Adele were pioneering pregnancy.

Sometimes she asked the most ridiculous questions, and her worries were pathetic little woes by comparison. Not once had she checked to see how Shaunna was, probably not even noticing that anything was different, because she was so caught up in herself. Shaunna's teeth ached from clenching them in her efforts to avoid saying what she really thought, and the notepad next to the phone was filled with harsh, angular doodles created with such force that they left an impression through several sheets below.

And so it was that Adele called to talk about her fear of developing varicose veins—innocent enough, other than it led to a discussion about older and younger mothers, with Shaunna arguing the case that regardless of age, any woman could survive pregnancy well with exercise, sensible diet and a little self-care. It was intended as an objective general comment only, a means of avoiding potential conflict, but it backfired terribly.

With her usual lack of sensitivity and empathy, Adele implied that older women were more responsible and therefore made better mothers generally, at which point Shaunna erupted and verbally tore her to shreds. Everything she'd held back since the start of the pregnancy came out in one long, bitter stream—how shallow Adele was, how little it mattered whether she kept her looks and figure, how she had totally the wrong priorities and, worst of all, how she didn't deserve to be a mother.

They hung up on each other at exactly the same moment. It would be a while before either backed down.

Chapter Seventeen:
The Wolf

Phil Spencer arrived two minutes late for his appointment with Josh, which wasn't a problem, but it was irritating. He was as over-enthusiastic as he had been when he came to book it, which was somewhat more annoying, bouncing in, so little like a person in need of therapy that Josh was instantly suspicious of his motives. However, he tried his best to take the man at his word and proceeded in his usual way, with a brief discussion about Phil's life, what he was currently doing, and the nature of whatever it was that had led him to seek counselling.

"The thing is, Doc," Phil started, "I've got this girlfriend."

Josh hid a grimace with a smile. "I'm not a doctor, Phil. Please just call me Josh."

"I've got this girlfriend, you see, Josh. Nice girl. Quiet, not as popular as me, but then, not many people are. Anyway, we've been together since just after she started uni. Then a few weeks back, she dumped me." He stopped talking and smiled expectantly, as if what he'd revealed so far warranted a reply.

"Go on," Josh encouraged.

"Well, there's not much else to tell. I want her back. I love her, see?" He sat, with his hands perfectly still, legs crossed at the ankles, head tilted slightly to one side, staring right at Josh.

"I see. And was there any particular reason why she called off the relationship, that you know of?"

"Yes, but I don't want to talk about it."

"That's fine, for now, but we will come back to it. Tell me—"

"Why? It's not relevant."

"Tell me about your relationship with your ex-girlfriend."

"I like to think of her as my girlfriend in remission."

"OK. Tell me what it is like."

"Sex-wise, very good. She's a looker. What bloke couldn't resist?"

"And socially, would you say you got on well?"

"As well as any man can with a woman. I mean, the conversation is hardly riveting, but we can't have it all, can we, Doc?"

"Josh."

"Sorry. She talks about the usual girly stuff, you know? Reading and art and all that crap. No interest in sport at all, but then that's par for the course, oops, bit of a pun there. I'm not into golf, by the way. I'm a footy man myself. How about you?"

"I can't say sport interests me. However, this is about you, Phil."

"Of course. Yeah, so, as I was saying, we get on all right. We go out and that. I even went shopping with her once. Terrible that was, won't be doing that again in a hurry, standing outside all sorts of shops while she fannied about with shoes and bags and stuff. She wanted me to look at a dress, cos my mum invited her to dinner. Well, I said, you don't need to get all dolled up, love, and got off."

"Got off?"

"Went home. Left her to it."

"I see." Josh made as if writing notes just so he could take it all in. He really couldn't stand this man, but had to admit that he shared his views on shopping. It was like having his soul slowly pulled out through his nose, in much the same way as the Egyptians removed the brains of their dead prior to mummification. That said, he envisaged that if he were ever to abandon Eleanor in the middle of a shopping spree, she would make what the Egyptians did seem like a reasonable alternative, dead or alive.

Notwithstanding his empathy for his client, or lack thereof, there was a job to be done. Josh faked a smile and soldiered on.

"Was this around the time that she called off the relationship?"

"No. This was weeks before. We were all right again after that. She didn't say much about it. Then there was this other girl. It didn't mean anything."

And there it was. Josh had heard more than enough. Phil didn't need counselling, he needed a good, hard smack in the teeth. What a hideous man, if he was being honest and all of this were true, which was doubtful.

"Sometimes, Phil, I have clients who don't know how to discuss what is really bothering them, so they either tell me about other, less important things that are going on, or they create stories that are, erm, quite frankly, untrue. Can I ask you, are you making this up?"

"Well—" Phil smirked "—that's for you to decide, isn't it? After all, you're the one who's done the training, knows what he's on about, and all that. Richard said I'd like you. He was right. So, that'll do for today, will it?"

"You do have another fifteen minutes yet," Josh pointed out, tempted as he was to lie and tell him that his time was up and then lock up and find new premises, just in case he ever returned.

"Ah, well. I'm done till next time, just needed to set out what I've been going through, really."

"That's fine, Phil. If you feel we have no more to discuss today, we can continue another time." A client trying to leave before the end of a session often meant they were finally working in the right area, and at such times, Josh would usually persevere as gently as he could. However, on this occasion, he wanted Phil out of the room as quickly as possible.

"Right then—*Josh*—see, got there in the end. Thanks for listening, and all that. I ring to make another appointment, do I?"

Oh God, he's coming back, Josh cried, in his head, where a battle of ethics was raging.

"No. We can arrange it now." He had to say it. It was only fair. Phil seemed pleased, at least, and they arranged for the same time the following week.

"Thanks, *Josh*," he called cheerily, descending the stairs.

As soon as he heard the click indicating the outside door had closed, Josh sank back onto his own couch and covered his face with his hands in absolute despair. There was no way that Richard would willingly have held a social exchange with this fool. Likewise, Richard was not the sort of person that Phil would befriend, considering his total intolerance of his girlfriend's different interests, if indeed there was a girlfriend.

Josh pushed his hair back from his eyes, and remained where he was for a while. He liked to do this from time to time, to take in the world from his clients' perspective, especially after a first encounter with a difficult or dislikeable individual. It didn't seem too threatening, he thought; he kept his own chair at a very low level so that the height advantage was barely noticeable. The room was tidy, but not to the extent that it was unwelcoming. It always smelled of coffee—he'd seen it used elsewhere as a deliberate ploy, and although it wasn't so in his own surgery, it did add to the general ambience. Even Dan commented that it was a nice place to be.

So why did people like Phil put on such a show? Usually, Josh was able to crack the hard outer shell very quickly, and he understood that many relied on it to even engage with life in the outside world. On brief reflection, he envisaged that digging below the surface this time, however, would lead to even greater, unrestrained arrogance and bigotry.

The sound of footsteps on the stairs brought Josh out of his trance, and for a moment, he panicked. Maybe the door hadn't closed properly. Maybe Phil had changed his mind and was coming to reclaim the rest of his session.

"Alright, mate?"

Josh peered over his shoulder towards the open door, where Dan's head and shoulders appeared, disembodied from the rest of him.

"I was just thinking about you," he said, relieved. He lifted his legs and put his feet down hard, gaining the momentum to stand. Dan took that as an 'OK' to come in.

"Nice for you." He raised his eyebrows in further query.

"Oh, no, only what you said about this place being welcoming. Nothing sinister."

"Well, it is. Very homely, kind of warm and safe," he said, looking around the room and nodding. "I've had an idea, and I want your opinion."

"About what we discussed?"

"Yeah. I was thinking…" Dan paused, unsure if what he was about to suggest was the right thing to do, or if it would serve any useful purpose.

Josh waited, but he had already guessed what the decision was.

"I'm going to talk to Shaunna," Dan said at last. "What do you think?"

"To be honest, Dan, you're going to do it, whatever I think. As soon as you say anything like 'I've had an idea', I know your mind is already made up."

"Am I that predictable?"

"Probably not to most people, but they don't know you the way I do."

"You're right, fortunately, or unfortunately, however you want to look at it. I'm just worried about how to deal with her when I do tell her."

"She might be relieved to know that it's someone she cares about and respects."

"There's been a bit of a development," Dan said cagily. "God, I make it sound like someone made a few simple adjustments to a building plan or something." He perched absent-mindedly on the arm of the couch.

"I'm sorry. I have no idea what you're talking about." Josh looked to him for further explanation.

That was true. What Kris had told Dan he had kept to himself, only briefly mentioning to Shaunna that he knew, after which she had more or less locked herself away from the rest of them, although Josh had known there was something going on when she'd called to make an appointment. At the time, he'd assumed that Adele's pregnancy, coupled with Krissi's imminent coming of age, had dredged up some of the old hurts of the past. However, no-one but Kris and Dan knew what this was really about, so none of them could possibly have thought to give Shaunna a call, or pop in, just to say hi and be there for her.

A long time passed, maybe as much as ten minutes, while Dan tried to find the best way to explain what the development was. Each time he tried to give voice to it, the swell of rage intensified in his gut until he was barely able to contain it.

"Kris said it wasn't consensual," he stated eventually, coldly, and with every ounce of control he could muster.

Silence.

Josh grabbed for the table behind him. He'd always thought that when actors on TV did things like that, it was utter nonsense, but the news had knocked him off balance.

"She was raped," Dan added, in case there was any possibility of misunderstanding.

"But surely, everyone's judgement was impaired," Josh reasoned. "We'd all had far too much to drink." He was trying to justify it in his own mind. *Poor Shaunna. All these years and she didn't tell anyone.* Yet he could appreciate why.

"That's no excuse," Dan said.

"We accepted it as Shaunna's excuse. I think you're being unnecessarily harsh."

"You're wrong. Even when I've had a few, I've still got enough about me to know that when a woman says no, she means it. What man in their right mind forces himself on a fourteen-year-old girl?"

"He wasn't in his right mind, was he? And he was only a boy himself at the time."

"It's still no excuse."

Josh was speechless—something that seemed to be happening to him a lot of late. He didn't know how to deal with this, what advice he could give to Dan. The whole rape aspect changed everything.

"Your thoughts, oh great counsellor?" Dan pushed wearily.

"I, err, oh Jesus! This is terrible. I need a cigarette." The declaration surprised Dan only slightly more than it surprised Josh himself, seeing as he'd given up smoking, with Jess, ten years before and never been tempted to start again. "You realise the implications of telling her?"

"Legally, you mean? Yeah, but I've to do the right thing. I've been involved in some shady deals, turned a blind eye to a lot of stuff I shouldn't have, but this? This is different. She's married to my best friend. In fact, she is one of my best friends."

"I understand. However, Andy is your brother." Josh gave himself a mental clip around the ear for stating the hideously obvious. That was, after all, what it had always been about.

"And maybe a rapist." Dan wagged his index finger at Josh, something that wound him up, regardless of who did it, but now was not the time to protest.

"And if I'm right, and I'm pretty sure I am," Dan continued, "then he's no brother of mine."

Chapter Eighteen: Breach

As soon as Dan left, Josh called the other client booked in for that afternoon to reschedule, locked up and set off for Eleanor's restaurant. This was something he could no longer keep to himself. He was still deep in thought and reeling from the shock when he arrived and almost walked into the door.

"Hi, Josh," Karen, one of the full-time waitresses who also doubled as relief manager, greeted him. "Eleanor's just popped out to the bank. Do you want a coffee?"

"I'd love one, thanks," he replied, and slumped into a seat at the usual table. For a while, he distracted himself with the antics of a young family in the next booth: a boy and younger girl of preschool age, a mum and possibly the grandmother. The boy was whingeing for ice cream, and his mother insisted he finished whatever was on his plate first. Josh couldn't see what that was.

The little girl was in a high chair, with all that was visible of her covered in tomato sauce flecked with oregano. She realised he was watching her, looked in his direction and stopped, a finger of half-chewed pizza crust in her hand. She smiled, and Josh smiled back. How sweet she was, and how much work it would be to clean her up later! She returned to the pile of food on her high-chair tray, swapping the soggy, naked bread in her hand for a piece with cheese on.

"You look like you've seen a ghost," Karen said, putting the coffee on the table in front of him.

"Do I? I just had some bad news, that's all." He searched the condiments pot for sachets of brown sugar. There was only one in there, and he came in often enough for Karen to know that if he had sugar at all, he'd need a lot more than that. She disappeared momentarily, returning with a handful of tiny sausage-shaped packets.

"Thank you." Josh gave her a watery smile and took the sugar, simultaneously ripping the tops off all eight sachets before tipping them into his coffee.

Karen nodded in acknowledgement and moved on to the family. She checked all was well and went back to what she'd been doing before he arrived, watching him out of the corner of her eye.

Josh had been stirring his cup and staring into space long enough for Eleanor to return. Karen indicated in his direction. "He's on the sugar," she explained quietly.

Eleanor studied him for a moment. "Can you manage on your own for a while?"

"Sure."

"Thanks." Eleanor approached Josh, but he didn't seem to have noticed. "Hey."

He glanced up. "Hey."

"You look like you've seen—"

"A ghost? Yes. You're not the first person to say that." Josh gave a hollow laugh. "That would be preferable."

Eleanor slid along the bench on the opposite side of the table and examined her friend. "What's happened?"

"Hold on to your seat, Ellie, it's going to be a bumpy ride." Hoping she would understand, he began to explain.

"Dan's been talking to me about this for a long time, but please don't feel that I've kept you out of it for any reason other than that it being in a professional capacity, so I couldn't share. Even now, I shouldn't be doing so, but I have to."

Eleanor nodded, eager to hear what he had to say whilst also wondering why he suddenly felt the urge to tell her now. Josh wouldn't admit that it was because he couldn't deal with whatever was going on, although it was apparent in his demeanour.

Josh sensed her curiosity and hoped she would understand why he needed to share. No longer could he be the only one involved, albeit indirectly. They were his friends, and it had been a hard enough burden to carry, without today's mind-blowing news. He took a deep breath and began.

"Most of the time, when Dan comes to see me, he just chats generally about things that are getting to him, making him angry. Sometimes it's about people he has to deal with in his work, sometimes it's about Andy. In fact, it's predominantly to do with Andy, if I'm honest. To start with, it was like he couldn't forgive him, as if he'd let him down, even though it was never certain that Andy was responsible, and I kept reminding Dan of that.

"The first time he booked an appointment to see me might even have been when he was still in London, and he insisted on paying for it. I guess he saw it as insurance of my silence, and I refused payment—not to wheedle out of keeping the confidence. When all's said and done, friends don't buy each other's trust. And there are so many occasions—when he gets all high and mighty—I've literally been on the brink of letting it slip. He turns on himself first and then me. Instead of Andy."

Eleanor listened quietly, her expression unchanged as Josh went on, even though the story so far was too cryptic for her to comprehend.

"As soon as Shaunna told us she was expecting Krissi, Dan was convinced that Andy was the father. I won't bore you with why, but the evidence was, if not conclusive, certainly substantial. I was the first and only person he told, and by then it had twisted itself into a terrible secret that had been tearing into Dan for a while. It was no longer about Shaunna, or what did or didn't happen at the party. It was about Andy's dependence on him in all respects. Dan's paid out for Andy's mistakes, given him a job…protected him from the truth.

"Then, today, he told me that Shaunna was raped, or rather, Kris says it wasn't consensual, which amounts to the same thing. Now Dan believes he has some moral obligation to inform Shaunna, or punish Andy, or both."

Eleanor remained calm—on the surface. Behind the scenes, the panic was rapidly mounting, but it wouldn't help Josh to see it.

"Can't you talk him out of it?" she asked in desperation. "Only, I can't see that it's going to help. Is he even sure that it was Andy?"

"Pretty much." The confirmation seemed so irrelevant. It was by no means certain that Andy was Krissi's father, based on the hard, solid facts alone, but Josh had spent so long listening to Dan that he couldn't rely on his own judgement anymore.

Eleanor shook her head, still struggling to comprehend what Josh had told her. "If he's wrong, he's going to destroy Andy for no reason. It'll kill him, unless…" She didn't want to say it, to put into words the thought that had flitted across her mind—that Dan might be right. Until that moment, she'd assumed Andy was an innocent party, which wasn't the way Josh was presenting it.

The family left; others came and went. Karen and Wotto soldiered away, glancing every now and then at their much revered boss, wondering how long they could cope without her assistance. They could see that whatever the matter under discussion, it was serious. She would never knowingly abandon them otherwise. Eleanor and Josh continued to talk in animated, hushed voices.

"The thing is," Josh said, "if Krissi starts up again about locating her father, then it will all kick off anyway, and I agree with Dan that this might be the best way to limit the damage. Mind you, he didn't seem too worried about that side of things. He was even angrier than usual, either with Andy for what he did, or himself for not saying something sooner, I'm not sure which."

"I'm amazed, you know. I just didn't see Dan as an angry person."

"Oh, believe me, he is. He's never got physical or anything, but you wouldn't want to hear the things he says. And now I've said too much."

"How do you do it, Josh?" Eleanor had wondered often. There were many times when he had confided in her about conflicts between his personal and professional life without revealing the issues behind them. If he, too, was angry with himself for keeping quiet, then he certainly didn't show it, and in the same circumstance she wouldn't have been able to maintain that professional stance. It wasn't as if he were a priest receiving confession. Shaunna was his friend. But then, so were Dan and Andy. "I wouldn't even know what to do in a situation like this," she thought aloud.

"Which is why a code of ethical conduct comes in handy," Josh said, "although it hasn't really been a problem until today. As far as I was concerned, Andy, possibly, had got drunk, done something he shouldn't and lost the memory to alcoholic amnesia. Either that, or he didn't do anything to forget and

Dan's paranoia fuelled it all. But I had no reason to suspect he had any more recollection of that night than Shaunna. Now there's the possibility he may have been hiding something all this time."

"But what if he's a—" Eleanor stopped and waited until Karen had walked past their table. "Shit. I've just realised how busy it is. I'll have to get back to work." She leaned in close as she rose from her seat. "What if Andy really is a rapist?"

"Then we cross that bridge when we come to it." Josh sighed. "I'll leave you to get on. Apologise to your people for me, for keeping you away from your duties." He stood and put his arms around her.

"I love you," she said, hugging him back. "You're fantastic. I hope you know that."

"And I love you, too, Ellie," he replied and kissed the top of her head.

She watched as he walked out of the restaurant, for the first time since she'd known him looking like the weight was too much for him to carry.

***

Dan hadn't acted on impulse, which was unusual. Generally, once he'd made a decision, he wasted no time in further pondering the best way of putting a plan into action. More often than not, it worked out for the best, because his decisions were of a business nature, and he had to act quickly to avoid missing an opportunity.

However, this was entirely new ground. In business, he was prepared to risk everything, investing in ventures with no track record, paying upfront without seeing the merchandise because he had a gut feeling that it was a good move. Business was everything to him, always the most important thing in his life.

To finally seal the contract on a tricky deal…well, it was how he got his highs, and his social acquaintances rarely surpassed that, with his friends and family sometimes left wondering whether they mattered to him at all.

His relationships with women were shallow, involving virtually no risk of his heart, because he only ever truly loved Adele—something that wasn't meant to be—and he had so many doubts about who he was. As his therapist, Josh seemed to understand the tightrope Dan walked, but the only person who had seen him fall was Kris, long ago, before the emergence of the super-confident alter ego, and Dan wasn't about to drop the act now, of all times.

No, this required careful execution and the guidance of those more emotionally competent than he was. He would need to ask Josh for a favour, see if he would talk to Andy about what he knew, maybe even try and break him down to see if he had been covering up. It was a possibility, considering his brother's personality was little different from his own, and his own was all affected.

After that, Dan would talk to Shaunna himself, in Kris's presence. But first, he was going to meet up with some mates and get hammered. He hadn't done it for years—didn't dare to with his closest friends, because they mattered. But there were a few people he'd worked with who lived out of town, and that was where he was heading, for a long weekend bender. *Then* he would deal with the rest of it.

***

Andy had agreed to keep hold of Dan's work phone for the duration of his jaunt. He hardly ever went off the radar and made sure there were no outstanding matters, so it was unlikely there would be much to do on that side of things.

Alas, he also had an enormous pool-like enclosure in his apartment, containing fifteen Japanese koi carp. That was more of a worry, because the instructions for caring for them were more complicated than any exam paper Andy had ever encountered, and they didn't need to be. He'd done it a few times, for odd days here and there, and with Adele's reluctant assistance, obtained by pleading with her until she caved. She'd lived with the things and knew what they needed better than he did.

Now, with Adele well into her pregnancy, and Dan's insistence that he didn't tell anyone he was going away, Andy would just have to get on with it and hope for the best. Dan had also left the car, with strict orders that any petrol used be replaced and a threat regarding the presence of even the slightest scratch on his return. Andy waved the warning away. He wasn't going to chance using the car unless he had to, and in any case, while Dan was gone, it gave him an opportunity to look for alternative means of employment.

***

Josh got home, warmed some milk, added a shot of whisky to it and went to bed with his laptop. He wasn't intending to tell George about the day's events; he just needed the distraction of chatting about unimportant stuff. In fact, the last thing he wanted to do was discuss the whole situation again, and the best way to avoid inadvertently driving the conversation that way was through instant messaging, so he was disappointed to find that George wasn't online. Nor was he answering his phone, but then, it was still mid-afternoon on the ranch.

Josh closed his laptop and decided to try again later, assuming he was still awake, which was very likely, the way he was feeling. He found the page in the book he was reading—

about the thirtieth piece of trashy fiction he'd got through since Adele's wedding—and settled back, mug of hot milk in one hand and book in the other.

Three chapters and an empty mug later, no nearer sleep, he went down to heat more milk, changed his mind, and took a glass and the whisky bottle back up with him instead. He hated drinking alone as a general rule, and placated himself with the idea that if he was chatting online, technically, he wasn't alone. Still George wasn't there, and he experienced a minor outrage, which was preposterous. It wasn't as if George was being deliberately evasive…he hoped.

The book was boring, there was nothing on TV, and Josh was still wide awake. He flicked back and forth through the music channels, stopping to listen to songs he liked or that were fitting to his state of mind, and paid no attention to the amount of whisky he was consuming in the process. As it took effect, his sense of time drifted, and it quickly became the early hours. Intermittently Josh glanced at his laptop screen to see if there was anyone at all worth talking to. At one point, Jess showed up as being online, but then she was gone again. He checked the clock: 2:38 a.m.

Drunkenly, he staggered off to the bathroom, emptied his bladder, and returned to bed, shoving his open laptop across the duvet so he could lie down. The world began to spin, and he sat up. He tried again, more slowly this time, and with some success. At least the whisky had made him feel a little dopey, so there was a chance of sleeping. Tomorrow, he was at the university, and in retrospect, drinking that much alcohol was not the best idea he'd had. The thought slowly faded.

***

Three email messages, several attempts to get hold of him via messaging and a missed phone call... George replied to the message but got no response. He checked the time in the UK. It was too late to return the call, and he wasn't sure what to do. Josh had been in touch a lot recently, but this seemed different, somehow more urgent, and he obviously needed to talk. But George had things to deal with himself, so for now, he let it be.

Chapter Nineteen: Time for Change

Jess felt so much better for handing in her notice. She had no idea how she was going to afford to pay the mortgage or anything else, but if she spent much longer in that place, she'd end up killing someone. She still had to work the month out and doubted she'd last even that long without stabbing her supervisor in the eye with a freshly sharpened pencil; the thought crossed her mind often enough.

She was finally ready to make the break and go for it. Talking it through with Andy had made her appreciate that her career was no longer under her control. The positions she'd taken in legal firms had always placed her in subordination to men, whom she had been happy to accept as her superiors in both love and work. Her modus operandi had been to keep moving on, to avoid awkward situations and the conflict she felt between the roles she adopted and who, deep down, she believed herself to be. Her life was being governed by others, and it had to stop.

So, partly, it was what Andy had said about how the accident had forced him to re-examine a few things, such as being independent and taking responsibility, something he had thus far avoided. More significantly, it had given Jess a new perspective on her own future.

Her lifestyle, whilst never as wayward as his and certainly lacking the daredevil escapades, needed a serious overhaul, because it could all just end one day, and she would look back with regret if she didn't at least try and realise her ambitions. They had both followed their own paths, yet somehow reached the same point in their lives at the same time and were looking to start over.

As a single, professional woman, Jess had saved a fair bit of money over the years, some of it frittered away through holidays and lending out to friends—specifically to Andy—but there was enough to serve as a nest egg. And when he was in between jobs, he promised to help out as much as he could. He knew a little bit of every trade, nothing well enough to be an expert in anything and still not a piece of paper to his name, excluding his third-class degree in civil engineering.

However, when it came to the crunch, Jess trusted him as much, if not more than she would a fully qualified, time-served tradesman, and that trust extended to every aspect of their relationship. So far, he'd kept his promise; since the accident, he hadn't embarked on any more dangerous adventures.

After persuading Jess to help him feed the koi, Andy went with her to look at properties on short lease. She wasn't convinced that an all-female firm of solicitors had any legs, she said, a turn of phrase that she wished she'd thought through in advance, as it resulted in some hilarious innuendo for the rest of the day, which was spent wandering from one musty, old building to another, hoping for that 'perfect' moment to occasion.

Most of the offices they looked at were drably painted in magnolia, with old, chipped desks and broken chairs left by their previous occupants. One even had an old telephone with a dial, although there was no active phone line to check if it still worked. The estate agent was very helpful, arranging their visits at short notice and driving them to each location, but none of the buildings were right. They were too big, too small, too old, too damp, had the wrong vibe, not enough rooms, or any other reason Jess could find not to move on with her dream. Much as she wanted it, she was terrified that it might fail.

On their way home, after the twelfth recital of 'entrance hall, main office, kitchen, small office, WC', Jess was noncommittal, even though Andy, who did not get excited about property and especially office buildings, was trying his best, enthusiastically pointing out what each place had to offer. She gave each review either an outright 'no' or scowled and grunted, until he reminded her why she was doing it. She finally conceded that the consequence of not doing it was worse.

By the end of Saturday, there were two places, out of the twelve they had viewed, that had potential. One of them was of a reasonable size but had no bathroom, and Andy assured her that he could sort that out. The other had a bathroom and a kitchen, on account of having once been a house, with little done to convert it to offices. The lease was for the whole building, and it was too big, although again, Andy came up with a solution, suggesting she could sublet one of the two floors. He even checked with the estate agent so that Jess couldn't use it as an excuse to strike that one off the very short list of possibilities.

Its biggest draw, though, was that it was next door to Josh's surgery, which was in a safe, friendly area and, like his building, there was parking space in front. The cost was slightly higher, but Jess was warming to the idea of subletting, providing that it was either to other women or to people that she knew. There was time to consider, as no other offers had been made yet, so they went to the cinema for the evening and forgot about office hunting for the time being.

They were like a pair of naughty children, giggling and throwing popcorn, having eaten several bags of sweets and drunk too much Pepsi already. The film wasn't all that great either, and unnecessarily long. Some of the audience had left early, leaving only a handful of people in the large auditorium. For Jess and Andy, where they went and what they did hardly mattered, as long as they did it together. They were both physically attractive, intelligent, fun people who had taken their relationship further on occasion but always returned to being 'just friends'. Neither wanted more commitment than that, nor did they want the fun to stop, as it had for Dan and Adele.

Miraculously, they made it to the end of the film without being thrown out, emerging from the cinema to find that it was pouring with rain, and darting from one entrance to the next. After a brief stop at a pub, they bought a kebab to share and strolled home under glowing streetlights that reflected in the puddles. It was still raining, but they had reached the point where they were so wet they didn't care.

They arrived at Jess's house and she went upstairs to change, throwing down a pair of old jogging pants and a t-shirt Andy had left on a previous visit. He dumped his wet clothes in the kitchen and took a couple of bottles of beer from the fridge, settling on the couch to wait for Jess to finish whatever she was doing.

Of the four women in their group, Adele took the longest to get ready for a night out, but when it came to deciding what to wear, Jess was the champion, regardless of whether the occasion was a big formal dinner or a couple of hours of slobbing on the sofa before bedtime. By the time she decided on a pair of red silk pyjamas and came downstairs, Andy had almost finished his beer and waited not so patiently for her to catch up.

Jess searched the room for the TV remote control, lifting Andy's legs to see if he was sitting on it and making him stand so she could check under the cushions. She couldn't find it anywhere, so gave up looking and was about to press the power button on the TV when he reached down and pulled it out of the leg of his jogging pants. She snatched it from him and sat down at the other end of the sofa.

Dan's phone played the tone that signalled a text message had been received. Andy tried to ignore it. He had done as he was asked, not even telling Jess that Dan was away for the weekend, so when she pressed for him to check his phone, he either had to do so or risk rousing suspicion.

Somehow, he persuaded her to go and get a couple more beers from the fridge so that he could safely take out the phone without her seeing it. Dan had lots of money and a lust for gadgets that even surpassed Josh's, making his phone instantly recognisable.

T OUT RING ME PLS A X

He read the message and then read it again, unsure whether he was seeing more to it than was really there. He heard the shuffling of bare feet coming down the hall and quickly shoved the phone back in his pocket, just as Jess pushed the door open. She eyed him suspiciously as she handed him a beer.

"One of your dangerous friends, was it?" she asked, knowing he'd checked the phone in her absence.

"Something like that," he muttered nonchalantly, making a big deal out of lifting the top off the bottle she gave him.

"You changed your text tone," she observed.

He knew she was probing and that he had been partly rumbled, but he'd done nothing wrong, so he made a joke of it.

"Yeah, so what? You're not the boss of me." He tickled her, and she giggled.

"But I liked the old one."

"Well, I like this one." He grabbed her leg and held it between his own. She slipped away, and he grabbed her again, this time pushing her silk trousers up so that she couldn't wriggle free.

"Get off, you big meanie." Jess squirmed and tried to escape, but it was no use. Andy had clamped down hard with both thighs. "So your leg's all better then." She laughed, but her laughter soon faded when his own phone received a text message. He took it from his other pocket and glared at it.

Jess jerked her leg free and reached for her beer. He read the message, locked the screen and put the phone back in his pocket, immediately focusing all his attention on the TV. There was an awful silence, the sort that follows the smashing of glasses in a bar or a dropped tray in a restaurant kitchen; it was the sound of breaking trust.

Jess pulled at the label on the bottle and spoke without looking up. "Can I ask why you've got Dan's phone?"

"I haven't," Andy lied uselessly.

"I knew I recognised that ring tone, I just couldn't remember where from. It is Dan's, isn't it? What's he up to that you can't tell me?"

Andy sighed. There was no point trying to keep secrets from her. He should have known that by now. "I've no idea what he's up to. Gone off with his mates for the weekend. That's all I know."

"Which is why we had to feed those horrible fish of his."

"Yeah. He asked me not to mention it to anyone. Sorry."

"Hmm. I wonder why?" Jess tried to think of any recent events that might have led to Dan needing to escape for a few days. She'd never known him to do anything like that before, although he could be up to all sorts when he was away on business and no-one would be any the wiser. However, he didn't explicitly attempt to conceal his whereabouts.

"I think he was trying to get away from me," Andy said, aware of how egotistic he sounded. He didn't know why, but Dan had been so off with him since his accident, or was it since Adele got married? He wasn't sure anymore, not with the text messages he'd received over the past couple of days. He took out Dan's phone, opened the last message and showed it to Jess. "Or maybe he was trying to get away from this."

Jess read the message and shrugged, but then she realised the significance of the initials. "You don't think…"

"I don't know. Read this one." Andy took the phone back, selected the other text message from 'A' and gave it back.

"Missed you after you left last night. Where were you? Text back. A, kiss," Jess read aloud. "That doesn't prove it's not Adele."

"No, but they haven't seen each other since the wedding."

"As far as we know."

"I'm certain they haven't. Adele's perfume is very distinctive."

"Trust you to notice that. I concur, however. When they've been together, he smells almost as strongly of it as she does."

"Yeah. If she's intent on getting up to any funny business, she might want to tone it down a little. It's a dead giveaway."

"She was still all over him at the reception, and I know we hug and smooch and all that jazz, but we're both still single. It's a bit different when you're attached. And pregnant."

"Someone needs to have a word with her about that."

Jess poked him in the ribs. She knew he was hinting that she should somehow involve herself in finding out whether there was anything going on, and in the event that it turned out to be innocent, impart a few words of wisdom about appropriate behaviour for a married woman.

"Forgive me if I'm being a little self-critical here, but don't you think there are people better qualified to give someone a pep talk on how not to flirt with men?"

"Hmm, now let me see." He pretended to think about the answer. She play-punched him, and he mouthed an 'ouch', rubbing his chest.

"I still think we might be reading too much into this, though," Jess said.

And frowned. "All right, if it isn't Adele, then it must be something I've done. I'm not sure how I could've upset him, but he's been vile to me lately."

"Maybe he just needed a break. After all, you're a hideous patient."

"That's not fair!"

"It's perfectly fair. You scared him like you scared the rest of us. He wants some time out. Do you think it could just be that?"

"Agh!" Andy threw his arms in the air. "Who knows what goes on in my little brother's head? There was a time when I did, but he's changed. There's something bothering him, and he's not sharing."

Jess linked her arm through Andy's and rested her head on his shoulder.

"He will. When he's ready, he'll tell you."

Chapter Twenty:
Will Out Itself

When Kris came back to bed at ten in the morning, Shaunna had a feeling it wasn't because he wanted to get romantic. He loved early Sunday mornings on his own and almost always got up with Krissi at seven, so that he could spend a few hours alone after she left for work. He took Casper for a walk, then, if the weather was good, he sat out in the garden with the newspapers, leaving them in pristine condition so Shaunna could also enjoy them when she finally decided to end her lie-in.

On the occasions when Kris did come back upstairs, it was either because it was a special day—someone's birthday or an anniversary—or he needed to talk to her about something. In the absence of the former, Shaunna listened with her eyes shut, as Kris placed a cup of tea on the bedside table and climbed onto the bed behind her. He spooned up and draped his arm over her. It felt cold, even through the bed covers.

For a long time, she pretended to be asleep, the thoughts roaming around her mind, not wanting to ask the question, knowing the answer already. That was part of what had got to her about Adele. All those little, niggling worries through pregnancy were just a preamble to the ongoing traumas of motherhood—the worries about stillbirth, choking, bumps on the head—it never got any easier. She'd always known that one day, Krissi would want to know who her biological father was.

It had been a lot longer arriving than Shaunna had anticipated, but now it was here, it was also a lot harder to deal with.

Finally, without moving or opening her eyes, Shaunna spoke. "Did you tell her?"

"Sort of."

"Meaning what, exactly?" She pulled herself up the bed and picked up her cup.

"That'll be getting a bit cold for you. Shall I make you another?"

"When I've finished this one." Shaunna sipped at the tea, which had only been there a matter of ten minutes or so, and was still pretty warm. The unspoken message had been clear; he couldn't waylay her.

"She brought it up again, I didn't," Kris justified.

"Goes without saying."

"She said she would have liked to have found out who her real father was before her birthday, not because she thought it would be lovely to have him there. She said that was 'sooo Disney'." Kris affected the gestures of the characters in the teen sitcoms that Krissi had loved when she was younger. Shaunna laughed, and he joined in—anything for some light relief.

"So why, then?" she asked.

"She wants to put it behind her, move on. I said, 'You know looking for your dad is upsetting your mum?' She said she just wanted you to be honest with her and tell her what happened—was it a boyfriend or a one-night stand? She said she doesn't care if it was someone really horrible, she just wants to know."

"Did you tell her about the party? Or that I don't know if he was horrible or not, because I don't even know who did this to me?"

The last four words fell into sobs, and Shaunna clutched the cup of tea as her body jolted. Kris took it from her and pulled her towards him, holding her tight until the weeping subsided and she relaxed onto his chest. He smoothed her hair gently from her face and waited for her to recover.

"I told her there was a party, and that we were all drunk. I told her that we love her very much, and that she was always wanted."

Shaunna nodded her understanding, and they both fell silent. This was it; there was no getting out of it. She had to tell Krissi what happened, or at least the version of events she had always chosen to believe herself. Only if it was absolutely necessary would she mention anything else, if her daughter was still so set on establishing her father's identity that there was no other choice.

***

As soon as Dan had checked that his fish were still alive, he went to Andy's house and rang the doorbell. He waited for a short while and peered through a gap in the blinds of the living room window. The TV was playing away to itself, which meant nothing where Andy was concerned. He left it on almost all the time and hardly watched it at all. Dan tried the doorbell again, waited a few seconds longer, and then used his spare key to take his car. He contemplated leaving a note to explain where it had gone but had second thoughts; his brother didn't deserve the courtesy.

He hadn't intended to come home until Monday, but he'd been churning it around the whole time. The alcohol only made him more melancholic, caused him to predict all possible, unbearable outcomes to the situation, so that by mid-Saturday evening, his friends were having to drag him from one place to the next and, try as they might, they couldn't even raise a smile.

In the end, Dan made some excuse about Andy still needing help after his accident and left them in a club. He found a hotel and lay there, sleepless, counting the headlights of passing cars as they flashed across the ceiling, until breakfast time, when he picked at eggs and bacon and soon after took the train home.

He wasn't used to this. True, since Adele married Tom, there was always this empty feeling, like something had died inside. He loved her enough to want her to be happy, he'd always believed that. And yet, now she was, it made him mad and destructive. He'd taken to going to the gym every night, and his knuckles were wrecked from hitting that damned punch bag, but he had no other outlet, no-one he could take it out on.

When Dan talked to Josh, he worked hard to contain it, always careful not to fully reveal himself, not mentioning the broken fingers and toes from lashing out at objects harder than he was. When Josh asked if Dan ever got angry, he told him, yes, he did, but he could control it, which was more or less the truth. He hadn't actually killed anyone, though he'd been tempted many times. However, keeping what he'd discovered to himself had been the biggest test of his self-control.

The morning after the party, when everyone had gone home, he and Andy frantically cleaned the house. It wasn't as bad as it could have been; no-one had thrown up anywhere, or broken anything. Andy was a lot more hungover, possibly even still drunk, but pulled his weight, polishing marks off furniture, taking empty bottles to the tip in an old newspaper delivery bag.

Dan went upstairs to check their parents' bedroom. All seemed in order, and it looked like their guests had followed the strict instruction that the room was out of bounds for all but coats. Dan straightened the pillows and pulled the bedspread straight. He hated the way they still had sheets and blankets, and his mum was so obsessive about every sheet being folded symmetrically, every pillow facing the same way, she'd know if anything was amiss. Dan double-checked everything was how it should be and left the room.

Halfway down the stairs, he remembered some horror story about knickers under parents' beds, and as an afterthought went back up to check, just in case, not thinking for one minute there would be anything there. And that was when he discovered them. Not knickers, but boxer shorts; unequivocally, Andy's boxer shorts.

In a house with three sons who were pretty close in age and therefore physique, his mother had long ago established a colour code for their clothing. Michael's underpants were green, Andy's were red, and Dan's were blue. They'd hated it, having no choice about what colour each got and no opportunity to swap because she said it would just get too confusing at laundry time. As they grew up, even their stepdad had to put up with it, and he was stuck with grey or white. Still, Dan thought little of it, and picked up the red boxers with the tip of a finger and thumb, carrying them at arm's length to the laundry basket. By the time Andy returned, any thoughts of stray underwear had slipped his mind completely.

Months later, when Shaunna's pregnancy was revealed, Dan asked Adele to tell him what happened, but she knew nothing. She and Shaunna didn't talk anymore, not the way they used to. Instead, Adele told him how much she missed their nights in, reading magazines and chatting about boys, and how horrible it was that they all had to grow up. Dan listened and comforted, offering to be her new 'girlfriend'. She took him up on it—he could still remember that first story she read to him, about a girl who fell in love with her boyfriend's best friend.

At first, Dan fidgeted and didn't listen, but soon he was totally gripped. These glossy magazines were a revelation to him. Girls liked sex, thought about it as much as boys, were hurt when boys misunderstood them, misread the complicated signals. Over time, he wasn't just reading them with Adele, he was buying them himself, trying to get to grips with the female of the species—he explained, when Andy caught him one night.

The times with Adele were the best, though. She would read the problem page to him, while he lay on her bed, listening, before giving his advice on what the girl in question should do. Then Adele would grade his response and read out what the agony aunt had to say. Usually, their reading sessions would end with some heavy petting, and once again, the mystery of Shaunna's pregnancy would be forgotten.

Finally, when he and Kris were away at university, Dan happened on the opportunity to fill in some of the gaps. Kris had also been at the party, and didn't drink much, although he was partial to the occasional joint. That night, Dan and Andy had made him promise not to bring any, let alone smoke it at the party. He'd agreed, and Josh and Jess also promised to go out onto the street to smoke. It was one thing to cover all traces of booze, but their parents drank every night, so there was always a slight whiff of alcohol in the house. It was another entirely to get rid of the smell of smoke.

Hence, Kris had been as close to sober as anyone got that night and he'd not had much fun. The more everyone else drank, the less fun it had become, and he'd decided to go home. Dan apologised retrospectively, for being such a rotten host, and they'd both laughed, as Kris recounted some of the antics he'd observed that night, before it ended with an almighty argument when he'd asked George if he ever got turned on by girls. George completely overreacted—considering they weren't together—and stormed off down the garden. Kris considered going after him but was intercepted by Jess and Josh, who said they'd brought pot to the party, and he was welcome to join them.

"I knew it!" said Dan. "I could smell it, and I was sure it was you."

Kris assured Dan; no, it wasn't him. He'd told them off, reminded them that they'd promised, and went to get his coat from upstairs, which was when he heard 'stuff' going on. He'd waited in Dan's room, with the door ajar, until he'd heard the door opposite open and close, and someone unsteadily descend the stairs. When he'd gone in to retrieve his coat, he'd found Shaunna. He took her home, and the rest was history.

It *had* to be Andy. The boxer shorts were the first clue, admittedly not enough on their own. Yet, when the two of them had walked into the labour room and first set eyes on Krissi, she seemed so familiar. It had made Dan uneasy, and Andy looked like he was experiencing a similar sensation. The dark hair, already copious and drying into curls, the olive skin tone—just like their own first photos. He was glad when the midwife shooed them out, and neither said a word about the baby's striking resemblance to their own family line.

With the story that Kris had told, Dan had at last been able to put it all together. Andy was Krissi's father—a hard enough secret to keep in itself. With the recent revelation, it had become a millstone he could carry no more.

He drove to the gym, changed into his sports gear and ran for ninety minutes straight, eventually staggering away to the showers, where he stood under the lukewarm spray, punching the tiled wall until he could barely feel his knuckles, tears of pain and rage mixing with the drops rolling down his face.

***

Krissi came home from work with a bag of goodies consisting of all the reduced-price items left when the shop closed. She did it every Sunday, and it was kind of fun, trying to create a meal from the lucky dip selection no-one else wanted. Sometimes it was fantastic and delicious; always it was bizarre. They had feasted on Camembert cheese and Lincolnshire sausage wraps, and spaghetti Bolognese and barbecued pork ribs on the same plate.

Today's offering was quite mundane, consisting of Indian snacks, Chinese ready meals and a bag of mixed leaf salad. There was no challenge, and Krissi apologised for it.

Shaunna hugged her daughter and took the plastic bag. "We need to talk, you and me," she said, emptying the contents onto the table.

"It's OK, Mum. I've been thinking about what Kris said this morning. I'll leave it, if it's going to upset you."

"Let's get this food on," Shaunna suggested.

They opened boxes together and loaded the various snacks and containers into the oven. Once they were finished, Shaunna indicated to Krissi to sit with her at the table. Casper came over and lay his head on Shaunna's knee.

"Kris told you there was a party."

Krissi nodded.

"And we were all really drunk."

Krissi nodded again.

"The thing is, hun, I don't remember anything else. Kris took me home and put me to bed. When he told Grandma and Grandad that he was your dad, they went ballistic."

"Sounds about right."

"So, I told them the truth. I don't know who your dad is, but I don't want you to think that's because I was sleeping around. Me and Adele spent most of the night sitting on the floor, bitching about the lack of talent, then it's all a blank. If Kris hadn't told me, I wouldn't even be able to say where I'd been, how I got home, or anything."

"What on earth were you drinking, Mum?"

"God, all sorts. Cider, Pernod and blackcurrant, probably. That's what we drank back then, before those dodgy vodka shots you drink now."

"Were you going out with anyone?"

"Ha ha, no. I fancied Dan. Everyone did, and that was before he got really hot."

"Ew. Dan's an old man."

"To you, maybe, young lady."

"Ah, yeah, I keep forgetting you're old, too," Krissi joked. "So, you don't remember anything at all?"

"Nothing. But—" Shaunna took a folded piece of yellowing paper from the back pocket of her jeans "—here's a list of all the boys—or should I say old men—who were at the party. It'll help, if you decide you want to do this."

Krissi removed the paper from her mother's hand and unfolded it. There were only eleven names listed, including Kris, Andy, Dan, Josh and George.

"Go and talk to Jess again," Shaunna said. "She'll help you work out what to do next. Kris said he'd help you, too, but I can't. I hope you can understand that."

Chapter Twenty-One:
At the Seams

Hi George,

Before you come over, I'll have to fill you in on a couple of things that are going on. It's pretty massive, and I'm glad you're going to be here for Krissi's party because we're going to need each other. I'll give you a call sometime, as I don't think email is the best way to tell you.

Let me know your exact arrival time, and I'll meet you at the airport.

Catch you later.
Josh x

====================

Hey Josh - wanted to let you know the flight's booked. Joe isn't coming, which I'm kinda glad about - he's getting on my nerves at the moment.

And tell Ellie I'm gonna be there in plenty of time for her to have me in full on slave mode.

I think the plane lands at 8 on Tuesday morning - will check this and get back to you.

G x

Josh clicked the 'Send' button and went to his outbox to re-read what he'd written. He was, surprisingly, very excited about George coming home for the party; he'd been missing him lately. It would have been nice to meet Joe, but perhaps that was best left for another time, when their entire friendship group wasn't in tatters.

Emailing George had lifted a weight from Josh's mind and seemed to have triggered his appetite. He went to the kitchen, filled the kettle and took a giant chocolate-chip cookie from the bag of four he'd bought earlier in the day. He wasn't sure why. Eating them always reminded him of the little cow-shaped cookies Krissi had made—a memory he normally pushed from his consciousness. For once, he allowed the nostalgia to wash over him, and his thoughts went back, to George's farewell at Kris and Shaunna's housewarming.

At the time, the house had been quite bare, compared to how it was now. Shaunna loved clutter, but it wasn't untidy, and there were always so many lovely smells. She worked far too hard at being the ideal mother, learning new skills, such as how to knit and bake, so she could do so with Krissi. The Johansson house was always filled with the smell of recently baked cakes, scones or biscuits—sometimes all three—and the kettle never went cold. The tea mixed wonderfully with the scent of potpourri and incense, which Shaunna insisted was to camouflage the stink of wet Labrador.

At one point during the afternoon of the housewarming, Josh had walked towards the patio doors, about to head out into the garden, where Kris was barbecuing burgers and George and Eleanor were sitting on a garden bench and chatting quietly. Krissi intercepted him.

"We mustn't go out there. Aunty Eleanor said so, cos Uncle George is crying. I don't think he wants to live in America."

She ran past, leaving Josh hanging in the doorway, from where he could see that Uncle George was indeed crying. Eleanor made eye contact, shaking her head just enough for him to detect it. He didn't want to be the cause of this but knew that he was. He could have asked George to stay—he wanted him to stay. He might even have managed to fake enough of a relationship to make it worth his while to stay. But it would have been wrong, and selfish. What he was feeling was simply guilt, for being the reason George was going—why the nine was about to become eight.

At university, a lecturer in psychotherapy had singled Josh out and given it back to him, word for word. *If you don't come to terms with your own insecurities, you'll eventually push away all of your friends.* It had made Josh all the more determined; he would do everything in his power to keep his friends together and make a liar of Professor Harrington.

The one thing Josh couldn't do was stop George leaving, but Eleanor had been right. It was never goodbye. Now they had rekindled their friendship, everything could have been back to the way it used to be, but for the situation with Shaunna and Andy—assuming Dan was right. This was bigger than anything Josh had ever had to deal with, and he wasn't sure he had it in him.

The kettle had long since boiled and switched itself off. Josh switched it on again and finally got around to making coffee. He'd taken one bite of the cookie when the phone started to ring, and he knew it would be George.

"You got me all worried with that email. What the hell's going on? Is everyone OK?"

"Yes, everyone is fine, as in no-one else has had an accident, or anything," Josh assured him, before going on to explain, at length and from the beginning, Dan's longstanding belief that Andy had sex with Shaunna at the party, Kris's account indicating that she had fought him off, and Krissi's desire to confirm the identity of her father. George listened in silence, in much the way Eleanor had, only speaking once Josh reached the end of the whole sorry tale.

"Man, what a nightmare! How're you holding up?"

"Me? It's not really anything to do with me, or not directly. What about Shaunna? And Kris? And Dan, come to think of it. I doubt Krissi's coping too well—"

"Josh, come on!" George interrupted. "You forget who you're talking to. Don't you think I've spent long enough watching and listening to you to know when you're struggling?"

Josh sighed. "Oh, George, it's so hard." He pinched the corners of his eyes to stop the tears that were prickling there.

"Because you can't save them all? Nobody asked you to." Josh stayed silent at the other end of the line. "You still there?"

"Erm, yes," he finally managed to utter.

The call continued for another half an hour, with Josh pushing George to talk to him about anything that would keep his mind off what was going on. Having already emailed the sketches of the house, George instructed him to open the images and gave him a virtual guided tour, detailing all the different features, however irrelevant. The house was scheduled for completion within a couple of weeks of George's return from Krissi's party, and he had to admit, he was pretty fired up about it, considering how long it had taken him to deal with the house in the first place.

When Josh pointed out that it had been Joe's doing, George agreed and went on to confirm that his flight arrival time was as stated, before ending the call to go on his evening check of the ranch. If Josh had been in a fitter state of mind, he'd have picked up on how George had kept the conversation away from Joe and made a quick getaway as soon as his name was mentioned. As it was, Josh said goodbye without giving it a second thought.

It was such a relief to have shared his troubles with Eleanor, his best friend, and George, who proved himself time and again to be someone he could trust with his life. Yet at the same time, it felt like he was letting them down by offloading on them, when the path was of his own choosing. However, as George pointed out, no-one had asked him to take responsibility for keeping his friends sane and together; nor had anyone forced him to become a therapist, although that side of things didn't usually give him any trouble.

Admittedly, he'd struggled with Phil Spencer, and perhaps that would have been true at any other time. But at the moment, Josh was not at his most tolerant. That party was inevitably going to come back to haunt them, purely through Krissi's existence, but it was almost as if her turning twenty-one, her official arrival at adulthood, truly signified the end of an era, and it was all tumbling down around their ears.

***

With Josh and Dan on the brink of total meltdown, and the Johansson household in emotional disarray, it was something of an irony that Andy was ambling along as usual, albeit with a greater sense of resolve to give some direction to his life. Jess was working overtime to leave the decks clear for her unlucky replacement at the CPS. Thus, she, too, had been kept in the dark, although it was intentional in some respects. Dan was avoiding social contact, and Josh had only confided in George and Eleanor. Indeed, the only person likely to tell Jess was Eleanor, and she would not betray Josh's confidence.

It wasn't just Andy and Jess who were oblivious to what was going on; Adele knew nothing either, which was as well. Her blood pressure had risen dramatically since the argument with Shaunna, and in her simple little world, that was what had caused it. Tom pointed out that it was probably little more than coincidence; what was important was that she did as the doctor advised, and rest. When she protested, he called Eleanor for backup, and she reiterated what their GP had said.

The risk was to Adele's own health, and by extension, the baby's, and she was officially off sick from work until further notice. Tom had already informed the department store's general manager, indicating that Adele's absence was likely to extend into maternity leave.

Adele had *thought* about contacting Shaunna to apologise, because she knew she was out of order saying what she did, but she hadn't got as far as doing so. She wondered if Shaunna was jealous. Maybe she wanted another baby—it would certainly explain why she was so bad-tempered. Even so, it was unlike her, and in Adele's own way, she loved Shaunna very much. She'd even forgiven her for pushing her away when she was expecting Krissi, and she could understand why now, too.

It had taken Adele much longer than any of her friends to grow up. When they were talking about boys, she was still playing with dolls. When they were thinking about degree courses, she was talking about boys. Now, at thirty-six, her best friend's daughter was more an equal than those of her own age. Tom said she was young at heart and told her it was why he loved her. No doubt he did love her, and she loved him, but she was desperate not to lose touch with her friends.

Eventually, Tom called Shaunna on Adele's behalf and without her knowledge. Kris answered and suggested that he and Tom meet up one lunchtime, as there were things going on that were best kept from Adele. They went for a drink in a pub near the department store, where Kris told Tom as much as he needed to know about the situation and asked him not to mention to Dan that they had spoken, until Kris had a chance to say something. Tom didn't really understand what Dan had to do with it, based on what he had been told, but agreed to keep it to himself. The next time Kris saw Dan, he didn't mention that he'd seen Tom. There was no point in further rocking the boat.

***

Dan had perked up considerably and was starting to have some doubts about what he thought had happened on the nigh of the party, although he still wanted Josh to talk to Andy. Dan firmly believed that alcohol was no excuse for behaving badly, and this was hardly just a little harmless fun. Thus, he didn't give Kris the potential lead that Krissi needed, even though he was sorely tempted when Kris explained that she was thinking of making contact with the male party guests and had decided there was no point going after her mum's closest friends.

From what Kris was saying, it was still doubtful whether Krissi would bother doing anything at all, and Dan decided he would only tell Kris if and when the real search began. For now, he'd keep it between himself and Josh. That way, there was a slim chance the matter might resolve itself without involving long unseen acquaintances and courts of law.

Two weeks had passed since Dan last went to see Josh, and he was shocked by how tired Josh looked.

"You not sleeping, mate?"

Josh shook his head and added an extra spoonful of coffee to his cup. The dream was recurring less, but only because he'd hardly slept in days; at last count, he'd had eleven hours in total over five nights. Calculating sleep deprivation somehow made it seem more manageable, or at least made him feel better about the bags under his eyes and the constant aching in his joints. Caffeine was the only thing keeping his mind ticking over, and even that was starting to lose its effectiveness.

Dan wavered in his resolve, but Josh had engaged the professional switch.

"What did you want to talk about?"

"Nothing. I want *you* to talk to Andy."

Josh nodded, as if he'd been expecting the request forever, but didn't pass comment.

"I—*we* need to know the truth."

"OK. I'll do it. On one condition."

Dan waited.

"You need to be in on it."

"No." He backed away with his arms raised. "No way. You know how I feel about him."

"I take it you've got past the whole 'I could really be her uncle' thing?"

"I'm not doing it. If I'm in the same room as him for any length of time—well, you know what'll happen."

Josh felt the colour rise up his cheeks, and his hair begin to bristle.

"Do I? Am I a mind reader now, as well as the fucking glue that keeps us all together?"

"I want to kill him, and I really mean kill him. Ever since that accident, I've kept thinking, why didn't he just die?"

That was all it took to send Josh over the edge. "What a load of shit!"

"I'm sorry?"

"Dan. I have, as has everyone, respected and admired you for a long time. You're a great person—successful, generous, understanding—but this thing with Andy. It has to stop."

"He's a rapist!"

"Oh, do me a favour! You've hated him for years, coming in here, droning on and on about how sick you are of holding him up, or digging him out. Has it ever occurred to you that he might not want you to? Have you ever stopped to think at all? I doubt it very much, knowing you as I do. Yes, I'll meet with Andy one-to-one—when, and only when, you've told him what's going on."

Even in his own seething rage, Josh picked up on Dan's change of stance, the anger that bubbled below the surface, barely contained, but he was going to say what he needed to, even if it meant getting a fist in the teeth.

"And before you threaten me, I know you have one hell of a temper. I've seen how well you control it. No doubt you could flatten me with one punch. Take a shot, if you like, if it will make you feel better. But I am not going to be the one to accuse Andy of rape. Because if you're wrong—"

"I'm not."

"If you *are* wrong then it will all be over. For every single one of us."

"And if I'm not, will it be any different?"

Chapter Twenty-Two:
Needing

"You didn't call me, El-e-a-nor." That distinctive accent, that deep and wondrous voice, drifted through the restaurant to where Eleanor was standing and facing the opposite direction. Mentally preparing herself and affecting what she hoped was a carefree smile, she turned to greet its owner.

"James. Has it really been a month already? It's absolutely flown by."

"Indeed, for it has been twice that. I come in here, and I think to myself, sweet El-e-a-nor, surely she will have missed me."

Eleanor giggled nervously. She had thought about him, that much was true, but with everything else that was going on, calling him had totally slipped her mind.

"I'm sorry, James. Life has been a bit hectic."

"Ah. My loss." He placed his briefcase on the nearest table and sat down. "We must arrange something for certain, but first, I have a review to take care of."

"Really? Oh, no! I thought you were supposed to tell me a week in advance."

"You have not received my letter? Then we should wait."

"No, you can go ahead. I'm always prepared for these things."

"I knew as much, my efficient, lovely El-e-a-nor. I wonder if you would fetch me a glass of water?" He smiled and then added more seriously, "I hope that my attention does not make you feel uncomfortable. I do not wish to. I find you a particularly attractive woman. Please, just say the word, and I shall flirt no more."

Eleanor blushed. "Nothing could be further from the truth," she said, and went to the kitchen for the requested glass of water.

"Wotto, you need to be on your best behaviour," she informed the chef, who was in the midst of taking on the entire of the Jackson Five with his 'Blame it on the Boogie' dance routine.

"I always am!" he protested, looking momentarily astonished that she would suggest otherwise, before breaking into a broad grin.

"Mr. Brown is here to complete my review, so none of—"

"Ow! I feel good," Wotto sang as he moved across the tiled floor, sliding one foot to meet the other, before picking up his wooden rolling pin and holding it to his mouth as if it were a microphone.

"That's exactly what I'm talking about. Make some garlic bread, or something," she pretended to chastise and backed out of the kitchen shushing him, but he was too busy singing to pay any attention. Only when she was halfway back to the table did she realise she'd forgotten the thing she'd gone there to get.

Returning from the kitchen a second time, and with the glass of water, she sat down opposite James, who had her personnel file open in front of him and didn't appear to have noticed Wotto's or her own silliness.

"Thank you, Miss Davenport," he said, taking the water.

Eleanor quieted the dippy schoolgirl within, having picked up on the change of address.

He continued, "I have spent some time looking through the files of all my managers, reviewing their figures—" he coughed nervously "—for the restaurant. I must say, you by far surpass the rest in many respects."

"Such as?" Being the sort of person she was, Eleanor wanted to know what she was missing to make it only 'in many respects'.

"As I said on my last visit, your stock-taking is second to none, and your staff retention is extraordinary." James leaned in towards her. "Your staff are incredibly loyal."

"You've spoken to them?" Eleanor asked, trying to recall any prior occasion where her staff had been questioned by her superiors.

"We sent them questionnaires. You have no problem there."

"Ha! They're not so loyal that any of them told me."

"Well, not to worry, Miss Davenport. Everything is fine in that regard. Considering the size and popularity of your restaurant, your profits are exceptional, which is due to your frugal use of both staff and stock."

Eleanor loved hearing the praise, yet there was still a little nagging voice in her head. "I sense there is a 'but' coming, Mr. Brown."

"You are too perceptive. There is indeed a 'but' coming. I must stress that it is no reflection on the way you work. I am a critical man, but I find you beyond repose."

"Well, thank you," Eleanor responded bashfully, at the same time having realised what he was about to tell her. "You're closing us down, aren't you?"

"Not exactly. We are merging you." The Pizza Place owned another restaurant three-quarters of a mile across town, and it was bigger and more popular than Eleanor's branch.

"Will you be merging my staff, too, Mr. Brown?"

"Yes. They will all be offered the same posts at our other branch." James paused, and then added, "Including you."

Eleanor frowned in thought. There was now a surplus of managers, and she wasn't sure she wanted to know what would happen to her counterpart. He was used to running a larger restaurant, and it made more sense to keep him on. "What about Zak Benson?"

"He has already been offered promotion and taken it."

Eleanor nodded her understanding and relaxed back against her seat. She had been asked to go for promotion herself, many times, and always turned it down. She wouldn't have minded being a regional manager, but the company had a habit of shuffling their staff around. No sooner would she have got used to one place than she would be transferred somewhere else.

She therefore had no reason to feel passed over, when it was her choice to remain a branch manager, and Zak deserved the promotion. They'd been at school together, and he'd been a bit of a weirdo, but that was long ago. Still, there was something that didn't sit well with her.

"I see you mulling it over," James said. "You need time to think, to talk to your friends. Your staff speak very highly of them, also."

Eleanor knew he hadn't meant it as a jibe, although their visits would undoubtedly dwindle if she took on the other shop.

"And I don't need your answer today," James added.

"How soon is this going ahead?"

"The restaurant will close in a month. Mr. Benson is taking up his new role in six weeks, when he has finished his training. He will be your regional manager."

"Oh." Eleanor was surprised and disappointed. "Where are you going?"

"Back to my proper job." James laughed and beckoned her closer. "I am the managing director."

"Oh," she said again, making a mental note not to do that the next time they met, but now he'd explained, she'd connected the dots. There was a James Brown on the company management structure diagram—she remembered laughing about it with Josh, years ago.

"I must leave you now." James closed the file and banged it on the table to straighten the pages before returning it to his briefcase. "If you could tell me your decision before the end of the week, it would be most helpful. I can give you until Monday if you need it."

At the same moment as James rose from his seat, Josh came tearing through the door in a clear rage. He stopped and checked himself.

Eleanor looked from Josh to James, unsure what to do for the best. James smiled and shook her hand warmly.

"Your friend is evidently in need of your lovely ear. I very much look forward to hearing from you, El-e-a-nor." He picked up his briefcase and left, giving Josh a courteous smile on his way.

Josh waited until the man was out of sight and stepped towards Eleanor. He felt like he was going to faint. Eleanor ran to him and half-carried him to the nearest seat.

"If I didn't know better, I'd say you were drunk," she said, still supporting him, as he eased his way along the bench.

"I kind of feel like I am."

"I'll get coffee, then I'll tell you all my news." Although it sounded selfish, it wasn't at all. Eleanor had never seen Josh quite this bad before, but when he was troubled, he wanted to talk about anything other than his own problem. He would get around to it eventually, once he had sorted it into some kind of order that made enough sense for him to explain it out loud.

"So, James Brown," she said, putting the two steaming cups on the table. "I don't know if you remember, it's unlikely, seeing as it was ages ago…"

She waited to continue. Josh wasn't listening to a word she was saying. He looked so ill—lines around his eyes, skin sallow, his hair much duller than usual—had the sleep problem really become that bad?

"Josh?"

"Sorry. What was that again?"

"James Brown. When I did the management training, and we were looking over the piles of paper they gave me to read. Josh!"

"I'm listening. Really."

"All right, I believe you. Actually, I don't, but no matter. He's the managing director."

"Who is?"

"Agh!" Eleanor didn't know whether she wanted to laugh or hit him. "James Brown!"

"James Brown? The sexy one?"

"Yes, who just left."

"Got it." Josh picked up his coffee and took a mouthful. "Ow. Hot!"

"You might want to give it a minute to cool down." Eleanor put aside her frustrations and rubbed the back of his hand. "Do you want to tell me yet?"

"No. Go on. James Brown, managing director…"

"Standing in as regional manager, or in the middle of a big company shake-up, or whatever. He's closing this restaurant and wants me to take on the other one."

"Right. Is that promotion?"

"No. It's a sideways move, though there are more staff to manage. But I'll tell you who has been promoted—Zak Benson."

"Why do I know that name? Zak Benson…Zak…ah, yes! The Freaky Stalker."

"That's him. Mind you, he's not so much of a freaky stalker these days. He is—was—the manager of the other restaurant."

"He was in Andy's year, wasn't he?" Josh said, and a vacant glaze passed over his eyes once again.

"Yes. I believe so." Eleanor stopped faking conversation. Josh was no longer listening and had regressed into his own thoughts. "Right, mister. Out with it. I don't care if it's a load of incomprehensible nonsense, you think you're overreacting, or any other bull you want to spin me. What's up?"

Josh put his head in his hands. "Oh, Ellie, I've just lost my temper with Dan. I mean *really* lost it, not just like when I've had a few. I said some terrible things."

"Ah."

"He more or less ordered me to talk to Andy."

"Right?"

"About Shaunna."

"I guessed that. So what did you say that was so awful?"

"What I've wanted to say for years. This thing with Andy, it… Oh, never mind."

"I do mind. Come on," she pushed.

He ran his fingers through his hair and laced them behind his head, squinting up at the light above the table. "He's been angry for a very long time. At Andy. Dan that is. He says he wants to kill him."

"Is that not kind of rational, though? He thinks his brother raped someone. If I found out one of my brothers had done something like that, I imagine I'd feel the same."

"That's just it. He's always felt like that. That's why he started coming to see me, well, that and—" Josh was about to completely disregard client confidentiality. "That, and a complete lack of belief in himself. The whole 'great Dan' thing? It's an act. He's very good at it, I'll give him that much."

"And *you* have given him that," Eleanor stated.

Josh nodded his acceptance. Maybe without his support and counselling, Dan would not be who he was today; Josh doubted he was that influential, but it must have been some help. After all, Dan kept coming back.

"Well, anyway—" he tried the coffee again, this time without burning his still tingling tongue "—I will speak to Andy, once Dan has told him what's going on."

"I'm sure Andy'll come straight to you as soon as he knows. I honestly don't think he did it. Or, at least, I think he could possibly be Krissi's father. He might be a lot of other things, but he's not a rapist. I'm certain."

Josh didn't know anymore. Eleanor was as convinced of Andy's innocence as Dan was of his guilt, and it was causing Josh so much distress, he didn't know how to deal with it. But even in the crumbling of his own sanity, he could see both sides. He would apologise to Dan; it was the right thing to do.

Chapter Twenty-Three:
Flying

"Legally, as I've said, you can't force them to provide a sample, but if they refuse, then you could possibly read something into that. The courts would interpret it as an expression of guilt."

Krissi sat in front of Jess, taking in every word of her careful reiteration and clutching a newly typed version of Shaunna's list. Kris had come with her and was listening in silence.

"But they might all refuse, which would mean nothing."

"That's very true. However, I think most of them will be willing. I'm happy to write you an official-looking document."

"Wouldn't that get you sacked?"

"I've handed in my notice, and no, it wouldn't. I can word it to state that it *may* be possible to obtain a court order to secure their sample. In some circumstances, that would be true. They don't need to know that these are not such circumstances."

"So, there's nothing I can do, then, if they say no?"

"Well, initially, just try asking them and see how far you get. You'll need to organise the tests first. There are plenty of companies out there that will provide you with the kit and instructions, but it's not cheap. And generally, the cheaper the test, the less accurate it's likely to be." Jess jotted a website link on her pad, tore off the page and handed it to Krissi. "This is a company I've dealt with in the past. They're very good—the tests are reliable and thorough. They also offer controlled testing for legal evidence, which is about double the cost and turnaround time."

"I'll have to get a loan," Krissi groaned, biting her lip. This was all so much trouble, and she kept wondering if it was worth it. It didn't really matter that much, and she had a dad. Kris had willingly volunteered to come with her to see Jess and to help her make contact with the men on the list. He loved her like she was his own daughter, and he'd always been there for her. She loved him, too, and it made no sense, but she just had to know.

"I've been saving up, Krissi, for your twenty-first," Kris said, the reluctance evident in both his tone and demeanour. "If you're sure it's what you want, you can use the money for the tests."

Jess looked from one to the other and then busied herself with putting papers in order. This was not a discussion she should be part of.

"Really?" Krissi asked. "Would you mind?"

"Not at all. It's your money, and to be honest, I have no idea what to buy you. You keep changing your mind about what you want."

He was lying—not as regards not being able to find a suitable birthday present. He'd thought long and hard about that. But paying for the tests: that he minded very much—for Shaunna, for Krissi, for himself. The sorrow was defeating him, for he knew she had decided that this was what she wanted. It was going to happen; all that was left was to tell Shaunna and ride the storm.

***

"Right, then." Dan untied the snowboards. "You want excitement? I'll give you excitement."

Andy looked around him at the open space of the airfield. He wasn't quite sure what was going on. Dan had hardly spoken to him in months and then he turns up at the house and tells him they're going to do things together, the way brothers do. It made no sense.

"Why are we at an airfield with snowboards?"

"I saw this thing the other week. Skysurfing, it's called."

"Are you mad? Skysurfing needs special boards. And training. Jay does it."

"They're close enough, unless you want to buy the real deal. Oh, sorry, I forgot, you don't have any money."

"OK, that was low. But you're scaring me for real now. What the hell's going on?"

Dan didn't reply. He handed Andy his board and set off in the direction of a small, distant building. Andy followed reluctantly. He'd promised Jess he wouldn't do anything dangerous, and he'd only been parachuting twice, paragliding once. He was a fairly accomplished snowboarder, but this was way beyond anything he wanted to experience right now. He'd never seen Dan like this, and everything inside him was telling him to refuse, but somehow he couldn't stop himself from going along with it.

From the office, they collected parachutes and soon after boarded a plane. Following a bumpy takeoff, they started to climb, and Dan attached his board, gesturing to Andy to do likewise. The pilot levelled out, the hatch opened, and they received the go-ahead to jump. Andy looked to Dan, and the blue beyond the opening. His face was stinging from the bitter wind.

"After you," Dan prompted smugly, "unless you'd like me to go first, as usual."

Andy shook his head and edged towards the hatch, an action made more difficult by the board. Terrified, he leapt from the plane and began to fall.

It felt much faster than parachuting, and he registered that it must have been because of the board, which was tilting backwards and making him spin, slowly at first, but gradually gaining momentum, until he was spiralling at speed through the patchy cloud and towards the brown and green expanse below. He tried to pull his legs up so he could release the board, knowing that if he deployed the chute, it would get tangled and fail to open. With this realisation, his first thought was how much he would miss Jess, closely followed by how many times he was going to punch his brother if they both got out of this alive.

In his attempts to reach the straps on his feet, Andy managed to slow the spin, and manoeuvred the board into a horizontal position, all the while trying to calculate how long he had left before he pulled the ripcord. He didn't even dare to glance around and see if he could spot Dan. In spite of himself, the adrenaline was now taking over and replacing fear with the familiar sense of exhilaration.

This still had to be the stupidest thing he had ever done, and he cursed himself for not refusing outright. He considered trying a controlled tip of the board, moved one foot slightly and felt the whole thing start to nosedive again, so pulled back. Searing pain coursed through his recently healed leg. Finally, he opened his chute, felt the wonderful tug of negative G-force, and settled into the rest of his descent to land. He now had the opportunity to remove the board, one of his most prized possessions. It had cost a small fortune, and it might survive the fall, but for the first time ever, it was more important that he survived. He unclipped it from both feet and watched his board fall away.

A moment after he landed, he saw Dan's parachute deflating on the horizon, which was relatively nearby, because

Andy had set down in the middle of a low-lying field. The endorphins had diminished the pain in his leg to a dull ache, and he tore off the parachute, shoving it aside as he marched in his brother's direction. It appeared that Dan had also removed his board during the descent and was standing in an adjacent field, attempting to untangle himself from the cords.

"You stupid, fucking tosser," Andy screamed from thirty yards away. "What the fuck were you thinking? We could both be dead. I might kill you yet, you bastard." He ran the rest of the way and took a swing at Dan, who ducked just in time.

"Whoa!" Dan grabbed his brother's arm. "You've got to admit, that was amazing."

"Amazing? I'll give you..." With that, his fist rose again, this time hitting Dan hard in the chest, sending him flying backwards and winding him. Taking a moment to get his breath, Dan got up and went straight back at Andy, throwing a swipe at his jaw. Andy's head jerked sideways, blood and spit flying from his mouth. He lunged for Dan, grabbing him around the waist and pulling him to the floor in a rugby tackle. Dan kicked him off and was about to stand up, when Andy kicked him in the back of the knees, making him fall flat on his face in the dirt.

Before he had the chance to come back at him, Dan was up on his feet and threw himself on top of Andy, pinning him to the ground, rage in his eyes, ready for the kill. Andy rolled him, putting himself on top, and Dan kicked up with both legs. Andy buckled in the middle and tumbled head over heels for a considerable distance across the muddy field. He scrabbled back towards Dan and grabbed his arm, but Dan twisted onto his side and stamped on Andy's outstretched fingers. Andy swore and pulled his hand in, giving Dan enough time to pin him down again. He pushed Dan off, and flopped onto his back, both of them lying there, panting heavily for several minutes.

"Better than sex," Dan said eventually.

"Definitely. We haven't fought like that since we were at school."

"And I still kick your ass, you soft bastard."

"Yeah, Dan. Whatever." Andy sat up, and attempted to brush the mud and grass from his jumpsuit. "Care to tell me why you tried to kill us just now?"

"Shaunna."

"What?"

"You. And Shaunna. Don't act like you don't know what I'm talking about."

"I really don't know what you're talking about. You've totally fucking lost it. Obviously, you're not paying Josh enough money."

"What's that supposed to mean?"

"I know you've been having counselling for a long time, not that you ever needed it. Until now, anyway. So what's this about me and Shaunna?"

"You were the one. At the party."

"Fuck off!"

"I've always known it was you. It turns out she didn't say yes, though. Not only did you screw her when she was drunk, she tried to stop you. You raped her."

"Hang on? Where's this coming from? You were as pissed as I was. Who's told you this load of crap?"

"It's not important. I fucking know it was you." Dan had been shouting the whole time. Now his voice became quiet. "It was you, Andy."

Andy looked at his brother, covered in mud, crumpled, defeated. He understood that what Dan was saying he believed with all his heart.

"Dan, I…" he started, but had no words. It was all too much to comprehend. The thing was, it was entirely plausible, now he thought about it. Krissi looked like him; he'd had a thing for Shaunna. He was really pissed. But even so, as drunk as he was, he would never hurt her, or any of his friends. Not in a million years. Not intentionally.

"We need to go find the boards." Andy got up. "When did you drop yours?"

Dan pulled himself to his feet. "I didn't, I took it off before I jumped."

"Arsehole," Andy muttered and started to walk away. Dan followed.

Chapter Twenty-Four: Descent

After locating Andy's snowboard, which had survived the drop with only a few surface scratches when its descent was slowed by a tree, they collected Dan's from the office and drove home in silence. They stopped outside Andy's house, and Dan turned off the engine.

"Will you go and talk to Josh about it?"

"I was thinking I might anyway. You have to believe me when I say I'm totally astounded by what you've told me. I don't remember going near Shaunna all night. But then I don't remember anything, and I've been trying to. I'm so angry she's suffered. If it turns out it was me, you won't need to kill me, I'll do it myself. I love Shaunna. Why would I do something like that to her?"

"I don't know." Dan fiddled with his keys. The anger had subsided enough for him to believe what Andy was saying. "That's why I think you should talk to Josh."

"Can I just ask you one thing? Not about Shaunna or what makes you think I did it. Are you still seeing Adele?"

"What? Don't be daft! She's pregnant, and she married Tom, remember? I think she might even love him."

"OK. Fair enough." Andy reached for the door handle. "Only those text messages while you were away, well, me and Jess put two and two together."

"You and Jess always were shit at maths." Dan took his phone out of the glove compartment. There were several missed calls and three unread text messages. He flicked through the new messages, read them, and then handed the phone to Andy.

T DOING MY HEAD IN. STILL UP 4 A
3SUM? TB A X

"The 'T' isn't Tom, it's Theresa, Alison's girlfriend." Andy looked at his brother incredulously. "Yep, that's right, she dumped me for a girl, and now they want to have some fun." Dan pondered for a moment. "Still, can't say I blame them."

Andy almost laughed, knowing his brother was joking and that whilst things were still awful, there was a chance that this might finally sort out their differences once and for all.

"I'll give Josh a call later," he said as he got out of the car. He took his snowboard from the rack and went inside.

Dan started the engine, but remained stationary for five minutes, trying to find a specific CD amongst the many stuffed inside both doors and the glove compartment. It had on it some of his favourite songs from his teens—songs that were also favourites of Andy's. He found it, pushed it into the stereo and drove away.

Andy watched from behind the blinds, took some strong painkillers, and went for a much-needed shower.

***

Adele knocked on Shaunna's front door and waited. She heard Casper barking and leaping about, saw Shaunna's outline through the patterned glass. The barks became muffled, and Shaunna opened the door.

"Adele!" She was stunned to find her friend—much larger than the last time she saw her—standing on the doorstep.

Adele waited to be invited in, and Shaunna did so with a wave of her hand in the direction of the hallway. They went through to the kitchen, where Casper greeted Adele with wagging tail and a tea towel he'd retrieved from the back of a chair.

"Oh, thank you, Caspy," Adele said, taking her gift and rubbing the dog's ears.

"Damn Labradors," Shaunna grunted, going to the fridge for orange juice. "The number of tea towels I have to wash, or replace, you wouldn't believe."

"But he's so lovely," Adele said in the dog's defence. She pulled out a chair and sat down; Casper settled at her side and peered up at her.

"Juice?" Shaunna had already taken two tumblers from the cupboard.

"Great." Adele stroked Casper and baby-talked him. He was used to it and loved the attention. When he was happy, he wagged his tail so hard that all of him wiggled.

"I think someone's missed you," Shaunna said, laughing at the ridiculous dog, who was now lying on his back, sweeping the floor with his frantically wagging tail, whilst Adele tickled his tummy with her foot.

Adele looked up at Shaunna. "I'm sorry I said those awful things to you. I didn't mean it. You're one of the best mums in the world."

Shaunna smiled and nodded. "I'm sorry, too. And Casper isn't the only one who's missed you."

"Besides, we had to make up before Krissi's birthday. It would have been mean on her."

Shaunna delayed to see if Adele commented further, trying to ascertain if she knew of anything else that had been going on. Apparently, she didn't. "Everything's organised, thankfully."

"Yes, Ellie gave us all jobs to do. I got a lovely selection of stuff from work. I even had enough for a Gucci bag to put everything in."

"She'll love it, Adele."

Krissi was a lot less feminine than either of them, but she still liked designer goodies, and Shaunna was certain Adele would have picked exactly the sorts of things Krissi would choose herself.

"You're looking great, by the way."

"Am I? I feel so fat."

"Yeah. I know that one. I remember going through that. It doesn't seem like twenty-one years ago. God, I could be a grandmother by now. How bad is that?" Shaunna laughed, but was secretly horrified by the possibility. Adele joined in.

"Though it goes without saying, you'd be the most glamorous granny ever!"

The two women chatted for hours, the way they had always done, although in the past it would have been about make-up and Wonderbras. Now it was about breastfeeding pads and the best baby cream. Shaunna said nothing of what Krissi was up to, and Adele didn't ask, not just because she didn't know anything about it. Shaunna looked troubled by something. She could tell that much, but it had long ago ceased to be her job to ask what was wrong, even as her best friend.

***

After his shower, Andy did as he'd promised and called Josh. There was no answer at his surgery, so he called his mobile and got voicemail. He left a rather cryptic message about needing to meet up, doctor-patient.

Andy didn't mention that he and Dan had spoken, but as soon as Josh picked up the message he knew that had to be the case. He'd been working with Alex the vampire, which served as a little light relief from everything else that was happening. In today's session, Alex had been explaining some weird and wonderful myth about virgin's blood, which had Josh totally enthralled, to the extent that he momentarily forgot he was the therapist and asked Alex to elaborate on a part of the story that wasn't even slightly relevant to his treatment.

As soon as his client had left, Josh called Andy and arranged for him to come in the following day. He went to his bookshelf, scanning each level in turn, looking for a book that contained a technique for tapping into long-forgotten memories. It would be a problem, now that Andy was aware of the accusation, for he would already be forming his own recollection of things that may or may not have happened at the party. There were ways of asking questions that could break through his reconstruction of events, if Josh could just find that book. He ran his finger along the neatly aligned spines, moving up a shelf at a time. It was nowhere he could see, but then another book caught his eye.

All this time he'd been having the dream, trying desperately to find its meaning, sharing with Eleanor and then George, in the hope that they would at least humour him, and perhaps even enlighten him. Now it was time to go back to the original—the great man who had inspired him to take up this career and would no doubt have the solution nailed in a couple of overly prosaic sentences.

He took an old hardback volume from the topmost shelf and brushed the dust from the cover, taking a moment to admire the binding and run his fingertips over the indented lettering. Josh carefully placed Freud's *Interpretation of Dreams* into his bag, turned on the alarm and went home to read.

Chapter Twenty-Five:
Landing

Kristian Johansson
Andrew Jeffries
Daniel Jeffries
Joshua Sandison
George Morley
Henry Hartley
Neil McCann
Zachary Benson
Stephen Payne
Martin O'Brierley
Robert Simpson-Stone

Kris looked at the list, pencil poised in hand, not knowing where to start. Krissi had asked him to rate the names in order of probability. The first one was easy, therefore, because he and Shaunna had discussed it before. Kris marked a number one next to Zak Benson and ran the pencil up and down the list again, leaving faint trails on the paper. It was impossible. He slammed the pencil down on the table and rubbed his eyes. It was far too early in the morning to be attempting something like this, but he wanted to do it before Shaunna was up, and lately she'd been struggling to stay in bed.

He made a cup of tea and picked up the pencil once more, chewing the end thoughtfully as he scanned the names. He stopped chewing and cringed. It was one of those pencils with an eraser on the end, or, rather, it had a metal ring around the top that once held a tiny cylinder of rubber. The thought alone put his teeth on edge. Returning to the list, he started at the top and struck off his own name. The tests were expensive enough, and there was little point in him having one, seeing as he knew for certain that he was not Krissi's biological father, however much he wished he was.

Next, he crossed off Josh's name, but then changed his mind. In the interests of fairness, they should all be tested. That's what Dan had suggested. That way, there was less chance of Zak—prime suspect—and the others refusing. Kris went to rub out the line, forgetting that there was no eraser on the pencil, and ripped the paper, scoring the table below.

"Bugger," he said, rubbing at the mark with a damp fingertip. Shaunna would be furious if she noticed. He heard movement upstairs and went to refill the kettle, listening for a clue as to the identity of the person who had arisen. It was seven o'clock, so it was likely to be Krissi—he predicted correctly. He heard the toilet flush, and she plodded downstairs in her slippers and dressing gown.

"Morning," Kris called cheerily. "Cup of tea?"

"I feel really ill," she said, flopping into a chair. Kris lifted her face with a gentle finger under the chin.

"You don't look too great, if I'm honest."

"Thanks." She turned the piece of paper so she could read it. "Not getting very far, are you?"

"Not really." Kris emptied a pot of buttons and other sundries onto the counter, found a small, fluorescent-green eraser, and removed the line he had put through Josh's name.

"Surely we don't need to test Josh. Or Andy, or—"

"Objectivity, Missy, that's what we need."

"Oh, all right, if you say so, but come on! Josh and George? How likely is it, really?"

"It's not, but then the same could be said for Andy or Dan. Not to mention Rob."

"Robert…" Krissi squinted at the last name on the list. "Simpson-Stone? Sounds posh."

"Yeah. He was really funny, actually. I remember him moaning about his name a lot. His mum and dad were called Elizabeth and Christopher, or something like that. When they got together, they went double-barrelled, and it took them ages to decide which name should go first. I had to agree with Rob, though, that Stone-Simpson was better, if they had to keep both."

"You don't half remember some rubbish," Krissi said, stretching and moaning with the pain. "Oh, I ache. I think I might ring in sick."

"Why don't you take your tea and go back to bed? I'll call in for you when the shop opens."

"Thanks." Krissi picked up the mug and shuffled off the way she had come, feeling really sorry for herself. "Love you."

Kris swallowed hard. It was so difficult to stay cheerful, with everything that was going on. "Love you, too."

"Oh, and why not Robert double-what's-his-name?" Krissi called on her way upstairs.

"He's black, you're not, last time I looked," Kris called back.

"Fair enough."

He picked up the list and started again, this time, putting them in order of physical similarity, which put Zak top, Dan and Andy next, followed by George, who was blonde but had very curly hair that he wore extremely short. He was of a similarly dark complexion, and whether he was gay or not was irrelevant for now.

Josh had dead straight, fair hair that had its own natural highlights and turned completely blonde in the summer, so he went to the bottom of the list, one place above Rob. Martin was third from bottom, being a short, ginger-haired man who these days worked in a bookmaker's in town. Neil had ginger hair too, so he went in eighth place, leaving Stephen Payne, who Kris sort of remembered as being fat, blonde and a bit dozy, and Henry Hartley, whom he didn't remember at all. He randomly placed the numbers six and seven next to their names and set down his pencil.

***

Josh hadn't slept. He'd gone to bed with his book and spent the night reading, attempting to get a couple of hours in before he left to meet George at the airport. It was only an hour's drive, so he didn't need to leave at six a.m., but he did so anyway, making a coffee in his travel mug beforehand. It was a chilly morning, still quite dark, and wonderfully quiet, with no more to contend with than a few lorries and one or two other cars.

The drive on the motorway was calming and gave him time to reflect on Freud's wisdom, even if he did doubt that his dream had anything to do with the innocent joy of childhood exhibitionism. At university, he had read as much Freud as he could get his hands on, spending his entire interlibrary loan allowance on books and papers his university library didn't stock. His dissertation had focused on a Freudian analysis of friendships—a subject on which his idol had surprisingly little to say, in spite of mentioning his many friends and acquaintances in his work.

Josh arrived at the airport, parked up and went to purchase a ticket. He read through the pay-and-display information and grumbled, searching his pockets for his bank card. The short-stay car park really took advantage of its monopoly, with fees extortionate enough to warrant the installation of a chip and PIN machine. He found his card, inserted it and prodded viciously at the keypad, before snatching the ticket from the drawer below and making the epic journey back to his car to deposit the ticket, and on to the terminal.

George normally made his own way from the airport, and on this occasion it was more to do with Josh's need for him than the convenience of a lift home. George's mum—he'd told them—had moved to a very small flat after he left home, so the friends alternated in letting him stay. Shaunna and Kris had put George up twice, and Dan at least that. Everyone but Josh had had George stay over, but none would have imposed it on either of them, in light of George's feelings and Josh's denial of them. This time, however, Josh had offered. He was ready to move on and rebuild their friendship. Some things were too important to let them fade away. He could accept that now.

Airports never sleep, and there was much activity to be observed. Josh searched the vast board in the terminal for George's flight number, located it and headed for the gate indicated, where he promptly found a coffee shop, bought a large cappuccino and settled in for some serious people-watching. It was another hour before George's flight landed, assuming it was still on time.

The first person to catch Josh's curiosity was a tall, slender woman with incredibly big hair, wound into an enormous loose bun on the top of her head. With every step, the bun bounced up, and then down again, in time with the clip-clop of her high-heeled boots. She was pulling a small, wheeled suitcase along behind her, oblivious to everything else, staring at the departures board at the end of the concourse, mouthing the flight number over and over again.

Josh lip-read the number, and peered up at the board, which was perfectly legible from where he was sitting, even though the woman was squinting, apparently unable to read it. She was headed for Milan, by the looks of it, and she looked the type to fit right in there. With her complexion, she could have been Italian, although she had mouthed her flight number in English, and Josh concocted a biography for her on the spot. *Ex-supermodel, now living in England, flying home for winter. Fortune earned and spent on expensive clothes and cocaine, still in receipt of Papa's allowance. Seeks filthy-rich, handsome man in early forties for friendship and romance.*

Next came a couple in their sixties, wearing hiking boots and big, woolly socks, and carrying rucksacks. *Toured the world since retiring; geography teachers—childless, of course—off to Istanbul, to traipse the ancient grounds of Topkapi Palace and admire the resplendent beauty of Sultanahmet, the Blue Mosque and Hagia Sofia. They'd seen some places, but so much more to do.* Josh checked his watch against the arrivals board: still on time, with thirty minutes to go.

He'd brought Freud along for the journey and had placed the book on the chrome table beside him, but then he'd got so carried away analysing passers-by he'd forgotten it was there, until he realised that he wasn't the only one playing the game. A young woman, in student attire, was sitting at the next table and watching Josh sip his coffee in his own voyeuristic, little world. He glanced across and smiled.

"Damn. I've been rumbled," she said in an accent that he placed as originating in Sydney, Australia.

"Looks like I have, too." He laughed. "Go on, then, tell me. What am I?"

"Right. I'd say, and I cheated a bit here, because I spotted the book? I think you're a psychologist. No, wait, not a psychologist. A lecturer, maybe? But definitely something to do with psychology. You're waiting for your girlfriend, who lives in Colorado. You're going to propose. You want her to accept and move back home."

"Hmm. That's very good."

"Really? Cool. Marks out of ten?"

"No, let me do you first, then we'll compare notes."

"All right."

"Let's see. You're a student, postgraduate. You've got a degree in—got to be psychology, maybe some philosophy in there, too—from an English university. You started your Master's last year, but you're homesick, so you're continuing at Sydney University. You want to be a clinical psychologist, and you've got a twin sister, who dresses nothing like you at all."

"Oh my god! That's so accurate. How did you know about my sister?"

Josh grinned. "I can see the photo in the back of your passport wallet."

"Ah, yeah. So how did I do?"

"Well, you were really close. I'm a therapist, which was maybe where your confusion lies. My friends have always said I look like a lecturer."

"Ace. And the girlfriend?"

"Well, I am waiting for a friend, not a girlfriend though, but they do live in Colorado. You were a bit off on the rest of it."

"Oh, well. Never mind. I love doing that, don't you?"

"Yes, it's good fun."

"This friend of yours, you've not seen them in a while?"

"Actually, I saw them a few months ago. Let's just say we haven't been close for a long time."

"Right. Me and my sis are a lot like that. When we're together, we fight all the time. When we're apart we miss each other like crazy. I haven't been home for two years. Can't wait."

"I bet." Josh looked at his watch again.

"When does her flight land?"

"Ten minutes," Josh said, then asked as an afterthought, "Why do you think it's a 'she' I'm waiting for?"

"I don't know really. You're kind of giving off a vibe. It's not a 'she', then?"

"No. George, his name is."

"Wow. What a coincidence, my name's George—Georgina, officially."

"How funny. I mean, it's a nice name, but how strange that I should come to meet one person called George, and talk to a random stranger with the same name. I'm Josh, incidentally."

"Pleased to meet you and so many coincidences, both psychologists, same names."

"Very true, though the more people you meet the more you realise it's like a magnetic thing—we psychologists must attract each other or something."

"That'd be right. Well, I need to get another coffee and head for my next flight. It's been really good chatting. Take care."

"Thanks. You, too. Bye." Josh watched as Georgina pulled her rucksack onto her back and bought another coffee before disappearing into the crowd, which had grown considerably since he last looked. He gulped down the rest of his own coffee, threw the cup into the next bin he passed and wandered over to Arrivals, where there was some movement already. He checked his watch against the enormous digital clock between the two boards; according to both sources, the flight was early, so there was no time to visit the loos.

Edging closer, Josh watched people pour through the doors, being greeted by friends and family. George would be at the back of the queue, having spent too long making sure that everything he started the flight with was still in his possession.

The flow of passengers began to slow, and finally George emerged, grinning from ear to ear and wearing a cowboy hat. He put away his boarding pass and passport and walked towards Josh, who found himself moving forward without any conscious effort.

"Man, it's good to see you," George said, throwing his arms around him and squeezing tight.

"You, too," Josh replied, not releasing his grip for a moment. "How was the flight?"

"Long. Boring. Bloody awful food."

"Same as ever, then. I'm parked this way," Josh motioned, taking one of the bags George was carrying. They had just set off, when someone called Josh's name. He turned to see Georgina running towards them.

"I forgot to get sugar, and when I went back you'd gone." She handed him his book.

"Oh! Thanks, George. I'd have been devastated to lose this."

"No worries. This is George, then," Georgina said.

"Yes. This is George."

She nodded at him. "Nice to meet you. Good luck." With that, she turned and ran back the way she had come.

"I'm not confused at all!" George said.

Josh chuckled. "That's Georgina. We met in the café before and did some people-watching on each other. It passed the time."

"George, short for Georgina. Got it. It's been a long night. Well a short one, actually, but I'm beat."

Josh led him to the car. It was daylight by now, which confused George's body clock even more. Everything internally said it was the middle of the night, yet here he was in the cool, bright morning. It would take a couple of days to adjust, not just to the time zone, but to the situation with Shaunna and Krissi, and to being with Josh. It was a lot to take in, now Josh was right there in front of him.

Josh drove back to the motorway. George opened the window a little, put his nose up to the gap and sniffed. After a couple of minutes, he closed the window and shivered.

Josh glanced at his passenger and laughed. "What in Christ's name are you doing?"

"Great British air. Nothing like it."

"I'm surprised you haven't got a black nose from all the pollution." Josh joined the motorway, after which George kept the window shut and turned in his seat so they could talk.

"So, how've you been?" he asked.

"Stressed. Not sleeping. You?"

"Ah, you know. Kicking back, watching the clouds roll over the mountains."

"Show-off!" Josh joked, although he was a little jealous and quite fancied the idea of escaping from all that was going on.

"How bad is it?" George watched Josh intently, noting a little of the familiar unease. "Hey! Remember what I said on the phone? Chill out, man!"

"Sorry. Old habits, and all that." Josh switched lanes to overtake a coach. "Are you asking about the insomnia, or all the other shit?"

"Both, I guess."

"Well, I'm still having the dream—when I get any sleep at all. I'll tell you the rest when we get home. It's too much to think about while I'm driving."

The motorway leg of the journey was relatively short, only passing four junctions, and the traffic was light, so they chatted about the arrangements for Krissi's party, and Eleanor's new love interest, seeing as these were the least complex happenings. As their turning approached, Josh indicated to switch lanes, and a car pulled out in front of him. He braked hard and swore at the driver.

George shook his head. "You really need to loosen up."

Josh brushed his hair out of his face and pulled into the inside lane. "Fat chance! I've had Dan on my case about Andy, who I'm seeing this afternoon. Jess has resigned from her job—"

"Same old Josh. Pick us up, put us back together…"

"You want to try being here for a while."

"I intend to. And I'll help you, if you let me," George said sincerely, although without realising what he was letting himself in for.

"I'll tell you the rest later, and you can reconsider your offer," Josh said ruefully, as he turned off the motorway and navigated the rush hour traffic into town.

When they got back to the house, George went for a quick shower, and then they sat in the living room while Josh brought him up to speed. Finally, Josh felt himself begin to relax.

Chapter Twenty-Six:
Mind Games

"Can't you do some sort of hypnosis thing?" Andy asked. He was feeling quite uneasy about having his mind hacked and was playing with the desk tidy, in much the same way small children play with toys in dentists' waiting rooms. Since he'd arrived, he had barely looked at Josh; he was beginning to understand what Adele meant when she said he had a knack of getting right inside your head.

"If only it were that easy. I could possibly put you into a relaxed state, and then we could reinstate the context, but we don't entirely know what that was."

"Do *you* think I did it?"

"I don't think you did it knowingly, if that's what you're asking."

It was the truth, Josh confirmed to himself, with relief. The Andy before him now was no different to who he was all those years ago—the little boy who couldn't quite manage naughtiness, always holding back for fear of getting into trouble. Yes, he was reckless at times and did things that to Josh and the others seemed utterly ludicrous. No doubt if Andy had been having the waterslide dream, he'd have found a way to purge it from his unconscious, simply for being tedious. However, what he'd always wanted, more than adventure, was approval from those he loved. Intentionally having sex with Shaunna, consensual or otherwise, guaranteed the absolute opposite.

HIDING BEHIND THE COUCH

"But you think I might have forced her to…you know. Oh God, if I did, I'll never forgive myself."

"All right. Don't panic. Ultimately, whatever we uncover in this session, or any other, I won't share without your permission. OK?"

"Yeah. I guess."

Andy wasn't OK at all. Far from it. He trusted Josh. Even if Andy came right out and confessed that he had knowingly, deliberately raped Shaunna, without his say-so, it would not pass beyond these four walls. It would almost be easier for that to be the truth, instead of this awful weight in the pit of his stomach, in many ways like the build-up to being dropped on top of a mountain, only this was a sense of foreboding rather than anticipation.

"First of all," Josh said, "I need you to relax, take some deep breaths. I don't often suggest this, but it may help to lie down."

Andy did so—gingerly, on account of his post-fight bruises—and closed his eyes. Josh gave him instructions, slowly, quietly, taking him through each level, until he reached a state of deep relaxation. His fists unclenched, and Josh began.

"I want you to think back to the party at your house. Do you remember the party I am referring to?"

"Yeah. Mum and Dad are in Paris."

"Good. Tell me what's happening."

"Dan's got a crate of beer. Can't see what it is, though. Says he bought it off a lad in sixth form."

"What else?"

"You and Jess have just arrived. He's telling you not to smoke in the house. Jess is shouting at him."

"Right, you're doing great, Andy." Josh remembered the argument between Jess and Dan. Jess had been really insulted by Dan's attitude, so much so that it had been hard to persuade her to stay.

"I'm talking to Kris in the garden," Andy continued. "He's drinking blackcurrant. He's telling me about an audition for a drama school."

"Who else is there? Can you remember?"

"There's some more people arriving just now. Neil, Jen, Zak, some other dude. Not sure who it is. Dan's really drunk already. He's talking to Adele and Shaunna in the living room. They've got cider, by the looks of it."

"I want to move you on a bit, Andy. After you talked to Kris, what did you do next?"

"Erm. Made snakebite for me and Rob. We went to sit behind the shed. Smoked a spliff. Rob brought it."

Josh almost passed comment on that revelation. Andy, and Dan, too, had been infuriatingly smug about being so clean-living when he and Jess were struggling to give up smoking. But he kept it to himself and pushed on. "After that, where did you go?"

"I can't remember. It's morning, and Dan's told me to take the bottles to the tip in my *Evening News* bag."

"OK. We're going to backtrack a little. You're sitting with Rob, by the shed. What can you hear?"

"You and George, talking about someone. You're talking about...Kris?"

Josh thought back through his own sketchy recollections of that night. He remembered something Kris had said that upset George, but couldn't quite recall what it was.

"Can you see or hear Kris anywhere?"

"No. I can hear another conversation, but I can't tell who it is or what they're saying. Someone's talking really loud. I think they're having an argument."

"The person who is talking loudly. Do they sound male or female?"

"Definitely male—maybe Kris. I dunno. It's stopped now."

"So, you're sitting by the shed. Can you describe anything else? Sights, smells, noises?"

"I can smell ganja and something else. Adele. She's sitting with us, she's having a tote."

Adele, too? Now that was a surprise. She wasn't much less of a control freak than Eleanor, so the idea of her smoking anything that would impair her judgement was a real turn-up. But then, they were only young. They did things like that when they were teenagers, and it didn't have to be in keeping with their adult personalities. Peer pressure, curiosity, rebellion, all played a part in those kinds of decisions, such as anything at that age was properly thought through.

Josh pulled himself away from his musings. "We're going to move forward slowly," he said. "What music can you hear?"

"Not sure. I don't recognise it."

"Never mind. It doesn't matter. I need you to stay with it until the next song comes on."

"Yep. It's Meat Loaf."

"What are you doing whilst Meat Loaf is playing?"

"Still smoking. Am really smashed. So's Adele. Rob's laughing at us. No, hang on, we're all laughing. Got the giggles."

"What time would you say it is?"

"Dunno. You and George have gone in cos it's starting to rain."

Josh tried to think back, but he couldn't remember it raining at all. "Are you going back into the house?"

"Nah." Andy started giggling. "We're just gonna sit here and get wet. Adele's moaning about her hair going curly. Me and Rob are taking the piss. Look at our hair! We've been sitting here too long, Rob."

"All right. We're going to leave the party now." Josh recognised the slip into the behaviours that gave stage hypnotists their fame and glory. Slowly, he roused Andy from his trance-like state, and Andy opened his eyes.

"Take your time. You might feel a little disoriented for a minute."

Andy swung his legs round and sat up. "Whoa! I feel stoned."

"Yes, you would do, you bad lad."

Andy thought for a minute and then grinned. "Ah, yeah. That was a bit naughty. No wonder I was suffering the next day. That's bloody amazing, Josh. Where did you learn to do that?"

"A course, a long time ago. Don't get to use it much. How are you feeling now?"

"Fine. Although we still don't know what happened."

"True. I'm going to ask George if he remembers what time it started raining, although you could have just added that bit yourself, and it might not even be relevant."

"Oh. I'd forgotten about George. Where've you left him?"

"At home, sleeping. He was shattered." Josh picked up his book and jotted a few notes. "Give me a second to write this down, and I'll read it back to you."

"OK." Andy settled back on the sofa, smoothing the plush fabric with his fingers and leaving a dark trail in the pile. "I like it here," he said.

"Do you?"

"Yeah. It's very restful. Kind of a home from home."

"Dan always says that."

Josh continued to scribble away without realising that, for the first time ever, he had accidentally breached a confidence, albeit in a very small way. Andy didn't react.

"Right. This is what I've got. You were outside in the garden, talking to Kris, who wasn't drinking. Neil, Jen, Zak and someone—a male whose identity you're unsure of—arrived. Dan was drunk, talking to Shaunna and Adele, who were drinking what you think was cider. You're still in the garden, smoking a joint with Rob. You can hear George and me talking about Kris, who you think had gone inside. Adele was with you. You heard a male engaged in an argument but couldn't tell who it was. By this point, you were very intoxicated and recall that it had started raining."

"Yep. That about covers it."

"Good. Given the circumstances, I'm going to type this up and get you to sign it, just in case."

"Shit, I never thought of that. D'you think she'll go to the police? Maybe I should do the right thing. Turn myself in. I mean, it was so long ago—"

"No, I don't think she'll go to the police, assuming you mean Shaunna. Even if she did, this kind of statement would be discounted in court."

"How come?"

"It's not guaranteed to be accurate. I tried to lead you as little as possible, but memory is a very fragile thing, as we all know."

"Very true." Andy rubbed his eyes and yawned loudly.

"Try not to worry about it," Josh said lightly, keeping his head bowed for fear he might give away how concerned he was himself.

DEBBIE McGOWAN

"I'll do my best. Thanks for that, mate. You know, I feel more sure than ever I didn't go near Shaunna all night, let alone have sex with her. But I'm guessing we'll need to do that again?"

"Perhaps. I'm going to see if I can find out who this mystery boy was. I wonder if anyone else knows? Or remembers an argument. Anyway, let me see what else I can piece together first."

Andy nodded, thanked him again and left.

Josh locked up and followed shortly afterwards. He had some investigating to do.

Chapter Twenty-Seven:
Do Not Argue

Kris showed the list to Shaunna and explained the numbering scheme. She paid very little notice, which was what he'd expected. The lab had said that the tests took up to three weeks to process, and with Krissi's birthday only four days away, there was no way she would have the results by then. She'd received the testing kits that morning, read the instructions six times and contacted the company who provided them to see if it really was necessary for her mother to provide a swab for every single kit. They said it was, which was enough to turn Shaunna's nonchalance into downright stubbornness.

What followed wasn't an argument as such, for Kris refused to get involved. Krissi pleaded with Shaunna, even turning on the tears and lamenting about how ill she was feeling, which was partly true, although she was feeling better than she had first thing. When that didn't work, she tried reasoning and eventually resorted to screaming and shouting.

Shaunna just sat with her arms folded, refusing to even engage in the discussion. Krissi gave up. The sample would have made for a more definitive result, but she didn't need it, and she wasn't going to raise the issue again. So, having decided that Rob definitely wasn't a blood relative and there was no point testing Kris, it was now time to start contacting the other nine men.

The first step was easy. She called Josh, who said he and George were popping over anyway. Both of them were more than happy to be swabbed. Next, Kris phoned Dan, who also agreed to come round with Andy at some point during the evening. As it happened, they all descended on the place at once, with Andy still feeling a little woozy following his hypnotherapy, and George very much in a state of jet lag. The pair of them engaged briefly in some polite conversation, before leaving the main group and going to sit in the living room, where they chatted for no more than a minute and fell asleep.

Josh observed that Dan was more his usual self, and they talked about Krissi's party, rather than anything relating to why they were all sitting or standing in Kris and Shaunna's warm, crowded kitchen. Shaunna was coping well, aided by Kris, who made drinks and suggested he go to the late shop to buy some snacks.

"I'll go," Shaunna offered. Kris could see she needed to get out of the way for a while, but it was getting dark, and he wasn't sure how to challenge her without causing a scene.

"I'll come with you," Josh said, having picked up the vibe. "Are you ready?"

"Yep." Shaunna grabbed her bag and followed him out to the car.

Neither spoke much on the way. Josh was wondering if he should call Eleanor and Jess and invite them over and was about to propose this, but Shaunna jumped in first.

"Maybe I should give Adele a ring and see if she fancies coming round?"

"Funny you should say that. I was thinking the same about Ellie and Jess."

"Good idea. We can phone them all when we get back."

They stopped and bought nuts, crisps, breadsticks and dips, and on the way back, Shaunna brought up the issue of the rape and the tests, although not in those words.

"I take it you know everything that's gone on?" she asked.

"With Krissi?"

Shaunna nodded. "I was going to come to talk to you about it, what Kris heard, but I couldn't face it. I think I've got my head around it now, though."

"My door's always open, Shaunna."

"Thank you. I just can't see how all of this is going to help Krissi."

"Neither can I, although at the same time, we all need to be able to identify our origins. I suppose none of us can truly understand what it's like to not know a parent."

"I guess. But why now? I've given her everything. *We've* given her everything."

"I'm sure she knows that."

"But still it's not enough?"

"I used to have a client who was adopted, and he really struggled with it. He'd met up with his mum, but not his dad, and it was very hard for him to let it go. He couldn't really tell me why, just that he needed to know."

"That's exactly how Krissi feels."

They arrived back at the house and stopped on their way to the kitchen, to look at Andy and George, fast asleep at either end of the sofa.

"They look like bookends, bless them," Josh said.

Shaunna laughed. "That's so true. But what's with Andy? I mean, I can understand George being exhausted."

"Probably still coping with all that healing," Josh lied, and nudged Shaunna onwards to the kitchen.

He didn't need to ring Jess; she was already there, so he called Eleanor, several times, with no success, and decided she was most likely at work. He left a message and handed the phone to Shaunna so she could call Adele. Tom answered and explained that Adele had gone to bed. Her blood pressure was up again, and her ankles were swollen, which he said was worrying her more than her high blood pressure, if only on an aesthetic level.

"So, Dan," Jess ventured, "what happened to Andy's cheek?" Everyone had noticed that both brothers were sporting cuts and bruises, but no-one else dared to ask.

"Interesting you should mention that." Dan looked a little shame-faced. "We had a bit of a scrap."

"Well done!" Jess said sarcastically. "How old are you?"

"Yeah, yeah. He started it. Kind of." Everyone looked at Dan expectantly. "Agh. We went skysurfing. It was an adrenaline thing."

"You went what?" Josh asked.

"Skysurfing. Like parachuting, but with a board. And bloody hard work too, apparently. I bottled it, left my board on the plane. Andy nearly shit himself."

"I'm gonna kill him," Jess fumed, and she sounded like she meant it.

"It was my idea, so don't give him too much of a hard time. He didn't know what I'd planned, which was why we had the fight. In a really muddy field!"

"You two are bonkers," Shaunna said, pouring herself and Jess another glass of red wine.

"Yep. I have to agree." Dan beamed.

Josh eyed him over, and Dan gave him a subtle wink. They'd obviously succeeded in beating each other up enough to be on civil terms again. Now if they could just get past this next hurdle.

"Did I hear my name mentioned?" Andy appeared in the doorway and stretched, taking a newly opened beer bottle from Dan.

"I was just explaining about our little jaunt yesterday."

"Ah, yeah. This...idiot thought it would be fun." Andy poked his brother in the side.

"Ow!"

"Sorry, bro," Andy said, only half meaning it. "We won't be doing it again, will we?"

"Err, no."

"You best not," Jess warned, aiming a gentle kick at Andy's behind, at which point, Krissi decided to bring up the tests.

"Before you all get too drunk or carried away, I need your DNA." She reached on top of the fridge and lifted down four boxes, carefully opening the top one and putting on the enclosed gloves. She passed a consent form to Dan, who happened to be standing closest to her "You need to read and sign this."

"Oh God, what have we agreed to?" he grumbled, watching as she opened the plastic tube and removed a long swab.

"Don't be a wuss, Dan," Shaunna said, handing him a pen, which he used to sign the form without reading it. Krissi advanced on him, instructed him to open his mouth, scraped across the inside of his cheek with the swab and returned it to the tube, sealing it with a numbered label. Once she'd carefully copied the number and filled in the details on the rest of the form, she took off the gloves, threw them in the bin, and repeated the procedure with the next box and Andy.

"This is cool," she said. "I feel like I'm on *CSI*." She did the same again with Josh and then went through to the living room with the last box.

"George." She shook his arm gently. "George." Still no response. She knew what would work. "Uncle George, wake up now!" She didn't even need to say it in a loud voice. It had always been enough to get his attention.

"Huh? Oh, hello, you." George smiled sleepily. "You've come to get me with your giant Q Tip, have you?"

She rolled her eyes. "You've been in America too long."

George compliantly opened his mouth and let her take a sample.

"So, you watch *CSI*, too?" she asked, returning the swab to its tube. He looked confused. "I had to explain to the others what I was going to do."

"Oh. I get you." George nodded. "Yes. I watch *CSI*," he added quickly, hoping she wouldn't ask him any questions about it, as he'd only seen it once or twice and understood the reference, but he wouldn't have been able to name a single character.

With the last of the four done, Krissi double-checked the labels and paperwork, sealed the boxes and left them on the table to take to the post office the following morning.

"Five to go," she said wearily. "Right. I'm off to bed. See you all Friday." She kissed Shaunna's cheek and hugged Kris.

"Night," everyone called.

"I'm going, too," Dan said. "I've got to drive to London first thing. You coming, Andy?"

"To London? With you? Not bloody likely."

"No, you moron. Do you want a lift home?"

Andy looked at Jess, who shrugged.

"Up to you," she said but meant the opposite. He shook his head.

"Cheers, but I'll stay. I don't think I've quite averted the risk of having my testicles ripped off." He looked sideways at Jess.

She smiled sweetly. "You'd better believe it, sunshine."

Kris walked Dan to the front door, where they stood for a while in quiet discussion. They'd completely forgotten George was in the living room, not that it mattered, as he knew everything they were talking about anyway.

"How are you holding up?" Dan asked.

"I'm fine. Krissi seems to be having a whale of a time. Not sure how she'll feel once she gets the results back. Or how Shaunna will take it."

"I know. Still, it was going to come to this, hey?"

"I guess so. Night."

"Night, mate."

Kris closed the front door and went back through to the kitchen. George waited until he was gone, and followed at a distance. As he passed the bottom of the stairs, he heard a door close quietly upstairs. He waited and listened. There were some muffled sounds of movement, not much, but enough to tell him that Krissi had also overheard Dan and Kris—not that they had said anything directly incriminating, but the conversation had implied that they knew more than they were letting on.

George joined the rest of them in the kitchen, where Jess was laying into Andy about something or other, and Josh was trying to explain what a Freudian slip was to Shaunna.

"What are you talking about?" George asked.

"Shaunna said she was going to get another bottle of bed from the living room."

"Gotcha. I wouldn't mind a bottle of bed myself."

"I understand now." Shaunna giggled and hiccupped. "I've had too much wine."

"Well, I guess we're off as well," Josh said, picking up his keys and shuffling a very dopey George towards the front door.

Not long after they left, Shaunna sent Jess and Andy on their way too and was asleep before Kris returned from a quick jog around the block with Casper.

Chapter Twenty-Eight:
Food for Thought

James stopped the car outside Eleanor's building and switched off the engine.

"It has been a most wonderful evening, do you agree?" He shifted his position so that he could face her.

She remained perfectly still, staring forwards and clutching her best small, black handbag with both hands, looking like she'd been caught in a freeze-frame.

"It's been lovely, James. Thank you for dinner." She fidgeted nervously with the clasp of the bag.

James's laughter filled the car. "You look terrified. Are you expecting me to suggest we go in for coffee?"

"No, no, nothing like that." Eleanor was pleased for the darkness.

"I am an old-fashioned romantic. It will not come to this— yet," James assured her, using the steering wheel to pull himself to face the front.

Eleanor took a breath, opened her mouth, and then let the breath go again. She was going to tell him, and she didn't know why. They'd engaged in conversation twice—on a professional level—and spent two hours in a restaurant. It was hardly a deep and meaningful relationship, yet here she was, revealing her darkest secrets, for the third time that night.

"I have a problem with food." She spoke so quickly that the words merged into one.

James let go of the steering wheel and sighed. "How inconsiderate of me." He turned towards her again; she seemed perplexed by his statement. "Here I am, trying to woo you, and I think to myself, this woman would surely appreciate dinner at the best restaurant in town. I am truly sorry."

"Don't be silly! This is my problem, not yours. I have no idea why I even told you. Look, how about that coffee?"

"I would like that very much, but only if you really do just mean coffee."

"Well…" She was uncertain which answer would ensure his continuing interest. "That is my intention right now, yes."

James shrugged and removed his keys from the ignition. He followed her inside.

"So far," Eleanor said, filling the kettle, "I've told you I'm a divorcee because I'm antisocial, left medicine because I lost my nerve, and I have an eating disorder."

"Yes, you have. Where would I find the coffee mugs?"

"In there." She pointed to the cupboard in question. "So why on earth are you still here? And what about you? You've not told me anything yet."

James placed the mugs on the kitchen worktop. "Firstly, in my defence, I would like to point out that you haven't given me a chance to speak. Secondly, I am a man of the moment, so your past is your past. It makes you who you are today—an attractive, intelligent woman. Now, where do you keep your coffee?"

"In here." She pushed a jar towards him. "And still you avoid the question."

"What can I tell you? I, too, am divorced, although for very different reasons. I have a son, Oliver. He is two years old. My ex-wife is a pleasant and reasonable individual who dislikes me intensely, for I work too many hours. I am thirty years old. A spoon?"

"Wow!" Eleanor took a teaspoon from the drawer and handed it to him. "Don't take this the wrong way, but I thought you were older."

"Men are lucky, I am told, for we become distinguished. Do you like it strong?"

"Not too strong, and I mean because of your being an MD."

"Yes. I am ambitious, that much is true. My parents migrated from Trinidad some time before I was born, and my father worked very hard for us. I have been both fortunate and unfortunate in receiving his example. Do you take sugar and cream?"

"I've got milk, no cream. And no sugar for me. Do you want sugar?" James shook his head. Eleanor took some milk from the fridge. "How so, your father?"

"It was my belief as a child, and as a man, that the way to love one's family best was to provide for them. Only when I found myself alone did I understand that one must do so much more. My loss, and a lesson learned. My father is not as wise as he thinks. Where shall we sit?"

Eleanor gestured towards the living room. "It was a different time then. Men were the breadwinners and women accepted that."

"Yes, you are right. Women have different expectations now. I am too traditional. In here?"

"Please, go in."

James entered and stopped in the middle of the dark room, while Eleanor located the light switch.

"Sit down." She indicated towards the sofa and sat next to him.

"I am intrigued. What are your thoughts on old-fashioned men, El-e-a-nor?"

"To be honest, I've not given it much thought. I suppose all women like the idea of being romanced and taken care of by a strong man. The reality is never much like the fantasy, though, is it?"

"You are a professional. A manager. Surely such an indomitable woman does not harbour a requirement to be taken care of?"

"I love my independence, but I'm not as tough as people think."

"Nor as confident as you should be in your self-belief. I have determined this evening that you wish to leave the company's employment. Is this correct?"

He had been staring at her intently throughout the evening, and she had found it endearing. Now she had to break eye contact. She hadn't said a word, but for the first time since she started working for The Pizza Place, today she regretted giving up medicine.

"Yes. You are right," she confirmed.

"Then you must make alternative plans for your future."

Eleanor looked back at him, and he held her gaze for a moment before breaking away himself.

"I would like very much if you would consider making me a part of that future, El-e-a-nor, if only for a little while, so that we might get to know each other better."

"I'd like that, too," she replied sincerely.

***

There was a storm brewing, evident in the stillness of the trees and the stony silence of their walk home. Andy kept his head down, occasionally glancing sideways at Jess, while she marched with speed and purpose, to beat the thunder and lightning, she said. It wasn't a metaphor, and they arrived at the house as the first clap resounded.

"Sit." She pointed into the darkened living room on her way to the kitchen. He did as he was told, listened for a moment to the bangs and crashes of kettles and crockery, switched the lamp on, and attentively awaited her return.

A couple of minutes later, hot coffee slopped over the sides of the mugs as they were slammed into the tabletop. Jess ignored it, perched herself on the edge of the chair across the room and folded her arms.

"Explain."

***

Josh was struggling to put the duvet inside the cover, not helped by the fact that it was brand new and therefore very thick and rigid. To make matters worse, the spare room was tiny, with a gap around the bed barely wide enough to walk through. So, he was essentially pinned against the wall, aggressively shaking the misshapen cover, when George came out of the bathroom. He took one look at Josh and burst out laughing.

"Well, I must confess. I didn't think anyone was worse than me at making a bed." Still chuckling, he grabbed one end of the duvet by the corners, and they flipped it up and down a couple of times in an asynchronous wave motion.

"See now, it's all twisted. We're going to have to start again," Josh moaned, pushing his damp, floppy fringe out of the way to wipe the sweat from his forehead.

"Don't say that like it's my fault."

"I didn't!"

243

"Give it here." George took the cover from Josh, pulled the duvet from it, and started again. "What we need is a system," he said and instructed Josh to take hold of one side. Josh grumpily complied, mirroring George's moves until they had succeeded in pushing the top corners of the duvet into the top corners of the cover, which really did seem too small. However, once they gave it a good shake, it finally started to look like a piece of bedding.

"There we are. See? Not so hard after all," George said, falling onto the bed.

"No. Piece of cake!" Josh replied crankily, picking up the plastic bag that the duvet had come in and heading for the door. "I'm going to warm some milk. Want some?"

"Sure, why not?" George kicked off his shoes and pulled off his socks. Josh disappeared downstairs, leaving him to undress, after which he followed in his t-shirt and boxers. Josh brought the warm milk through to the living room and turned the TV to a music channel for quiet background noise.

"I don't know what I'm going to do if I can't sleep tonight. I'll have no-one to talk to."

"Well, you can always wake me up," George suggested, at the same time hoping he wouldn't hold him to it. "I can't believe you're still having that dream."

"Nor can I. And it's always the same—almost, anyway. There's always people there waiting for me to take my turn, and I'm always naked. In fact, the only thing that I know changes for sure is that sometimes I jump into the tube of my own free will. Most of the time I'm pushed."

"Who are the people?"

"No idea. I can't see them. I just know they're behind me."

"Weird," George said. He crossed his legs underneath him and sat, elbows resting on his knees, with the cup balanced on his feet. "What does The Master have to say about this?" Josh looked questioningly at him, and he nodded towards Freud's book.

"Ah." Josh grinned.

"You drove us mad when you were at uni, do you know?"

"Yeah. Sorry about that. Well, he says—"

"Let me guess, it's something to do with your mother not bathing you enough."

"Not far off. He says it's to do with childhood, obviously. The nudity bit is related to the blatant exhibitionism of the young child, before we must endure clothing. Therefore, being naked in the dream is related to me wanting to express an inner part of my self, yet I don't want others to see it. I haven't looked at the symbolism of the platform and tube yet, although Adele did a nice little analysis on me."

"Would you hate me if I said it was a load of bollocks?"

"Hey, I make a good living out of this load of bollocks, if you don't mind," Josh said in mock offence.

"More fool the loonies who pay you."

"You might have a point there, although it was really helpful today, with Andy, which reminds me. You know 'The Party'? Do you remember it raining at all?"

"Um…" George wracked his brains, trying to recall. "Yeah, it did rain. Just after Kris stormed off."

"Don't suppose you remember what time that was?"

"I could take a guess. It was dark, I know that much."

"What was up with Kris, anyway?"

"Can't remember, but he was such a flouncer back then, it could have been anything." George drank the rest of his milk. "Anyways, I'm off to bed. Hopefully, I'll be working on Greenwich Mean Time by the morning, but I doubt it. Good night."

He took his empty cup to the kitchen and went to bed, leaving Josh nursing his own cup and watching music TV, waiting for that elusive sensation of sleepiness. *So, it was raining that night, and Andy was outside, otherwise he wouldn't have known that.* Slowly but surely, he was putting together the pieces. Whether it was any use was yet to be seen.

Chapter Twenty-Nine:
Girl's Best Friend

Kris came in, threw his keys on the kitchen table and collapsed onto a chair, still wearing his jacket, his arms dangling at his sides. Shaunna pulled the jacket down off his shoulders and started massaging them. He groaned and wriggled into a more comfortable position.

"Well, that's got to be the worst commercial I've ever done. I did tell them it was a little difficult to feign excitement for sushi, considering the last time I went near the stuff it almost killed me."

Shaunna tutted.

"How's your day been?" he asked.

"Quite productive. I called Ellie about Krissi's party. She's totally done it all. And she's met this guy called James. She couldn't stop talking about him. What else? Oh, I took those boxes to the post office for Krissi, tidied the house, booked a hotel for your mum and dad and your million other relatives. And guess what?"

That wasn't what he'd been asking, but it was apparent Shaunna was taking a practical stance and didn't want to talk about how her day really was.

"I've ordered a limo for Saturday," she chattered on. "It's going to pick up Krissi's mates on the way here. It was really cheap, as well."

"Fantastic. She'll love that." Kris decided it was best to let it go.

"It's pink, which I know isn't really her thing, but never mind."

Krissi was one of those teenagers who had lived in black, baggy clothes and had only recently started to wear colours. She was definitely 'one of the girls', though, and her friends would distract her from focusing on the outside of the limo. It was their suggestion, with the intention being that they all club together to pay for it. They'd called Shaunna to check she hadn't had the same idea, which was when she offered to pay, as a treat for them all. As most of them were still students, they jumped at the offer, rather ungraciously, but she assured them that she didn't mind at all.

Kris reluctantly got up from the chair and made some lunch, as was usual when he came home during the day, and later Shaunna would make dinner. She'd only recently taken up a new part-time job in a hairdressing salon, although she and Kris had always shared the household chores. In the past, her job had been caring for Krissi. Kris doted on them both and never begrudged his voluntary responsibility—not even now, with everything that was happening.

Kris had arranged to meet up with Josh that afternoon to discuss rape counselling, not that Shaunna knew anything about it, and he was only going to find out more about it, because he didn't know what else to do. On the surface, Shaunna was coping well, but there were little things that had changed, like waiting until everyone was out before she'd have a shower, drinking every evening, buttoning her tops right up to the collar. She wasn't aware that Kris had noticed, and he wanted some advice on how best to support her. He had a terrible feeling it was going to get far worse, and he wanted to be ready.

"Right. I'm going back to work," he said as soon as he'd finished eating. He rinsed his plate and put it on the drainer.

"See you later." He kissed her on the top of the head. Normally, he would lift her hair back off her shoulders and kiss her neck, at which she would pretend to become annoyed, but it didn't feel right.

Shaunna acknowledged him with a smile. "See you. Pick up some takeaway on the way back?"

"Will do."

***

When Kris arrived at Josh's surgery, George was there, too, and Kris didn't want to make him feel unwelcome, but he didn't want to discuss Shaunna in front of him, either. He didn't know Josh had confided in George, or, in fact, that they both knew more than he did.

"I was just about to go see Ellie, anyway," George said, taking the hint. Once he was gone, Kris followed Josh into his consultation room and closed the door.

For Josh, it wasn't a problem keeping confidences, so when Kris explained that Shaunna had been raped, he was easily able to act as if this were news to him, whilst also utilising the opportunity to ask a few questions and fill in some details in the timeline he was building for the night of the party. Kris could remember the whole night vividly—from his own point of view—the disagreement with George, shouting at Jess and Eleanor, going up to get his coat and hearing Shaunna, before he took her home.

When Kris had finished, Josh explained the various reactions women displayed to rape, particularly in circumstances such as date rape, where they were uncertain about what had happened to them. It sounded like Kris had little to worry about. Shaunna's behaviour was temporary and more to do with the shock of the news than a response to rape, and taking on the part-time job was possibly part of it, a way of trying to regain control over her life.

Josh said there were lots of ways Kris could help that process, like not trying to take over, reassuring her, listening and not belittling her experience. Kris was aware that he had always taken the lead, and he needed to step back a little. However, doing so would make Shaunna suspicious, so it was a case of being aware of his behaviour and easing back gradually.

**

To give Kris as much time as possible, George took the long route to and from Ellie's restaurant, and by the time he arrived back at the surgery, Josh was alone and sitting at his desk, scratching his head with the sharp tip of his pencil as he pored over his notepad.

"So, Holmes, what've we got so far?" George asked, rubbing his hands together to warm them. He was used to cold weather and being outside, but he was still suffering from jet lag, so his body thermostat was a little out of kilter.

"You shouted at him because he asked you if you fancied girls," Josh said incredulously—more at the fact that George had shouted at someone than at Kris's question. "And when I say shouted at him, what I mean is really laid into him."

"Did I?" George sounded equally surprised but then vaguely remembered something. "Come to think of it, he asked me if I ever got turned on by porn—girl-on-girl porn, that is. I don't think I'd seen any porn at all at that age!"

"Well, anyway, I can't see how it could have been Andy. Kris just corroborated his story—that he was behind the shed, getting stoned with Rob and Adele—on top of which, Andy recalled our conversation about Kris. After you shouted at him."

"Adele smoking cannabis? Who'd have thought it? Although, it does explain how whoever it was managed to get Shaunna on her own."

"Kris also left this list of names. That's all the boys from the party." He handed the list over. "He wondered if we were still in touch with anyone."

George scanned the sheet of paper, mouthing the names written on it. "Who's Henry Hartley? He wasn't in our year, was he?"

"Shaunna says she can't remember him at all. On balance of probability, I'd say it's the same person Andy mentioned."

"OK. We need to look into that. Neil McCann went to college with me, and I'm pretty sure he stayed in Aberdeen. Zak Benson. He was a strange guy at school."

"Of course! The Freaky Stalker! I knew that name rang a bell. Ellie was talking about him—he runs the other pizza restaurant. I wonder if she's friendly with him, being fellow managers, and all that?"

"She's coming round later, you can ask her. Ugh. Stephen Payne. He was in my form, sat behind me, stinking of BO. I've not seen him since before sixth form, I'm glad to say. Nor Martin—he was in my form as well."

"He works at the bookie's in town, Kris tells me. He was going to go and see him on his way home. They're not bothering with Rob, seeing as he really is the most unlikely candidate."

"You know nothing about recessive genes, do you, Joshua?" George teased. Josh snatched the list back.

"Regressive, maybe, but no. I'm sure if I changed career and became involved in the breeding of large mammals, then it would come in very handy." Josh folded the list inside his notebook and checked his watch. "Well, it looks like my client isn't going to turn up, so I'm done here."

"That happen a lot? People not turning up?"

"Not really, as they get billed whether they do or they don't. This guy is a pest, though—came for his first appointment, left after fifteen minutes. He's rescheduled his next appointment three times, and now he's not showed, I'm pleased to say." The client in question was Phil Spencer.

"Good stuff. I vote we go shopping and get something really nice for Krissi," George proposed, zipping up his jacket.

"If we must," Josh lamented.

"You sound just like a little boy being dragged out to buy new school shoes."

"Ha. I was that little boy of whom you speak. God, I despised going for new shoes—still do!"

"Interesting. Tell me about your childhood," George said, with a grin.

Josh locked up without comment and soon they were headed for the shopping centre, stopping to buy coffee and cake on the way. George more or less had to drag Josh from one place to the next; he really did hate shopping, to the extent that there was rarely any food in at home. The only shops that generated any enthusiasm sold gadgets, none of which were going to make for a special birthday gift.

George, on the other hand, loved shopping, and had bought enough clothes to re-stock his wardrobe before they'd reached the second floor. He stopped short of trying anything on, because there was no way Josh would stand for it.

After three and a half hours of griping about carrying bags when he didn't even want to come here in the first place, and with twenty minutes to go before the centre closed, Josh pointed at a jeweller's store.

"There. They'll have something, I'm sure of it," he said, marching towards the shop, glad for the opportunity to put down the bags. George shrugged and followed him over to the window full of dazzling gemstones, all shown to greater effect by the extensive white floodlighting around the display cases.

"What's the chances of that bracelet having twenty-one stones?" George wondered aloud, pointing at a white gold and diamond bangle."

"Hmm. It's possible. Let's go and ask." Josh went to the door and pressed the button, sounding an old-fashioned doorbell.

"Jesus, this is gonna be expensive!" he muttered. They heard a buzzing sound, indicating the door was now unlocked, and went inside to enquire about the bracelet.

"I'm afraid, sir, that it only has twenty diamonds. A gift for Her twenty-first is it?"

"Yes, it is," George replied as solemnly as he could, with Josh snorting to himself, back turned against the jeweller, who sounded like he'd walked straight out of a comedy sketch.

"We have a number of tennis bracelets set with differing numbers of stones, but none with twenty-one. Would sir like to see something else? Perhaps the lady would appreciate a diamond pendant."

George was desperately trying to keep a straight face, not helped by the fact that Josh was laughing so much he was crying and received an elbow in the ribs.

"Please forgive my friend," George said through gritted teeth. "It's a very emotional time for us."

With that, Josh lost it completely and let out the loudest, most raucous guffaw, before going to look at a rotating, cube-shaped display cabinet in an attempt to regain his composure.

"What about this?" George called a couple of minutes later and received no response. "JOSHUA!"

Still giggling a little, Josh managed to hold it together and went over to see. The bracelet was all the more sparkly through his wet eyelashes, but he could clearly make out the nine different precious stones set across the front of the white metal bangle.

"This, sir, is a platinum bangle bracelet, set with—" the jeweller pointed with his pen at each stone in turn "—diamond, topaz, ruby, aquamarine, emerald, amethyst, sapphire, garnet and citrine."

"Platinum," Josh repeated.

"Nine stones, though."

"Ooh. Yes. That's perfect. I'll just phone the bank to arrange a re-mortgage."

"How much is it?" George asked, not expecting the response he received. Between them, they could just about scrape it together, and now that they'd seen it, they had to have it. George paid using his credit card, and the jeweller polished the bangle, packaged it in a box that looked as if it would cost a week's pay on its own, and passed it over the counter.

"I'm sure the young lady in question will be ecstatic with delight, sirs," he assured them.

George nodded in agreement, thanked him quickly and pushed Josh out of the shop before he started snorting again.

"Was he for real, do you think?" Josh asked, choking on his own saliva. George was laughing, too, by this point.

"I do believe he was. But that is the perfect gift for our little Missy Kissy." George opened the box, as if to check that the bracelet was definitely in there. He stuffed it deep into his inside pocket and then they were heading homewards, chatting all the way about possible combinations of stones that could match the initials of the members of their friendship circle. It was no surprise that the most precious of all was the only stone they could think of for Dan; the diamond: hardest substance known to man, loved by all women.

Chapter Thirty:
Reconnecting

Eleanor closed the till, said goodbye to the customer who had just paid and picked up the phone. It had been ringing for quite some time.

"The Pizza Place. Eleanor speaking."

"Hi, Eleanor, it's Zak. You called me this morning?"

"Yeah. Hi, Zak. How are you?"

"I'm fine. I'm on the regional managers' course, which is not so great, but there you are."

"I heard. Congratulations, by the way."

"Thanks. So what can I do for you?"

"I'm ringing on behalf of Shaunna Johansson—you probably know her as Shaunna Hennessy?"

"Oh! The lovely Shaunna. Has she still got that glorious copper hair of hers?"

"She most certainly has. However, this is a pretty serious matter, Zak."

"OK. My apologies for being flippant."

"Firstly, I need to tell you that Kris Johansson was not the baby's father."

"Well, no. We all knew that."

"And her daughter has decided she wants to locate her real father, the only problem being—"

"Shaunna was so drunk she can't remember. Aye, 'tis the stuff of legend, that."

"Well. I can confirm that it is more than legend. She genuinely has no recollection of who she was with that night, so we're helping Krissi, her daughter, by contacting all of the male guests at the party."

"Right." Zak went very quiet.

"You were at the party."

"I know."

"The more DNA samples we have the higher the probability of an accurate result," Eleanor hedged, hoping that it would help persuade him, just in case he was about to refuse.

"Do I need to give blood or something?"

"No, just a swab of cells from your mouth. It's painless, so the others said."

"Yeah, all right then. I've got no problem with that. I'm back home for the weekend. I'll pop in on Friday night, if you're on shift."

"Aren't we always?"

"I don't know about that. There's a rumour down here that a certain MD has been spending a bit of time in our neck of the woods."

"Yes, well I wouldn't take too much notice of gossip, if I were you."

"I was just—sorry. You're right. I feel awful, Eleanor, I never knew."

"About what?"

"Shaunna. Everyone said she was sleeping around, and that's why she didn't know who it was. You and the gang always said she'd been drunk, but we thought it was bull. I'd love to meet up with you all again and catch up, especially Shaunna. I had quite a crush on her for a while, but I never had the courage to speak to her."

"Yes, I remember. Look, I must go. I'll see you on Friday, Zak. Bye."

"Bye, Eleanor. Don't work too hard."

"I'll try not to."

She pressed the button on the phone to hang up, still holding the receiver in her hand. Her immediate thought was to call Josh and let him know; she had a strong feeling that they were on totally the wrong track. Zak might be a bit smarmy these days, but as he said, he couldn't even speak to Shaunna, let alone force himself on her. Still, he'd agreed to the test, so eventually she'd know if she was right or not. The arrival of another customer meant she'd have to leave telling Josh until later.

**

Andy's job hunting was going quite well, in that he had found two or three posts that sounded right up his street, and he'd been invited for two interviews already. The third job was the one he wanted, as it involved working for three-month stints labouring in Dubai, followed by two months at home. He'd already discussed the possibility of renting a room from Jess and letting his house go; he'd never needed a whole house to himself, and it wasn't by design. It was just that as his university buddies grew up and moved away, he didn't. He still had absolutely no intention of moving away, or growing up, apart from the compromise with Jess over his dangerous lifestyle.

Jess's answer had been yes—he could rent a room, on the one proviso that he stuck to his word, even if Dan tried his best to get him to do otherwise. He also had to agree to be her official handyman when he was in the country. Entering into a deal like that with any lawyer was likely to be a legally binding contract; entering into it with Jess was as good as sealing it in blood.

He was still working with Dan, or for him, depending on which brother was asked. However, Dan had gone to London and was yet to return, even though he'd said he was going to drive back late and not stay over. Andy wasn't really that worried about it, as Dan often stayed away on business longer than planned. But with all that was happening, Andy felt a strange need to have him around. Jess said she wanted time to herself; Josh had George staying; Kris and Shaunna could do without the burden of a thirty-seven-year-old teenager just now; Eleanor was either out with friends or working; Adele was on prescribed bed rest.

He was bored and lonely, and there was nothing he could do about it. So he went on the internet and looked up self-hypnosis. Most of the advice outlined a process similar to what Josh had done with him, and it had been pleasant enough, if not a little draining emotionally. Nonetheless, Andy decided to give it a go. He turned off the light and lay on the sofa, with music playing quietly.

It was a weird experience, drifting off into a state not dissimilar to daydreaming, and he could hear the trickling water of the spring he had created in his mind. As a means to improving his recollection of anything, it turned out to be absolutely pointless, as within ten minutes, he was asleep, dreaming about fields filled with buttercups, bluebirds and all manner of things he would never admit to, all the while being slightly aware of his real surroundings.

The next thing he consciously recognised was the sound of milk being delivered to the house next door. Checking the clock, he discovered he'd been lying there for ten hours. It was still early morning, so he dragged himself upstairs and into bed, where he went to sleep—properly.

***

Dan hammered on Andy's front door again and then tried his phone. He had to be in. It was only ten o'clock, and his bedroom curtains were shut. Assuming his brother was in the shower, Dan walked back to his car and called Andy a second time. Still voicemail. He propped himself against the bonnet, chewing the top of his mobile phone. If Andy *was* in the shower, he wouldn't be too long, Dan reasoned. He decided to wait a couple of minutes before trying again.

A net curtain twitched, and the woman next door sneaked a quick glance at who was loitering outside, saw it was Dan and gave him a cheery wave, which he returned. It made him smile, to think that people liked him so much when he loathed himself. These days, he knew it was part of the problem he had with Andy—because they were so alike. The only real difference between them was that Andy had dreadful friends at school, who got him into all sorts of trouble, whereas Dan got lucky.

If it hadn't been for Kris and the others, Dan quite possibly would have ended up on drugs, in prison, or worse. In the end, 'The Circle', as Tom had called them, had managed to rein Andy in too—or enough for him to not go the same way as his other mates. Indeed, were it not for Dan's friends—and they were *his*, not his brother's—neither of them would have achieved much at all.

Dan walked back up to the front door one last time and banged on the glass so hard that it shifted in the frame. Finally, a window opened upstairs, and a head came into view.

"What the hell? You trying to break the door down, or what?"

"I've been knocking for half an hour. Ask the woman next door. Are you gonna let me in, or shall we stay here like this?"

Andy closed the window and went down to open the front door. "What are you doing here?"

"I need to talk to you."

"Right. Important, is it?"

"Not really." Dan pushed his way into the house. "To tell the truth, I'm having a bit of a problem dealing with all this."

"You, too, huh? I was cursing you last night for not coming home when you said you would."

"That doesn't mean I want to get all pally with you, Andy. JOu.st that I want to hear your side of things. You talked to Josh, I take it?"

"I did. It was very enlightening. I got stoned. Can you believe that? I hardly ever touch the stuff, and I was totally off my face."

"So, what does that mean?"

"It means while the party was going on, I was pissed up to the eyeballs, sitting in a marijuana-induced time warp behind our garden shed, that's what. I wasn't even in the house when it happened."

"And you know this for sure?"

"More than I know anything else about that night."

Dan punched the wall right next to his brother's head; Andy didn't even flinch.

"I suppose we're just gonna have to be patient," Andy said.

"Because we're so good at that, aren't we, bro?" Dan snapped. He'd hoped that talking to Josh would have brought the answer closer, not sent it further away, and he was sick of waiting. He couldn't shake this rage until he knew, one way or the other. He spent a moment trying to rein in his temper and then had an idea. "D'you fancy coming the gym?"

"Might as well. Let me get some food first, though. You eaten?"

"No. What've you got?"

"Cereal, mostly." Andy walked towards the kitchen. Dan followed.

"Nothing with any protein, then?"

"Doubt it. I might have some eggs." He opened a cupboard containing a box of cornflakes, a bag of porridge oats and what turned out to be an empty bran flakes box.

"Nah," Dan said, reaching for the cornflakes, "I'll settle for these." He poured a large mound into one of the bowls Andy set down and looked at him expectantly. Andy nodded to signal that he should also fill the other one.

The two brothers ate breakfast and headed for the gym, where they spent the morning trying to outdo each other and lifting beyond their weight, capping it off with a test of endurance in the steam room. If they could have stopped being so competitive, just for a moment, they might actually have started to enjoy themselves.

Dan emerged from the changing room first, showered and fully clothed, and prodded at the vending machine buttons while he waited for Andy, who was only a minute or so behind.

"Drying your lovely curls, were you?"

"What do you think?" Andy retorted, shaking his head, like a wet dog does, and spraying Dan with droplets of water. "Actually, I was having a problem getting my shoe on. My leg's swollen again." He pulled up his trousers.

"Bloody hell! You want me to take you to the doctor's?"

"No need. It's nothing serious."

Dan poked the distended skin around Andy's calf muscle and raised an eyebrow in disbelief.

"Really," Andy insisted. "Let's just go home. No. In fact…"

Instead, they bought fish and chips and headed for a pub. They talked about nothing, really, the strange association of families tied by genes and seemingly little else. By seven o'clock, they were both so drunk from trying to go one better that the barman threw them out and shortly after called the police to move them on from the pavement outside, where they were throwing badly aimed punches at each other. After some resistance, a van took them to the police station.

Dan made such a deal of emptying his pockets, taking out one thing at a time and dropping it into the envelope. He was reluctant to part with his phone at all, and now the police officer, whom he was sure he recognised from somewhere, wanted him to turn it off. He was so drunk that most of the fuss was really a means of hiding the fact that he couldn't find the power button to turn it off.

"I am not turning off my phone. I may miss an important call," Dan slurred.

"Turn off the phone, Mr. Jeffries." The police officer—a sergeant—continued to hold out the open envelope in anticipation that he would comply, at which point Dan was reminded of the schoolboy, a couple of years older, standing before him with upturned palm awaiting payment, and suddenly he remembered who he was.

"All right, Aitch. How's it going?"

"Given the circumstances, I don't think now is the time for chitchat. Your phone, please."

Dan shrugged, staggered a little, but somehow succeeded in turning off his phone and putting it in the envelope. Andy had already been taken to a cell, and Dan was placed in the next one along. They were there for the night, and for all of their persuasive powers and contacts, there was nothing they could do about it. Either that, or they chose not to.

***

Josh arrived home from work to find George spread out across the living room floor, eating toast with one hand and typing with the other.

"You'd best not have got any crumbs stuck in my keyboard."

"On the contrary. Oh, that's your line. Anyway, I've cleaned your laptop. It was disgusting."

Josh ignored that. There was no way his laptop would have been 'disgusting'. "I need coffee," he said and went out to the kitchen to put the kettle on. "So what've you been up to today?"

"I'll show you in a minute," George called back.

When Josh returned, he peered at the screen, which was displaying George's profile page. "Someone could steal your identity, the amount of info you've got on there."

"Fair comment. Although on this occasion, the fact that we all seem hell-bent on sharing our lives with the rest of the world has paid off. Look what I found." George sifted through his friends and clicked a name. The browser started loading another page, and a new window opened. It was for a cancer charity. He closed the window and went back to his friend's profile page.

"This is Kathryn Payne," he explained. Josh looked puzzled. "Stephen's sister."

"Oh!"

"He died from testicular cancer fifteen years ago."

"Bloody hell."

"You might well say that. How bad do I feel? After all I said about him being smelly. He'd had it since he was thirteen."

263

"Poor guy. Well I guess we may never know."

"It can't have been him. I was reading that other page." George clicked again, and the previous window was redisplayed. "Apparently the treatment would have made him infertile."

"How sad. At least it's one less for us to worry about. Nice work, Watson."

Chapter Thirty-One:
Turning a Corner

Dan and Andy were discharged by the morning shift with no more than a caution for disorderly conduct and a reminder not to set foot in that particular pub again. After retrieving the car—a good three miles' walk from the police station—they went to a café and ate a full English breakfast, before Dan dropped Andy back home at his request. They'd both had very little sleep, although Andy was suffering far more than his brother—luckily for Dan. He had a video conference organised, and with half an hour to get home, shower and shave, he tore through one set of changing traffic lights when he should have stopped and nearly caused the car behind to hit him when he decided at the last second not to do the same at the next junction.

Josh heard a horn and looked to see what the fuss was about, observed a rather angry driver mouthing expletives, and glimpsed into the car to his left, where Dan was impatiently drumming on his steering wheel and edging forward. He must have sensed he was being watched, as he looked across and wound down his window. Josh did likewise.

"You're going to give yourself a coronary if you keep on like this."

"Bloody lights. Every single one on red. I've got a meeting in fifteen minutes."

"You look like you had a rough night."

Dan nodded and mimed drinking from a glass. The lights changed to amber, and he sped off into the distance.

"See you later," Josh muttered to himself. He, by contrast, was in absolutely no rush to get to the university and face the usual onslaught of angst-ridden undergraduates, so he turned off the main road and headed the back way, where no lunatics like Dan were to be found, urging him to drive faster than his current twenty-five miles per hour.

As he ambled past The Pizza Place, he tooted his horn at Eleanor, who was running a squeegee down the outside of the giant front window. She jumped and almost fell off the chair she was standing on. Josh laughed guiltily as he pulled over and reversed back up the road.

"Sorry, Ellie."

"It's not funny, you toad. I could have broken a limb!"

"But you didn't. Are you all right?"

"Yeah." Eleanor adjusted her clothing, mostly for effect. "I've been meaning to call you for the past couple of days, but I haven't had a chance, with the party and work and whatnot. Zak's agreed to being tested. He's coming in tonight, so I'm going to pop to Shaunna's in my break and pick up a box."

"Good stuff. I take it you couldn't get the night off?"

"Afraid not. I've already had two off this week, three with tomorrow. Not to worry."

"All right. Well, I'll see you in the morning at The Legion, then."

"Okey dokey. Have a nice day." Eleanor smiled sweetly, knowing that Josh hated Fridays with a passion.

"I won't," he groaned. "Bye."

Arriving at the university any time after eight in the morning, there was virtually no chance of finding a parking space. Josh slowed right down as he waited for the security guard to indicate where he should go, although the guard didn't look like he had a clue what he was doing. Meanwhile, a long row of cars was drawing up behind him.

Finally, the guard pointed in the general direction of the back of campus, which was ten minutes' walk from the room they had set aside for Josh. He crawled around the one-way system, avoiding students who walked out in front of him, whilst still on the lookout for any stray spaces. Eventually, he gave up and drove down to the overflow car park, the gravel bouncing up and hitting the sides of his car, even though he was doing, at most, five miles an hour.

On the walk back to his 'office', he heard a dreaded and familiar voice, followed by the sound of jogging feet.

"Crap," he mumbled under his breath.

"Hi, Doc."

"Hey, Phil, how are you?" He kept walking, refusing to look at his companion at all, in the hope that he would take the hint and go away.

"I'm pretty good. Me and the missus are back together."

"That's good news," Josh said, adding 'not for her' in his head.

"I might pop in to see you later, just to chew the cud and all that."

"I'm booked pretty solid today."

"Oh, well. Another time then." Phil started to jog away. "I'll give you a call and re-book that appointment," he called, and off he went, around the side of the building.

"I think I might change my number," Josh muttered, adjusting his grip on his bag before taking a detour via the campus cafeteria. A large dose of caffeine was definitely in order. He had the feeling it was going to be one of those days.

***

"Good morning, sleepy head," Kris said, kissing Krissi on the top of her dark, tangled mass of hair. "Happy Birthday."

"Thanks," she replied through a yawn, and sat on the last free chair at the kitchen table. With the huge, multicoloured pile of envelopes before her, it took her a minute to realise that Matt from work was sitting opposite.

"What are you doing here?"

"Charming!" he remarked, a little offended. He was her very new boyfriend, whom she'd mentioned to Kris but not to Shaunna, but apparently her mum knew already, by the fact that she had just placed a cup of tea in front of him.

"Thanks, Mrs. Johansson." Matt beamed. He knew the drill.

"Shaunna!" she admonished.

"Shaunna," he repeated obediently.

"You still haven't told me what you're doing here," Krissi said. Everyone stared at her, grinning inanely. "What's he doing here?" She directed the question at Kris—the easiest one to break—but it was her mother who replied.

"We're going out for the day, as a family. And we thought it would be fun if we invited Matt."

"Nice to be asked what I think," Krissi grumped.

"At least he gets to see your true colours," her mum remarked, quickly turning away to rinse the cups she had only just washed. Krissi wasn't the friendliest person in the mornings.

"So where are we going, or have I got to go blindfolded?"

"No, not at all," Kris said, smoothing his stepdaughter's hair. "We're going to a theme park."

For a moment it looked as if she wouldn't give him the response he'd anticipated, but then a huge smile broke across her face.

"Excellent. I love theme parks."

"We know!" Kris and Shaunna exclaimed in unison and with just the slightest tinge of relief.

With that sorted, she started ploughing through the envelopes, reading the cards contained within and passing them around the kitchen. Some of them were incredibly rude, others were covered in flowers, like the one from Adele, handmade from lace and pressed rosebuds.

"You need to get a move on, Missy," Shaunna said, clearing the empty envelopes from the table. "Don't forget we need to be back by seven." The table at the Chinese was, as always, booked for eight, so for the first time ever on her birthday, Krissi did as she was told and was showered and dressed in ten minutes, her hair hanging in tight, wet ringlets.

The nearest theme park was by no means the best, but it was only forty minutes away on the train, allowing seven and a half hours for Krissi to drag her less-than-willing fellow revellers onto roller coasters, giant platforms that plummeted vertically at massive velocity, and all other manner of terrifying rides. There was also the advantage of coming on a weekday, when there were fewer people, shorter queues and longer rides—something which pleased Krissi far more than it did anyone else.

At one point during the day, after he'd ridden The Tartarus—a coaster that plunged into a concealed opening in the ground—Matt turned a definite shade of green and had to sit at a picnic table for quite some time before he even felt up to walking. Krissi bounced up and down with excitement and somehow persuaded Kris to go back on with her. When they emerged five minutes later, he didn't look much better than Matt.

"Whose idea was this?" he said, staggering back to Shaunna, who grabbed hold to steady him. It had, of course, been his, and for all that he was suffering now, one look at how much fun Krissi was having wiped every regret from his mind.

As they journeyed home that evening, Krissi was still buzzing and talking incessantly at Matt, disagreeing with herself about which ride was the best. Kris realised that it was the first day in two weeks that she hadn't mentioned the paternity tests.

***

Meanwhile, George spent the day trying to track down Neil McCann, who had stayed in Aberdeen, as he'd suspected, but then moved to Somerset and, he eventually discovered, now owned a dairy farm. Neil had come in for a great deal of criticism in the local press about his farming methods, and George read the reports with interest. He looked up the number for one of the newspapers and spoke to the journalist concerned, who said she couldn't give him Neil's number but would pass on a message.

The journalist was as good as her word, and a couple of hours later, Neil called. He didn't sound too pleased that George had found him, although they'd never been more than classmates, so it wasn't surprising he thought it odd that he should have tried so hard to track him down. When George explained why, Neil became flustered and said he needed time to think about it. After he hung up, George picked up the list and wrote 'guilty as the day is long' next to Neil's name, although guilty of what, he wasn't sure.

***

Josh had little time during the day to ponder over the list, or how they were going to track down everyone on it. He knew George would be hard at it, but he didn't expect him to be getting very far. But then, he mused, as he set out on the expedition back to his car, George had been full of surprises recently. Not only that, but he was starting to preoccupy Josh's thoughts a lot of the time. It was to be expected, he reasoned, when he was currently more than a little dependent on him—not a sensation he was accustomed to. At other times in his life, he'd have done anything to avoid it; yet right now, it was a real and welcome comfort.

When he arrived home, he took one look at the list and burst into fits of laughter. The idea that Neil McCann—the freckly, gangly, ginger streak they went to school with—could have anything to do with the fathering of Krissi was absurd.

"You're right, as usual," George agreed. "Although I didn't mean it was him. But he's definitely up to no good."

"Well, you seem to be getting it right more often than me, so maybe you're on to something."

"That wasn't what I was talking about." George sighed. "Anyway, go and get ready or we'll be late."

"Yes, Dad," Josh grumped, skulking from the room.

"And don't call me Dad," George shouted after him.

After a quick wash and a change of clothes, Josh returned, folded the list and put it in his jacket pocket.

"I think a discreet update will be in order this evening."

"I agree," George said. "Should we take Krissi's present with us, or leave it till tomorrow?"

"It's her birthday today. We should take it."

George nodded and picked up the bracelet box. "I hope she likes it."

Josh raised an eyebrow. "She better bloody had!"

***

Dan didn't bother getting out of the car. Instead, he called Andy's phone to say he was waiting outside. They were picking Jess up on the way.

"Don't mention last night, will you?" Andy pleaded as he got into the car beside Dan and put on his seat belt. "She'll kill me. Or worse."

"Does it get worse than that?" Dan asked, but then saw Andy's expression. "No worries, bro. I've no intention of bragging about getting kicked out of my local."

"And getting beaten by your big brother for the second time in a week."

"Yeah, right!"

"Seriously, though, I can do without the aggro right now."

"Can't we all?" Dan retorted. That familiar anger starting to course through him again, he turned up the stereo and drove on to Jess's, where Andy climbed into the back of the car so that she could sit in the front. She glanced from one to the other and knew instantly they'd been up to something. Both of them tried to look innocent.

"What?" Dan asked.

"Nothing," Jess snapped and turned her glare on Andy. "I'll talk to you later."

Had it not been for the dance music pumping from the bass bin in the boot, the rest of the journey to the restaurant would have been in stony silence. When they arrived, Jess got out and went straight inside, leaving Dan and Andy looking sheepishly at each other.

They followed at a distance and sat at the opposite end of the table, as far as possible from Jess. Kris, who was already there with Shaunna, Krissi and Matt, took one look at Dan's face and thought better of asking. A minute later, Josh and George arrived, followed by Adele and Tom. Jess still looked none too happy; Adele took the seat next to her—where Andy would usually be—and offered her a friendly smile. The moment passed, and they went to fill their plates.

Once they all had food, the friends took turns to pass their gifts to Krissi. Even though they had clubbed together to buy her something, they had each individually bought her a small present.

Krissi hated being the centre of attention, but loved the boots her mum and Kris had bought, the mood-stone ring from Matt, and Adele and Tom's makeover voucher from the department store. Dan and Andy had gone in together and bought her a magnum of champagne, which was lying in an ice bucket to the side of the table, but the best was yet to come. When she opened the box from George and Josh and saw the bracelet inside, she gulped and her eyes became wide.

"Nine stones," George explained. "One for your mum, Kris, and each of your adopted aunts and uncles."

"Wow. That's amazing! It must have cost so mu—"

"It doesn't matter. Do you like it?"

"Uncle George, I love it. Thank you. And you, Josh." She put the bangle on and held her arm aloft so that everyone could see. It shimmered in the light, casting multicoloured sparkles over the tablecloth.

Josh watched proudly and nudged George to get his attention. "Worth every penny," he said.

George nodded and smiled and tucked into his food. The others followed suit, holding their own little conversations throughout the meal, pausing every so often to refill their plates.

On the way back from her third visit, Jess stopped alongside Andy. "You gonna tell me yet?"

"Honestly, there's nothing to tell," he said, with a little too much conviction. Dan coughed nervously.

"No problem. I'll get it out of you, sooner or later," Jess assured him loftily and went back to her end of the table.

"God, you're in trouble," Dan chuckled.

"Fuck off," Andy hissed. He pushed his chair backwards with force and walked off.

"Oh, come on!" Dan called after him.

"More champagne?" Krissi went on a timely tour of the table, topping up glasses where required.

"I really miss this," George told anyone who happened to be listening. It was Kris who caught it.

"The Chinese food or the get-togethers?"

"Both, I guess."

"Ever wanted to come back?"

"I've thought about it, but I don't know. I love the mountains."

"Yes, I recall they were very beautiful."

"I'm used to it there now. It's home. But I do miss you all a lot." He smiled wistfully.

Kris nodded in understanding. "Where's Josh gone?"

"Getting food, I think."

"Oh, right. How's he doing with the list?"

"Not bad. We've discovered that Stephen Payne died, a while back now, from cancer. I spoke to Neil McCann today—he always was an odd bugger—he's 'thinking about it'. I think he might be in a bit of bother, to tell the truth."

"What sort of bother?"

"I'm not sure. He owns a dairy farm—one of the big factory farms supplying supermarket chains. According to the articles I was reading, a group of local farmers took him to court over labelling some of his produce as organic when it wasn't. It turned out they were right, and he was fined, as was the supermarket, but then there was some controversy over the claim that he was also injecting his cows with growth hormone, although apparently, no official action was taken. I'm boring you, aren't I?"

"No, not at all," Kris replied, stifling a yawn and laughing at the same time.

"Sorry. How did you get on with Martin?"

"I went in to see him the other day. He was more than happy to oblige. He seemed sort of honoured to be asked. So, his test went off this morning. Who's left?"

"Ellie said Zak was going to do his tonight, which just leaves what's-his-name. Oh, it's on the tip of my tongue."

***

Andy strolled out onto the street, hands shoved deep in his pockets. He kicked a bottle top into the gutter; he'd had as much as he could take. First Dan nearly kills him and accuses him of rape, and then gets him arrested. And after he'd been so certain, Andy was now beginning to doubt his own innocence. The promise he'd made to Jess was starting to look impossible to keep, and she'd avoided him all week. He needed her to believe in him, now more than ever before.

Andy suddenly realised he wasn't the only one struggling to cope, for there, in the next doorway along was Josh, smoking a cigarette.

"Oh, dear. That bad is it, mate?" he asked, walking over.

"Andy. How are you holding up?"

"Not great, I must confess. Last night me and Dan got arrested."

"What for?"

"Being drunk and disorderly. We got locked up for the night and I was lying there, the room spinning—"

"As it does."

"Yeah. I hate that. Plus, I was starving."

"What time did they let you go?"

"This morning." He paused, unsure if he should continue. He'd thought about keeping it to himself, but there was no escape, nothing to be gained from staying quiet, other than suffering his doubts alone. "I remembered something else about the party."

"I see," Josh said, blowing smoke and feeling a little woozy. He wasn't convinced that anything Andy remembered now would be accurate, not after talking about it with other people.

"We got the munchies, and I went back inside to raid the cupboards."

"Are you sure?"

"Yep. I don't know what happened after that, mind you. Funny, though, it just sort of came to me."

"Memory's a curious thing. That's what I was saying the other day, about reinstating the context. Probably being drunk and hungry triggered something."

"I wish it hadn't. I'm right back where I started."

Josh put out the half-smoked cigarette. "It still doesn't mean it was you."

"Maybe. Do me a favour, Josh. Don't mention the arrest or anything."

"Tell you what, if you don't tell anyone I was smoking, I won't say a thing."

"Deal." They shook on it and went back inside.

***

"Henry Hartley," Shaunna said without looking up from her bowl of ice cream.

"Henry Hartley. That's it!" Dan exclaimed. "I've been trying to think of his name since last night. I can't believe I couldn't remember it. We were good mates at school. Bit dense of me, too, actually, seeing as we used to call him 'Aitch Aitch' and then shortened it to 'Aitch'."

"I remember Aitch," Kris said. "Do you know where he is?"

"Sure do—in the local nick. He's a copper."

"Aitch is in the police?" George asked incredulously.

"Yep. He's a—"

"And you know this how, exactly?" Jess interrupted, putting down her champagne glass and pushing up her sleeves.

"It's not a very interesting story," Dan muttered cagily. Jess glared at him, and everyone fell silent.

"Let's not forget this is someone's twenty-first birthday," Kris said loudly—a cue for the waiter to bring the cake. Josh and Andy made it back to the table just in time to see her blow out the twenty-one candles and join in with a rather tuneless rendition of 'Happy Birthday To You'. Stuffed as they all were, they had to eat cake.

"I'm never going to lose all this weight," Adele lamented, putting a large chunk of vanilla sponge in her mouth.

"Don't be daft. You're allowed to get fat, for the baby," Jess comforted, gently patting Adele's bump. "Are you feeling any better?"

"I feel fine. It's just my blood pressure and the swelling. Look at my fingers!" She held her chubby hands up for Jess to inspect. She'd had to remove her wedding and engagement rings with sunflower oil, but she still had perfectly manicured and polished nails.

"Poor you," Jess sympathised, watching Andy out of the corner of her eye. He'd promised to walk her home so they could discuss what he was hiding, or at least, she would interrogate him, and eventually he'd just give in and tell her. He was putting his coat on. "Going somewhere, Andy?"

"I wouldn't dare. I don't feel too good." He sat back down and shivered.

"Good. Serves you right," Jess responded cruelly and continued her previous conversation.

Tom had barely spoken all evening, but it suited him just fine. For as much as he loved Adele, it was tiresome reassuring her that everything was all right every two minutes, all day, every day. It was such a nice change to be out for the evening and drop in on the different conversations going on around the table.

"Yeah," Matt grumbled, "it's lovely."

Tom refrained from smiling at this. Poor Matt. It had to be the twentieth time Krissi had wafted the bracelet in his face and asked him what he thought.

"You did a mighty job there," Kris talked across Shaunna to George.

"Hey! What makes you think it was all his doing?" Josh protested, not really remotely offended by the suggestion.

"It wasn't all down to me," George said. "True, I had to drag him screaming and kicking to the shops, but he actually chose which shop."

"Well it is beautiful, both of you," Shaunna reassured them, and Tom realised it was the first time she'd spoken for ages. The whole thing with Krissi wanting to uncover her father's identity was getting her down. Even he could see that and, he only knew her from the few times she and Adele had met up since the wedding.

"Faking the flu to get out of a bollocking, though," Dan said, peeling apart the stem of one of the flowers that had been in the vase at their end of the table. Andy shivered and gave his brother a watery smile.

"Leave off, Dan." Josh tried to say it amiably, although it didn't come across like that. For once, Dan didn't rise to the challenge, and George tutted quietly at Josh.

"You were smoking."

"Shush," Josh urged. He'd hoped he'd get away with it, but they were sitting close in a confined space, so he had no hope. "You can shout at me later."

Adele placed her hand on Tom's arm, bringing him back to his senses. "Would you mind awfully if we go home?" she asked. She was starting to feel tired and uncomfortable, so they made the first move, although it was getting late.

Tom helped Adele with her coat, and they said their goodbyes, wishing Krissi a 'Happy Birthday' once more. Jess agreed to Dan driving her and Andy home, conceding that Andy's paleness and violent shivering was compelling evidence that he was genuinely ill. When they stopped outside Jess's house, she let him go, with a promise that she would have the truth out of him by the end of the weekend.

George and Josh walked home together, chatting about the list of names and congratulating themselves on how well they were progressing in their detective work. In reality, George had done most of it, and Josh appreciated his support. He'd been dealing with things on his own for so long, it was a wonderful thing to have someone at his side. It had crossed his mind several times to ask George if he was planning to rush straight back to the States after Krissi's party, but he didn't want him to think he was pushing him out. Nothing could have been further from the truth.

Shaunna and Kris took a taxi, leaving Krissi and Matt in town for a night of clubbing with friends. Shaunna warned her not to stay out too late, or it would spoil her enjoyment of her birthday party. Krissi waved her away.

As soon as they got home, Shaunna went to bed, leaving Kris to deal with Casper and lock up. He expected her to either be asleep or pretending to be when he followed her upstairs ten minutes later and was surprised to find her awake and waiting for him.

"What's up?" He sat on the end of the bed and took off his shoes.

"Nothing," she replied, climbing behind him and wrapping her arms around his neck. "Just wanted to tell you I love you. That's all."

Kris turned his face towards her and kissed her. "Let me get my clothes off, and I'll be right with you."

"Ha ha! I tell you I love you, and you think your luck's in," she joked, throwing a pillow at the back of his head. He picked it up and threw it back. Within seconds, it escalated into a full pillow fight.

"I'm gonna get you, Mrs. Johansson," Kris said, crawling up the bed on his knees, dangling a pillow by its corner from each hand.

"Not if I get you first." Shaunna laughed and leapt over him, grabbing his pillows on the way past.

"A-ha! The element of surprise!" He reached down to pick up a pillow that had fallen on the floor, but too late! Shaunna now had all of the pillows and was swinging one above her head, ready to launch. "Noooo!" he yelled, backing up against the headboard, where she bombarded him with all four of them, before climbing onto the bed and straddling his legs. He rubbed her thighs with the palms of his hands.

"OK. You win," he submitted between the kisses.

"Of course! I always do."

At three in the morning, when Krissi and Matt returned, Shaunna and Kris were only just drifting off to sleep.

Chapter Thirty-Two:
Party Plan

Krissi woke up and lifted her head to check the time. It was only just after eight, and she sank back, grateful that she was off work for the weekend, but annoyed by the fact that she was so much in the habit of getting up early that she had woken anyway. Matt was taking up more than half of her single bed, and it wasn't very comfortable, but there was no way she was relinquishing it. She shoved him with her knees, and he snorted and grunted in his sleep. She turned her back against his, reclaimed her share of the duvet, and went back to sleep.

***

Kris, ever the early bird, had already been up for an hour, and was sitting in the kitchen in silence, reading the newspaper and drinking tea. Casper had been for his walk; the dishwasher was empty; all was well with the world. Shaunna was in the bath, so hopefully wouldn't be too grumpy when she came down—it made him smile to think how alike she and Krissi were in that regard—and he had already made her a cup of tea and set out a cereal bowl, knowing that these simple things would soothe the beast within, which was always at its worst first thing in the morning.

***

Shaunna put a special treatment on her hair, wrapped it in a large towel and lay back in the water, sliding down the bath as far as she could without getting the towel wet. She'd heard Krissi and Matt come in at three, made a mental note to have words with her daughter, who might be twenty-one now, but still had to ask for people to stay over. Not to mention the fact that she hadn't even told her about Matt; she'd told Kris, and Josh, and George. Had Shaunna become so unapproachable that her own daughter couldn't tell her about her new boyfriend?

***

George had also risen bright and early and was ironing shirts, wearing only his boxers, and singing to himself. When Josh came downstairs, George took one look at his face and knew better than to ask if he'd slept well. It was becoming a serious problem, and it worried him. He'd heard movement around the house on several occasions during the past few nights and estimated that Josh was getting, at the very most, three hours' sleep. The situation with Shaunna and Andy, and by extension, Dan's state of mind, really wasn't helping. And then there were all the other burdens he chose to carry. But there seemed to be more to it. He wasn't sure even Josh knew what it was, and so far, he'd resisted George's efforts to help in anything other than practical ways.

***

Josh re-boiled the kettle, which was still warm, getting to his first fix of the day more quickly than usual. He put four slices of bread in the toaster and waited. He wasn't even hungry, but breakfast was a habit he'd forced on himself, as the food seemed to counter the sleep deprivation a little. Much as he was a great believer in non-pharmaceutical treatments, it had reached the point where he was contemplating asking the doctor for pills. He took his breakfast through to the living room, where George was battling with the creases in his trousers—a task he gladly put on hold for a slice of toast.

***

Dan laid the dead fish on a newspaper and returned to the others. It was very odd that one of them had died suddenly like that. There didn't seem to be any evidence of disease. The others were all happily swimming about, some of them coming over to his location to see if he had food. He tickled their backs and then gave the dead fish a thorough inspection. It didn't sadden him; there was no real emotional attachment. Koi were expensive and showy—that was their major pulling power— and it felt more like losing an investment than a pet. Nothing seemed amiss, so he wrapped up the fish and placed it in the freezer until he could figure out what to do with it. It was a tad too big to flush down the toilet, as he had done with his goldfish when he was little.

***

Andy lay in bed, sniffing and coughing, holding a tissue under his dripping nose, but considered, on the plus side, that he didn't feel anywhere near as bad this morning as he had last night. The bed had been wringing wet when he awoke, and he assumed he'd sweated off a fever, leaving him with a severe cold, but nothing more than that. He'd been downstairs, taken some painkillers and was now waiting for their magic to take effect, after which he thought he might go for a run and head over to see Jess. It would save a lot of bother if he just came clean and told her about the arrest before someone else did.

***

Jess pulled the large brown envelope free from the letterbox and turned it over to check the sender was as she'd expected. It was. She picked up the rest of her mail from the floor and plodded back to the kitchen. This was it: the final contract for the lease. She could still change her mind, but there was little point when she had come this far. The farewell night out had been good fun, and she would miss the girls she'd worked with, but it was a relief to know that she never had to return to the place again. It was the shortest she'd stayed in a post in her entire career, and the first time that her leaving wasn't because of a man.

She opened all the smaller envelopes and checked through their contents: bills, flyers, the usual junk. Finally, she took a knife and slit the top of the big envelope, removed the legal documents within and placed them on the breakfast bar, reading each page carefully before flipping it over and moving on to the next.

***

Adele was in a terrible state. The swelling had subsided overnight, but whatever Andy had, she had it, too, and didn't dare take anything. Tom phoned the GP on-call, who confirmed that she could take paracetamol, but she was determined to be a martyr for this baby. Instead, Tom dutifully brought her tissues, applied vapour rub, made cups of hot blackcurrant, changed the TV channels and cooked breakfast—all before he was due to leave for work.

Right at the last minute, Adele started to cry and asked him to stay home. Fool that he was for her, he called in sick, all the while fearing that this would be the thing that led to the threatened disciplinary. There was a bit of victimisation going on, for by and large, he was professional and reliable. However, the general manager was the son of one of the directors, and she was a formidable woman. In short, Tom's manager was scared of his mum.

***

Eleanor picked up the box containing Zak's DNA test, locked the door and set off in the direction of Shaunna's house. There was still so much to do that she was beginning to wish she hadn't agreed to organise the party.

This was normal. The morning of Adele's wedding, she'd called her mother and cried about people not pulling their weight, in response to which she'd received the usual lecture about the hardships of bringing up seven children, and how she couldn't assume that anyone would help. Eleanor knew it was a poke at her dad, who was probably sitting a few feet away, taking in the whole conversation with no intention of changing his ways. Neither of them was wrong, for it had been hard on them both, with her dad working overtime and her mum always up to her elbows in nappies and washing up. When James had talked of his father's hard work, it had rung true of her own experiences.

"Good morning," Kris said, opening the door before she'd got as far as knocking. "You're here early."

"Ah. You know me," Eleanor replied, stepping into the warm hall and inhaling deeply. "Your house always smells so lovely."

"Does it? What does it smell of?"

"Loads of things. Potpourri, perfume, baking, tea…"

"I've just put the kettle on. Again!" Kris beckoned her to follow him to the kitchen, where Shaunna was drying her hair.

"Oh. That's what I can smell!" Eleanor said, placing the test box on the table and walking over to Shaunna to sniff her hair."

"WHAT?" Shaunna shouted over the buzz of the hairdryer. "Your hair smells wonderful!"

"THANKS! I PUT AN INTENSIVE TREATMENT ON IT IN THE BATH."

Kris laughed. "Oy, noisy!" He shoved her along the kitchen so he could get a mug out of the cupboard. It was utterly useless trying to talk over the noise, so he and Eleanor sat and waited. Finally, Shaunna turned off the dryer and twirled to face them, deliberately letting her hair spin out.

"Gorgeous." Eleanor nodded approvingly.

"Thank you. It's some jojoba oil thing Adele bought me ages ago."

"It's very nice," Kris said. Shaunna sat next to him, and he snuffled in her warm hair.

"What's that incredible smell?" Matt was standing at the kitchen door.

"Shaunna's hair," Eleanor replied, wondering who on Earth he was.

"This is Matt, Krissi's boyfriend. Matt, this is Eleanor," Kris explained, as Matt also came over to have a sniff.

"Oh, Lord. This is going to be fun!" Shaunna groaned, gently pushing his face away. "Krissi not awake yet?"

"Yeah, she is, but she said she wanted her bed to herself for a while. I hope it was OK me staying last night. I promise we behaved ourselves."

"I know. I was listening," Shaunna said. Eleanor and Kris looked at her as if she had committed some terrible crime. She shrugged. "It's a mother's prerogative."

"I was going to sleep on the couch, but Krissi thought that would annoy you more."

"That's very true," Eleanor agreed, although it was Kris who was the intolerant one when it came to mess, and he would

286

have been silently steaming all day if he'd come down to find bedding and shoes all over the living room.

"Right. I need to go home and shower and things," Matt said. "Thanks for letting me stay, or at least, thanks for not kicking me out in the middle of the night, and for yesterday. I guess I'll have to get used to all that."

"The thrills and the spills…" Kris grinned.

"Definitely the spills." Matt mimed throwing up. Eleanor looked puzzled again.

Shaunna explained, "We went to a theme park yesterday, and Matt had loads of fun going on the rides with Krissi."

"Ah, yes! I know that feeling. She's always been like that. I remember me and Josh nearly passing out after going on The Waltzers with her six times in a row. She wasn't even old enough to be on the damned things."

"Great." Matt rolled his eyes. "I'll look forward to that one. See you later." He waved and let himself out.

"Seems nice," Eleanor remarked once the front door had closed.

Shaunna nodded. "He is. She's still my baby girl, though." She suddenly burst into tears. Both Eleanor and Kris watched, feeling hopeless and sympathetic at the same time. "Ignore me. I'm just feeling a bit soppy today. How silly." Kris passed her a tissue, and she wiped her eyes, laughing at herself at the same time as crying.

Eleanor rubbed Shaunna's arm. "Hey, it's not silly. I can't even imagine how you must be feeling at the moment, but you should be very proud. You have an incredible beautiful daughter. You are the best mother I have ever known—the best parents, in fact. No-one could feel more loved. She's so well-balanced. I mean, she even picked a nice, sensible boyfriend, not like us lot." Eleanor paused and looked at Kris. "Present company excepted."

Kris nodded in acceptance. "Although I had my fair share of dodgy boyfriends once," he joked, but he understood what she meant. He was a little choked by her words, because it had never occurred to him to be anything other than what he was. Shaunna and Krissi literally were his life.

"So, without further ado," Eleanor moved the conversation on, "we have a party to put on."

That galvanised the three of them into action. They all downed their tea in one, and Shaunna left a note for Krissi, to let her know they had gone to The British Legion to set up the room.

***

Krissi got out of bed just before midday and spent the afternoon in her dressing gown, pottering around the house, listening to music, manicuring her nails, plucking her eyebrows, waxing her legs, and generally pampering herself. She'd bought a floor-length black dress some time ago and high-heeled shoes to match it, but now she wasn't so sure about the shoes. For a start, she didn't wear heels very often, and when she did, she ended up taking them off halfway through the evening. Also, Matt was only an inch taller than her, and the shoes had three-inch heels.

Her mum's feet were much smaller, so she couldn't borrow any of hers, and it was too late in the day to be rushing around the shops and searching for a new pair. She had an idea; she picked up the phone and called Jess.

"Hi. It's Krissi."

"Hiya. You all right?"

"Kind of. I have a shoe problem, and I remember a conversation ages ago about me being the same size as you."

"Size seven?"

"Yep. Don't suppose you've got any black shoes I can borrow for tonight? They need to be quite flat."

Jess had a lot of shoes, almost all with high heels, but with her thing for shopping, she was bound to have something.

"I think I've got a couple of pairs. Do you want me to bring them round?"

"No, it's OK. I'll come to you. Be there in about twenty minutes?"

"Great. See you then, then."

Krissi hung up, took a picture of her dress with her phone, and slung on some jeans and a t-shirt. By the time she got to Jess's, every black pair of shoes Jess owned was lined up against the bedroom wall, like invisible soldiers.

"Wow! That's a lot of shoes!"

"You don't want to know," Jess groaned. "Although I do have more black ones than any other colour."

Krissi tried on several pairs before deciding on flat, satin slip-ons with velvet bows on the top, because they were the most comfortable. Some of the others were crippling to wear, even for a few minutes. Jess confided that most of them had not seen daylight since she bought them, indicating the expanse of mirrored doors that lined the adjacent wall, concealing a wardrobe stuffed with clothes and shoes, with every single door slightly ajar.

"You can keep them," Jess said, on their way back downstairs. "I'm going to have to get rid of some stuff soon, anyway."

"How come?"

"If Andy gets the job he wants, he's going to give up his place and rent my spare room. It'll do us both a favour."

"Oh, right. That's cool. Well, thanks, Jess, you're a life-saver. See you later."

***

"Give me that bloody thing." Eleanor snatched the balloon inflator from Josh, releasing the end of the balloon he was holding. It fired off chaotically, making a rude noise.

"I was doing just fine."

"You've been at it for half an hour, and what've we got? Four, eight, eleven...fifteen balloons. That's two minutes per balloon."

"There's no rush. You've done everything else."

"And I'd like to be out of here before six o'clock, so I have time to go home and get ready." Eleanor pumped manically and handed the inflated balloon to Josh by its neck.

"See, now that's the easy bit," he grumbled, struggling to tie a knot in it. Before he was done she was ready with another one.

"Honest to God." She tied the end of the balloon she had just inflated, watching him and shaking her head. She blew up and tied another three while Josh was still fiddling with the first one, which was now tied, but not very well, and it was leaking air.

"Need a hand?" George sauntered over. "I've put out all the tablecloths and snack bowls."

"Here." Eleanor passed him a balloon, which he quickly tied and threw to the floor with the rest of them. Josh gave up and passed the balloon he was holding to George, at which point he was saved by the DJ, who appeared at the entrance, struggling with flight cases of various shapes and sizes.

"Hi there," Josh called, grateful for a reason to leave his two friends with the balloons. He was frightened of them anyway, always worrying one of them was going to explode in his face. He smiled as he registered that he felt the same way about balloons.

***

Just after six o'clock, they locked the room, now covered in banners and all manner of decorations, and returned the keys to the barman. Everything was ready, and Eleanor had precisely fifty-five minutes to go home, shower, change, do her make-up and get back to meet the caterers. In the unlikely event that she didn't make it, she'd left notes on the buffet table to indicate what should go where. Josh dropped her off with a promise to be back on time, and George reassured her. Neither of them would dare risk her wrath when she was in full party organiser mode.

Chapter Thirty-Three:
The Key

"Oh my god! Mum! That's amazing! Pink, but amazing." Krissi was standing in the doorway, staring in disbelief at the stretch limousine that had pulled up outside the house. Several neighbours had also come out to take a peek. The chauffeur opened the nearside rear door, and Matt stepped out.

"Your carriage awaits, Mademoiselle." He gestured to the interior of the enormous car.

"This is the best." Krissi hugged Shaunna and Kris. "Thank you so much. For everything," she said, her voice cracking with the threat of tears.

"Don't you dare cry!" Shaunna scolded. "Your mascara will run, and you look stunning."

"Yes, you do," Kris seconded.

They watched Krissi bounce down the garden path towards the limousine, looking for all the world like the little girl they remembered leaving for her first day at school. Shaunna sniffed, and Kris put his arm around her shoulders.

Krissi lifted her long skirt, climbed into the back of the limo and shrieked at the discovery of all her friends already sitting in there.

"Come on," Kris said. "We need to get a move on." Shaunna nodded and wiped her eyes. "And you know what you said about mascara?" He gently wiped a smudge from under her eye.

"Mum. There's room for two more!" Krissi shouted.

Shaunna was about to refuse the invitation, but Kris answered before her. "Why not?" He turned to Shaunna. "You ready?"

"Let me get my things," she said, and went back inside, appearing a minute later with a small clutch bag and a wad of tissues.

"Woohoo!" Krissi cheered. She and her friends shuffled along the leather seat to give Kris and Shaunna room to sit.

"This is so cool!" Shaunna said, looking around the car in amazement. She'd missed out on the limo to the sixth-form ball. Kris had invited her as his guest, but as always, she'd refused to go out and leave Krissi with her parents. When he had deliberately bought a house near theirs, he'd hoped it would change, and then Shaunna's mum had been ill. Now that Krissi was officially an adult, he was optimistic Shaunna would give it up and finally live her life a little.

The chauffeur drove them the longest way possible to the party venue—up the high street, all the way around a roundabout and out of town into the suburbs, before returning in a complete circle, past their house and on to The Royal British Legion club. He pulled up in the crowded car park and opened the door.

Kris climbed out and helped Shaunna, who was followed by Matt, Krissi and her eight closest friends: seven young women, scantily clad in pale pastels of varying lengths who clip-clopped in their strappy high heels, and one young man, wearing a fifties-style black suit with a faint pinstripe, and a black trilby pulled down over his face. As he passed Shaunna, he tilted the hat, revealing heavily made-up eyes.

"Thanks, Mrs. Johansson," he said cheerily, and then returned the hat to its previous position, resuming his moody demeanour.

"You're welcome, Jason," Shaunna replied, chuckling as he slouched along behind the chattering, tottering girls.

Jason was Krissi's best friend and had been so for many years—the one who had led her astray with goth clothing and goth attitude, giving rise to many arguments about too much make-up, hair dye all over the bathroom carpet and ridiculous statements about 'being so alone'. It hadn't been an easy time, but Shaunna could smile about it now. Krissi had moved on, stopped dying her hair black—not that she'd ever needed to—and sold her ridiculous big boots with the spikes on the toes. Jason was a good guy, even if he had always been slightly strange, and studying music production at university had only reinforced his 'arty' side.

The chauffeur closed the door and thanked Shaunna for the payment, which included a generous tip. She and Kris followed the others inside, to where the room was already buzzing with people. Krissi dumped her friends to go and circulate and was currently talking loudly to her great grandfather—Kris's grandfather—who was quite senior in years, but not deaf.

"She's always done that." Kris laughed. His grandparents had a good command of the English language, and his father was fluent, yet since Krissi was little, she'd been in the habit of shouting at them 'because they come from Swedeland'. They also insisted on calling her Kristina, which had never been her name, and she kept telling them. To a four-year-old so used to having people hang on her every word, it had served as conclusive proof that Farfar was indeed deaf.

"This makes me feel so old," Shaunna complained, pulling her shrug up to hide the saggy arms she was convinced she was getting.

"Well, you *are* closer to forty than thirty now," Dan said.

She turned to find him standing right behind her and poked him hard in his solid chest. "Which means you are, too."

"I prefer to think of it as my mid-thirties," he said with a wink. "Alright, Kris. I see you've brought the clan."

It was true. Kris's entire extended family was in attendance and monopolising Krissi's attention. As far as all but his parents were concerned, Kris was her father, in spite of her looking distinctly non-Scandinavian. She was now deep in conversation with Lars, Kris's older brother, who was much fairer and more heavily built than Kris. He had bought Krissi a huge teddy bear, and she sat it on one of the chairs at the nearest table, where Lars' wife was trying to contend with their two teenaged daughters. Both of them were arguing that they should be allowed to have an alcoholic drink, until Lars shouted, at which point they became quiet and thereafter spent the evening alternating between sulking and winding each other up.

Shaunna spotted Adele and Tom sitting in the quietest corner of the room, Adele with her legs up on a stool, and Tom fussing around her, making sure she was comfortable, had enough water, and so on. Shaunna went over, leaving Dan and Kris to queue at the bar and trying her best to hide her irritation at Adele's hypochondria on the way.

"Hiya, hun, how are you feeling?" She smiled cheesily and leaned forward to kiss Adele's cheek.

"I'm OK. I've got a stinking cold, though. And fat ankles and sausages for fingers. Bet I look really sexy!"

"You always look lovely. Stop fretting so."

"As do you. And Krissi. That dress really suits her, which is great, as she's not really a dress person, is she?"

"No, I suppose not. She ended up borrowing shoes off Jess. The ones she bought to go with the dress were too high, she said."

"Oh." Adele looked hurt. "I thought they would be perfect."

"And how's that baby treating you?"

"She's a nuisance! Keeps kicking me in the bladder, which is most unkind." Adele rubbed her bump. "Oh, I'm going all lightheaded again."

"She'll be pressing on your spine. You need to sit up a bit, or shift on to your hip. So you know it's a 'she', then?"

"Not for sure, I just have a feeling, you know?"

Shaunna remembered that feeling, although her own instinct had been way off. "Well, you never know. I got it totally wrong. All those little blue suits I bought, as well!"

"No. This is definitely a girl. I'm convinced. Not lazy enough to be a boy." Adele blew a kiss at Tom. He looked harassed almost to death. He briefly met Shaunna's gaze, and she offered him a sympathetic smile.

"I'd better go and socialise," she said. "I'll catch you later." She kissed Adele again and returned to the bar, grateful for a reason to not sit around listening to her moan about how terribly pregnancy was treating her. As Shaunna approached Dan and Kris, they did an appalling job of discreetly changing the subject, and she caught the words 'test results'. She took her drink and went to see Eleanor, who was busy shuffling trays of food around.

Dan waited until Shaunna was out of earshot before he asked, "Is she really OK?"

Kris shrugged. "She's coping. That's all I can say for the moment." He glugged the rest of his lager and ordered another two pints.

"You've got a thirst on you tonight," Dan observed with more than a little concern, as Kris rarely drank alcohol, and he'd just beaten him to finishing a pint.

"I'll slow down in a while, give you a chance to catch up," Kris said with a wink.

Andy and Jess had arrived and were standing at the bar next to them. Andy's nose was all red and shiny from the constant wiping all day, while Jess looked as glamorous as ever. Once they all had a drink, they found a table and made sure that at least one of them remained there for the rest of the evening.

Eleanor took a step back and looked over the buffet table. She smiled. "That's better."

Shaunna raised an eyebrow. "If you say so, although I thought it looked fab before. Thanks for everything, Ellie. I really appreciate it."

"No need to thank me. I love doing it. You're also much easier to please than Adele."

They both glanced over to the corner, where she was now lying on the bench seating, fanning herself with a beer mat.

"She does look a bit flushed," Eleanor remarked, and Shaunna nodded.

"You're right, but knowing her, she's done it with make-up, just for the sympathy."

"Still pissing you off, is she?"

"A bit. It'll pass. I don't suppose she means to be insensitive, or even realises she is being. She still doesn't know about Krissi, or the…thing."

"Well, let's not dwell on that tonight. It's a party. I think we should get a bottle of wine."

Shaunna nodded in agreement, and they went to purchase the first of the four bottles they had consumed between them by the time the party finished.

George followed Josh outside, knowing he'd gone to smoke. He didn't mind; it was Josh's decision, and he had no real part to play in it. However, he recalled how difficult it had been for him to give up the last time he relapsed, and he'd asked them all to nag him if he started up again. Therefore, out of a sense of duty, George had to keep on at him, before he was totally hooked for a third time.

"So, apart from the fact that they stink and cost a fortune, what is it you like about that particular brand?"

"Stop it already!"

"You told us we had to, so there's no getting out of it, Joshua. Put it out right now."

"No way."

George tutted but didn't lecture him anymore. "I never understood the attraction of them. Especially in this country. They're pretty cheap in the States."

"Well, if I do get hooked again, I'll be coming to visit a lot more often."

"You're not smoking in my new house! I told Joe that. He rolls his own, and they really do stink."

Josh looked at George and said nothing.

"What?"

"That's the first time you've mentioned Joe since you got here."

"Is it? There's not much I haven't told you already."

"That may be so. However, there are still seven people in there who don't know about him, and whilst I'm very good at keeping confidences, don't you think they'd be pleased to hear you've met someone?"

"I'm not ready to tell them. It's—let's just say it's complicated and leave it at that for now."

"As you like. I know there's something you want to talk about, but whenever you're ready, George. Whenever you're ready."

In fact, there had been several occasions, before and since he'd been staying with Josh, where George had wanted to say something. He hadn't even been sure Josh had picked up on it until now.

"I will tell you," George said. "Just not here, not now. OK?"

"As I say, when you want to talk, talk, and I will listen." Josh put out the cigarette and pushed the stub into the bin on the wall before going back inside. George followed, his head starting to fill with all the old feelings again. Falling for Joe had only ever kept them at bay, and since Tuesday, he'd found himself slipping back, with the return of that familiar butterflies sensation every time Josh was near him.

***

Predictably, Adele left early, and to be fair, Shaunna appreciated how difficult it was to keep up appearances almost six months into pregnancy. Tom looked a little disappointed to be going home, but he was more concerned with Adele's happiness than his own. If it was what she wanted, then he wanted it, too.

Shaunna gave Adele a hug and promised to pop over during the week, watching from the doorway as she dragged herself wearily out to the car, with Tom trailing right behind, carrying her bag and a large bottle of water. Shaunna shook her head in dismay and went back inside. If this was what Adele was like now, she'd never cope with the last four weeks, when even turning over in bed was a huge effort. The beached whale analogy didn't even come close.

As Shaunna came back in, the assorted grandparents left, with a request for slices of birthday cake at a later date. Krissi promised she'd send on the cake—if she could bring herself to cut up the fondant replica ghost train. The cake was hidden under a layer of black icing, with pictures of bats and skeletons and a sign on the side that read 'Ride If You Dare!' At the front, there was a track and a tiny moving carriage, with a pair of proportionately tiny people inside. There was even a ticket booth with a button on the top, which when pressed, sounded the ghost train siren.

By the end of the night, Krissi was the most sober person left, having had little time to stop and drink. Her friends stayed until they were kicked out, and she'd had a slight disagreement with Matt regarding Jason, so Matt had left, too.

Eleanor roped in the whole crew to tidy up—a task that took far longer in light of their sum total alcohol consumption—and Dan decided it would be fun to pop the balloons with a cocktail stick, until one burst right behind Josh. At first, he laughed, but after four more loud bangs in quick succession, he went for Dan, and George had to verbally pull him back.

It happened so often when they got into this state that the others automatically concocted conversations to distract both parties from scrapping. One mumbled an apology, and the other responded with an equally insincere acceptance. They were the most strong-willed members of their friendship group, and it was to be expected that they would come to blows from time to time. That said, both men were acutely aware it was happening a lot more at the moment, and not just because of alcohol.

When the hall was finally tidy, and the leftovers had been divided, everyone went their separate ways. Dan, Andy and Jess shared a cab, dropping Dan home first before going on to Jess's house. Eleanor, Josh and George shared a second cab. Shaunna, Kris and Krissi got a lift home from the barman, who was an old friend of Shaunna's dad. The last time Kris looked at the clock before he fell into a drunken sleep, it was almost three in the morning again.

***

"You do realise," Josh observed on his way up the stairs, "this is usually when I wake up. It's going to totally screw my body clock."

"Because it's not screwed already! Night," George called, heading for the spare room with a glass of water in his hand.

"Good night."

***

Dan walked through his living room in the dark, but for some reason he backtracked and turned on the light.

"What the hell?"

There was another dead fish floating on the top of the water. He removed it and put it with the other in the freezer, setting a reminder on his phone to call his mate in London, who was a koi expert.

***

Jess ushered Andy inside and closed the front door. It was almost as cold in the house as it was outside, but before she got as far as the heating thermostat, he pinned her against the wall by her arms and kissed her hard on the lips.

"I don't want your germs, thanks," she said, trying to push him away and make a joke of it, but he kept hold and pressed his body against hers.

"You were perfectly happy to share them on the way home," he said, letting go with one hand and pushing her bolero jacket back to reveal a bare shoulder.

"Andy! What are you doing?" With great effort, she struggled free and shoved him away with such force that he hit the opposite wall.

"Don't be like that, Jess."

"I'm not being like anything. I'm just not in the mood tonight."

"You think it, too, don't you?" Andy accused, slumping back against the wall. He ran his fingers through his hair and grasped two handfuls at his crown, clinging to them as if his life depended on it.

"I'm not having this discussion with you now," Jess said pointedly. "We've both had a lot to drink. Let's just go to bed, shall we?" She staggered and stooped to remove her shoes.

"I don't blame you. I don't even know anymore." He tugged at his hair and banged his head back.

"Andy, please can we go to bed?"

"I might as well give it all up now." He slid to the floor, still holding his head in his hands, and looked up at her. "You think I raped Shaunna."

"Don't be ridiculous," Jess yelled in frustration. When he made no attempt to move, she scooped up her shoes by the ankle straps and stepped over him. "I've had enough of this. I'm going up. Are you coming?"

He stared at her a moment longer and then turned away. She threw out her arms in exasperation and started to unsteadily climb the stairs.

"Maybe you're all right," he said. He waited until she reached the top of the stairs, hauled himself to his feet, and left.

Chapter Thirty-Four:
Finding the Door

The morning after the party, Kris awoke with a start, his eyes flinging themselves wide open without his permission, pain ripping around the sockets in response to the dimmest daylight patterns cast on the ceiling by the curtains' gentle movement. He groaned, squinted at the clock until it momentarily came into focus, and forced his eyes closed again. Four hours of sleep and the sensation that a family of small animals had taken to nesting on his tongue during that brief period of unconsciousness... He needed water, his brain told him; his mouth and throat agreed. His stomach wasn't so sure.

He couldn't bear to stay in bed, but it was terrible getting up, too. Somehow, he made it to the bathroom, ricocheting off the walls a couple of times along the way. Post-shower, he returned to the bedroom in a somewhat more linear fashion, and dressed in the most comfortable clothes he could find, all without throwing up, but it was by no means certain that this would continue. Getting fresh air seemed the best policy, even though his head was thumping so hard that Casper's lead pulling almost finished him off completely.

On the plus side, the longer he walked, the better he felt, so he kept going, until he reached the shop, conversed reluctantly with the newsagent and took the long way home. Alas, the improvement was short-lived, with a new wave of nausea hitting him as soon as he set foot in the house. He slowly lowered himself into a chair and sat at the kitchen table, newspaper spread in front of him, his hands cupping his pounding head.

Kris hated hangovers and wasn't accustomed to getting them, but he was reassured by the words of wisdom from more experienced others, who'd said that it would go away if he could keep down water. Better still, a cooked breakfast. For now, however, staying absolutely still was all he could manage, and with that stillness he started to nap. Every so often his arms would give way, jolting him awake again. Eventually, he gave up, crossed them and allowed himself to gently slip forwards onto the table.

That was much better. It reminded him of his exams in sixth form, where Andy spent most of the allotted time slumped over his desk directly in front of Kris, unless Dan was also taking the same exam. Looking back, it was a miracle the three of them got into university at all. Unlike Andy, he and Dan worked hard, but the subjects available didn't exactly present an opportunity for them to play to their strengths. All three of them took maths, as did Jess, with advance warning that it was a difficult subject. Poor Jess really struggled and just about scraped the grade she needed, although her other grades more than made up for it. In contrast, the Jeffries brothers seemed to have a natural aptitude for the subject, and Dan aced the exam. Andy failed.

Later, at uni, Kris apologised for being such a dope, as Dan more or less tutored him through the course. Dan had been dismissive, arguing that it was the reason he had done so well himself, glossing over the fact that his other exam results weren't exactly shameful. Only in engineering did Andy get a higher grade, and why? Because Dan did the coursework for him—a point of contention that came to a head just before the written exam, prompting Andy to produce such a thorough and overly critical evaluation of 'his' product that he subsequently achieved an 'A'.

Funny the things that come to mind. That was the first of many occasions Kris recalled Dan bailing his brother out, often without being asked to, which Kris pointed out once, in response to Dan's complaints about Andy's dependence. It hadn't been mentioned since, so maybe it had sorted itself out. Over time, most things do.

Movement from above disturbed Kris's dreamy train of thought. He carefully pulled himself upright and kept his jaw firmly clenched. Refusing to be thwarted, he fetched the frying pan, bacon and eggs and started to cook, all of which took mammoth effort on his part, but it had to be worth it for the possibility that it might make him feel better.

Krissi, who had no hangover whatsoever, bounced downstairs and greeted him loudly, and then kept an eye on the eggs, while he made an emergency dash for the bathroom. When he returned, she carried a plate of food up to her mum, who took one look at it, grunted ungratefully, and buried herself under the duvet.

The last thing Krissi wanted was to stay at home with hungover parents on her first Sunday off since starting work. She called Matt, discovering he was in pretty much the same state and still smarting about Jason, thus refused to get out of bed. Under the guise of getting back at him, Krissi phoned Jason next, who sounded typically indifferent to the idea of getting together for the day but was secretly delighted she'd called. He'd only come home from university for the week and was feeling very put out by her new love interest.

By the time Krissi had hooked Casper's lead to his collar, picked up his Frisbee and walked to Jason's house, Jason was already waiting outside, leaning against the garden wall, looking as cool as ever.

"Please tell me *you* aren't hungover," she implored, planting a kiss on the pale cheek closest to her.

"Hangovers are for the weak," Jason said and fell into step beside her.

She peered under the rim of his hat, spotted the laugh behind the line and smiled to herself. Same old Jason.

They mooched along as slowly as the dog would let them, his Frisbee clenched purposefully in his teeth as he led the way to the park. They spent a few hours there, talking about nothing in particular and playing fetch. Casper was having the time of his life and looked like he'd really missed their Sundays together.

"I've finally found my vocation," Jason said, throwing the disc for the hundredth time. Casper dutifully lolloped off after it, flipped it with his nose and returned it once again.

"If your friends could see you now," Krissi joked, watching Jason wipe the dog slobber from his hand.

"My credibility is diminishing by the second." He launched the Frisbee and lifted his hat back so he could look at her properly. "Don't tell anyone, but I'm loving every minute of it."

"I'm glad you're here."

"Me, too, although Matt isn't, is he? And this sun is causing me dreadful pain."

"Get a life, gothboy." She pushed him. He pulled his hat down, folded his arms and pretended to ignore her. It was great fun being together, and she suddenly realised how much she missed him when he was away.

***

Jess called Andy over and again, alternating between his house and mobile phone, but to no avail. Eventually she gave up and left him a text message to contact her, followed by another to say she was coming to talk to him. Still she received no response, so she went round and knocked on the door. The upstairs curtains were open, and the view through the letterbox was of an empty house, meaning either he was already up and out, or he hadn't gone home the previous night. Deep in remorse for the way she'd treated him, she walked to Dan's house, not really paying any attention when he opened the door with a phone in one hand and a large net in the other.

"I'll call you back," he said into the phone and then put it away. "Alright, Jess? What're you doing here?"

"Can I come in?"

Dan moved to one side so that she could pass and followed her into the living room. She stopped to take in the drenched floor and the dead fish lying on newspaper.

"What's all this?"

"I've lost three fish in the past two days."

"Oh dear. Why's that?"

"That's why I was on the phone—trying to figure it out."

"Any luck?"

"My mate reckons it's KHV—a strain of herpes. I got a new fish a while back, but without testing the dead ones, there's no way to know, so I'm thawing them out to take samples. I tell you what. I'm sick of bloody tests at the minute."

"I know exactly what you mean," Jess agreed absently. "Anyway, I only popped round to see if Andy was here."

"Nope. I haven't heard from him this morning."

"Neither have I, and I upset him last night." Jess went on to explain what had happened, and Dan listened, all the while lifting carp out of the pool and checking their gills for signs of the virus.

"I wouldn't worry, Jess. He's probably hiding upstairs, pretending to be out. I'd leave him for a while. He'll call you, once he's stopped acting like a child."

"Seriously, though, Dan. D'you think he could have done it?"

"I really couldn't say," he lied, as he was still convinced of Andy's guilt, regardless of what Josh had been able to get out of him.

"Well, I guess I'd better leave you to it. If you see him, will you tell him to call me?"

"Sure." Dan let Jess out and returned to inspecting his fish, furious with himself for thinking that the last buy was a bargain. He should have realised it was too good to be true, and now he was paying for his stupidity.

Jess tried Josh's house next, where he and George were sitting in their pyjamas and playing video games. They hadn't seen Andy, either, and suggested he might be at Dan's, but, of course, she'd already been there, and she couldn't think of where else he might be. It just wasn't like him to disappear, not without telling someone where he was going. She returned home and checked the phone: no messages or missed calls.

After trying him once more, she decided to stay in and wait to see if he got in touch, convinced that he would, sooner or later. She felt so awful for reacting the way she had. After all, there was nothing different about him trying it on last night. They'd both had a lot to drink, which always, inevitably, led to sex. But the possibility, however slight, that he had forced himself on Shaunna, had made Jess think twice about his motives, and she was starting to see a pattern that simply hadn't been there before.

The next day, when she still hadn't heard from or seen him, she used the spare key to get into his house, checked the living room first, and then went upstairs. His bed was made, there were no clothes in the linen basket, the bathroom sink was dry. There were no signs at all that he'd even been home. She went back downstairs, turned the latch on the front door to leave—

She stopped and held her breath, unsure if the noise she heard was imagined or real. It was most likely wishful thinking on her part, but she decided to check the kitchen almost on a whim, and it was as well she did. For there he was, sitting on the kitchen floor, wearing the same clothes he'd been wearing on Saturday night and nursing an empty vodka bottle. She gently took the bottle from him, inspected it and put it next to the sink.

"How long have you been here?" she asked.

"Go away, Jess. Please?" He refused to look at her.

"No. I won't."

He didn't respond or react in any way.

"I'm sorry, Andy. I truly am."

"I accept your apology, and I know you mean it, but it makes no difference. You thought it. You're my best friend, and even you think I'm capable of...it."

She had no defence. Whatever she said would make no difference, but she had to try. "A fact that has more to do with my own insecurities and shortcomings than yours."

"Maybe, but even I don't know if I did it. When you pushed me away, I thought..." He stopped.

He still wouldn't look at her. She sat down next to him on the cold tiles. "What did you think? Tell me."

"It doesn't matter."

"It does matter, to me at least. You should go and shower—it'll make you feel better. I'll make you a coffee, and then we can talk."

"What's the point?"

"Because we need to. I hate seeing you like this. I love you, and I can't just leave you to fall apart. I won't desert you." She got to her knees and moved in front of him, gripping him around the wrists and pulling. "Come on, now. Get up."

He resisted for a second but then allowed her to help him up. She put her arms around him and brushed his hair with her hand.

"Even if it turns out it was you, I won't love you any less, you know." He sniffed and rubbed his nose on her shoulder. "You'd better be crying and not using me as a handkerchief," she warned. He sniffed again and laughed half-heartedly.

"It was a bit of both," he said, pulling away and rubbing his eyes. "I'm sorry."

"For what?"

"Everything."

"If you mean this thing with Shaunna…"

"Not that. Well, yes, that, and for being such a bastard."

"You're not."

"When you pushed me away, I realised. I do come on too strong."

"There's a big difference between coming on strong and having sex with someone against their will. No. I simply can't accept that. You don't even know that Shaunna was…forced, let alone whether you're responsible. Not for sure."

He sighed and let his head rest on her shoulder. "I'm going for that shower you suggested."

"Good. I'll put the kettle on."

"Don't abandon me, will you?"

"I won't. I promise. Now go and shower!" She pointed to the stairs, and he compliantly plodded away.

"By the way," he called back, "there's no milk."

Jess slammed the kettle down and went out to buy some.

When she got back, Andy was showered, wearing jogging pants and t-shirt, and looking far more human.

"Here." She handed him one of the sandwiches she'd bought, knowing he wouldn't have eaten since Saturday night. He smiled his appreciation. She went to get the coffees, returning to find him still standing where she'd left him, holding the sandwich. She put the cups down and sat on the sofa, patting the cushion next to her to signal that he should sit, too. He sat in the armchair. She considered telling him not to be so silly, but then she noticed the look in his eyes and thought better of it.

**

Kris was about to leave for work when the phone rang.

"Good morning. Would it be possible to speak to Kris Johansson?"

"Speaking."

"I'm calling from PatSure. It's regarding the tests you sent last week."

Before Kris had time to interject and explain that it was Krissi she needed to speak to, the woman continued with her question.

"Is it possible that the samples you sent cross-contaminated in any way?"

"No, I don't think so."

"Or that the child is related to one of the donors, other than through paternity?"

"What do you mean?"

"The child's sample matches one of the donors on a number of markers. Without a sample from the mother, it's difficult to conclude paternity at this point, although there is a strong probability that the child and the male donor are related."

"I'm still not quite sure what you mean. Two of the samples we sent are from brothers. Would that make any difference?"

"Not really, as we only compare the potential father to the child. However, it would have been helpful if it had been noted on the form. In the absence of a maternal sample, there are additional tests we need to run."

"Sorry about that."

"No problem. However, it's important we take this into consideration, particularly as there may be markers in both samples indicating paternity. Do you have the reference numbers to hand?"

"Hold on." Kris put the phone down and went to the kitchen, found the list of names and numbers and returned. His hands were shaking. The pieces were falling into place. "Hello?" he said.

"Hello again," the woman replied. "The sample reference is LA41267-P."

Kris scanned down the numbers. "Yes. It's one of the brothers."

"OK. I'll make a note of that."

"Does that mean one of them is the father?"

"Well, we can't confirm the match without further tests. However, our two labs have reported the same results independently. You should hear from us by the end of the week."

"But it indicates paternity?"

"There is a high probability that the male donor discussed is related to the child. Bear in mind, this is not a formal conclusion at this stage."

*

Kris remained there, holding the phone, for quite some time after the woman had gone. Then he picked up his keys and walked out of the house.

Chapter Thirty-Five:
Morsels

"Did you want that train, son?"

The question zapped Kris out of his thoughts, and he found he was sitting in the station, waiting for the train to work, with little recollection of how he'd got there. Bewildered, he looked up into the inspector's face. "Is it the Beacon Hill train?"

"No. That left five minutes ago. I thought you must be waiting for this one. You're in your own little world there, aren't you, mate?"

"Err…" Kris scratched his head. "When's the next train to Beacon Hill?"

"Twenty-five minutes. I'd stay alert if I were you. There's folk who'd take advantage."

"Yeah. Thanks."

Still in a daze, Kris watched the inspector walk up the platform all the way to the front of the waiting train. He blew his whistle, and the train departed, chugging slowly, gathering speed, becoming a blur as it passed out of view.

Kris pulled his paperback from his pocket and tried to read, registering each page turn simply because the wind was against him. The words were gobbledegook, mashed together in a swirling mess of black and white. He tried to concentrate, but after reading the same paragraph five times, he gave up, returned the book to his pocket and walked to the edge of the platform, where the train had been, maybe seconds, maybe minutes ago. Everything had gone haywire in his head and nothing made sense.

Perhaps he'd misunderstood—he hoped, tried hard to convince himself that this was the case, all the while knowing it was pointless. He'd heard very clearly, asked her to repeat it, checked to see if she was sure. One of them had been there in that room, that night, forcing themselves into Shaunna, when she was too drunk to push them off. She'd said no, over and again. Still they had continued. For almost twenty-two years, one of them had been living with the secret, the lie, pretending to be his friend...*their* friend, someone they trusted. They might even both be in on it.

All those nights in London, Dan never so much as hinted he knew anything. Surely it couldn't be him? But then Andy, impulsive as he was, however irresponsibly he acted at times, seemed equally incapable of committing such an act. Kris started to question his recollections of the night of the party. He could be wrong; it was so long ago, and only recently had he told anyone what he heard. *Yes*, that made more sense, such as any of it did.

One thing was for sure, though: there was no way he could go to work in this state. He left the station and set off in the opposite direction to home, to do as they all did in situations like these.

***

Josh was in the middle of hearing about Alex's night at a vampire club—something he'd advised against some time ago. It was too close to turning fantasy into reality for Josh's liking, but Alex seemed to have enjoyed it. His account of the evening was enthralling...how he'd found himself surrounded by 'real' vampires—people who went the extra mile and had cosmetic work on their teeth to extend their canines. They wore terrifying contact lenses and drank thick, dark liquid from delicate wine glasses.

A girl Alex had spoken to on the club's website recognised him from his picture and greeted him enthusiastically, introducing him to the others. And he soon realised that they were all like him, all sharing the same fantasy of immortality. He had so much more to learn, and Lileth, as the girl called herself, offered to be his guide.

Josh found it fascinating and had to admit the effect on Alex was both profound and positive. He was about to probe him for more information when Kris burst into the room.

"I'm sorry, but I need to speak to you. Urgently," he said, panting from having run all the way from the station.

Josh quickly weighed up the situation. If Kris had said 'it's an emergency' rather than 'I need to speak with you urgently', he'd have sent Alex on his merry way. "Can it wait ten minutes?" he asked.

"Oh. It's OK, Josh," Alex said, already getting up from the sofa. "I can leave it for today."

"Are you sure?"

"I'm sure."

"Well, thanks for being so understanding. Next week then?"

"Yes, bye for now."

Alex, a small, quiet man who had always reminded Josh of a mouse, put on his coat and left, looking bigger and stronger than ever before. Josh closed the door behind him and turned to Kris.

"Sit down," he ordered, aggravated by Kris's lack of manners and the interruption to the only aspect of his work he was currently enjoying.

Kris didn't move, so Josh steered him to the couch and gently pushed down on his shoulders. His legs gave way and he sat, staring straight in front of him.

"What's the matter?" Josh threw his notepad onto his chair and sat at the opposite end of the sofa.

"The lab called."

"The lab?" He thought for a second. "Wow. That was quick. I thought it was going to be two or three weeks."

"They needed to confirm something. Asked for Kris, instead of Krissi. How am I going to tell her?"

"OK, slow down." Josh adjusted his tone, now he'd realised the state Kris was in. He could be quite melodramatic, but he wasn't inconsiderate. Nor did he usually seek Josh's counsel. "Tell me what they said."

"They called to confirm whether any of the samples came from people who were related to Krissi, but not her father. You know what that means, don't you?"

Josh's heart missed a beat and then overtook itself, thumping so hard and fast he was certain it was visible through his shirt.

"It's one of them. Dan or Andy," Kris continued unnecessarily. "If one's related but not the father, then the other has to be."

Josh was lost for words, and Kris's were a scramble of thoughts escaping aloud.

"How could they pretend? Go on as if nothing happened? I don't understand it. Dan's my best friend."

"But it might not be Dan," Josh reasoned.

"So it's Andy. We trusted him, too."

Josh could see that Kris was devastated by the very idea that either of them could be Krissi's father. It would have been bad enough had it been a distant acquaintance, but a close friend? It was the worst kind of betrayal.

"There's also another possibility," Josh said in a desperate bid to soften the blow. He knew there was little point in the long term, but it might be enough of a diversion for the time being.

"That the result's wrong? That I misheard? No. I asked her to confirm what she said."

"Where was Michael? During the party, I mean."

"Michael? Wasn't he away at uni?"

"It was January. He was on a semester course, so he might have been home."

"I don't remember him being there. In fact, I'm pretty sure he wasn't. Oh, what am I saying? I'm not sure of anything anymore."

"You need to calm down a little, Kris. There's time to look into it before the results are returned."

"Four days, we've got, at most. She said they'd be back by the end of the week. But she was very clear. Either Andy or Dan is Krissi's father."

"She didn't say that," Josh pointed out uselessly, for if Kris had been listening to him at all, he certainly wasn't listening now.

"Dan was my best man. Surely it's not him? He wouldn't do this to me, or to Shaunna."

It was true, then. After all these years, Dan was going to be proved right. What a hollow victory that would be.

***

Josh had two clients in that afternoon: the insufferable middle-aged woman, followed by her equally insufferable and middle-aged friend. They made an outing of it, waited for each other, no doubt went for cream teas afterwards and compared notes. He could scarcely tolerate them at the best of times, because there was nothing wrong with them. They harped on and on about the awfulness of their comfortable, secure lives, the trial of searching for some meaning to it all… Today, he felt like telling them they were actually meaningless and should stop threatening and take assertive action, put everyone out of their misery.

He didn't say anything of the sort; he was far too professional, but by the time he arrived home, he felt like he'd gone several rounds with a heavyweight boxer. His head was banging, and his teeth were hurting from lack of sleep and caffeine, the latter of those being at George's suggestion.

In lieu of his defence, George had dinner ready: chicken and chips, which was Josh's current favourite meal, although he did wonder how George knew that. But Josh wasn't going to complain, seeing as George had also bought him coffee. Decaffeinated coffee.

"What's the point?" Josh sipped and grimaced at the barely palatable substance that bore only a vague resemblance to his usual beverage.

"I read some stuff about addiction, and it said a big part of it is the habit. So I figured, you break the chemical addiction and keep the habit, you're halfway there."

"But I *like* coffee. I like caffeine."

"Good for you. Do you like getting three hours of sleep a night as well?"

It was a valid point, and Josh was too close to exhaustion to fight. He'd give it a go, and if it didn't work—well at least he could say he'd tried. He set the 'coffee' aside and got on with his meal. It was delicious.

"So, George," he said through a mouthful of chicken, "you might think, based on my calm exterior, that today has been a fairly ordinary day."

"Right," George said cautiously, waiting for the 'however'.

"However."

"I knew you were going to say that."

"This is really big, George, shush a minute." Josh swallowed the food already in his mouth and put down his fork. "I was in session with Alex the vampire this morning when Kris burst in, and I mean, literally walked straight into the consulting room. No apology, no backing nervously out the door."

"That's not like him." George frowned.

"True, but it's infuriating, nonetheless. So, this morning, he took a phone call that was meant for Krissi. It was from the DNA lab. Some of the tests have already been processed."

"And?"

"It looks like Dan was right."

"Hang on. They could only have had the samples, what? Five days? And that's counting the weekend."

"Well, they phoned to check if there were any genetic connections between the samples, as there was a possible match with Krissi, but not to her father."

"No shit!" George absently rubbed his chin. He was shocked and not at all convinced. For all that Josh had told him about Dan's suspicions, there was something amiss. He just couldn't put his finger on what it was. But then, he also knew from very recent experience that DNA tests were pretty conclusive these days.

"You been up to much today?" Josh asked.

"Not really," George said vaguely. "I collected my email, that's about it. Joe says the house has arrived. There was some trouble clearing the plot, as it was a bit bigger than we'd been told, but it's in place and partly secured."

"Excellent. So it's not all bad, then?"

"No, I guess not." George desperately wanted to tell him about Joe. Judging by the way he was being scrutinised, he was sure Josh had picked up on it, but there was too much going on. "So what's going to happen next with these tests?" he asked, making a point of examining the morsel of food on his fork.

Josh eyed him carefully, wondering what the big secret was. George clearly wanted to share, but either he wasn't ready to, or he didn't know how to put it into words. There was always the possibility that it was a repeated declaration of George's undying love, in which case he'd also rather not discuss it right at that moment, or indeed ever. He stopped theorising and answered George's question, at the same time reloading his fork.

"According to Kris, the results will be back by the end of the week, and it'll all be over." He crammed the food into his mouth. "This is bloody marvellous, by the way."

George gave Josh a rueful look. "Or just beginning."

Chapter Thirty-Six:
Bric-a-Brac

Monday was spent in deep and painful dialogue. Jess had decreed they move proceedings to her house, and Andy obeyed without protest, following her like a lost puppy, sitting where he was told to and speaking on command. It wasn't conversation really, as Jess would ask a question, after which there would be a long pause, until she prompted him and a torrent of information would pour forth. He was struggling to hold it together, and she still felt guilty for having abandoned him for most of the previous week.

"Dan's everyone's favourite. The life and soul." It had taken Andy even longer to marshal a response this time, and he'd regressed. "Mum's no different in treating him that way." He brushed invisible dust from the knees of his jeans. "Sometimes you could almost forget he's the baby and Mike's the eldest. Other than the sheer size of him, anyway. He's so immature, even more than me, all the massive tantrums he throws, just because he doesn't get to stay out till eleven or some other stupid thing."

It had long been apparent to Jess that the Jeffries brothers shared the same self-destructive personality, although for Michael it manifested itself in his relationships. His wife had to be the most tolerant and understanding woman on the planet. Every other person he had been involved with, including his own parents and siblings, were potential targets, with Andy—

his junior by three years—coming in for more than his fair share of abuse over the years.

To some extent, as 'the baby', Dan had been cushioned by his mother, who hadn't doted on him as such, but she did spoil him, gave in to him more often than not, and almost always took his side in fights.

Andy continued, "It got a bit easier as we got older and bigger. If Dan and I ever had cross words, we dealt with it ourselves, but she always had to intervene. We were the same size from when we were about five and soon caught up with our Mike. It helped, but Mum always threw the same old rubbish at us—'if only I had a man around'... That first idiot she married—not Dad, the other one—was all right on stuff like that. He used to say 'boys will be boys' and leave us to beat the living crap out of each other. We didn't know it was because he wasn't interested, until she kicked him out."

Their mother had remarried twice, the first time, it was a long-term relationship that had little impact on any of them. Their father, when he was around, paid no attention to their emotional needs, although he couldn't be faulted on the amount of time he dedicated to his three sons, but it was the fun stuff—taking them to football matches and supporting them in athletics tournaments. He treated them all the same, with no consideration of their differences at all, which was as bad as their mother's favouritism.

"When Mike went off to uni, me and Dan started to get on a bit better, because there was no-one there stirring and winding us up. Even then, he was a moody sod. I can't remember how many times he moved his bedroom around to hide fist marks in the walls. I never knew what his problem was—he wouldn't talk to me, so how could I possibly know?"

All of this was not news to Jess. Andy had talked about it many times before, but never like this. It was like he couldn't snap out of it; he didn't have the mental resources, and seeing him so low was traumatic. Andy was the fun-loving, impulsive extrovert, always up for a laugh—hardly the same person as the man sitting before her, pouring out his soul and wishing he were dead.

Jess made him cocoa and put him to bed, grateful for an excuse to go to the bathroom, where she cried, silently, until she herself could hold it together again. When she returned to the bedroom, Andy was fast asleep, and she curled up behind him, draping her arm over his vast yet strangely childlike body. He gripped her hand in his sleep and didn't let go, until she forcibly had to remove it in the middle of the night to shake off pins and needles.

The next morning, she commanded him to get up and shower. She'd woken with ideas that could solve a few of their problems. The first was to contact his landlord and give notice to quit. He hadn't paid the rent for two months, not wanting to ask Dan for money, and not being able to work because of his injuries. Thus, Jess decided, regardless of whether he got the job or not, she was going to suggest he moved in with her, which would be a help to them both, financially at least. Then there was the issue of Krissi, but until the paternity test results were back, there was no point in worrying.

When Andy finished in the shower, she sat him down with some breakfast. "I've been thinking," she said, having planned out what she was about to say word for word, although in the rehearsal, the audience looked like they were watching the show. "Regardless of what happens with—" she struggled to find the best way to phrase it "—with the whole Krissi and Shaunna thing, I'm here for you. You've always been my best friend, and I'm sorry if I made it more difficult last week by avoiding you. It was all a bit of a shock."

"Jess, you don't have to do this. Live your life. You know I'll get by. Somehow. I always do."

"You always *did*, but this is different. So, if I may go on?" He nodded his consent. "What I suggest is this. Give your landlord notice, I'll pay the back rent and you can move in here. If you get the Dubai job, great. If you don't, no problem. There will be others."

She stopped and waited for him to protest. He didn't. Instead, he pushed the dregs of breakfast cereal into a tidy pile in the middle of his bowl, bashed them flat with the bottom of his spoon and dropped it into the bowl, where it clattered and bounced several times before coming to rest.

He pinched the corners of his eyes and spoke into his hand. "I love you, Jess. Part of me wants to tell you not to do this for me, because I don't deserve it. But the truth is, I really need you. I can't do this on my own. If I did do what Dan says, I'm not sure I'll be able to live with it."

"*I* can live with it. We'll get through it together." She took his hand across the breakfast bar and gave it a squeeze. He nodded again. "Good. Now that's agreed, we've got a lot to sort out today. And don't try telling me you're not up to it. I'll keep you so busy you won't have time to worry about anything else. How much of the stuff in your place is actually yours?"

Andy thought for a minute, mentally visualising each room of his rented house. The furniture all belonged to the landlord. "The TV, DVD player, stereo in the living room. And the beanbag. The kettle and toaster are mine. The bedding. That's it."

"Right, well, we won't be needing a van or anything for that lot. I'll give Dan a call and see if we can borrow his car. It'll only take a couple of trips."

"I'd rather you didn't." He would have justified his resistance by pointing out that there was hardly any room in a two-seater sports car, but she didn't let him get that far.

"I'm sorry, Andy, but he owes you. He's your brother, and you've done more than enough for him already. He's used you, and yes, I appreciate he's paid you handsomely, but all the dirty work you've done for him? Whether you're guilty or not, he should be standing by you."

She picked up the phone to avert further protest and called Dan. She didn't say why, just that she wanted to borrow his car. He agreed, with no questions or snide remarks at all, and even offered to drive it over to the house. Jess accepted and thanked him with convincing sincerity.

"Is that how you get your defendants off?" Andy asked. "'Of course this man is innocent, Your Honour.' Juries fall for all that smiley bull, do they?" He managed to smile so she knew he was teasing, although he was surprised how nice she'd been to Dan, after what she'd just said.

"It would be, if that was my area. Now, get those cornflakes eaten. You have no idea how much stuff there is in my spare room."

Andy swallowed the last soggy remnants of his breakfast and washed his bowl. "See? You've trained me well." He gave her a weary wink, more thankful than she could possibly imagine.

They went upstairs to the spare bedroom, and Jess pushed hard on the door, which opened part of the way and then sprung back, the bags behind it resisting as if they knew their time was finally up. Edging their way into the room, unable to go back or move forward without falling over, they found themselves pinned against the wall by the mass of bags, shoe boxes, suits and dresses. In the midst of it all was a rail of clothes, complete with their tags, and a cardboard box with a mound of smaller, coloured, metallic boxes in it, all containing perfumes that Jess had bought and worn once, at most.

"Whoa!" Andy paused to take in the scene before him. "When you said you liked shopping, you meant you really, *really* like shopping. Where are we gonna put all this crap?"

"Excuse me! This is a collection of very expensive designer items. And I don't know where I'm going to put it. That's why it's in here."

"Is that how it's going to be?"

"What?"

"I?"

"I don't follow."

"You said 'I don't know where *I* am going to put it', not 'we'."

"You're clutching at nothing, Andy."

"Am I?"

She didn't reply. They'd never been 'we', but this one occasion of not thinking about her wording signified so much more about what she was really thinking. If someone in the stand had done it, she would have jumped on it as quickly as Andy had.

"eBay," he said, trying to gloss over his momentary outburst and what he hoped was nothing more than his paranoia surfacing again.

"What? Are you serious? I didn't buy all this to sell it to someone else for 50p!"

"You could make loads out of this lot, even at 50p a pop."

"You know what I mean. I won't get back anything like what I paid for it."

"But it's not doing anyone any good in here, is it?"

Jess sighed. He was absolutely right. She had to get rid of it. "OK. For now, we'll stick it in the living room. Later, I'll sort it into stuff I want and stuff I don't, and you can put it all on eBay for me, seeing as you suggested it."

"Cheers," Andy said drolly as he stepped over the shoe boxes. He grabbed an armful of clothes and lifted the hangers free of the rail, stepped back over the shoe boxes and sidestepped out of the room. "I'll leave this lot on the sofa," he called on his way downstairs, repeating the action twice more before the rail was empty.

Jess carried down the shoe boxes and piled them in the corner of the room, while Andy brought the large plastic sacks of posh bric-a-brac, swearing when a bag containing lingerie and nightdresses burst halfway down the stairs, making him slip on a silky something or other. He just caught his step and launched the bag at Jess, who was standing at the bottom of the stairs, waiting to take it from him. She scooped up the knickers and bras and put them in a new bag, leaving him to retrieve the final few items from the spare room. There was just time for a quick drink before Dan arrived.

"You know something?" Jess said from across the living room, peering over the mounds of varying colours and textures. She'd been looking at it for quite some time, calculating how much she must have spent. "It's like we're both moving forward now."

Andy glugged the last half pint of orange squash in one go before answering. Even in his state of mind, the evidence had been clear throughout the morning's activities. "Does that mean you're going to stop shopping?"

Jess felt a pang of unease. What kind of man was he to understand that her shopping represented a far greater need than just running out of perfume?

"Did Josh say something?"

"As if he would!" Andy frowned and folded his arms. "So Josh knows you've got a shopping addiction?"

"It's not an addiction," she snapped defensively. He raised an eyebrow. "Even if it is, I wouldn't be about to broadcast it, would I? Not even to Josh. He and Ellie are always going on at me about it. They try to talk me out of shopping trips and confiscate my credit cards."

"Ellie, too?" Andy mused thoughtfully. Much as he appreciated he wasn't the sort of guy people usually confided in, they were still best friends, and it hurt.

Dan's instantly recognisable knock at the door stopped them both worrying any further, and as neither of them wanted him to come in, they grabbed their jackets and keys and went straight out to the car. He seemed in good spirits and still didn't question why they needed the car, which was odd. Since Andy's accident, Dan had sniped at every given opportunity, although it didn't take a genius to see that Jess was even less tolerant of him than usual, or how drained Andy looked.

Whatever the reason, they chatted as if the events of the past few weeks hadn't happened at all and dropped Dan off at home before going on to Andy's house, where there were two envelopes on the hallway floor. One was written and delivered by hand; the other had a London postmark. Andy stepped over them and went straight to the living room, where he started unplugging electronics, leaving Jess to pick up the letters.

"Shall I open these for you?" she suggested.

"If you like."

She followed him into the living room, and he peered at the handwriting. "That one's from the landlord."

Jess opened it first. "Yeah, it is."

"Another threat of eviction?"

"Actual eviction. I'll give him a call." She took out her mobile phone and dialled the number on the letter. Andy continued packing, listening in to the conversation.

At first, the landlord refused to talk to her, until she said she was his lawyer. It wasn't entirely a lie; she was *a* lawyer, and she was often called on by her friends for legal advice. She arranged to drop off a cheque for two months' rent, even though it was closer to four that was due, including the month's notice. Jess told Andy's landlord to keep the deposit and they'd call it quits—an offer he accepted, seeing as how she was a lawyer and he was used to tenants leaving his properties in a terrible state, whereas this one was in good condition.

"He's a cheeky bastard," Andy said, lugging the TV out into the hall. "He knows I've redecorated. And fixed the leak on the water tank. And replaced the loft insulation."

"No matter. It's sorted now." Jess opened the second letter. "Oh!"

"What?"

"Interview. Tomorrow."

"That's short notice. Where is it?"

"London."

"Shit." Andy put the DVD player down next to the television and went back into the living room. "Well that's that, then."

"Oh, stop being so bloody defeatist. We'll go back to mine and book a train ticket."

"Do you know how much it'll cost to get a train ticket for tomorrow? It's cheaper to fly."

"And more exciting, no doubt. No. You can borrow Dan's car again."

"If that's the case, I'm not going. I'll see if they'll rearrange it."

"Do you want this job or not?"

"Of course I do, but I'm not asking Dan. I'm not owing him anything."

"You don't. He's the one paying the debt. If he'd said something back at the beginning, then we wouldn't be in this mess, would we?"

Andy could see there was no point in arguing. "You can ask him, then, because I'm not."

"Fine. I will. Now, where are we up to?" Without waiting for a response, Jess stomped up the stairs to Andy's room, pulled a suitcase down from the top of the wardrobe and started packing his clothes. Andy took his TV, DVD player and surfboard to Jess's place and came straight back. As much as she'd annoyed him, she was doing all of this for him.

Apart from an occasional 'sorry' when they got in each other's way en route to the car, they worked on in silence and were all done in less than two hours. Andy squashed the last bag into the boot, and Jess went back to check they hadn't missed anything, moving the sofa and chairs away from the wall to check nothing had fallen behind them. The only thing she found was a framed photo of the two of them, taken at her graduation ball. Andy's hair was almost down to his shoulders, like it was now, and he was wearing a large gold hoop in his left ear, much bigger than the one he wore these days.

Jess held the picture to her chest, allowing a few memories of those times to flood her mind, smiling as she recalled one occasion when he'd fallen 'in love' with one of her housemates, who dumped him soon after. It was the closest she'd ever seen him to how he was now, but it had meant nothing, and he'd moved on to a new girl before the weekend was out.

Still clutching the photo, she closed the front door and walked out to the car.

"All done," she said.

"Yep." Andy started the engine. "The end of an era."

Chapter Thirty-Seven:
Turnings

Dan was more than agreeable to Andy borrowing the car for his interview, because it meant he could go with him. He'd now lost a total of six fish, and he was taking a couple down for his friend, the koi specialist, to look at. Jess offered to pay half the petrol money, but Dan declined, saying he would rather Andy helped him out with some work while they were there.

Much as he didn't want to, Andy agreed to this one last job—providing it was the very last. When he asked what it was, Dan told him he'd explain on the way. With the transport sorted, Jess and Andy went home and phoned to confirm his attendance at interview.

"You'd best get to the barber's," Jess advised, knee-deep in bikinis in the middle of the living room floor.

Andy groaned. "I like it like this." He pulled his fingers through his long, curly hair.

"It is very sexy, I'll admit, but you'll look scruffy in a suit with that mop. You can always grow it again, after you get the job."

"All right," he huffed, "if I must, although I'm already feeling a bit like Samson, and that was *after* his haircut."

For all his moaning, Andy still did as he was told. If it weren't for Jess directing his actions, he wouldn't have had a clue what he was doing, and when he returned from the barber's a short while later, looking more than a little sorry for himself, she climbed out of the jumble sale that was her living room to rub his head.

"That's good, too," she said and kissed him. He soon forgot he was supposed to be sulking when she handed him the first page of the inventory she had been compiling in his absence. He was beginning to wish he hadn't suggested putting it all on eBay.

***

Shaunna dropped everything and raced to the hospital, replaying all of the cruel thoughts she'd had, everything she'd said, the reassurances that made a liar of her now. The bus seemed to take forever, and she kept looking at her watch, as if it would somehow make the journey quicker. She ran from the bus stop to the hospital entrance, slowing to a trot as she passed straight through the reception and on to the antenatal ward, where Tom greeted her with a hug and a very shaky 'hello'.

"What's happening?" she asked, keeping a gentle yet firm grip of his arms, for her own sake as much as his.

"They've managed to get her blood pressure down, but it's still very high. She's all over the place, not making any sense." His anxiety was evident in his face. "She's been asking for you."

Shaunna nodded calmly, fighting to keep it together. "I'll go and find a midwife or someone," she said and left him standing in the corridor. The staff let her into the ward; two doctors emerged from a side room on her left, followed by a midwife, she assumed, from the dark-blue uniform. The doctors were talking in quiet voices. The midwife made a beeline for her.

"Are you Shaunna, by any chance?"

"I am, yes."

"I thought so. Adele was just telling me all about you. She's not fully aware of the seriousness of the situation, and it's probably best that way. She has preeclampsia, and we've put her on a drip to try and stabilise her condition. However, there is still a risk that she could suffer a stroke or a heart attack. Now, at the moment, baby is fine, but if Adele's blood pressure rises further, we'll have to perform an emergency caesarean section, for her own safety and the baby's."

"Oh my god," Shaunna gasped. Adele was only twenty-five weeks pregnant.

"What's really important now, Shaunna, is that Adele doesn't pick up on how worried you are. Normally, we would only allow Dad on the ward outside of visiting hours, but Mr. Kerry isn't coping too well, as I'm sure you could see, and we don't want to upset Adele any further. So, I'll give you a minute to compose yourself before I take you in. Would you like a cup of tea or coffee?"

"I, err…yes, please. A cup of tea, two sugars."

Shaunna spotted a row of chairs along the wall and sat down, taking deep breaths and trying to slow her racing pulse. How she was going to keep this to herself, she didn't know. But as the midwife said, somehow she'd have to, for Adele's sake.

"Here you are, my love, take a few minutes. I'll be back shortly." A plastic cup was deposited in her hands and partially brought her out of the hysteria building inside. She thanked the midwife and watched her walk briskly back up the ward, where she stopped at a trolley to collect a plastic apron, which she hung around her neck, before disappearing into another side room.

Shaunna sipped at the hot tea, wishing she'd asked for more sugar, but at least she'd calmed down a bit, and felt almost ready to see Adele. It was only now she realised how much she cared. She needed to be strong for her. Nothing mattered more than that.

The midwife came into view again, laughing as she called back through the opening she had just emerged from. *How dare she be cheerful*, Shaunna thought. But then, whilst Adele was suffering in one room, in others there were new mums with their new babies, feeling that indescribable joy she remembered so vividly it could have been yesterday. The midwife beckoned; Shaunna got up and followed her through a doorway and beyond some curtains, to where Adele was lying back on her pillows, picking at the Velcro cuff on her arm.

"Hey, you!" Shaunna said, making her way around all of the equipment to give her best friend a hug. "You were determined to get into this place, weren't you?"

"And it's *so* boring!" Adele grumbled, returning the hug. "Everything keeps beeping at me. Doesn't it drive you mad, Jane?" she asked the midwife checking the monitors.

"I don't notice anymore. It's when they stop beeping you have to worry." She half-winked at Shaunna, who couldn't decide whether the double bluff was a wise move. "See you later," Jane said, and off she went again.

"It's my blood pressure," Adele explained with an airy sigh.

For the first time since entering the room, Shaunna made eye contact. "Oh? Why's that, then? Too high or too low?" She tried not to stare, but Adele's face was so swollen that her eyelashes, with all their mascara, were hardly visible in the puffiness.

"It's too high. They're going to monitor me for twenty-four hours then make a decision. Did they say anything to you about it?"

"Not really," Shaunna lied. "But I don't think they're allowed to give information to people who aren't family."

"Oh, yeah. I never thought of that." Adele smoothed her bedspread and examined her chubby fingers, poking down a mostly buried cuticle with her thumbnail. "This is a bit like old times, isn't it? If you'd brought a magazine, it would be just like when we used to sit in your room all night."

Shaunna gulped back tears at the memory. It had been so easy then: no babies, no jobs, no houses to clean. She pushed away the thought that this might be the last chance to relive those days.

"I'll go and buy one in the shop in a minute," she suggested. "What do you fancy?"

"Anything. I don't mind. Just make sure it's got a problem page and some true life stories."

"Righteo."

"Is Tom still here?"

"Yes, or he was when I came in. He wouldn't go and leave you here, would he? Not…" Shaunna had been about to say 'in your condition' and managed to change it with hardly any pause at all. "…when he's so excited about being a daddy."

Adele didn't notice. "I suppose. He was a bit put out that I wanted you here, plus that jumped-up general manager is on his case again."

"Well, he seemed fine. Do you want me to go and get him?"

Adele nodded. "When you go for the magazine, send him in." She stopped talking for a moment to think, biting at her bottom lip. "He's been good to me. So patient."

"Yes, he has. More patience than me, that's for sure." They both laughed lightly at the truth of it.

Adele continued, "He's a good man, reliable, sensible. And he works so hard."

She didn't need to say anything else. Shaunna had heard it all many times before. Each time Adele had been in a serious relationship with anyone other than Dan, there came a point when she knew it was better to stay where she was but had to talk herself into it. This time, though, she didn't have much choice.

"I'll go for that magazine," Shaunna said, gently squeezing Adele's hand to indicate she understood. She went off in search of the shop, letting Tom know on the way.

Regardless of Adele's concerns, Tom felt a lot better for Shaunna being there, if only to share the stress. It was another day off work, and his boss was after him as it was. He was supposed to have a meeting this afternoon, to discuss his performance, and the word 'disciplinary' had been touted. When Tom called to explain he needed to cancel, and why, the boss warned him it would mean rescheduling and escalating, clearly expecting him to back down. Tom only just stopped short of telling him where to stick his disciplinary proceedings and his job.

Shaunna returned with an armful of magazines and suggested to Tom that he go home. There was no point in both of them staying, and she'd call if anything changed. He was so exhausted he quickly agreed and went home to sleep, promising Adele he'd be back early the next morning.

The two women settled in for an evening of bitching about celebrities and trying to beat agony aunts' advice before the ward staff sent Shaunna away a little after midnight. She arrived home to find a plate of sandwiches in cling film and a note from Kris to say he'd told Josh, George, Jess and Eleanor what was happening and gone to bed.

***

James was determined to make up for their first date, even though Eleanor insisted it had been a wonderful dinner. After spending the early part of the evening at the theatre, they strolled through the park and went to a jazz club, where the background music was provided by live musicians who came together in various combinations to perform. The venue was furnished with low-backed sofas and chairs in small groupings with beech coffee tables between. James found them a corner away from the bar traffic, where they could chat quietly and see the performances. He ordered a bottle of house white, and sat beside Eleanor.

"Do you like jazz music, El-e-a-nor?" James talked into her ear, his breath disturbing her hair and sending a shiver down her back.

"I can't say I've listened to it much," she replied, her voice wavering with the thrill of him sitting so close. "I've definitely never listened to it like this."

"It is the only way to listen to jazz." He took her hand and reclined against the sofa, his eyes shut, head moving slightly, in time to the lilting rhythm of the double bass. Eleanor rested against his shoulder and allowed herself to be drawn in by the music, the resonance exaggerating the effects of the body contact.

At the end of the piece, the sparse audience applauded, and musicians exchanged places, this time creating a piano, sax and female vocal ensemble. James released Eleanor's hand and leaned forward to pick up the wine glasses, passing one to her.

"You are a very beautiful woman. Have I ever told you?"

She giggled. "Yes, you might have mentioned it."

His expression remained sincere. Eleanor steadied herself and put the glass to her lips, sipping slowly. James did the same, watching her all the while.

"There is a sparkle to your eyes I find most enthralling. Like the moon scattered across the surface of a lake."

If any other man had attempted to describe her in such a way, she wouldn't have been able to take them seriously, but the way he said it was alluring.

"I also find you very attractive, James. I have really enjoyed this evening."

"Even the terrible play?"

"Oh, it wasn't so bad."

James smiled gratefully, so sure that he had made another bad choice.

"I don't want tonight to end," Eleanor said, staring into her wine.

"Then we shall keep it for a while longer." James took her hand once more, this time cupping it between both of his. He gently caressed her fingers, sliding smoothly up one side of each finger and down the next.

She moved her face towards his, hesitating to see how he would respond. He placed his palm on her cheek, guiding her forward. Their lips touched and remained in contact for a long time. Slowly, she pulled away, slightly breathless, a tingling sensation flooding her body. James drew her close again, and she rested her head on his chest, her own heartbeat quickly falling into synchronicity with his.

***

George pulled the duvet up and tucked it under his neck, sure that the slight draught coming through the air vent was the source of his stiffness, but then, he'd been sleeping on a lumpy spare bed for a week.

And still he hadn't told Josh about Joe. He'd almost got there tonight, but then Kris had phoned about Adele, and once again the moment passed, the problem getting smaller and smaller with every new thing that happened. It was never-ending.

He drifted off, vaguely hearing Josh move in the middle of the night, but otherwise sleeping soundly until the morning, when a house martin must have miscalculated its landing approach and hit the window.

***

From the bedroom window, Andy saw Dan waiting in the car, engine idling.

"I'm going." He leaned over the bed to kiss Jess's cheek.

She groaned and rolled onto her back. "What time is it?"

"Two minutes to six."

"Umph."

"Have a good day."

"You, too. Good luck," she yawned, lifting her arm to brush Andy's chest. He left, and she drifted back to sleep. Later, she and Eleanor were going shopping, but not for clothes this time. They were going to buy furniture for the new office.

"Alright, bro?" Dan greeted Andy cheerfully. "The interview's at twelve-thirty, yeah?"

"It is."

"Nice haircut, by the way." He checked the rear-view mirror and pulled out.

"You would say that," Andy muttered.

"It's served me well over the years."

"Nah. It suits you, but I hate mine being this short." Andy fastened his seat belt, sat up, and sniffed. "Ugh. What the hell is that smell?"

"Fish."

"Fish?"

"I've got seven dead koi in the boot—in a cool box. Hopefully, they won't stink us out before we get there." They headed for the motorway.

There was plenty of time, considering the journey only took three hours, but it was better to be early, and Andy needed to get the train into the city, so Dan put his foot down and stuck to the outside lane all the way.

***

James stayed over and, much to Eleanor's dismay, slept on the floor. She'd offered the sofa, but it was only a two-seater and he was at least six feet in height. She'd suggested the bed, but he thought it too forward for a second date. So he'd slept on the living room floor—not that anyone would have known. He'd been up only ten minutes, he said, yet there was coffee and toast all neatly laid out on the table, with a knife and marmalade.

Aside from his old-fashioned nature, Eleanor's only regret was that spending time with James meant she now had to work Friday and Saturday night, but it was worth it for this. He kissed her lightly on the lips, leaving the scent of his aftershave lingering on her chin. She watched and waved as he drove away and then closed the door, unable to shift the big smile from her face.

Later, when she and Jess stopped for lunch, Eleanor told her all about James, her frustration that they hadn't slept together, her worries that she was falling for him big time, that she'd told him too much about herself, talked her way out of her job, but how wonderful it was to have big, strong arms around her.

Jess teased her about it, warning her she'd be married with two children before she was forty. Eleanor laughed, even though she was starting to rather like the idea.

After a while, the conversation drifted from James, to Andy and his interview, and then on to the offices and what to do with the other floor of the building.

"There are no other female solicitors who want to join me," Jess complained. "I can't say I blame them. It's a bit of a gamble."

"What about dentists? Surely there must be at least one female dentist in town. Or you could try ringing the colleges and touting."

"I suppose, though there's a dentist under Josh's surgery, isn't there?"

"True, but he's a man, and I'm sure some female patients would rather see a woman. I know that's the case when they visit the doctor."

"Maybe. Actually, there was one female GP who looked like she might be interested. Of course, I'd have to take the upstairs rooms."

"Really? Anyone I know?"

"You might know her, although I think perhaps that James Brown fellow knows her better."

"Pardon?"

"You, Ellie. I'm talking about you."

"Oh, please! I haven't practised for years. I only just finished my general practice before I quit."

"Yes, but you said it yourself. You don't want to take on the other restaurant. Isn't it about time you went back to what you're good at?"

"I don't know, Jess. I mean, I'd need to go on courses to get my knowledge up to date. I'd probably need to retrain."

"But you haven't said no, have you?"

"I just don't know if it's too much effort, or even if it's possible."

"So, look into it. I'm in no rush. And if you decide you're up for it, I'll keep the space free. What do you think?"

"Oh…hell, why not? It won't hurt to do a bit of research," Eleanor agreed, with mixed feelings. She'd thought about it a few times over the years—more so of late—but not with any real conviction. Maybe Jess was right, and now was the time.

***

"Stay with me, Shaunna," Adele pleaded from under the oxygen mask. She was already in a surgical gown, with all her hair piled inside an elasticated cap, a few golden strands peeping out at the temples.

"Am I allowed to?" Shaunna asked the porter pushing the bed out of the side room.

"I don't know. You're best asking the nursing staff."

Shaunna tried to pull away so she could do as he said, but Adele refused to let go of her hand.

The porter smiled and sighed. "Hang on a minute." He walked over to the ward station and asked the doctor who had checked Adele earlier. They chatted briefly and quietly, and the porter returned.

"We've just got to wait for a nurse to accompany us, but she didn't think it would be a problem, seeing as Mr. Kerry isn't here."

"He's waiting outside. Maybe I should go and get him instead," Shaunna said, trying again to pull away.

Adele's grip tightened. "No, Shaunna. Please?"

"OK, hun. At least let me go and tell him what's going on. I'll be right back." She snatched her hand from Adele's grasp, dashed out of the double doors and found Tom, explaining as tactfully and quickly as she could. He took it well; he'd been dreading the caesarean right from the start and was relieved not to have to be there.

The porter wheeled the bed onto the main corridor that ran through the hospital, where Shaunna and Adele had bumped into Dan and Andy only a few short weeks ago. A nurse walked alongside Adele, talking to her in a quiet, soothing voice. Shaunna remained close to Adele's other side, listening to the nurse and ignoring the panic bubbling under her skin.

Adele went straight into an operating theatre, where another young nurse helped Shaunna put on a gown, hat and shoe covers and then found her a chair. She placed it next to the top end of the bed. Adele was attached to even more equipment, which bleeped and flashed and printed wavy lines onto reels of paper. One of the doctors checked a screen and noted down the readings before showing another doctor.

"Mrs. Kerry, how are you doing?"

"OK," Adele confirmed shakily.

The surgeon offered a warm smile at odds with his serious tone. "As you know, we're going to deliver your baby today, because there is a serious danger to your own health if we don't. I'm going to make an incision across your lower abdomen, so you should still be able to wear a bikini when I'm done."

"What about the baby? She's too early." Adele started to cry.

"Our special care unit will take your baby straight away. We need to make sure you're around to look after him or her." A nurse came over and wiped Adele's eyes, indicating to Shaunna to follow her away from the bed.

"We think Adele may have had a kind of mini stroke yesterday. Once she's delivered, we can investigate. Now, at the moment, the baby's heartbeat is erratic. However, this might be due to interference from the other equipment, but you need to be aware of the situation."

Shaunna nodded solemnly to confirm that she understood, and prayed silently that this would all turn out the way it was meant to. She returned to Adele's side and held her hand while they prepared the epidural. Shaunna had been offered one when she was in labour and had nearly passed out at the words 'long needle'. She was trying her hardest not to focus on the same long needle being inserted into Adele's back.

Thankfully, the anaesthetist was very efficient and was done in seconds. Shaunna heaved a sigh of relief and switched to chatting idly about Krissi's party, the women who came into the salon, anything and everything she could think of to pass the time while the epidural worked its magic, and then to keep Adele's attention away from what was going on behind the green sheet shielding the lower half of her body.

The surgeon continued, almost oblivious to the conscious person at the other end of the bed, signalling to his team to hand him various tools, apply suction, swabs and so on. Shaunna could feel her hand slipping away from Adele's with the sweat, unsure whose it was. She adjusted her grip and continued her monologue, waiting for a sign that the baby was all right. It seemed to be going on forever, and she was struggling to find things to say.

Suddenly, Adele started to shake, only slightly at first, as if shivering with the cold. The spasms increased, becoming more violent, and the nurse asked Shaunna to move so that she could turn Adele's head to the side, all the while watching the surgeon. The convulsions rattled the bed, and the anaesthetist grabbed the frame to steady it, until they slowed to an occasional twitch. A trickle of blood came from the corner of Adele's mouth.

"OK," the surgeon said. He lifted the tiny, seemingly lifeless form, clamped the umbilical chord and carried the doll-like being to the other side of the room. Two of his team quickly packed Adele's abdomen with dressings, and the nurse turned her fully onto her side, holding her and waiting until she became completely still again. It lasted a few seconds, not even a minute, and Shaunna was helpless, frantically looking from the staff dealing with Adele to those tending to her baby. No-one was talking, and the hysteria she had battled to contain began to rise inside her.

"Please will someone tell me what's happening?"

Another person entered the room, pulling what looked like a giant fish tank behind her. The doctor who had operated was still working on the baby and signalled to a nurse, who wiped his brow with a cotton wool ball. Adele stirred slightly and coughed.

The doctor placed the baby in the incubator and turned to Shaunna. "She's fine. A good size too—nine hundred and thirty grams—but we've had to put her on a ventilator as her lungs aren't ready yet. Does she have a name?"

"Shaunna," Adele uttered, her voice a vague, rasped whisper.

"I'm here, hun." Shaunna grabbed her hand again. "The baby's OK. It's a girl, like you said."

"Her name is Shaunna," Adele said again. Shaunna squeezed Adele's hand harder. She could contain it no more.

"Oh, Adele. You brave, brave girl." She collapsed onto her friend, sobbing uncontrollably.

"Shaunna it is, then," the doctor confirmed. A nurse wrote on an impossibly small hospital band and placed it on baby Shaunna's ankle. "Your due date was wrong, Mrs. Kerry, fortunately for this little lady. I'd say from the size of her, you were closer to twenty-eight weeks into your pregnancy." He thanked his team and left. Another doctor was in the process of stitching Adele, and one of the nurses chatted quietly in Shaunna's ear.

"We're going to take Mrs. Kerry up to Intensive Care," the nurse explained. "She may have a blood clot or a small bleed. If you like, you can go with her once she's done here."

Shaunna nodded and tried to stand, but her legs buckled, and she had to sit down again.

"Oh, dear me. Come on, sweetheart," the nurse said, gently taking Shaunna's arm and easing her to her feet, bearing most of the weight. "Now then, Adele, I'm just going to take your friend here for a cup of tea, OK? She'll be back to see you soon."

The nurse steered Shaunna from the operating theatre and into an office opposite, depositing her in a chair. "I'll just get that tea for you." She called to someone unseen in the corridor and then perched on the corner of the desk. "That was very hard on you, wasn't it, my love?"

Shaunna nodded but was sobbing too hard to speak.

"Well, it's all going to be just fine." The door opened. "Ah. Here's that tea now." She passed the cup to Shaunna.

"Thank you," she said, lifting the cup shakily to her lips and gulping the sweet, hot liquid. It burned her tongue, but it didn't matter. "I need to tell Tom—Mr. Kerry."

"Once you're on your legs again, I'll go and find him for you. You just sit there and rest a minute."

Shaunna accepted her kind words and did as she was told, not that she thought for one minute she'd be able to stand of her own accord.

This had to be the most terrifying experience she had ever endured—far worse than the discovery of her own pregnancy. Even waiting at the clinic for her mother's diagnosis to be confirmed was nothing compared to this. She had known what was coming then, and in a strange way, it was easier to lose a parent than face losing a friend. She replayed those horrible few weeks, when she had hated Adele for all her fretting about something going wrong, shuddering at her dismissal of maternal instinct, or whatever it was that had taken hold of her oldest friend. And for all that they had, at times, distanced themselves from each other, Adele would always be her oldest and most dear friend.

After a while, when Shaunna felt ready to move and the nurse had confirmed that Adele had gone up to the ICU, they went to find Tom. He was standing outside the main entrance, tracing his finger around the bricks of the hospital wall. The nurse informed him he had a daughter and that Adele had been taken to the ICU.

Shaunna watched on, trying to control the emotions threatening to erupt again and giving up when Tom grabbed her and almost crushed her with a tremendous hug borne of relief and gratitude.

"Thank God!" he cried. "Thank God, and thank *you*, Shaunna." He kissed her on the forehead—the only bit of her face that wasn't wet with tears. They hugged and cried a while longer and then forcibly pulled themselves together so they could visit Adele. They went via the special baby unit so that Tom could meet the miniscule, beautiful girl. He was shocked to see all the tubes attached to her, but the midwife explained what they all did and why they were needed, which helped. He put the gloved tip of his little finger on the tiny palm and held it there. Shaunna rubbed his arm.

"Let's go find Adele."

Tom said goodbye to baby Shaunna and went to see the wonderful woman who had been through so much and whom he loved more than anything else in the world.

Chapter Thirty-Eight:
Detonation

"That's sorted that little problem," Dan said gruffly, stopping to shake his throbbing hand now he was clear of the building.

"I think we should just go, don't you?" Andy had overtaken him and was already at the car.

"Yeah. Good idea. I think you're gonna have to drive, though." He managed to get his keys out of his pocket but had to switch hands just to press the button to unlock the car.

"For fuck's sake." Andy stormed around to the driver's side and snatched the keys from his brother. The pain made Dan draw breath through his teeth. "Just get in the car," Andy snapped, barely waiting long enough for Dan to do so before he revved the engine and took off with a wheel spin. The passenger door slammed shut with the force.

"Steady on!" Dan shouted, still struggling with his seat belt.

Andy ignored him, only speaking once they were safely on the motorway some fifteen minutes later. "Was that really necessary?"

"Was what necessary?"

"Doing him over."

"That's ten grand's worth of koi down the pan. Well, not literally, obviously." Dan laughed. Andy didn't. "Oh, lighten up, will you?"

"No I won't fucking lighten up. You just beat someone to a pulp over a bunch of overgrown bloody goldfish. You need your head examining."

"Ha! Look who's talking! A job in Dubai? Running away from your responsibilities again? I've tried, Andy, given you work, paid your debts, even hidden the truth. For you. You've had me going to Josh for years. I mean. Someone like me, in fucking therapy!"

"For what, Dan? Let's see, could it be the whole 'my brother the violent rapist' line, or are we going to move on to you now?"

"Don't even get me started."

"You want to know why I went for the job? To get away from *you* and this bloody power trip you're on. This is it. The end of the line. I'll come clean, tell Shaunna what you—what everyone—thinks I did. You can find some other idiot to manipulate from now on."

"And that will solve everything, won't it?"

"Of course it won't, but you'll have nothing on me. Not anymore." Andy switched on the stereo and turned the volume up full. That's where it stayed for the rest of the journey home, until they stopped outside Dan's house and Andy turned the ignition key, instantly killing the noise. He left it dangling in the ignition and walked away without looking back.

***

Josh put the phone down and swivelled to face George, who had been lying on his belly on the floor with Josh's laptop in front of him, until he caught the gist of the conversation, at which point he closed the laptop and sat up.

"Adele's all right, isn't she? And the baby?"

"Both stable. Which is more than can be said for Shaunna or Tom, by the sounds of it. Kris has got everything under control, I hope. It's distracted him from the test results, anyway."

"Man, you never know the minute, do you? I was only thinking last night how everything's gone a bit mad. And I thought at least nothing else can go wrong, then this happens."

"Welcome to my loony little world."

"George Morley, trainee therapist," George mused, and they both laughed.

Josh stood up and patted his pockets. "Speaking of which—" He frowned and looked around the room. George sighed. He was still waiting for him to finish his sentence. "Ah!" Josh retrieved his cigarettes from the mantelpiece and talked on the move. "On Friday, I'm at the university, so I'm going to let Kris know you're up to speed, if that's all right, in case he needs the moral support."

"Sure thing."

"Think you can handle it?"

"No worries." George grinned and settled back on the floor. He cleared his throat to speak but then thought better of it. Josh either didn't notice or chose to ignore it.

"I'm going to the garden for ten," he said on his way out.

"Addict," George shouted after him.

He ignored that, too.

***

Andy arrived back at Jess's and went straight past the living room, where she and Eleanor were watching what sounded like a cheesy American sitcom.

"I'm back. Dead tired. See you in the morning," he called as he ran up the stairs and slammed the bedroom door.

Eleanor cringed. "Oh dear. Doesn't sound like the interview went too well."

"Either that, or he and Dan have been at it again. Give him five minutes, and he'll be back down to tell us all about it."

Sure enough, after no more than five minutes, a rather sheepish looking Andy came downstairs and flopped into the armchair.

"What you watching?"

"*Friends*," Eleanor said.

"Any good?"

"Repeats. Adele's had the baby," Jess told him.

"You're kidding!"

"They had to do an emergency caesarean because of her blood pressure. They're both OK."

"Well, that's something, I guess." Andy got up again. "I'm going to get a beer. Anyone want one?"

"No thanks." Eleanor lifted her glass of red wine.

"I'm fine as well." Jess drained her glass and filled it again, waving the bottle over Eleanor's half-full glass and topping it up on her say-so.

"So what's up, then?" she called after Andy. He came back with two cans of lager, downed one and immediately opened the other. "Bloody Dan. You know his fish got a virus? He thought he'd go tell the guy who sold him the last one how upset he was about it."

"Andy! What have you done?"

"Nothing. I swear. I was there for reinforcement, but the guy just took it. He didn't even fight back."

"And the interview?" Eleanor asked.

"Not too bad. They're recruiting a whole team—surveyors, engineers, bricklayers, joiners, plumbers—wanted to know why I hadn't applied for the supervisor post. I told them I didn't know there was one advertised. They asked if I'd be interested if it was still available, and I said I might. It's more money, but I don't fancy the extra work. Anyway, they're going to 'let me know'."

"Fingers crossed, eh?" Eleanor said.

"I'm not bothered, to be honest." Andy shrugged and turned his attention to the TV.

Eleanor looked at Jess to see what she was thinking, and she shook her head—an unspoken 'leave it be'.

***

Dan held the bottle of beer between his legs and tried again to prise the lid off. This time, there was a hiss of escaping gas. The bottle opener slipped, and his left wrist rammed into the serrated edge of the bottle top.

"Fuck!" He put his wrist to his mouth and tried again, at last succeeding. He sat back, swigged at the bottle and then put it down to check his phone. No voicemail; no text messages; nothing on the house phone either. It was a welcome change. He found the remote control for his vast plasma screen TV and put on the news.

***

Josh didn't need to phone Kris. The next morning, after Krissi had gone to work and Shaunna had left for the hospital, he called to tell Josh his plan. He was going to intercept the test results and keep hold of them until Zak's came back. Then he was going to switch all the numbers. There was nothing to be gained from Shaunna and Krissi knowing the truth, and once she had an answer, Krissi was bound to let it go. He'd even concocted a story about Zak's career being ruined if the company found out he'd fathered a child when he was fifteen. As Zak was moving away, there was no reason to suspect he'd ever find out about it. Kris was also going to tell Shaunna he'd lied; she hadn't been raped at all. He'd made it up out of jealousy.

Josh listened to Kris's idea and spent a long time trying to talk him out of it, but he was adamant. The prospect of carrying yet another secret on behalf of his friends was not one Josh relished. More than that, he didn't believe it would work and said as much. But Kris was beyond thinking rationally, so Josh decided to drop the matter, until the tests were returned. By then, he'd have hopefully come up with a way to deal with Kris.

Except the following day, when the results arrived by recorded delivery, Josh was at the university, out of reach and powerless to intervene.

Chapter Thirty-Nine:
Shock

It wasn't often that George lost his temper. He was a very mild man—some may even have described him as a bit of a pushover—but this was a step too far. He'd willingly signed over fifty acres for rodeo, and another fifty for a pony trail, and that should have been the end of the matter. He'd evidently been too trusting, and he'd taken Joe at his word. Now, he was out of the country, and there was nothing he could do. If he hadn't been so furious, he'd have realised that he didn't actually want to do anything about it. However, the only reason he hadn't fired off a scathing email to his lawyer was that Josh had taken his laptop with him.

Rather than sit and stew, George decided to go and see Eleanor and left a note on the door to say where he'd gone, in the unlikely event that anyone came looking for him.

Eleanor had only just opened up, and was in the process of counting the float into the till.

"Hey, George. How's it going?"

"Ah. You know."

Eleanor stopped, a pile of pound coins balanced between her forefinger and thumb. "I recognise that tone. Want to share?"

"Not really. I need distraction therapy. And ice cream."

She laughed. George was the only man she knew who resorted to ice cream when in need of a little comfort.

"OK. Let me finish this and I'll go get some."

He shuffled from one foot to the other, watching as she placed the piles of coins into their respective compartments in the till.

"Talk to me or sit down!" she commanded, and George automatically went to the table—the one they all went to whenever they came here.

"I'm going to miss this place," he said, absently playing with the sugar and ketchup in the condiments pot.

"Me, too." Eleanor continued to count under her breath.

"What you gonna do?"

"I'll tell you in a minute." She huffed in agitation at having lost count for a third time. George took the hint and stayed quiet until she had finished. "Right. What flavour?" She reeled off a list of highly imaginative but not very descriptive ice cream names, none of which he recognised.

"I dunno. Something with chocolate in it?" he suggested, when she finally came to a pause.

Eleanor went to the freezer, returning with two individual pots of ice cream and spoons.

"There you go, cowboy." She slid one of the pots along the table, saloon-bar style, and took the seat opposite. George stared at her. "What did I say?"

"Oh, nothing. So, you were going to tell me your plans after this place shuts."

"Hmm." Eleanor sucked the ice cream away from her teeth. "My word, that's cold," she said, and they both giggled at her statement of the obvious. "You know Jess and I went out buying office furniture the other day?"

"No?"

"Well, we did. She suggested I go in with her. Open a general practice."

"Cool."

"Hang on, I didn't say I would."

"But you *are* considering it." George scooped a big chunk of ice cream onto his spoon and put it in his mouth. "I can tell you're definitely thinking about it. Aghhh! Brain freeze!"

Eleanor waited until he stopped rubbing his nose. "I've been thinking about it for a long time, to be honest. But things have changed so much. I was talking to the ex."

"I didn't know you were still in touch."

"We are. We just don't talk often. We get on all right, but, well, you know. We never had anything in common to begin with."

"But he's a GP?"

Eleanor nodded. "Shares a practice with another doctor. He was really helpful, and I now know what I've got to do if I decide to go ahead."

"I think you should. You're wasted in this place. Even what's-his-name—your new guy—must see that."

"James, you mean? He doesn't care what I do as long as I'm happy."

"And I've not seen you look this happy in ages, Ellie. He's obviously good for you."

"Yeah, I think you're right. Look at me! I'm eating a normal sized pot of ice cream, and I have no intention of going to throw up afterwards. All right, so it is only ten in the morning, but who cares?"

"I'll eat to that," George said, and they clanged their spoons together in a toast.

***

Josh greeted his first client the day—a first-year undergraduate, who was finding life at university exceptionally difficult. For many like her, it was their first time away from home, with very little money behind them, trying to hold down a job, stay on top of the study load and have a good time. If it had been like this when Josh was a student, he doubted he'd have lasted the first term.

Compared to all that was going on with his friends, her troubles were small, but he had all the patience in the world for people like her. She wasn't the same as the moping women. They hyped their own misery as if it gave them the right to declare their lives awful, whereas this girl was genuinely struggling. If she kept going long enough, she'd learn to cope. For now, all she needed was someone to listen. How tragic that Josh was the only one willing to do so.

After the student left, Josh sent a text message to George's mobile phone to ask if he'd heard from Kris and received no reply, which was strange, as he usually replied so quickly that Josh didn't have time to put his own phone away. He was probably in the shower or something and hadn't heard it, Josh reasoned, and decided to write up some case notes whilst waiting for his next appointment. As it happened, he completely forgot about the unanswered message until lunchtime. George still hadn't called or replied, so he sent another message, and after getting no response to that, he tried phoning but was diverted to voicemail. He hung up and went off to the cafeteria for lunch.

Waiting in the checkout queue, he heard a familiar and dreaded voice behind him. Phil Spencer. But Phil didn't seem to have noticed him, thankfully. Josh kept his head down, quickly handed over the money for his coffee and sandwich and headed for the door. Alas, it was too late; he'd been spotted.

"Hi there, *Josh*!" Phil called across the cafeteria, and several people paused mid-conversation to see who this 'Josh' was.

Phil strode towards him, closely followed by a girl whom Josh recognised but couldn't immediately place.

"Hello, Phil. How are you?"

"I'm very well. This is the missus, by the way." Phil stepped to one side and pushed the girl forward. She smiled nervously.

"Laura! Hello again!" Josh suddenly realised who she was. He was utterly astounded and knew at once he had to do something about it. There was no way Laura was socially aware enough to be two-timing Richard, who had reported only two days ago that things were going well between them.

"I was going to call in and see you later," Phil stated as a matter of fact. It was one of the many things he did that made Josh want to knock him out on the spot. However, where Josh would normally have done everything in his power to put Phil off, it was clearly a very different matter now.

"Yes. Please do. I'm free between two and three. You know where my room is?"

"Of course. See you then!" Phil beamed and headed back across the cafeteria, with Laura in tow.

***

Kris had been nursing the envelope all morning. When he'd signed for it, he could hardly wait to close the door on the postman so he could tear it open and finally know the truth. That was five hours ago, and Krissi was due home any minute. He held it out in front of him, turning it over and over in his hands, but there was the sound of a key in the lock. He shoved the envelope down inside his shirt.

"Hey," Krissi called, coming in and dumping her bag on the nearest chair.

"Hi. A good morning?" Kris asked, trying to sound normal.

"Yeah. It was all right. Really busy. Loads of old biddies buying biscuits reduced to ten pence a packet. I mean, how do they all know?"

"The first one gets on the phone and tells all her friends," Kris said, filling the kettle. "Then they phone all of their friends, and so on, and so forth."

"Are you not at work today?"

"Nope. Not till Monday."

"Has the post arrived?"

"Err…no. I saw the postman earlier, but I don't think there was anything for us." Kris could feel the colour rising in his cheeks.

"OK. I guess it'll be next week, then. I just thought it might be a bit quicker, you know?"

"Looks like it," Kris replied absently. He needed to get out of the house. "I think I might go out for a walk."

"Can I join you?"

"I—yeah. Sure." He really didn't want her to. "We can take Casper up to the park." On hearing that, the silly Labrador started bouncing round in circles. "You're not supposed to understand words." Kris sighed and tickled the dog's ears.

"I'll make a sandwich or something. I'm starving." Krissi opened the fridge and looked inside. "Do you want one?"

"No, I'm fine. I'm just popping to the loo." He was already out of the kitchen door.

Kris took the stairs two at a time, dived into the bathroom and locked the door. His hands shook as he fumbled his shirt buttons in his haste to remove the envelope, the source of the burning itch he'd passed off as a figment of his imagination. But there, on his chest, was a red, L-shaped rash, and it was spreading. *Something in the gum.* He loosened the bath panel, put the envelope behind it, flushed the toilet and went back downstairs, heading straight for the medicine box.

"What's up?" Krissi asked.

"Feeling a bit snotty," he said, sniffing for effect. "Seasonal rhinitis." He downed a couple of industrial strength antihistamine pills and waited, hoping it wasn't going to get any worse. "Just in case," he said, reaching into his pocket and pulling out his epi-pen. "You know what to do."

Krissi took the pen from him. She looked terrified, but she did know what to do. They all did.

Kris turned away and peered down his shirt. The rash now covered his chest, and it looked severe, but it was only skin contact, not ingestion. A minor reaction—he hoped. However, he wouldn't know for sure for at least the next half hour.

"Sit down and I'll make the tea," Krissi offered. Her eyes were wide with concern, and his guilt started to get the better of him. *Surely she has a right to know? And Shaunna.* In an instant, he changed his mind. He would open the letter, go and confront whoever it was and make them suffer for what they had done. Then he would break the news to Shaunna and Krissi.

Chapter Forty:
And Destruction

Jess was overjoyed with Eleanor's decision. She hugged her and kissed her, right there, in the middle of a pizza restaurant full of customers. It had to be the first time ever there had been this many in at once on an ordinary Friday afternoon, and only Eleanor and Wotto were working.

"We're going to have so much fun," Jess said.

Eleanor frowned and continued with the drinks she'd been preparing before Jess arrived. "Once I've done all those bloody courses, maybe."

"Definitely. I can't wait. Let's ring Josh and tell him."

"Can't. It's uni day."

"Ah, crap. Well, let's ring George."

"He knows already. He's kind of responsible for my decision, actually. He said he'd never seen me look so happy, and I realised it's not just because of James, although he's a big part of it."

"Good for George, that's all I can say. We could tell Kris and Shaunna." Eleanor rolled her eyes. "What?" Jess said. "I'm excited!"

Eleanor laughed. "Fine. Whatever." She picked up the phone and called Kris and Shaunna's house. "Hm. No answer. Although Shaunna will be at the hospital, and Kris is probably working."

"Oo-ooh—I want to tell someone."

"So, call Andy."

"Ha! Not a chance! He's in a foul mood today. I left him at home with his DVDs. I think he might have heard about the job."

"That's a shame. Hey, maybe we could employ him as a receptionist. A bit of eye candy." Eleanor raised her eyebrows suggestively.

"Nice idea, but it's definitely going to be a man-free zone."

Eleanor picked up the drinks and took them over to a group of uni students having an animated discussion about what to order. She returned to Jess, who was still watching the students. "They've only got enough money for one pizza between them and can't decide on two toppings they all like."

Jess nodded philosophically. "How simple life was when we were their age."

"Don't say things like that! You're making me feel old!"

"That's because you are. We all are."

"Hm. Older, but not wiser." Eleanor acknowledged a customer who had called for their bill.

"I'd best leave you to get on," Jess said. "Call round some time, and we'll talk rent and stuff."

"Okey dokey."

Jess reached across the counter and hugged her again. "I'm so happy. It's going to be amazing."

Eleanor laughed at her friend's ridiculous over-enthusiasm, as she watched her almost skip her way out of the restaurant, only checking herself when she passed James in the doorway. She paused outside the window to mime fanning her face and fainting. Eleanor shook her head and waved her off, and then turned her attention to James.

"Good afternoon, my lovely El-e-a-nor."

"Hello, you," she greeted him whilst printing out the customer's bill and sending an order through to the kitchen. She glanced up at him and smiled.

"I see I have arrived at a bad time," he said, looking around the busy restaurant. "There is only one thing for it."

With that, he took off his jacket, hung it behind the counter and went over to the students to take their order. Eleanor watched on in awe. If he hadn't previously won her heart, then it was most certainly his now.

***

Phil knocked on the door. Josh could tell it was him by the thoroughly irritating, loud, rhythmic rap.

"Come in," he called, making sure he was looking at his notes when the dreadful man walked in. It always worked a treat when someone needed bringing down a peg or two. Phil shut the door behind him and remained on his feet. Josh glanced up briefly. "Sit down. I won't be a second."

Phil sat and waited for Josh to finish 'writing'.

"Right, Phil," Josh said, finally. "You wanted to see me?"

"Yeah... *Josh.*" He paused to emphasise the use of the name. Josh didn't bat an eyelid.

"About?"

"I want your opinion on something."

"You do?"

"Yeah, one professional to another."

"I'm sorry?"

"Well, being a mentor, as you know, I do have to counsel the undergraduates I take under my wing."

The penny dropped. "So, you work with students with learning difficulties?"

"Students with special needs. Like Richard."

"And Laura?"

"Yep."

"I see." Josh scratched his scalp with his pen and took a deep, silent breath, releasing it slowly, slowly—

"She's a nice girl," Phil said. "A bit too quiet."

"You said you wanted my opinion, as a fellow...professional."

"That's right. It's this thing with Laura."

"Yes. I appreciate your...dilemma." Josh didn't know how else to put it. What Phil was doing, if he had it right, was a hell of a lot more serious than a simple moral dilemma.

"Excellent." Phil sat back and folded his arms. "So what's my best move, then?"

Josh couldn't wait to wipe that smug smirk off Phil's face, but he took his time, casting a slow, critical eye over the man before him—the trainers on feet set wide apart, the ill-fitting jeans with bulging pockets, the faded, misshapen t-shirt, the grubby stubble... *He wouldn't know professional if he fell over it.* He looked Phil in the eye. "You end it now, and I don't get you arrested."

"I don't know what *you're* talking about, *Josh.*" That same rage-inducing over-emphasis again. "But *I* meant how best to tell her I want to finish with her."

"As a fellow *professional*, as you call yourself, you should know that engaging in a relationship with a student is an unacceptable abuse of your status and breach of trust."

"Oh, she's all for it."

"I very much doubt that, Phil. I have no choice but to take this to the student welfare officer."

"I've done nothing wrong. She's an adult. And what about client confidentiality?"

"It doesn't apply. Laura is protected by law, and I have a duty to report it. You end it now, and not because you want to dump her, but because, as a *professional*, you should never have let it happen in the first place."

"You can't make me."

"End it and resign, or I tell the police. Your call, Phil."

He finally seemed to get the message, and his body language changed instantly, but Josh wasn't falling for it.

"You're right," Phil sighed, assuming a more subdued disposition.

"Out," Josh said, and returned to his notepad.

"I'm an evil man."

"Goodbye, Phil. I'll be checking with personnel for that resignation when I come in next week."

Phil stayed a moment longer and then left, slamming the door on his way out.

Sure enough, by the following Friday, he'd resigned and left the campus, and Josh saw to it that Phil Spencer would never work with vulnerable people again.

***

The phone stopped ringing. Kris checked that none of the missed calls were from Shaunna and went to the bathroom. Two hours had passed since his allergic reaction, which had started to calm down as soon as he took the antihistamines. Matt had called, and, after some reassurance, Krissi had gone out to meet up with him. She'd been pretty miserable for most of the week, with them not being on speaking terms.

And so, here he was, alone with that terrible letter. He removed the bath panel and fished it out. Carefully avoiding the gummed edges, he put it on the floor to clip the panel back in place. It lay there, that brown, A5, typed envelope, so innocent and benign, as if it wouldn't bring an end to his world.

He picked it up by the corner and went down to the kitchen, where he turned on the kettle and held the switch with one hand, positioning the glued edges over the spout. The steam scalded and he let go, hoping the envelope was unstuck enough to slide a knife into. The flap peeled back easily, and he tugged at the contents, his hands shaking with fear—of touching the glue and what he was about to uncover.

He closed his eyes and opened them again, slowly unfolding the wad of paper. *I could just shred it. No-one need ever know.* He could almost reach the shredder from where he was standing, and he moved closer, dangling the papers above the slot. An inch lower, and the decision would be out of his hands.

He read the first page.

It was a covering letter, explaining how to interpret the results. The fact that it was clearly addressed to Krissi made him feel even worse about prying, but he had come this far; he had to do it. He put the sheet to the back and moved on.

The remaining four pages were all in the same format: a table across the top with a name, a number, and at the end of the row, the words 'EXCLUDED' or 'NOT EXCLUDED', along with a percentage for the probability. The first set of results gave a percentage of 23.9 and were marked 'excluded', as were the third and fourth, both with '0%'. Only the second of the four sheets was marked 'not excluded'. *This is the one.*

With a sudden calm, Kris folded the papers in half, placed them back in the envelope and into his pocket. It was time to pay someone a visit.

***

Josh was caught in traffic all the way home, extending a twenty-minute drive to almost double that. By the time he pulled into his road, he was even calling harmless pedestrians every rude name he could think of. Luckily, the car windows were closed. He drew up outside the house, and took his foot off the clutch without putting the gearstick into neutral. The car jolted forward, sending him into a rage. It was ridiculous he was so aggravated by that hideous man, but what Phil had done equated to sexual abuse.

As soon as Josh stepped into the hallway, the smell of coffee and chocolate cake filled his nostrils, chasing all angry thoughts away—until he remembered he'd been trying to call George all morning. And there he was, lying on the floor, *reading Freud*.

"I called you. Several times. And sent you text messages."

"Yeah, I know. Sorry. I left my phone here, but I did text you back. Didn't you get it?"

Josh took his phone out. Sure enough, there was an unread message. "I didn't see that there." He read the message; it was a reply to his 'Where are you?'

"I was at Ellie's."

"Yes. I just read that."

"Then I came home."

"To read Freud. What's that? A laptop substitute?"

"And to bake muffins," George added quickly.

That was enough to get Josh back on side. "Fabulous. Where are they?"

"On the cooling rack." George got up and went past him into the kitchen. Josh followed.

"I didn't know I had one of those."

"You didn't, until this morning. I bought it from the hardware store next door but one to The Pizza Place. I saw it in the window and thought, I'll buy that and go make double chocolate muffins."

"As you do," Josh humoured him, picking up one of the large cakes. They were still warm to the touch. He pulled the paper case down and bit into the side. It was heavenly. "Oh, George. These are fantastic."

"Thank you." George handed him his mug. "That's real coffee, by the way. I figured you deserve it, seeing as it's Friday, and all."

"You're a star." He took another bite of the cake and washed it down with coffee. "Although you were right. I have slept much better this week."

"Well, you need to keep it under control. Moderation in all things, and all that."

"Mmm," Josh sounded through a mouthful of cake. "You're not having one?"

"Later, maybe. I had a tub of ice cream with Ellie this morning. That's my chocolate hit for the day."

"For your benefit or hers?"

"Mine. And no, Freud isn't a laptop substitute, but now you're back, can I borrow it? I need to email my lawyer."

"Sure." Josh gestured towards the living room, and they both went in. George took Josh's laptop from its case. Josh sat on the sofa. "A problem with the house?" he asked.

"You could say that, yeah."

George lifted the screen and made a bigger deal of pushing the power button than he needed to. The pressure was of his own making. Josh was trained to coax information out of people, but not his friends—unless they asked him to. He wasn't sure whether that was what George was trying to do. He needed to be much less subtle if it was.

"It's Joe, you see." George continued the procedure of booting up the laptop. "It's like this." He started to fidget with the keys. "Let me send this email, then I'll tell you."

"Whatever." Josh sat back and ate the rest of his muffin. "Where did you learn to bake like this? I don't recall you being that accomplished as a chef."

"Now, I wonder if that was because you avoided me from the time I left uni till I went to the States?"

"OK. You win."

"That easily?"

"For now." Josh slurped at his coffee and sighed.

George opened the browser and navigated to his webmail account. There were five unread messages in his inbox, all from Joe. He could guess what they would be about.

For several minutes, George typed, whilst Josh watched the TV, glancing over every now and then to see if he was done. It was either a very long email, or he was delaying, and the amount of backspacing indicated the latter. Finally, he stopped typing, clicked a button with a flourish and closed the laptop.

"Do you want me to ask you about it, George?"

"Oh, it's not that I don't want to tell you." He was thinking. *How am I gonna put this?* "I'm just a little concerned about what you'll think."

"Does it really matter what I think?" Josh asked rhetorically and immediately wished he hadn't. Of course it mattered. It always had.

"This is a bit—my relationship with Joe? Well, it's, err, unusual. Not your normal run-of-the-mill kind of thing."

"In what way?"

George didn't answer.

"You know, George, I meet some really whacky people in my job. Take Alex, for example. He thinks he's a four-hundred-year-old vampire and believes he'll die if he doesn't feed on human blood once a decade. Or Phil. He's been sleeping with a student with a learning disability, who couldn't possibly have given consent. Then there's Richard—he counts everything in multiples of three. I could go on, but I'm sure you get the point. My tolerance of what constitutes 'normal' is pretty high."

"But they're your clients. They come to you because they're not quite right in the head."

"All right. Look at Dan and his anger management issues. Or there's Andy, who's spent his life in Dan's shadow. Shaunna—we all know she slept around. Yes, we kept it to ourselves, but we saw her, at every party, drunk with some boy or another. She was 'a slut', even if she's brainwashed herself into believing she got caught out on her first time. Then there's Ellie's bulimia, Kris doting on Shaunna and Krissi and repressing his sexuality, Jess sleeping her way to the top and punishing herself for doing so. Adele—Daddy's little princess who never grew up, hiding behind the make-up and fake tan and designer clothes—"

"And you, hiding behind your couch."

Josh was taken aback, but it was true, for it was his only defence. "Perhaps you're right. But my point is not one of us is 'quite right in the head'."

"Joe's my half-brother," George said bluntly.

"Joe as in…"

"Joe, as in the man I've been with for the past five months. And yes, I knew when we got together. I know it's wrong. And before you say anything, I did have feelings for him, but he has to go, or I do."

George waited for Josh to speak, but he said nothing. He had no comeback, for every question had been pre-empted and answered.

"So," George said, "how's your tolerance of 'normal' doing?"

The silence filled the room, only the bleating of a local news reporter cutting through. Josh started to laugh.

"It's growing all the time, George. Growing all the time."

***

Kris cut across the park, dodging the children's play area, where Krissi and Matt were gently swinging back and forth. They were deep in conversation and didn't see him. On he went, along the high street, glancing into the crowded pizza restaurant. On again. Josh's surgery was in darkness…there was a 'To Let' sign on Andy's house…

Breathless from running, he only slowed when he finally reached his destination and leaned a hand on the wall while he fought to regain control. Now and then, a head would come into view through the curtainless window and then disappear again. He began to walk towards the door.

His father's advice echoed in his mind: *never pick up a knife when you're angry.* It had been in an entirely different context, and he'd always thought it a curious thing to say. Until now, with the blade slicing through his pocket lining. Lifting his hand, he formed a fist and hesitated. Was it too late to turn back? He'd be less than a man if he did. And what if it were merely an excuse to avenge himself? No. He was doing this for Shaunna, and for Krissi. It was the only way. He knocked on the door, and waited.

The dark-haired figure was visible through the obscure glass and could be heard calling back to the other in the room beyond. The door opened.

"Alright, mate?"

Kris pushed past into the house, freeing the knife from his pocket. He threw open the door of the living room and lunged. Over and again, he plunged the blade in, aware of his hand slipping further along the handle with each thrust, someone trying to pull him back.

*

Dan couldn't keep his muscles tense anymore. He toppled backwards, landing on the floor next to the row of newly removed koi, all dead. Andy had finally secured Kris in a headlock and held tight until he stopped fighting. He released his grip, and Kris looked down at Dan, sneering, yet horrified at what he had done. He dropped the knife and backed out of the room. Then he ran. And he kept on running, until he could go no further and fell to his knees with his head in his hands and yelled.

*

Andy called an ambulance, using his free hand to pull drawers open in an attempt to find a towel, a rag—anything to slow the bleeding. He grabbed a silk cushion off the sofa and pressed down on it as hard as he could.

"The knife, bro. You've got to get rid of it!" Dan urged, trying to hold the cushion against his chest.

"How?"

"There's a floorboard under the koi pool, by the pump. Throw it in there."

Andy did as instructed, swiftly returning to Dan's side to take over the task of holding the cushion. It wasn't the easiest thing to keep his grip on the slippery cover, with Dan writhing in pain, a red lake spreading across the wooden floor.

"You're gonna be all right. Just hold on."

"Of course I am, bro." Dan smiled, but he was getting weaker by the second. He'd lost so much blood. Andy tried to turn him onto his side, but he was a dead weight and was starting to drift.

"No! Stay with me, you bastard!" he cried, shaking his brother's limp body.

Dan coughed and opened his eyes again. "Protect Kris," he pleaded. "He's out of his mind. Call the others. Tell them. Just clean up this mess for me."

"The ambulance will be here in a minute." Andy glanced frantically at the window. Dan's hand gripped feebly at his arm.

"What we've got is bigger than me, or you, or Kris. Just this one last job. Promise me." Blackness was filling Dan's field of vision from the bottom up. He shook his brother's arm.

374

Andy held the desperate eye contact and nodded. "All right. I promise."

Sirens and blue lights outside. The paramedics packed wounds, attached drips, shocked him back to life three times, lifted him onto a stretcher and rolled away, down the path. Andy slammed the front door and climbed into the ambulance with his unconscious baby brother. *I've got your back, bro...*

Chapter Forty-One:
Red Koi

Adele sat on a vinyl-covered hospital chair, reading the problem page aloud, in an attempt to drown out the familiar sound of bleeping monitors, glancing up between paragraphs to see if anything had changed. She was fed up with this place. It was hot and stuffy, with nothing to do but read, or drink the terrible tea and coffee they provided every few hours to break up the long and monotonous day.

She'd been told she could go home after the weekend, and she wanted to, but it would mean leaving baby Shaunna behind. Still, it would be at least three months before she could finally show her the beautiful nursery Daddy had promised her, and the pine cot Grandad had made.

Dan stirred and groaned, separating his dry lips with his tongue. He opened his eyes and squinted at the ceiling lights.

"All right, you," he mouthed, but the words didn't sound.

Adele put down the magazine and held the cup of water to his mouth. "You're in my bed," she said. It was true. When they had brought Dan to the ICU after surgery, they had placed him in the bed she had recently vacated.

"How long have you been here?" He tried to pull himself up, grimacing with the pain but fighting as he always did.

Adele put her hand on his shoulder. "You need to stay still until someone sees you. I'll tell them you've come round."

Dan complied and relaxed his arms. The pain was almost unbearable. Adele went in search of a nurse, and he closed his eyes again, trying to remember what had happened.

"Mr. Jeffries." A deep voice brought him back. "How are you feeling?" The nurse checked the blood pressure cuff around Dan's arm and the tube attached to the bag of blood.

"Hurts," he uttered.

"It will do. You were stabbed six times. Lucky you've got strong pectoral muscles, or you wouldn't be here at all. I'll show you how to use your PCA."

"PCA?"

"Morphine," Adele interjected. "With a button you press when you want it." She'd already asked what it was. The nurse explained the device in more technical terms to Dan and then pressed the button.

"I'll see you next time," Adele said, as the drug took hold, and Dan's eyes sagged shut once again. She kissed the back of his hand, left the magazine on the bed—still open on the problem page—and went back to her own ward, via the special care baby unit. Little Shaunna was fast asleep, twitching every so often, still looking more like a doll than a baby. Adele placed her palms against the incubator, yearning to hold her daughter, but they said the risk of infection was too great.

***

Eighteen hours ago, someone had almost killed Dan, Andy explained to Josh, George, Eleanor and Jess, whose presence he'd requested, at their earliest and most urgent convenience. The knife had missed his major organs and aorta by mere millimetres, his intensive workouts affording him a natural shield that stopped the blade driving too deep. He was in intensive care…critical, stable, had lost a lot of blood…

The assailant was out of control, caught them by surprise, fought so hard neither of them could stop him. The police weren't involved, had to be kept out of it. There was a wooden floor to replace, a knife to be disposed of. For the assailant, they all knew before the name was spoken, was Kris.

He hadn't been seen since, Andy continued, as the five friends began lifting the floor, piling the boards against the wall. Shaunna had called Dan's mobile that morning to ask if Kris was there. Andy had lied, told her Kris and Dan had gone out together. It was only a matter of time before the truth came out, but for now, Andy was busking it and hoping for the best.

Jess smoothed his arm on her way past with Eleanor. They set the board down on a plastic sheet in Josh's boot and returned for another.

All the fish were dead, the last three floating on the surface. The pump bubbled on, oblivious to the horrors of this room. George turned off the power and carefully lifted the bodies, one by one, onto newspaper. The pool had to be emptied and disinfected, all the equipment disposed of.

Josh stuffed the cushion in a plastic bag, hid it under the passenger seat and went back to help George with the pool.

"Are you going to tell them?" George whispered.

"Later." Josh located the drain and unscrewed the plug covering the outlet.

Eleanor rolled up the newspaper with the fish inside it and took the bundle out to Dan's car. Andy said they needed to be incinerated; a friend had offered to sort it out. All the floor was up and loaded into both cars. With the cleanup operation almost complete, Jess stopped to make drinks for everyone.

"OK." Eleanor looked around the room to check they hadn't missed anything. They were standing on the concrete foundation, legs straddled over joists. The knife was gone. There was no blood anywhere to be seen.

Jess handed Eleanor a mug of tea. "We need to find him. Where to look, though?"

George stared at his feet. Eleanor went to the kitchen for sugar.

"I know where he is," Josh said.

"Where?"

"In hiding. He thinks the police are looking for him. He's convinced they've been chasing him all night. I don't need to tell you he's not of sound mind."

"Well, that's obvious," Andy snarled. "As a general rule, sane people don't come at their best mate with a knife."

"He had good reason, not that I'm saying what he did was rational."

"Damn right, it wasn't fucking rational. Where is he, Josh?"

"There are things you need to know before I tell you."

"Don't bullshit me, just tell me where he is. I'm gonna kill him, and I won't be needing a knife, either. I'll tear him apart with my bare hands."

"Hang on, Andy," George said. He could see Josh was struggling. "No-one's going near Kris until we've got the whole story."

Jess held out her hands in confusion. "Is it just me? Only I'm not really following this."

"Kris knows who Krissi's father is," George explained. "That's who he was after." He paused to let that sink in before going any further. "He opened the test results. Shaunna and Krissi don't know."

"You have got to be kidding me." Jess's eyes blazed with anger. "After all this time, and what he's put you through." She was addressing Andy, but he wasn't listening. "That stupid skysurfing stunt, the arrest—not to mention everything that came before it. I can't believe we're covering up lies, because of him."

Andy hadn't heard a word. He was looking at Josh and shaking his head. "He wasn't after Dan, was he?" The realisation turned him cold. Josh looked away. "It's me, isn't it?"

Josh could cope no longer. He grabbed his jacket and went outside. George and Eleanor collected the empty mugs and took them to the kitchen. Only Jess and Andy remained in the room, motionless and silent. She had dreaded this moment—hadn't actually believed it would come to this, and it was more awful than she could possibly have envisaged.

"Go if you want," Andy said, totally defeated.

If there had been words to give to this moment—of comfort, or sympathy, or anything but this judging silence—it would have made no difference. He'd been offered the job, and even as he'd accepted, he sensed it was because he had to get out of Jess's life, out of all their lives. Shaunna, Krissi, Kris…they'd be better off without him. And Dan.

Dan. The brother he loved and respected, broken by the secret he had carried for so long. *His* secret. It was the right thing to do; to leave and never look back.

"I'll pack up my stuff and walk away."

It sounded so simple, the way he said it. He could just leave. No house. No family, really. Shaunna would want nothing to do with him, and it was still so new, living with Jess, he'd hardly become a part of the furniture. Everything was changing. If he were to leave, now would be the easiest time to do so.

But, thought Jess, *nothing's ever that easy.*

"You will do nothing of the sort. A promise is a promise." She moved towards him, clambering awkwardly over each joist, and couldn't help herself. She started to laugh. "How bloody silly do I look?" She stepped over the last one and stumbled. Andy caught her and held on.

"I've taken the job," he said. "I'll be gone by the end of the week."

Jess nodded. "And thank God for that job."

Andy stared deep into her eyes, trying to make sense of the contradiction. She'd said she would stick by him, but he could understand if she had to break that promise now. She was telling him to stay, yet thankful he was going. It was all so confusing.

"I love you, Andy." She ran her hand over his short hair. "I know this sounds terrible, but if you hadn't gone for that job, if I hadn't insisted you went to the barber's first, it would have been you, not Dan. I'm so glad you got that haircut. It probably saved your life."

He looked down into her face, still trying to figure out what she was saying.

"You're a tough nut and all, but you're nowhere close to what you were before your accident, and Dan's been punishing himself forever. Your chest, however well honed and defined—" she ran her fingers down his torso and smiled "—and it is both of those things. But it wouldn't have shielded you the way Dan's protected him."

Now he understood. As children, their mum was asked all the time if he and Dan were twins. With no earring and his hair so short, like Dan's, it was easy to see how Kris, in his state of mind, could have mistaken one for the other.

Andy rubbed his hand up and down Jess's back. "I need to see Shaunna," he said. "Will you come with me?"

"Of course. I'll give her a call, let her know we'll be round later."

"No. Right now."

Jess released her grip. "I'm not sure if—" She stopped, his expression enough to impart that it needed to be now. "I'll go and tell Josh." She kissed him gently on the lips. "Don't do anything stupid while I'm gone."

"Anything else stupid, you mean." He held onto her hand until she was too far away.

*

Josh inhaled and blew the smoke in the opposite direction.

"I knew it." She leaned against the wall, next to him. "I could smell it as soon as you came back into the restaurant."

He shrugged.

"I'm going to visit Shaunna, with Andy."

"I see."

"Don't pull that therapist thing on me, Joshua. Now is not the time."

"It's never the time, is it? All these years, I've done this, 'the therapist thing', for all the right reasons. Where has it got me?"

Jess turned to face him, waiting for him to look at her before she spoke. "You've carried us all, at one point or another. Without you, we wouldn't be here now, all still friends." She paused an backtracked. "Well, I don't mean *here, now*, obviously. This whole situation is the pits. But we'll get through it." She linked her arm through his. "We always do. With your help. Now it's time to let us help you." She studied the cigarette in his hand. "Savies?"

Josh's face slowly broke into a grin. "That brings back memories." He took a drag on the cigarette and passed the 'savies' to Jess—the last half inch before the filter tip. She put it to her mouth, drew in the smoke, and choked.

"Uck! That's vile!" She threw the cigarette end on the floor and stamped on it in disgust. "You are so giving those up. Again!"

Chapter Forty-Two:
Broken

Kris simply didn't stay out all night, which had made Krissi reluctant to go, but Shaunna convinced her that he was at Dan's and sent her off with Matt to the cinema. Until now, with Jess and Andy standing at the front door, she'd been happy to believe it herself. It was better than worrying where else he might be. But she could see from Andy's expression that something was very wrong.

"Oh my god!"

"It's all right, Shaunna," Jess comforted. "Kris is safe. He's with Josh."

"What's the matter? What is it?" She beckoned them inside and through to the kitchen, where she automatically started filling the kettle and preparing cups.

"It's about the party."

"Krissi's party?"

"No," Jess said. "Come and sit, Shaunna."

"Oh. You mean 'The Party'?" she asked casually, as if this were small talk while she made the tea, and placed teabags in the cups. Her treacherous trembling hands gave her away.

"Can you come and sit down. Please?" Andy asked.

She did so and stared at him expectantly, whilst at the same time dreading what he was going to say.

He closed his eyes for a moment and then opened them again, forcing himself to meet her gaze. "This is really hard for me. But you must understand, I have no recollection of it at all."

Shaunna shrank back into the chair. She didn't want to listen, but she had to. She had to know.

Andy rubbed his chin self-consciously. "I didn't believe it when Dan first accused me. I tried to remember—Josh even hypnotised me. Then the results came yesterday. Kris must have signed for them."

Shaunna put her hands over her face. "Oh, no. No. Please don't tell me any more."

"The thing is, I was stoned. And drunk. I can kind of remember being in the garden with Rob and Adele."

"She promised she'd stay with me so I didn't do anything stupid," Shaunna cried, reliving the grief of her betrayal at Adele's hands. Every party, every night out always ended the same, and Adele had sworn she'd stick to her like glue, wouldn't leave her alone, not even if Dan tried to lure her away.

Andy shook his head. "Not your fault. I'm so sorry, Shaunna, for everything. I'd never do anything to hurt you. Please believe me."

"When I turned you down—it was to be fair on you and Dan."

"It was nothing to do with that. I had such a crush on you, you know that, but I'd have never..." He shrugged helplessly. "I couldn't."

"What Kris heard? I tried to push you away."

"So it seems." Andy covered his eyes and banged his elbows down hard on the table. "Shit, Shaunna. What did I do?" He started to sob, which set her off, too, and Jess. It was a while before any one of them was composed enough to speak again.

"Dan's in hospital," Jess said, sniffing. "Kris attacked him. He thought he was Andy."

"Is he going to be OK?" Shaunna gasped out each word in between sobs.

"Yes. He'll be fine."

"Can I go to Kris?"

"I don't know." Jess wiped her nose on her sleeve. It was so unlike her to do something like that, it made them both laugh, in spite of themselves and through their tears. "I'll call Josh," she said and took her mobile phone from her bag. "Damn. The battery's flat."

"Use the house phone," Shaunna suggested.

Jess went out to the hall to use the phone, leaving the door open—not because she didn't trust Andy. It just didn't seem right. Casper followed her, wagging his tail, looking bemused by it all. "Poor Casper." Jess stroked the dog's smooth head. "You don't understand all this nonsense, do you?" He licked the salty tears from the back of her hand and waddled back to the kitchen.

"I don't ever expect your forgiveness, Shaunna."

Andy's voice was muffled by his hands, and she could barely make out the words.

"I wouldn't even ask for it. But I've got a new job in Dubai. I'll take the supervisor post and send you money for Krissi. I owe you."

"Don't be ridiculous." She pulled his hands down and wiped a tear from the corner of his eye. Shaunna's knack for pulling herself together in seconds kicked in. "Kris put me on this pedestal, but I know what I was at school. Everyone did, and I'm grateful to you all for keeping up the lie. Now Kris will have to accept the truth." She got up, turned off the kettle and found a tissue for Andy.

"He's a lucky man," he said. He wiped his eyes and blew his nose loudly.

"Yeah, if you say so." Shaunna was unconvinced. She scooped up her hair and pushed it back over her shoulders, watching Andy sniffle into the tissue.

"Truly, he is. All of this? He did it for you and Krissi."

"I was never worth that much. You would know better than most."

"You think I came on to you because—"

"I was an easy lay?" Shaunna waited, not for a response as such, but for her words to settle.

"No. I never saw you that way. Kris wasn't the only one who held you on high. There were times I had to stop myself from telling you I loved you. I always will."

"As a friend, you mean?"

Jess came back into the room.

"Yes," he confirmed quickly. "As a friend."

"We're to go round to Josh's," Jess said. "That's where Kris is."

***

When Kris had first turned up on the doorstep, covered in blood and with a mania in his eyes, George immediately thought the worst. Josh was in the shower, and for a minute he didn't know what to do. He had to physically lift Kris into the house. His hand was badly cut, and he was completely outside of himself. George fetched a bowl of warm water and sat him on the sofa, kneeling in front of him to wipe the wounds on his hand. He was rambling, saying the same words over, and over again.

"Kris, you're making no sense, man. You thought who was who?"

"Thought it was him," he repeated, pulling his hand away from George. He reached into his jacket and took out the bloodied envelope. George put it to one side.

"Let me dress this first." He dried Kris's hand and wrapped it in gauze bandage.

Josh came into the room and stopped. "Jesus! What's happened?"

"I don't know. He's off his head."

Kris was rocking, still muttering the same thing. George passed the envelope to Josh, who took out the contents and read them.

"Oh, hell. Look after him, George. I'll be back as soon as I can."

Still wearing only his bathrobe and socks, Josh grabbed his keys and dashed to the car. He drove to Andy's house and saw the 'To Rent' sign, so he raced round to Jess's. The place was in darkness. He went on to Dan's, turning into the road as the ambulance pulled away with sirens wailing—a good sign the victim was still alive.

"OK," he said to himself, "at least he's getting medical attention." He drove back home.

"How is he?" he asked George.

"A bit calmer. I was checking for any other injuries." George opened the front of Kris's shirt, with no resistance or even awareness from the owner. "See this?"

Josh moved in to get a closer look. "Looks like hives."

"It's definitely a reaction to something. I gave him two of your hay fever tablets." George indicated to the empty epi-pen lying on the sofa. "And that. We should call an ambulance."

"We can't. See those wounds on his hand?"

George nodded. "I put the bandage on. It was like the damage Joe did when he was boning a joint of beef and the knife slipped. Ah." It dawned on George all of a sudden.

"We're going to have to deal with this. No ambulance, or the hospital might call the police."

Instead, Josh did the next best thing: he called the pizza restaurant. "Ellie, I can't explain, but can you get away?"

"Not really. It's dead busy, and James is here."

"It's urgent. Kris needs medical attention. You need to come."

"Hold on." Eleanor's voice became muffled. He heard her talking to a man, presumably James. She came back on.

"I'm on my way. Your place?"

"Yes. Bye." Josh ended the call. "She's coming."

Soon after, a taxi arrived, and Eleanor ran to the front door. She took one look at the rash and Kris's mental state, and she knew straight away.

"Allergic reaction, plus side effects of the antihistamine. I've seen it before. What have you given him?"

George showed her the packet. "And his epi-pen."

"Right. Well, let's just give it a while and see what happens. He's not anaphylactic, so hopefully those have counteracted whatever he took. How long since you called the ambulance?" When no-one answered, she looked from one to the other in horror. "You *have* called an ambulance?"

They shook their heads in unison, their mutual expression enough to tell her that dialling 999 herself was not a good idea. She sighed loudly and sat next to Kris, taking the wrist of his uninjured hand to measure his pulse. It was fast, but that was to be expected with the adrenaline shot. Next, she peered under the bandage. He needed stitches, but she had nothing to stitch him with.

"Who's managing the restaurant?" George asked.

"James. I told him there was an emergency, and he took over. Told me not to come back. He's going to pick me up later."

"That might be a bit of a problem," Josh said cautiously, and George glowered. "Everyone's going to find out, sooner or later."

Eleanor frowned. "Come on, people, spill it now!"

"I think Kris has stabbed Andy." Josh passed her the paternity test results.

"Oh God. I see why you couldn't call for help now."

"Not Andy," Kris muttered. All three looked at him. "Dan. I thought it was him, but it was Dan."

"Is he still alive?" Eleanor asked.

"I think so," Josh replied, even though she had been addressing Kris. "They had the sirens and lights going on the ambulance."

"I could call the hospital? Say I'm his mother or something?"

"You could do," George said. "It's pretty unlikely she will, and they won't know, will they?" He went online and found the number. Eleanor dialled it; the call went straight through to A&E, where they told her 'Mr. Jeffries' was being stabilised for surgery, and his brother was with him.

"Can you tell me which of my sons has been injured?" Eleanor asked. "Only there was some confusion. It was a terrible attack."

"Andy's just here, now," the nurse said. "Would you like to speak to him?"

Eleanor hung up. "It is Dan. They're taking him to theatre."

"Right. At least we know where we are," Josh said, rubbing his aching eyes with his fingertips. He was so tired it was getting tricky to stay awake. *Stress response*, he analysed and shook it off.

"Would anyone like a muffin?" George asked.

Josh glared at him. "Are you kidding?"

"Go on, I'll have one. And a coffee." Eleanor gave George a smile of encouragement. It was a coping strategy—something she recognised and Josh failed to, as always when it came to George.

Dutifully, George went to the kitchen and made coffee for his two closest friends, tea for his first real boyfriend—the attempted murderer—and himself. He returned with a plate of muffins and four cups on a tray. The three of them conversed superficially around Kris, and Eleanor phoned James to tell him she didn't need a lift. He gently insisted he was coming to take her home, completely misunderstanding her intentions, although she managed to persuade him to wait outside. In time, she would tell him everything, but not yet.

After Eleanor had left, Josh and George stayed up with Kris in shifts, encouraging him to drink water, changing the dressing on his hand and giving him pills every hour, as advised. As it started to turn light, he fell asleep, his breathing now back to normal and the hives almost gone. Josh filled the kettle again and went to rouse George.

Later, when Andy phoned, requesting their presence at Dan's, they had expected the worst kind of news and had to respond with shock to his narration of what they already knew. Of the four of them, there was only Jess who wasn't in on it. Andy had reported that Dan was stable, having undergone extensive surgery through the night, to repair nerve and tissue damage. They'd cleaned up. Shaunna now knew everything and was on her way to see Kris.

***

Kris was sitting perfectly still and trance-like when Josh and George returned from Dan's. Josh tried to cajole him into taking a shower and soon realised he was mentally and physically incapable. He took him to the bathroom and helped him wash and change into borrowed clothes. They were very plain, compared to the patterned shirts Kris usually wore, making him look even more washed out. He accepted the cheese salad offered to him, picked at a muffin afterwards, and went back to sitting on the sofa, staring into space. That was how Shaunna found him. George and Josh vacated the room to give them the chance to talk.

"Shaunna," Kris said, holding his arms out to her. She hugged him in a motherly way and sat beside him. He stroked her hair and opened his mouth to speak, to confess all his sins. She put her finger to his lips.

"I know everything. It's all right." He leaned towards her, and she pressed his head to her breast. "Don't you worry. It's all going to be fine." She rocked him like a baby, and he cried quietly, holding his wrist to avoid further damaging his hand.

"Andy," Kris murmured, lifting his head.

"I talked to Andy," she said.

"It was him. He—"

"He made a mistake, like I did—lots of them, in fact—and you saved me from all that. Now you must stop worshipping me, like I'm some perfect saint. Let it go, for Krissi, and for me."

Kris didn't reply, but his silence was enough for her to know he had taken it in and was starting to recover the facts, allowing them to reconstruct the fiction he had lived for all of his adult life.

Chapter Forty-Three:
Starting Over

"She's so beautiful." Dan traced baby Shaunna's outline with his finger. "Look at her tiny feet. And her hands. Those nails. How are they even possible?"

"She really is a miracle, but there's a long way to go yet. And I've totally forgotten how awful last week was already!" Adele turned Dan's wheelchair away from the incubator to take him back to the ward.

"No surprises there, then."

"Ha!" She poked him in the chest and then realised what she'd done. "Oh! Oh! I'm sorry!"

Dan grimaced and got the pain back in check. "How's Tom coping?"

"He's thrown himself back into his job, as you'd expect. That manager is still gunning for him, but it'll all settle down, now I'm not there. I think he always knew she was yours."

"Yeah. We do seem to have very distinctive genes, us Jeffries boys. Do you remember when we first saw Krissi? I nearly fell over. She looked the spit of Andy's baby photos." Dan reached forward and turned the door handle. "He nearly caught me out, you know—that text about the threesome? I told him it was from Alison—said she and Theresa wanted to get down and dirty with me."

"You made a big nasty sex thing out of our day at the beach?"

"I could hardly tell him the truth. That wouldn't have gone down too well, now, would it?"

Adele ignored him and wheeled the chair out onto the corridor.

"My turn," she said, clapping her hands excitedly. Dan eased himself to a standing position, and they swapped places.

"What sorry parents we are," he said and started pushing the chair. "Go!"

"One, two, three, four," Adele counted the seconds while Dan groaned with pain and the chair moved slowly along the corridor.

"All right. I give in," he said, having covered about five yards.

"That was rubbish! Forty-six seconds."

"Don't get smug. I'm only three seconds behind you!"

"But you're a lot heavier than me. And they nearly cut me in half."

"Oh, my poor ickle Adele!"

They swapped again, and Dan counted as Adele pushed. She got to thirty-four seconds this time. They played the game all the way back to the lift at the end of the corridor, with Dan taking what was hopefully the last stretch of the journey.

"Fifty-one, fifty-two…" Adele said. He slowed to a stop by the lift doors.

"And he takes the lead at the final hurdle." Dan raised his arm in victory and inhaled sharply. Adele giggled and gave him his seat back, expertly steering him into the lift. As the doors closed, he reached up—more carefully this time—and pulled Adele down so he was looking into her face, upside down and above his. He kissed her nose. She sighed in contentment.

"I almost gave you up, Dan. I tried really hard."

"I know. So did I. When Tom asked me to be best man, I made the decision it was over."

The lift stopped, and Adele pushed the chair out. "And now I have to live with those bloody fish again," she grumbled.

"You don't," he said sadly. "They're all dead."

She didn't say a word. She was no use at all at keeping secrets and knew anything she said would give it away. For right at that moment, as she was wheeling Dan back to his bed, Andy was supervising the re-stocking of the pool, now fitted with a solid mesh for when baby Shaunna was older. He'd already laid the new floor and everything was back to how it was before. Well, sort of.

***

Krissi brought in a bucket of plants and placed them next to the pool.

"I can kind of see what it is about them," she said, leaning over and dangling her hand in the water. A little gold and white fish came up and mouthed gently at her finger. "They're quite cute. Even when they get as big as the others were. And they're so friendly. I could definitely get attached to them."

Andy nodded. "You'd love reef sharks. They're really friendly. Not too big, either."

"Cool. I always fancied swimming with sharks."

"It's great fun. We should go do it sometime," he suggested, stroking the back of another inquisitive koi. Only after the words left his mouth did he realise the significance of what would once have been no more than a passing remark.

"Don't you dare go all 'dad' on me," Krissi said quietly.

Andy looked away in shame, wishing for the hundredth time that he could take it all back. "I'm sorry. I didn't mean it like that."

"I know." Krissi picked up the empty bucket and absently stared into it while she organised her thoughts. She put it down again. "Mum explained it all to me. It's just a bit weird at the moment. Well, *a lot* weird. I mean, you're Andy, my parents' wayward mate."

"Not anymore. I'm going to make it up to you, and your mum. I promised." He glanced sideways to see her reaction. She turned and held his gaze for a moment.

"Seriously. Don't go all 'dad' on me." This time, it was said in jest, and she pushed him to emphasise the fact. He lost his balance and toppled backwards. Were it not for the safety mesh, he'd have fallen into the pool.

"As if!" he protested, but knowing had changed everything.

***

Eleanor signed the form and put it in the envelope, then took it out again to double-check she hadn't missed anything.

"Now, El-e-a-nor. You must seal it right away, and I will take it to the postbox for you." James watched over her to make sure she did it and took it from her before she could change her mind.

"You're sure I'm doing the right thing?" she asked, putting her arms around his neck. He put his around her back.

"Only you know the answer to that."

"Is anybody going to help me with this desk, or do I have to do everything myself?" Jess grumbled, pulling at a large, flat cardboard box that was wedged firmly in the doorway. James immediately released Eleanor and stepped forward, but she pulled him back.

"Not you." She knew her friend only too well. This place was to be built completely free of male interference.

"You modern women. There is no place in this world for men like me."

"There is," Jess said, heaving the box into the room, "just not in my office!"

***

Shaunna picked up the scissors and cautiously began snipping. It was a long time since she'd done this.

"Will you please just cut it!" Kris groaned, turning to look at her. She put her hands on either side of his head and turned him back.

"Keep still, then." The snipping resumed, with a little more conviction. She could do it, she remembered how. She smiled to herself. "Something for the weekend, sir?"

"No, thanks. I have something already." He grabbed her and disarmed her of the scissors before he pulled her onto his lap.

"I'm going to highlight you next week."

"I don't think so." He kissed her, and she pushed his face away.

"And a perm the week after that."

"Not a chance," he warned jokingly but then became serious. "Are you OK?"

"Yeah. I'm fine. Are you?"

"I'm getting there. It's hard, you know?"

"I know. We'll be all right, though. Won't we?"

"Yes," Kris said. "I hope so."

***

George logged in to his bank account and checked the balance.

"Hallelujah!" he shouted.

Josh jumped and sprayed him with jam-and-cream-filled scone. "Jesus, George! There's no need for that!"

"It's all gone through. I officially no longer own a ranch. I'm coming home, Josh. Woohoo! I'm coming home."

"I see."

"Oh, what's that I hear? The sound of a counselling session coming on?"

"Piss off!" Josh threw scone at George's head. It missed. "So it's finally all Joe's?" Josh asked.

"Pretty much."

"Which is precisely what he played for, the scumbag."

"Yeah. I should've figured it out long ago. Man, I was a fool. Still, he's bought me out now, so I don't ever have to talk to him again."

"I don't think you're a fool, George, just a bit too trusting. Giving him and Ray the lease for the rodeo was a good idea."

"But it was a slippery slope from there. I had no grounds to fight him. He should have inherited fifty percent of the ranch by right—maybe more than that."

"And you gave him the other land for the pony club," Josh reminded him. "That should have been it. Quits. A fifty-fifty split."

"I know. I let him walk all over me. But relocating the house to his side of the boundary, when he knew there was nothing I could do?"

"I'm guessing he sacked Ray, once he found out he'd told you?"

"Yep. But my lawyer's going to make sure he pays for that. A nice little severance package—as in it's not quite a two-hundred-acre ranch anymore."

"Whatever, it's way more than Joe deserves. You know, I still can't quite get my head around you and him being together."

"No. He's definitely not my type."

"That wasn't quite what I—"

"I know what you meant, Joshua. But he doesn't look like me, or anything."

"Thank God for that! Imagine if there were two of you! I've always had enough trouble dealing with just the one."

George located the piece of scone Josh had thrown at him and threw it back.

"Thanks," Josh said, fishing cream out of his hair. "And I do mean thanks. For everything."

"No need. It's what we do, isn't it?"

"It's what *we* do. I'm not too sure about the rest of the world."

"According to Freud…" George started.

"Don't, or I'll kill you. Right here and now."

"Seriously, you should read some of his books. Oh, yeah." George grinned. "You did already."

"You're not funny, George."

It came to something when the only way to stop a recurring dream was to have everything Josh valued in his life start to slip away, and without George, he wouldn't have held on to it. Now they'd fixed everyone else, it was time to turn to himself—a task he didn't relish, but George was going to be there every step. Even so, there was no way he was going to have him quoting Freud at him forever more.

"So," Josh hedged, "now you're staying in the country, you'll need to find somewhere to live. I'm grateful for everything you've done, and your cooking is fabulous, but you can't stay here."

"Ha!" George replied, pretending to take offence. "Well, I don't need to. I'm moving into Andy's old house. It's already sorted. And if you're very nice to me, I might even invite you round to dinner from time to time."

Josh considered for a moment and smiled. "And I might even accept."

Epilogue

"Now, if you could lie down on the couch and make yourself comfortable."

"I told you. I'm not lying on my own couch."

"Just do it, goddamn it."

"OK, OK." Josh lay down, but then started messing with the pillow, fluffing it up, briefly resting his head on it, pulling it from side to side, fluffing it up again… After several minutes of this, he lifted his head, removed the pillow completely and threw it on the floor.

"*Joshua!*" George chided.

Josh huffed, picked up the pillow again and placed it behind his head. He took a few deep breaths and tried to relax. "Couldn't we do this at home over coffee and a cake? It'd be much nicer."

"No, we can't. Too many distractions."

"But it's just so—"

"Quit stalling. We're doing it here, and we're doing it now." George was very stern.

Josh pulled a face and wriggled further down the couch, aware that his delaying tactics were no match for his companion's determination. "All right. I'm comfortable, you may begin." He closed his eyes.

Hang on a minute, I'm the therapist. Who does he think he's talking to? George clamped his teeth together, refusing to be drawn. It had already taken twenty minutes to get Josh to lie down. "Thank you." George crossed his legs and placed the notepad on his knee, pen poised above the blank page "Now, I want you to think back—"

Josh opened one eye and looked at him.

"Oh, what now?"

Josh started to laugh and sat up. "I'm sorry. I can't do this."

"You can. And you will."

"All right. But I'm not lying down. That's far too vulnerable."

"Good. Now we're getting somewhere."

Josh was about to answer back but decided against it. He would do this.

"If I may continue?" George carried on without waiting for a response. "I want you to think back to your first recollection of the dream."

Josh closed his eyes and searched his mind for the very first time he had awoken with the memory of the water chute.

"The day of Adele's wedding. It was 5:14. No wait—it was earlier than that." Josh opened his eyes again. "It was the day I opened this surgery."

"You're saying that the first time you had the dream was over ten years ago?"

"I'd forgotten entirely. I put it down to worrying about paying for the lease. That, and the fact that we'd been to that bloody water park a couple of days before where I wouldn't go down the slide, because I'm terrified of heights. The night before the wedding must've been the second time."

"And can you remember the dream clearly from that first occasion?"

"Not really."

"I see."

"George."

"Yes, Josh?"

"Don't say 'I see' like that."

"Like what?"

"Like—well, like I say it."

George ignored him and continued. "So what would you say causes this irrational fear of heights?" He scribbled something on the pad.

"It's not irrational. You fall, you break your neck. How is that irrational?"

"The likelihood of falling and breaking your neck at a water park is very slim."

"No, it's not. I'd say with all that water about, it's an even greater risk than—"

"We appear to be evading the issue," George interrupted. "Let's return to your first clear recollection of the dream. Tell me what happens."

"Right. I'm standing on a high platform, and in front of me is a massive blue plastic tube with water running through it. It's about three or four feet in diameter—"

"Can you be more specific?"

"You know, George, you mustn't keep butting in like that. You have to give the client the opportunity to explain in their own words."

"My apologies. Please continue." George spoke without looking up from his note-taking. It made Josh feel very uneasy.

"Yes, well, I can see the swimming pool below, and it looks very small. I think there are people behind me, because I can sort of hear them talking. Then I look down and realise I'm stark naked. Someone pushes me, and I fall into the tube. Then I wake up."

"Hmm," George said, chewing the end of the pen.

"What?"

"You said you can sort of hear people behind you. Can you remember anything they said?"

"I can't make it out most of the time, although I remember something about the place shutting at six, and a child asking their mother what I was doing."

"Did they say anything else?"

"Jeez, this is hard." Josh closed his eyes again and tried to relive the dream from the early hours of Adele and Tom's wedding day. "OK. There are three different voices. The first one says something like 'For God's sake, hurry up'. It's a male voice, and it's kind of familiar. Then there's another male voice, followed by the child."

George scribbled some more notes.

"What are you going to do with all that rubbish, anyway?" Josh tried to look over the rings binding the pages. George pulled the pad up towards him.

"Three weeks. That's how long I've spent reading Freud's *Interpretation of Dreams*, Joshua. Figure it out for yourself!"

"He was wrong from time to time, you know."

"Surely not? You know you're just trying to distract me, so let's move on."

"I still think a chat over coffee and cake would've been more productive. And anyway, you're the one who's always messing around on my laptop."

George glared at him. "Are you done yet?"

"I'm just pointing out that I'm not the one who creates diversions. For instance—"

"You're doing it again."

"Doing what?"

"You know what. Just stick to the questions. Do you think you can manage that?"

"Right you are, Doc. Oh God, I can't believe I just said that."

"Tell me about the next time you had the dream."

"Erm, well, I think…" Josh drummed on his chin with his fingers and looked to the ceiling as he backtracked through the previous six months and the many occasions he'd had this same dream. Trying to locate the memory of its second occurrence was virtually impossible.

"Think about what you were doing at the time," George suggested.

He'd evidently been reading up on more than just basic psychoanalysis, and Josh was impressed, but he wasn't about to say so.

"Did you dream every night? Or were there some nights where you woke with no memory of it?"

"The next time I definitely had it was after Jess wanted to go clothes shopping for a dinner party."

"Was there anything different about the dream on that occasion?"

"Not that I recall. The first time it changed for sure was after I'd spent hours reading research reports about Asperger's Syndrome and interpersonal relationships. That was when I jumped instead of being pushed."

"What syndrome?"

"Asperger's. A form of autism. One of my clients fell in love, and I was researching how best to counsel him on the matter."

"Do you think there was anything about that day that would have led to the dream changing in nature?"

"You really have been overdoing the Freud there, haven't you?"

"Answer the question please, Josh."

He sighed. "Not really. I told the client I'd do some reading on it, and he thought it was odd that love could be studied empirically. He asked me if I'd ever been in love. I said I hadn't. I saw a couple of other clients and went home."

"Interesting." George paused to write again. He was beginning to see a pattern.

"I can also remember having the dream after Dan overheard Krissi saying she wanted to find her biological father. That was the night I phoned you. After that, it all kind of blurs into one."

"Yes, I can see why it would." George pondered, tapping the pen on his teeth.

"Would you stop chewing my bloody pen!"

George took it out of his mouth and smiled an apology. "Why don't you go make some coffee, and I'll have a look back over my notes."

Josh got up. "You know, having talked it through, it's starting to make some sense."

"Is it? Oh, good. We can compare interpretations over coffee. Go!" He shooed Josh away with his hand.

"There'd best be nothing about tubes representing vaginas in there."

"Ah. Now there's something I hadn't considered." George grinned. Josh growled at him.

When he returned with the coffee, he saw *The Interpretation of Dreams* was open on the desk. He put a mug down next to it and sat back on the couch, watching as George alternated between running his finger down the printed page and jotting notes in the pad.

"You'd have been as well to have borrowed Adele's dream book, for what that's worth," Josh said dismissively.

George raised an eyebrow but otherwise gave nothing away, and after ten minutes or so, Josh started to become impatient.

"I want a cigarette."

"You don't."

"I do."

"No you don't. Stay right where you are. Stop fidgeting."

"Well, hurry up!"

George closed the book, took one final look over the pad and resumed his seat in Josh's chair. "OK. Are you ready?"

"I suppose so."

"Then I'll begin. The first issue is your fear of heights, which, as you suggest, has a partly rational aspect to it, although the fact it appears in your recurring dream indicates there may be a deeper meaning attached to it. I will return to that in a moment."

"Good grief," Josh muttered and was instantly silenced with a glare.

"The dream itself carries a number of important symbols. The nudity is significant, as is the water. However, the three distinct voices represent—"

"I only heard them once, and I'm not even convinced that there were three of them, or that what I think they said was what they actually said."

"Shut up and let me get on with it!" George snapped. Josh smiled apologetically and pursed his lips together. "Right." George tried again. "I'm going to whizz through this as quickly as I can, so keep that know-it-all mouth shut and listen. Can you do that?" Josh nodded and put his finger on his lips. "Good. Then I'll continue.

"Every time you clearly recall having the dream, it's been related to an event where you felt vulnerable. When you first took on this place, Adele's marriage to an outsider, when your client asked you if you'd ever been in love, Krissi wanting to establish paternity. On each occasion it was something which threatened to break down the imaginary wall you've built around yourself and your friends. The nudity relates precisely to that. On the one hand, you want people to recognise your emotional vulnerability. On the other you work hard to repress it.

"As the events and circumstances became more intense, less subject to your control, you needed to take the literal leap, symbolised by jumping into the water chute. However, regardless of whether you were pushed or chose to jump, you consciously stopped yourself from falling.

"The three voices you heard were your own. The sense that you were running out of time is apparent, as is your fear of losing three members of our friendship group—the notion of it shutting, or stopping, at six. I hypothesise that the three are yourself, Ellie and me, and it wasn't just the lease for the surgery. It was the other things going on at that time. I went to the States, and Ellie left medicine.

"As your ability to suppress your desire started to crumble, the dream became less frequent. You finally started to accept that you are not solely responsible for the well-being of your friends." George flipped the cover of the notepad and closed it, placing the pen on top.

"Very good," Josh said, applauding. "I have taught you well."

"Thank you. However—" George paused to switch out of role "—whilst I'm not totally convinced by most of it, the one thing I do believe is what I told you a long time ago. No-one asked you to save us all."

"I know. And I do now accept that I can't."

"About bloody time, too."

"So, can I see your notes?" Josh went to take the pad and George pulled it away.

"Nope."

"As your client, I am entitled to see my records."

"Put it in writing."

"Give me the pad, George."

"I won't." He held it above his head, and Josh tickled him. George switched hands and tried to keep his grip on it, but it was pointless. He was far too ticklish. Josh snatched the notepad victoriously and flicked through to the one and only page of George's notes.

The letters were illuminated with doodles of cats, fish, an old-fashioned pram, a stethoscope and a judge's gavel. They formed just seven words:

Sometimes a cigar is just a cigar

Josh started to laugh.

"My dear friend, you have much to learn," he said.

George winked and took back the notepad. "That may well be the case, Joshua, but so do you."

They locked up the surgery and went home for coffee and cake.

The story continues in…

No Time Like The Present
(Hiding Behind The Couch Season Two)

Sometimes a murder mystery is the least of life's challenges…

* * * * *

Not the typical murder scene: no dark, rainy street, with concealed doorways, grim, spooky nooks where dangers lurk, imagined or real. Not even a place devoid of other people, who might witness such grisly events with relish. This, an average office in a busy, multistorey block, in the middle of the day—a bright and unseasonably warm one at that—and the usual staff milling around, mostly temps, armed with reams for photocopying, or otherwise glued to the nothingness of their computer screens. No-one heard, saw, suspected anything out of the ordinary.

The coffee was ghastly, and he'd poured it into the drip tray almost before it registered with his taste buds. Bitterness sensed by the tip of the tongue, cup tossed carelessly into the bin. Would they look there for evidence? Unlikely they would look at all. Yes, ironically the coffee was beyond disgusting today—a perfect day for dealing with the one and only enemy a man ever had. He dragged a towel across his hands, appreciated the possibility that they may find him by this act, and stuffed the towel into his briefcase, along with *The Guardian*, a sheaf of papers, his diary and the seven-inch knife he had taken from the fisherman down by the canal.

* * * * *

"Would you please stop playing with my tree!" Josh slapped the back of George's hand, and he immediately retracted it.

"But it feels so nice."

"Ha! And you said it had no therapeutic value. Anyway, what do you want?"

George grinned again but said nothing. Since he'd started the counselling course, he'd had to ask Josh for more favours than even the strongest friendship could withstand, and it was truly the case that every time they met up he needed something else.

"You know after Christmas? I have to increase to twelve hours of one-to-one, no hand-holding allowed, et cetera?"

"Which you're doing at the hospital."

"Which I *was* doing at the hospital, but there aren't enough places available."

"And?" Josh asked, but went on before George could respond. "You do realise all the goons on your course are my competition?"

"I know, you said already. The thing is that the hospital asked me to ask you if I can do more hours here instead."

"By the hospital, you mean that bloody Tierney idiot again, don't you?"

"Well, Sean suggested it, yes." George flapped the fibres of the tree, and they responded in a little wave of light, bouncing gently up and down for several seconds through their own momentum. He was about to do it again, but Josh was frowning and blowing air out of his nostrils so hard it was a miracle he wasn't snorting. He glared at George, who obediently folded his arms.

The truth was, Josh didn't really mind at all. It would leave him with tons more free time that could more usefully be put to planning lectures for the course. That's what made it a double-edged sword, seeing as he'd avoided teaching at the university for the past ten years and utterly loathed the place, even if it did pay the bills. Then Sean Tierney had started his latest bullying regime, by proxy, because he wouldn't have dared to suggest it to Josh directly.

"I'll get you an apple every single day," George offered, unhelpfully.

"I don't want a damned apple."

George knew the answer was 'yes' and was about to say thank you when the sound of shuffling up the stairs distracted him. Both men stopped dead and held their breath, waiting like hunted-down teenagers in a horror movie, knowing all the while that the rustling of bags, the low-volume grunting, signified one thing: Eleanor was coming, and she was in a very bad mood.

*****

"Hey, Alice! How's it going?" The familiar voice called her back to reality, rapidly followed by the cascade of colours that signified Dan Jeffries was in the building. These sensory registers always kicked in a couple of moments after her stomach flipped. Silly, really; she was old enough to be his mother.

"Good morning, Dan. I imagine you've heard the news about Mr. Campion?"

"News? No, I've come straight from the airport. I've been in Dubai visiting my brother. What news is this?"

Alice liked to think she was one of those who took no joy from sharing gossip; nor was this an occasion for smug, warm, newsworthy chit-chat.

"He's dead," she said.

Dan reeled slightly, though it wasn't that much of a shock. He waited for more information, and when it wasn't forthcoming he prompted, "A heart attack, presumably?"

"Oh, no. Nothing like that, or at least the doctor who pronounced him dead said that was probably what killed him, due to the excessive blood loss."

"I'm sorry, Alice, but I'm not following. Did Alistair have an accident of some sort?"

Alice nodded solemnly. "Yes, an accident, of some sort." She stopped, as if she had been put on pause, the plate hovering in her hand. Dan frowned.

"I don't think so, no," she said, thoroughly attending to wiping the plate with a paper towel. "He was stabbed." She opened the cakes and carefully placed them, one by one, on top of the perfectly centred doily.

Available from:
www.beatentrackpublishing.com/notimelikethepresent

About the Author

Debbie McGowan is an author and publisher based in a semi-rural corner of Lancashire, England. She writes character-driven, realist fiction, celebrating life, love and relationships. A working class girl, she 'ran away' to London at seventeen, was homeless, unemployed and then homeless again, interspersed with animal rights activism (all legal, honest ;)) and volunteer work as a mental health advocate. At twenty-five, she went back to college to study social science—tough with two toddlers, but they had a 'stay at home' dad, so it worked itself out. These days, the toddlers are young women (much to their chagrin), and Debbie teaches undergraduate students, writes novels and runs an independent publishing company, occasionally grabbing an hour of sleep where she can.

Social Media Links

Website: debbiemcgowan.co.uk
Newsletter Signup: eepurl.com/b8emHL
Blog: deb248211.blogspot.com
Facebook: facebook.com/DebbieMcGowanAuthor and facebook.com/beatentrackpublishing
Twitter: @writerdebmcg
YouTube: youtube.com/deb248211
Instagram: instagram/writerdebmcg
Google+: plus.google.com/+DebbieMcGowan
Tumblr: writerdebmcg.tumblr.com
LinkedIn: uk.linkedin.com/in/writerdebmcg
Goodreads: goodreads.com/DebbieMcGowan

By the Author

Stand-Alone Stories
Champagne
Sugar and Sawdust
Cherry Pop Valentine
When Skies Have Fallen
Coming Up ~ co-written with Al Stewart
Of the Bauble

Checking Him Out Series
Checking Him Out (Book One)
Checking Him Out For the Holidays (Novella)
Hiding Out (Novella - Noah and Matty)
Taking Him On (Book Two - Noah and Matty)
Checking In (Book Three)
The Making of Us (Book Four - Jesse and Leigh - exp. 2017)

Seeds of Tyrone Series
~ co-written with Raine O'Tierney
Leaving Flowers (Book One)
Where the Grass is Greener (Book Two)
Christmas Craic and Mistletoe (Book Three)

Sci-fi/Fantasy Light
And The Walls Came Tumbling Down
No Dice
Double Six

General
'Time to Go' in *Story Salon Big Book of Stories*

Hiding Behind The Couch Series

The ongoing story of 'The Circle'...
Nine friends from high school;
Nine friends for life.

The Story So Far...
in chronological order:
novellas and short novels are 'stand-alone' stories, but tie in with
the series. Think Middle Earth—well, more Middle England,
but with a social conscience!

Beginnings (Novella)
Ruminations (Novel)
Class-A (Short Story)
Hiding Behind The Couch (Season One)
No Time Like The Present (Season Two)
The Harder They Fall (Season Three)
Crying in the Rain (Novel)
First Christmas (Novella)
In The Stars Part I: Capricorn–Gemini (Season Four)
Breaking Waves (Novella)
In The Stars Part II: Cancer–Sagittarius (Season Five)
A Midnight Clear (Novella)
Red Hot Christmas (Novella)
Two By Two (Season Six)
Hiding Out (Novella)
Breakfast at Cordelia's Aquarium (Short Story)
Chain of Secrets (Novella)
Those Jeffries Boys (Novel)
The WAG and The Scoundrel (Gray Fisher #1)
Reunions (Season Seven)

www.hidingbehindthecouch.com
www.debbiemcgowan.co.uk

Lightning Source UK Ltd.
Milton Keynes UK
UKOW03f0251210517
301637UK00001B/36/P

415

Beaten Track Publishing

For more titles from Beaten Track Publishing,
please visit our website:

http://www.beatentrackpublishing.com

Thanks for reading!

Hiding Behind The Couch Series
The ongoing story of 'The Circle'…
Nine friends from high school;
Nine friends for life.